THE UNASSUMING ASSASSIN

LES ARNOTT

Cover Photographs of Handsworth Cemetary (C) Les Arnott

British Library Cataloguing In Publication Data

A Record of this Publication is available
from the British Library

ISBN 1846850258
978-1-84685-025-7

Published January 2006 by
Exposure Publishing, an imprint of Diggory Press,
Three Rivers, Minions, Liskeard, Cornwall PL14 5LE
WWW.DIGGORYPRESS.COM

Dedicated

To my Dad, Donald who left us on the Fourth of November, 2004.
A great man: full of integrity, brave, kind and true - never to be forgotten.

Acknowledgements

I wish to thank my wife, Pauline, for her advice particularly with regard to her toning down the worst eccentricities of my punctuation.

Thanks are due to Mr. G. Burton for advice on 'fire'.

I should also like to thank all those family members and friends who have encouraged and assisted me to produce this novel.

FOREWORD

I think that the 'The Unassuming Assassin' serves as a warning to politicians that fanciful theorising is no substitute for remaining in touch with reality.

The individual always matters more than utopian idealism. This is a deceptively profound yet nonetheless frightening story which will strike a chord with most thinking people as it demonstrates that ill-conceived actions as well as inaction at the highest level both have their consequences.

Let us pray that ordinary, decent people never find themselves pushed to the extremes seen in this novel.

A truly remarkable work.

Godfrey Bloom MEP

BIOGRAPHICAL NOTE

Les Arnott was born in 1951 in Scunthorpe and is a fanatical Scunthorpe United supporter. He has been involved in soccer commentary for Scunthorpe Hospital Radio from the Old Show Ground and latterly, Glanford Park, over a period of thirty seven years.

He lived in Burton upon Stather, which features in the novel, for six years as a teenager.

He was educated at John Leggott in Scunthorpe before departing to study Spanish at Sheffield University and for a year, at the Universidad Autonoma in Madrid, where he also became a Christian.

He preached in a variety of denominations for over a quarter of a century but has now retired.

He worked for fifteen years full time at Wales High School in the Rotherham L.E.A. at various times as: Head of Careers, Head of Year, Head of House and as a Languages teacher. For the next twelve years he worked there on a part time basis and in The Handsworth Christian School, Sheffield, also part time.

In 1986 he co-founded the above school with his wife Pauline who became its first Head Teacher. Les has been Chair of Governors, Consultant and teacher of Careers, Spanish and R.S.

He became a Sheffield Magistrate in 1996 and a Chairman in 2004 until stepping down in July 2005.

In 2001, he stood for the Westminster Parliament for the Hallam Constituency in Sheffield on behalf of The UK Independence Party.

In Spring 2000, he became 'The Grand Final Champion' in Channel Four's series of 'Fifteen to One'.

He is a prolific writer of: letters to newspapers, articles and commissioned pieces on political matters; principally on the need to abandon this nation's connection to that body of sleaze and corruption known as the EU, although in all other ways he is very pro-European, with considerable numbers of friends throughout the continent.

He owns a property in Spain which he visits whenever possible and is currently living in Sheffield Handsworth.

'The Unassuming Assassin' is his first novel.

AUTHOR'S NOTE

This work does not approve of murder, assassination or the work of vigilantes.

The author is wholly committed to the Rule of Law and as a former J.P. has laboured to ensure that Justice is done wherever possible. He swore an oath to "Do right" and believes firmly in that as a principle.

This book is written however, as a warning to those whose out-of-touch ideals and failed social experimenting have jeopardised the safety of the nation.

If Justice is not done and *seen* to be done, this author believes that there will be consequences, some of which may be as extreme as what is seen in this work - and some perhaps worse.

If we ever reach a point where the 'law-abiding' feel they have 'lost' then that is the point when decent, ordinary, honest people may well choose to take the law into their own hands and their blame may then be considered limited.

This author fears that we have been approaching that critical point for some years and believes that of late, our nation may be getting very close to social disaster on a massive scale.

Mel, Lucy and Jerome are, by and large, sympathetic characters. Many readers will find much to agree with in their attitudes. If you do not or cannot, then maybe Society is not as close to the brink as this author believes. One possibility is that maybe *you* are living on a different planet or are maybe one of those causing the problems in the first place. Another is perhaps happily, that this work is an overstatement of the problems, in which case, we can all breathe a mighty sigh of relief - that being so, I hope that you, dear reader, will enjoy this as a simple work of fiction.

INTRODUCTION

'The Unassuming Assassin' is a searing indictment; a salutary tale; a parable of a decadent society which is controlled by a powerful 'liberal elite' who are totally blinded to the consequences of their own actions and beliefs. They are fast to condemn violence and murder but utterly fail to grasp that it is their own ever-failing policies which are largely responsible and as a result they are quick to resort to gimmickry, always 'successful' pilot projects and wild theorising. They have little or no understanding of human nature, or where they do - they simply do not care. One might have thought that the proof of half a century's soaring crime figures, the remarkable success of 'Zero Tolerance' - *properly* enforced - in New York and the corroboration of their own eyes and intellects might have offered a few clues but sadly, not so.

That politicians, senior judges, university-based social commentators, the leftwing media and many social workers have lost all touch with reality is self evident. Their inherent belief in the 'basic goodness of mankind' is worrying in the extreme and in direct contrast to Christian teaching. Their personal finer feelings, sensibilities and intensely political agendas are more important than the welfare of all the rest of us put together.

It is into this context that this work considers the outcome from the point of view of two genuine victims: Mel Roberts, the protagonist and Lucy Saddleworth. Both have suffered dreadfully at the hands of criminals and this book attempts to unravel their thoughts, motivations and consequent actions.

Initially 'revenge' seems the key but as the pattern of violence increases and reaches a remarkable crescendo, this idea is lost as Mel tries to discover what life means to him. His is a mental and spiritual odyssey combined with a fundamental yearning for Justice and Vindication.

In the midst of all the mayhem a simple love story unfolds.

This mild-mannered, gentle, kind, generous, profound, caring man embarks on a savage, successful but nonetheless amateurish campaign which will ultimately rock the very heart of government as it mirrors the actions of a clandestine group which seems to be acting in a professional and cohesive fashion contrasting with his own one-man crusade against the violent, criminal classes.

We examine his driving force and he is only different to us in that he is capable of taking the advice of The Oracle to 'know thyself'. Therefore, we enter his thinking and must follow the line of those innermost thoughts. We appreciate his reasoning and at times, are perhaps horrified that we find his logic so unassailable and attractive. The book forces us to ask ourselves how *we* would react in similar circumstances.

Ironically, the principle reason why Mel acts as he does is precisely because he is *not* filled with those couldn't-care-less attitudes which

11

currently prevail in a post-modern society and because he *is* essentially an extremely socially-minded individual who easily passes our customary test of 'would I want this individual living next door to me'?

He makes a brutally honest exploration of his faith - or rather the lack of it - and hovers around the issue without ever quite being able to embrace it. Undoubtedly, the quest itself has a significant influence on him and produces many challenges and answers but equally poses new questions and in this readers are challenged to abandon any traces of spiritual apathy in their own lives.

J.J. Benson

"Do not take revenge, my friends, but leave room for God's wrath, for it is written: It is mine to avenge; I will repay," says the Lord.

Romans: 12, verse 19.

PART ONE

CHAPTER ONE

The noise of a pub in the late evening of a Sheffield Friday is deafening unless it is one of those many hostelries where the exuberant young congregate in order to tank up their alcohol levels prior to going clubbing - when the drinks are always prohibitively expensive. This particular watering hole tended to keep its clientele who were readily attracted by some very reasonable prices on strong, bottled lagers.

The clatter, raised voices and inebriated laughter suited him well. The noise from an inferior standard band in the room next door made it difficult to hear. That too suited his purposes.

He sat looking downwards at his emptying pint glass but dare not buy another. It was as well to minimise all personal contact. Safer.

From his peripheral vision he could see a group of loud and oafish twenty-somethings, all male, who were swapping details of alleged sexual conquests at the top of their raucous and somewhat unconvincing voices.

They were the kind of young men you would find in most pubs and clubs throughout the city; freeing themselves from the cares and exertions of the week gone by. They consisted of those very ordinary people who: were generally good to their mothers, tolerable employees, more or less honest and sometimes violent when fuelled by excessive alcohol or drugs.

His eye concentrated on the young man three from the left in an unnaturally straight group of eight. He wondered why pub seating was always so ill-designed.

The young man's fair hair was long and undulated freely. His eyes were a deep blue contrasting with the pale blue of his sweatshirt which sported a dark lion motif.

That he was wildly attractive was undeniable but a streetwise hint of almost psychopathic coldness disturbed the viewer. Whilst his friends indulged themselves in hilarity he watched; somewhat aloof and detached from the proceedings. He was a part of the group without doubt, but never an integral component of it.

That this man would prove sexually irresistible to some was evident.

He watched and waited for the opportunity that had to come. This was the third consecutive weekend to have found him in the roomy saloon bar of 'The Martyr's Crown' - watching. He remained unobtrusive, knowing that the time when this Pretty Boy detached from his friends would have to come. Patience.

There had been two occasions in the past when this man had gone to the toilets alone and his rising excitement had come to naught as, in both instances, a second member of the group had got up, more or less as an afterthought, in order to accompany him.

He had settled back into his less-than-comfortable seat to await the chance that would surely come. He thought it would be tonight but had no rational basis for this line of thought. He concentrated on keeping a low profile, making every effort to go unrecognised.

On that one occasion when this Pretty Boy had caught his eye, the previous week, there had been no hint of recognition - it was amazing how a shortened hairstyle combined with a theatrical prop moustache could be so successful in covering identity. Would he recall him anyway? The young man looked around most of the time, not so much from nerves but more from a nervous energy. There was something different about him. The neutral observer was unable to say what this 'difference' was but was able to recognise that it existed. He would go minutes at a time without saying a single word but this was not from any detectable shyness. It was more a kind of self-assurance; arrogance even.

No. When they met, he did not want his target to know him immediately. He required several seconds in which to savour his advantage. It was an almost spiritual high he was expecting. In the meantime, it was important that he was not spotted in this pub by anybody who might know him and so he often hid his face behind tonight's Late Edition of 'The Sheffield Star'.

His watching never ceased, however. He was fortunate not to see anybody whom he recognised but the root of his problem was rather that others might know him. He was sufficiently well known in parts of the city to be spotted by others without him even realising.

This was simply a risk that *had* to be taken. Some things just had to become a question of priorities.

The dregs of his drink had gone flat but he did not care. Savouring the so-called real ale was of little interest today.

Pretty Boy moved as if to get up. He tensed but the target was only adjusting his clothing in a most unseemly fashion for a public place.

He wondered if Pretty Boy was popular with the yob group and thought from their body language that there may have been a sense of wariness and caution in their attitudes towards him.

Knowing the young man's character meant that he was able to share any suspicions they may have experienced. He was strangely comfortable that he could feel so cool under the circumstances. There was simply no explanation for that.

Pretty Boy was on his feet! He was heading towards the toilets.

He knew that they were empty as he had been counting bodies in and out. They would not stay empty for long on a boozy Friday evening.

He delayed standing in order to establish whether or not the man was going alone.

Of the group of eight, he was the sixth to go for a leak and one weak-bladdered type had already been three times.

Nobody else moved. He rose carefully to his feet and headed for the toilets trying to avoid all attention and eye contact; head down. He was seven or eight seconds behind Pretty Boy pushing on the heavy wooden door which he did with his sleeve and followed through the second door marked 'Gents'.

The third urinal was occupied and the man was already in full stream. Unnoticed, he walked directly behind him and it was only when he stopped that there was a slight increase in tension.

"My name is Roberts!" he shouted, so that his victim would understand just why a six-inch stiletto was piercing the baggy sweat shirt, slipping in between the ribs and entering his heart.

Time went into slow motion. He had not expected that. He had supposed that such expressions were merely the artistic devices of writers and cinematographers. How did he even have time to think on such matters at a time like this?

The corpse crumpled and fell backwards soundlessly until the back of the skull bounced on the polished floor tiles and he could not help thinking that a coconut would have made an identical, hollow thud.

He remained calm, thoughtful and focused on his plan as he pulled a plastic bag out of his side pocket. He shook the contents onto the floor at the side of the body. They were seven small bags of assorted drugs which he had bought on a special trip to Nottingham a month earlier.

He slipped the gory weapon into the plastic bag and thence into the same deep pocket.

With a single tug, he dragged the body over, facedown on top of most of the packets of drugs.

He avoided treading in the gathering pool of blood and was suddenly struck by the vision of the rather pathetic, dripping, flaccid penis which he had glimpsed as he turned the gruesome cadaver. He shuddered.

The desire to cut it off and place it, Mafia-style, into the mouth, was quite overwhelming but he resisted the temptation and besides, the knife was designed for stabbing and not for cutting. Time was pressing.

He reached into the opposite pocket and removed a piece of A4 paper wrapped in a giant red cotton handkerchief. Was he taking too long to accomplish all these tasks? Ensuring that the paper did not touch his hands he used the handkerchief to shield his hand from any direct contact with the door handle as he pulled it open.

Unfolding the paper inside the handkerchief, it was revealed that there was a small blob of new Blu-Tack on each of the corners. Still using the handkerchief as a shield he pressed it onto the outside of the door just under the brass plaque announcing that this was the 'Gents'. The sign simply said 'Out of Order' in extremely thick lettering. He had ensured that he had left no DNA when pulling the Blu-Tack apart and had deposited the almost full packet into a bin in a street a long way from his home.

The handkerchief was pressed into service yet again to pull open the outside door without any direct contact with the handle.

He was out. The general hubbub carried on in the pub and he was certain that his departure had gone unnoticed. Escape was possible. The plan had been a good one, albeit rather risky. Even if he were caught, the fact that it was 'mission accomplished' still made it all worthwhile.

There was an enormous temptation to change the plan and to head through the nearest exit door which was only two or three paces from the toilet entrance but he resisted the temptation. Even if it improved his chances of freedom only fractionally, he had to keep to the strategy.

He eased his way through crowds of bodies to allow him to leave the pub on the far side which bettered his chances of escape.

As he slowly moved the fifty five feet across the wide bar he was reviewing the killing and concluded that it just was not humanly possible for it to have gone more efficiently. It would have all the hallmarks of a professional drugs hit.

What he could not realise, was that from entering the toilet to leaving it, everything had been achieved in just twenty eight seconds. Had he been asked, his misconception of the time would have suggested at least three times that amount, possibly more.

The far door and triumph were now just three paces away. He kept his head down and noted that as he was now well away from the bar, the congestion was considerably less.

He did not want to touch this door handle either and was preparing to use his handkerchief when it suddenly occurred to him that he had left his glass unattended and there had to be fingerprints on that. Amidst all the meticulous planning, how could he possibly have forgotten that? He wondered if he should go back. It rather depended on how long the body remained undiscovered. The glass was all but empty and would surely be cleared within a few minutes. After all, they tended to be so quick clearing glasses in here you could hardly manage to finish a drink before some overworked barman was snatching the glass, almost out of your hand on some occasions. Mind you, Sod's Law......

So the risk was a minor one. He moved to the door and his blood turned to ice in his veins as a hand was laid on his upper arm.

He was relieved to hear a *female* voice but horrified to be called by his name.

CHAPTER TWO

THE Prime Minister looked at his twenty one cabinet members and felt distinctly unimpressed.

The days when semi-educated union officials could poke a nose into a Labour Cabinet were long gone.

Today he had to contend with lawyers, bureaucrats and public servants. Even allowing for his own legal career history, he would have killed to have a few 'real' people to help them through the present crisis - but that was maybe an inappropriate way to look at things - *and* he had to remember that an election would be due in well under two years, at least if he followed the popular precedent of four year terms.

He simply could not believe the plummeting standards available to him.

Too many student-leader types who had never grown up, too many Champagne Socialists and too many people with no concept of how ordinary voters felt because they had become political researchers the day they abandoned the Ivory Towers of Academia.

Every one of them would be hell-bent on taking a liberal, politically-inspired stance on the crisis and their gut feelings might ultimately bring down his administration if the likes of 'The Mail' and 'The Telegraph' conveyed the genuine lack of substance in his government's response to disaffected Labour voters.

"We could bring back the death penalty." The P.M. looked in stunned disbelief at the most unlikely person in the whole of recent political history to utter such words and his heart welled with admiration for such a groundbreaking and refreshingly straightforward way of 'thinking outside the box'.

Surely Frank could not be serious. No Secretary of State for Education had ever uttered such a daring challenge since, since, ...well, in a very long time.....ever.

He settled back in his leather chair better to be able to view this sacrificial lamb being torn apart by wolves. The politically correct - of whom there were more than a few - would soon have Frank's guts on a spike. He knew all too well that there was nothing in the whole wide world more spiteful, venomous and viciously aggressive than a politician with liberal tendencies who had perceived that one of their sacred cows was being threatened. There must be no opposition; no discussion and certainly no hint that democracy might be brought into play.

The P.M. decided that he would gain a better view of the kill by sitting forward - but quite astoundingly, nothing of significance happened.

If there had ever been a greater surprise in his political life, he was unable to recall it at this point. Most simply spoke against Frank calmly and surprisingly rationally.

Ann Chambers, the most junior of those present, muttered that there was the possibility of gaining enormous kudos and no small amount of credit by offering a referendum to show how democratic Her Majesty's Government was being.

"Human rights legislation," muttered an unidentified voice from further along the table.

In the event the idea just fizzled out. 'Thinking outside the box' had to be 'put on the back burner' whilst they 'touched base' on 'more workable solutions'.

The problem which the Government was facing was a major outbreak of vigilante attacks on known criminals. It offended the sensibilities of the liberal-types who tended to throw up hands in shock and horror. The more leftwing members of the Cabinet always objected on principle if anybody was undertaking any task unilaterally and this was seen as "some troublemakers usurping the role of government" - their *own* particular function, in fact. Of course, nobody bothered to ask why such attacks were taking place at all as deep down inside, they already knew. These were acts of desperation in places where the lives of ordinary people were being made an absolute misery by the local, usually untouchable, criminal hordes.

The customary way to deal with such acts would be to wait until the seemingly inevitable beating or even murder of an innocent took place and to isolate the perpetrators with the resultant negative and wonderfully disproportionate displays of outrage by the Fourth Estate. At this point, the attacks were many more than had ever been seen in modern times and were remarkably well directed. Matters were not helped by knowing that there had not been a single arrest.

Maybe it was just luck. Maybe it was that this time the vigilante element was better led and coordinated but there had been eighty three violent beatings of assorted child molesters, local yobs who were laughing uncontrollably at their ASBOs and of burglars who targeted their own communities. All of this without taking into account the extraordinarily large numbers of drug dealers beaten to a pulp, presumably by angry parents.

Five rapists, two 'kiddie-fiddlers' and an arsonist who had murdered six people in an Old Peoples' Home only to be released on licence - and was strongly suspected to be responsible for the death of a local child in a subsequent fire - had all been found hanging from trees in local parks and woodland.

One had been in Norwich, one in Warwick, two in small Devon towns, one just outside Newcastle, one in Withernsea and two in Rochdale.

The executions had been efficient and had all used 'the long drop' which resulted in extremely lengthened necks but deaths which had clearly been near instantaneous. As far as Police Forensic Pathologists were able to assess the times of death, most had occurred at around three a.m.

It was hardly possible that these were not being selected; indeed coordinated at some central point.

The customary platitudes of the need to respect Law and Order, 'blah, blah', were uttered by senior politicians and police officers whilst the opposition proffered a worthy "tut, tut".

The Prime Minister spent many a happy hour in various chat rooms under the alias 'Super Bunny' and was more than a little astonished to find out just how little sympathy the victims of lynchings were able to gain from the majority of people who just wanted to see an end to the scum who were making everybody's lives a total misery.

It had suddenly dawned on him the previous evening that he might possibly be staring an election defeat in the face as this would be the unavoidable consequence of 'losing the streets'.

The Right would have a field day. He had no possibility of re-election if the Law was being administered more efficiently - and even he had to admit to himself, more justly - by self-appointed, 'Judge Roy Bean wannabees', as guardians of public security.

It was at precisely this point that he realised why he was P.M. He may only be average in his own sight but he had to confess that there were sublime moments when he became the fount of great ideas - and *this* idea resolved it all.

A wonderful, wonderful idea for which he would take all the credit personally. Yes. He considered it and saw that it was good.

He turned his mind off from the murmur and self-aggrandising twittering of his trusted colleagues as he considered all the possibilities and ramifications of his sudden stroke of genius.

"Eureka!" - he shouted and the entire room descended into a puzzled silence with every eye scrutinising him for signs of incipient insanity.

"I have it!" - he declared without facing the danger of some facetious retort from those present but only because he was the 'Boss'. "J'y suis" he said in order both to assert mystical authority and to baffle. After all, he was the Prime Minister. It was expected.

Those who had grasped the depths of the problem looked expectantly, wondering if the idea might save their somewhat tenuous hold on Cabinet positions and in several cases, their very seats.

He explained his idea of bringing back transportation.

"The Aussies might object, this time," said a dubious little voice, only to be rebutted by the explanation that they would be able to use a deserted Scottish island in The Inner Hebrides, or similar, for genuine Life Sentences. The isle waters would be patrolled as a regular exercise by The Royal Navy. There would be a garrison of Naval Officers on the 'free' side of the island who would monitor provisions, medical attention, electricity supply etc and the prisoners would live openly in rapidly constructed prefabs on the other side.

The idea was revolutionary and might well offer attractions to the reactionary Right without upsetting the Liberal Elite as much as the re-introduction of The Death Penalty would be guaranteed to accomplish.

It would prove to a sceptical public that Labour cared and, provided the intrusive and meddlesome Human Rights Act did not get in the way too much, it could well work.

It had the extra value of undermining the work of the vigilantes. His enthusiasm was infectious and within minutes there was a brainstorming session in play in which ideas and developments were outlined to the gathering.

By the end of a lengthy session the plan was finalised and a third of a billion pounds had been put to one side.

Parliamentary time would be made available and the bill would be pushed through - no irony intended - even if they had to use the guillotine. All serious opposition would surely stem from The Upper House.

It was decided to undermine *that* straight away. A breakneck timescale of just five months and The Parliament Act could always be dusted down and abused again if the democratic process happened to get in the way of a stupendous idea - particularly one which had emanated from the PM himself.

CHAPTER THREE

Mel Roberts drove his ageing Mondeo through the succession of linked pot holes which passed for a car park in the enormous Comprehensive where he had spent the most depressing hours of his working life.

Before alighting from the vehicle, he paused and stared at the huge, grey impersonal buildings and his heart sank, not merely at the prospect of yet another wasted day attempting the impossible but also because his heart went out to the one and one half thousand young people who were so ill-served by this allegedly pedagogical production line.

"You get more options and facilities in a big school," he muttered mockingly between tightened lips.

Mel was greeted warmly and in jocular fashion by at least a dozen pupils with a cheery 'Good morning, Sir,' and was ignored by at least twenty times that number. He chose to ignore the staffroom and simply signed in before taking a walk not far short of a quarter of a mile to his recently refurbished, glass-surrounded classroom which invited every passing pupil to peer in at what was going on in his class with unconcealed interest. He felt rather like a lab rat but without any of the advantages.

He had half an hour to prepare himself for the day and he thought about his many colleagues who would consider that he had arrived rather late for a Monday morning.

There was a kettle wisely hidden away in the happily spacious stockroom, so he mixed himself a Gold Blend, cursing himself for yet again having forgotten to bring milk. It happened too often and so he was prepared with some fairly revolting, powdered substitute which was disgustingly reminiscent of wallpaper paste.

He took a sip and the melted caffeine gave him an immediate lift. He was relieved but saw from his timetable that he had a full day. Five solid hours of stress. Three lessons of History and two of R.E. He could not face it. Fourteen years of this had been more than enough. Just one 'free' in the day could have helped make it more bearable but they were becoming increasingly rare these days.

He questioned what he was doing and more to the point, why he was doing it. What was he achieving?

There would be five lessons of crowd control, several confrontations and at least three nasty incidents, were he to attempt to teach; to make his subjects vibrant and exciting to young minds.

Today he would use the teachers' desperate fallback, that of having them copy out large chunks of textbooks. He supposed an OFSTED Inspector would be horrified that a teacher should be anything less than a miracle worker and might, on occasions have to resort to survival strategies. Too many of his colleagues had burned out.

He would impress upon his groups the vital importance of getting a substantial amount copied into exercise books - and they would fall for it. For psychological reasons he could not fathom, it seldom failed.

This would allow him time to get his work up to date and give him time to think.

He was surprised that pupils never seemed to latch onto the fact that the more troublesome they were the more boring their lessons became.

Still. That was not his problem today. It was theirs.

The Year Nine Group who were first to join him had a reputation as being amongst the worst in the school; belligerent, foul-mouthed, confrontational and antagonistic and that was just on a good day.

Maybe they were beset by Monday morning blues. He neither knew nor cared, but they were decidedly subdued and got on with their copying with a hardly a growl. It was quite possible that they had spotted that taking on Mr. Roberts today would not be a good idea - sometimes an attitude given at the front had an immediate consequence where the response of a given class was concerned. It was perhaps in his brusque, no nonsense approach at the beginning of the lesson where they had been able to detect a subtext of danger signals and had therefore decided to avoid risk and adopt a low profile.

This was potentially the most difficult lesson of the day. He would be on top hereafter and the day would be his; a simple triumph over adversity.

The lesson was under way in less than five minutes and he wondered why he did not aim to bore pupils into submission every day of his working life.

That he was profoundly unhappy in his chosen career was self-evident and he decided that something was going to have to be concluded and now was as good a time as any to do some serious thinking.

He wondered what criteria he had to use and was quick to determine that he wanted to avoid the unpleasantness of the present daily grind, be his own man, be socially useful and more than anything else, find fulfilment.

He was appalled to recall how many months notice he would have to give and decided to approach the Head and see if there was anything he could do to be released relatively rapidly. Under his circumstances he was almost certain that he would get his way.

Never usually one for sudden or rash steps, he came to a swift conclusion.

After two lessons, it was break, and he walked over to the Senior Staff Suite and asked to see Doctor Tom Beaker, or Dr Who, as he was rather unimaginatively called by his minions; a tag latched onto by the pupils but with little grasp of the origins of the nickname.

He decided to be open and honest and admit that he was struggling to cope. He felt that he could be heading for some kind of breakdown.

Dr Beaker, a tall, angular man with a shock of red hair was noted for his care for his staff.

He listened carefully to what Mel had to say and would not even allow him to finish making his plea.

"You can finish today if you wish. I shall be deeply sorry to lose such a talented member of staff and may I say, a particularly effective one. Your results over years have been impressive."

"I am most grateful......" Mel began but Beaker interrupted.

"Nobody who has been through what you have had to undergo should ever have to be put under pressure again. I am just grateful that we have had four years or so more excellence from you. I must confess that I was surprised to see you weather the trauma as successfully as you have done. Finish today, we shall get a supply teacher in for tomorrow and you can leave with our blessing and best wishes. Is there anything else we or I can do to help?"

"No. I don't think so. Thank you. Just thank you."

Beaker went on to ask him how he would live and Mel explained that he was not without resources. Beaker seemed relieved as he could not see where else Mel could get a job under the circumstances but decided to keep that thought to himself.

"How do you want to leave? Shall we have a farewell from all your colleagues in the staffroom at lunchtime?"

Mel felt unable to refuse even though he found the prospect somewhat unappetising.

Thus ended a fourteen year teaching career and by the end of the day he left the buildings for a final time without a single regret or even an emotion.

He clambered, laden, into his car wondering how they had managed to get so many cards signed and so many gifts together in such a short time span.

The one problem he had not managed to resolve was, of course, what he was going to do next with his life.

He had spent an interesting weekend and wondered if that offered any clues for his future. He would certainly enjoy the short term advantage of a lie-in tomorrow morning.

A now ex-history teacher with a history and with secrets, started the car engine. For the first time in nearly five years he possessed an inner satisfaction.

It was arguable that life was becoming acceptable. The dreary, pain-filled existence of recent years was beginning to recede.

He had to draw a curtain over this life which had brought him so much grief. When he gave it some thought he realised that he had not known any period of contentment since his days as a spotty sixth-former.

University had been ruined by falling into the clutches of the deeply disturbed woman who had gone on to become his wife and the loss of his much-loved parents. In addition, he had made a shockingly poor choice of career and life had simply deteriorated from this point.

All the signs were in place to indicate that there had been a new dawning in the past three days.

CHAPTER FOUR

Mel entered the 'White Rose' in Handsworth as was his wont on most Mondays in the early evening and ordered a steak and a pint of Sheffield's own, Stones. He first checked to see that the brew was the Creamflow which he considered superior to the original. The texture was so much better.

He glanced with some interest at a news item on the TV which displayed an insipid photograph of the Prime Minister as some bimbo newsreader was breathlessly outlining the Government's new anti-crime initiative.

The Tory leader was interviewed and described the idea as "archaic, ludicrous, unworkable and a knee-jerk response." He also managed to imply that soaring crime rates were a direct consequence of Labour's policies.

The Liberal Democrat spokesperson achieved the difficult combination of appearing both mealy-mouthed and shocked at the same time, whilst condemning this as an "outrage" in a modern, civilised society.

Passing members of the public were interviewed in a series of five second clips. Nobody could be found to condemn either the vigilante action or Labour's response to it.

The Programme Editor cursed quietly to himself and promised that he would never again take street interviews 'on the hoof' without editorial control over the content. As a practising Lib Dem, he was horrified that it was the Lib Dems who were the only ones to emerge from the news item looking weak and wishy-washy.

Settling back in his seat whilst sipping his pint, Mel collected his thoughts and memories from his rather eventful weekend. It had not been quite what he expected, but he was pleased with the unexpected directions his life was taking. His mind returned to the chill he had experienced when, in a different hostelry, that hand had touched his arm. He had turned far too quickly and found himself staring at a somewhat pneumatic, bottle-blonde whom he simply did not recognise.

"Mr. Roberts," the voice had said and he knew instantly that she had to be one of the many hundreds of ex-pupils he had taught over the years.

He had not known what to do. There was still the glass with his fingerprints troubling him but somewhat fortuitously for his peace of mind, glancing up, he glimpsed a young barman collecting the glasses and he was sure that he would have his glass on the pile within seconds. Good. Perfect.

He returned his gaze to the blonde and rather weakly said, "Oh. Hello."

The barman had the glass. He was certain. He did not want either to delay his departure or appear suspicious. If it were ever to become known that he had been in this pub on the night of the stabbing, his arrest and probably his conviction too would become assured.

Having no real idea of what to do he indicated that they should go outside and said, "I'm finding it awfully stuffy in here. Can we talk outside?"

She had assented and in that moment he realised that she was a pupil called Mandy something-or-other whom he had taught six or seven years previously.

His mind calculated that she would be about twenty three now and having no idea what to say, he stammered, "I am desperate for a bit of fresh air and I was just going down to the Chinese in Bramley because I haven't eaten in hours. Would you like to join me?"

It was only at this point that he realised that this was going to sound like a come-on. They were already some one hundred and fifty yards from the pub at this juncture and he was anxious to put as much distance between it and himself, so if he did, at thirty six, sound like a 'dirty old man' then that was tough. But how was he going to escape the inevitable problem that she knew that he had been in the pub? As a problem, that certainly dwarfed the unlikely connection to him by means of an anonymous glass.

To say he was concerned was a massive understatement.

The distance to the Chinese was well over a mile but she seemed unfazed by this. He was glad that she was not wearing high heels. There would have been no way that he would have dared use his mobile to call for a taxi. Locating where he had been would have been far too easy for any investigator.

He explained to her that his house was on the Bramley Estate and they could pop round there and order by phone if she preferred.

Just how long had it been that he had been out of circulation where women were concerned? This was a second come-on, however inadvertent. Still, it was not as if she were a schoolgirl. She was a mature and attractive young woman. Perhaps something might develop. Surely not.

How inappropriate the timing of these juxtaposed events had been. His mind was left in a complete turmoil. To make things worse/better (?) she had acquiesced willingly.

"Mandy. It must be more than six years since I last saw you. If I remember, you passed History GCSE and didn't stay on to do 'A' Levels. I am sure you would have done well at 'A' Level." In his mind he couldn't quite recall whether she had been any good at his subject or not but thought that a little flattery could do no harm and she was clearly pleased not only to be remembered but to have been seen as a good student.

As they turned off to the right, a Police car screeched around the same corner hurtling towards 'The Martyr's Crown', all lights and sirens blaring.

He had never seen a Police vehicle move so fast and within a minute, five more were converging into a single direction. An ambulance accompanied them making even more noise, if that were possible.

"Something must be happening," he observed lamely.

It had not escaped his attention that at the point when the first siren had startled them she had taken hold of his arm and had not relaxed her grip at any point on the remainder of the walk to his house.

As he let them in through the side door, he was fairly certain that no neighbour had spotted them arrive.

The house was warm and comfortable. He asked her what she wanted to drink and they shared a quality bottle of Chablis while they awaited the arrival of the Chinese food. He had experienced problems with the order because the person answering the phone spoke English particularly badly.

She had asked him if he were still teaching and he had confirmed that he was but was no longer enjoying it. It was too much like hard work, he had told her.

She brought up the names of some old classmates but he could only remember about half of them. If a pupil did not have two heads they usually had to be very good or very bad in order to be remembered - and that applied as much to quality of work as to behaviour. It was a shame how many of the average were simply lost in the mists of time.

He remembered Mandy because she had always stayed behind to ask him questions and she obviously liked him. He was able to recall that at the time, he had often found himself humming Sting's 'Don't stand so close to me.'

As a highly moral man, the attentions of hormone-afflicted schoolgirls had been far from welcome. Perhaps things were different now. Very different. He no longer had a wife and the dripping of the sands of time had made acceptable what would once have been unthinkable.

They talked easily and he became conscious that she was a considerably more attractive young woman now. Shapely, buxom and with the clearest skin he had ever seen, she was voluptuous. Her features were clean cut and her manner was relaxed. Further things would happen on this amazing night, there was now no doubt about it.

"I must get changed," he said leaving her for as long as it took to thrust all his clothes and trainers into the washing machine, to take a rapid shower and to scrub his nails with the greatest of care.

He would have quite liked to have got rid of the trainers but it suddenly occurred to him that the knife was still in his pocket. He rushed into the kitchen in his dressing gown and stopped the wash cycle, not without considerable difficulty and a certain amount of mess, and extricated the weapon.

In his slippers, he darted through the back and squeezed into the garden next door through a rickety board fence. Mr. Silver, an ageing bachelor and all round good neighbour, was visiting a 'friend' in S. Australia for three months. He concealed the knife under his shed as a temporary measure along with the false moustache from the other pocket.

Coming back inside, he found Mandy in the kitchen viewing him with a degree of puzzlement perhaps wondering about the on/off moustache as well as the pools of water on the kitchen floor.

"Putting the rubbish out," he explained tamely.

Before anything else could be said the other doorbell rang and he went to collect the food.

He returned to the kitchen table and he realised that it was the dressing gown itself that had caused her surprise and not so much that he had been wandering around outside in it. She really must have thought that this was yet another cack-handed sexual overture and he was embarrassed.

He invited her to set out the food, indicating that he was prepared to eat anything and he departed to throw on jeans and tee shirt.

Back in just a few moments, he helped her to complete setting out the plates and found some trays so that they would be able to eat in the lounge. He took it through after uncorking a second bottle of wine.

They settled down to eating and chatting and he thoroughly enjoyed the meal - almost as much as the company. The adrenaline was still coursing through his veins and it was true that he was feeling quite aroused in the presence of such a lovely young lady.

She turned the conversation by asking how he had been and a certain tension arose when she finally said, "I heard about what happened and I've often thought about you. How have you managed to cope with it all?"

He was unwilling to discuss and settled for a non-committal reply on the lines of; "Well, you learn to get by."

Finishing her last piece of Hong Kong Chicken, she had stood to her feet and kissed him slowly and deeply on the lips.

He took a long pull on his pint and tried to re-live precisely the sequence of what had happened.

Passion? - Yes. There had been passion - never experienced like this. Excitement? - Definitely. She had taken over as she was considerably more experienced than he. Discovery. Touch. Kissing - and what kissing! Deep. And smells. Her perfume had been so well-chosen - especially for one like himself who tended to find such fragrances a touch sickly. Her own natural odours adding to the passion. Tenderness. Oh so tender. Climax. Ah! Certainly. Climax. Afterglow. Deepest contentment. Slight discomfort from such vigorous exercise on a full stomach. Partially-restored belief in life.

But then that most unwelcome interruption as the doorbell rang. He had initially chosen to ignore it but realising that the lights were on all over the house, when it rang a second time he threw on his jeans and muttering angrily, looked at the clock to see that it was twenty five past eleven.

"Who the......can it be at this time.?" He mumbled to himself and then suddenly he realised that he never got visitors at this time and he tensed up. His guts gradually knotting, he put the chain on and partly opened the door.

"Evening, Mel," said a disembodied voice.

"Who is it? This is *not* a good time!"

"Jerome Kemp," said the voice.

"Sergeant! What can I do for you at this time of night?"

"If I can just come in a moment, I can explain. I saw your lights were still on. Oh. And it's Inspector now."

He opened the door and C.I.D. Inspector Jerome Kemp crossed his threshold, closely followed by a gangly, soft-featured young lady who was introduced as D.C. Calver. He stared at her and found little connection to anybody he might have recognised from *The Bill*. He wondered if he should make a joke but thought better of it.

Kemp walked into the lounge where Mandy, who was just about decent, was sitting in an armchair.

Both Police Officers sat down without invitation and waited for him to do the same.

"We have news," said Kemp and Mel tried to feign a cross between interest and the anger of a lover disturbed.

Kemp was in his early fifties and had the kind of face that Chandler might have described as 'lived-in'. Although very tall, he was, in fact, several inches shorter than his sidekick. Neither had been slow to use powers of deduction to ascertain what had been happening in the room just prior to their arrival.

"Malone's dead!" he announced with emphasis on the word 'dead'.

"Good riddance," was the reply injected with venom. "Drugs?"

"Not exactly," said Jerome. "Somebody stabbed him tonight in 'The Martyr's Crown'. I thought you'd want to know."

Hoping above hope that Mandy wouldn't say anything incriminating he butted in with: "The Martyr's Crown? Isn't that over in Woodthorpe?"

He dare not catch her eye.

"No. It's further across in Birley."

"Yeah, thought I knew it. What happened?"

"Well, we don't really know. A barman found him dead in the toilets."

"Good. I hope he has commenced an eternity rotting in hell. Would you do me a favour? When you catch the bloke can I send him money and offer him my lifelong support and permanent friendship?"

"I'd be all too happy to oblige Mel - just as soon as the person with the strongest motive known to man is eliminated from our enquiries."

"Me?" - he asked hoping to sound a little surprised.

"Just for form's sake. You do have to be eliminated as a suspect."

"Okay. When did this happen?"

"Just under two hours ago," said the policeman, thoughtfully.

"Right. I've not had my car out of the garage today and Mandy was here with me a couple of hours ago." He dare not suggest longer. He was hoping above hope that she would be unable to put the chronology together. That she wouldn't notice the pub's name where they had met. That she would keep *stumm*.

No! There was no hope. She was no fool.

"I've been here since about five thirty," said a sexy voice which was as welcome as it was unexpected. He tried not to look relieved and continued to avoid her gaze.

Kemp signalled that his assistant should take her details and putting a solicitous arm around Mel's shoulder he said, "I am just so happy for you - and the rest of civilisation - that the bastard is dead. Of course nobody thought it was you. There's plenty more out there who wanted to stuff him and between thee, me and the gatepost, it has all the hallmarks of a drugs killing. I wanted to be the one who came and told you what was happening. No point in you getting it all second hand. I'll try to keep you updated."

Whereupon he nodded to the D.C. and the two had left within seconds.

He did not know what to say to Mandy. He just offered her another drink and when she didn't ask the expected question, he merely said "Thank you." At this she asked what was in her heart. "I assume that it was this Malone who.....?" As her voice trailed off he nodded and she gave him a big thumbs up, told him that the alibi she had just given him would never be shaken and completed everything by saying: "Now that's made me randy. Bed, is it?"

They made love intermittently throughout the whole weekend. Without any doubt it was the best weekend of, not only his life, but of his wildest dreams.

* * *

There, in The White Rose, he finished the remnants of his steak which had not quite reached the usual standard and drained his pint before heading home to watch TV.

Life simply got better. Mandy was due to call next Friday evening and to be honest, he needed the break in between.

Nice girl!

CHAPTER FIVE

The three, rather distinct 'adrenaline hits' had dried up by the Tuesday morning. Bedding a beauty, ditching a detested job and achieving his life's single ambition with a stiletto did not really hack it for him.

The 'rush' had departed and descended into anti-climax, almost bordering on depression. He was unable to read his daily paper and had to force some cornflakes down him just to line his stomach.

He was unable to explain why he felt as if he were in a kind of spiritual vacuum. There seemed no reason for it. The sense of exhilaration had departed and he could only hazard a guess that adrenaline worked like any other drug and that coming down was an inevitable side effect. Perhaps gaining your heart's desire was just another, deeper glimpse into the hell that life had already demonstrated to him with devastating efficiency and unmitigated cruelty.

He decided to visit the Handsworth Cemetery and the walk took him about twenty minutes. He said a breezy 'hello' to two young men called Aasim and Nasir whom he knew slightly, as they walked past in the opposite direction. He felt a little better for the exercise and he was delighted to see that the grass was dry. He had brought a cagoule to sit on but it would be easier as there had been no rain.

He laid the fluorescent-orange garment next to the grave and looked at the two inscriptions. The plot he was sitting on was empty. He had bought it for himself.

The words read: - *Jenny Sophia Roberts, snatched from us. Aged nine years.*

He was cross that he had forgotten to bring flowers. How could he have done that? He blamed himself and swore. She deserved flowers but then he remembered that he had something better. "That man is dead." He told her. "Dad sorted it all out for you, my diamond." And he wept, gently at first then gaining power, the sobs rocked his body for minutes on end.

Eventually, he regained some semblance of control and read the second caption on the headstone: - *Miriam Adele Roberts. Died aged thirty five.* Looking at the grave of the woman who had been his supposed 'soul mate' he felt a total absence of emotion and had Jenny not been lying in the same grave he knew that he would never have visited.

It was difficult to find any feelings for the woman who had sucked the very humanity out of him; the one who, after Jenny's passing had dedicated her life to making him as miserable as was humanly possible.

To say he despised her was to miss the point. Had it not been for her having given birth to his beloved daughter, he could have wished that her life had never even been inflicted on the planet.

She was despicable and he had shed not the smallest tear for her but had undergone an enormous sense of relief, almost bordering on

34

pleasure, on the day she died. He seldom thought ill of others and felt guilty.

He left the Burial Ground and without thinking caught a bus into the City Centre. He sat next to an attractive young lady with an agreeable smile whom he knew slightly. Her name was....... oh, dear.....erm......

Rebekah....Mawson.....Lawson....Dawson.... or some such. Upon arriving , he was mildly surprised to discover where he was and could hardly recall having caught the bus.

He alighted onto the path and walked aimlessly for more than an hour. Spotting a coffee shop, he stepped inside for some much needed caffeine and to use the toilets.

He stared aimlessly through the window, drank his excellent filter coffee but was too absorbed to notice the high quality of the significantly overpriced beverage. Reinvigorated, he got up and carried on his ill-determined route to nowhere in particular.

Finding himself standing outside a small Church he walked in like an automaton and sat down. The place was plain which led him to believe that it was either very low or possibly some kind of evangelical Church. There was nobody about but sounds of cleaning could be heard from somewhere to the rear.

He relaxed and felt as far removed from God as it was possible to feel. Having taught both R.E. and R.S. he had a good knowledge of the mechanics of Christianity but no sense of how it really worked for the 'born again' believers whom he had met in surprisingly large numbers throughout his life.

He was certainly not a believer but neither was he an atheist. He supposed that that made him some kind of agnostic but that would mean that he had no belief at all. He wondered if his general belief in a First Cause made him a deist - but then, he was quite taken by Christ's teaching; a moral base for living which surely had never been bettered in recorded history.

As he tried to get his mind around these trying concepts he felt a hand gently touch his arm provoking, for a whole half second, a numbing sense of *deja vu.*

The same as before, he turned to find a friendly face; a youngish man perhaps in his late twenties or early thirties. His relief was palpable.

"Can I help, at all? - I'm Pastor here."

"Do you talk to people about their problems?"

"Yes, but I only have forty minutes right now. If you need longer it will have to be an appointment."

"Forty minutes would be perfect. More than sufficient, I'm sure."

"Super. Come on back into the Vestry and I'll ask Maisie to get us a coffee. Okay?"

He was only too pleased to agree and the Pastor who announced himself as Bri, arranged for the coffees.

They sat opposite each other in a pair of ancient but astonishingly comfortable leather armchairs.

35

"Well, Bri. I have immense hatred in my heart for two people and they infest almost every one of my waking moments. How does that equate with being what your God would want me to be.? Does that condemn me to hell? Shall I ever be free of them?"

"The Lord's Prayer tells us that there is a balance - that in learning to forgive, we can be forgiven. Christ bought our salvation from hell on a cross. All we have to do is repent and ask Him in."

Mel interrogated his man trying to see how he *should* be feeling.

"So without repentance it *is* hell? Without forgiving others it is hell? So, how is this achievable, this salvation? You are asking the impossible."

Bri replied "You know, there is a story in the Scriptures where a man has not got enough faith and......"

"Yes, and he claims to believe and asks Jesus to forgive his unbelief. I know it"

"Then apply it. But if you don't really want the salvation which is on free offer, God will not force you - it is all your choice. Freewill and all that."

"Do you have to forgive dead people? The people who have wrecked my life are dead."

"Simply stated. Yes. Yes, you do. Forgiveness is about *you,* not them."

"But is there such a thing as 'a just hatred' a 'just revenge'? Is vengeance okay, ever?"

"The problem is that God is the only One pure enough to take revenge. When a court acts that is retribution which is only defined as the same thing in a bad dictionary. 'Retribution' implies 'righteousness'. Vengeance, for us, is ultimately selfish."

He left quickly not wanting to delve any deeper at this stage but promised to seek out Bri if he ever needed more help.

"Vengeance is selfishness" he declared to himself. "That is the key." Quite clearly, the killing of Malone had been wrong, he supposed. Then why did he feel so good - so very good - about it?

Mel liked the Pastor and thought that he might visit in the future and checked times of services as he exited. It wasn't as if he had a whole load more other things to be doing. That was going to be one of his problems now that he had quit his job.

Just what was he going to do with his life? He rather assumed that he would not be spending a significantly large portion of it in prison. Anyway, if that happened it would have definitely been worth it, although he did not think that the Pastor would be agreeing with him on that one.

Brian was not to know that his well-meant and immaculately delivered advice would be taken by his visitor and used in ways which he might not have anticipated.

CHAPTER SIX

He went straight up to his bedroom with a mug of instant coffee and a packet of biscuits.

He could smell the faintest of hints of Mandy on the bedding but he refused to allow this to distract him. That made it tempting not to change the sheets until just before her next visit. How he was looking forward to that. There was something positive in his life for a change and what a jewel to have covered for him like that. In spite of this, he needed to think; to plan out the future as best he could. He had to sort out the general direction of his life, at the very least.

He decided that he would have to start with his finances. He had known when he had seen Beaker that he would probably have more than enough to live on but he had simply never bothered to find out just how much. Money held no great importance for him, unlike for Miriam who had been quite grasping in her attitudes. He really would have to try to think up some positives about this tragic woman. He tried hard for several minutes and the whole process was an abject failure. He analysed himself and tried to see if it was just his perception then he remembered how all his old friends had tended to avoid the house as if it had been subjected to an outbreak of Black Death. Indeed, where were all his former friends now? He still had friends, of course, but distance had been put in place between them and it was more than possible that this had been achieved calculatingly by the unlovely lady.

He sat at the abnormally large, old-fashioned, roll-top desk where he kept his laptop and logged onto the Internet. He had set the same password for all of his accounts. The money had all been invested carefully on the advice of a good friend who was a financial manager.

Money had poured into the household in recent years. At Miriam's death he had received a large sum from a Life Insurance Policy through her job, he had received a lump sum of her pension contributions, they shared a hefty Joint Lives Policy taken out when they got married, she had money from the estates both of her parents and grandparents and he had a significant legacy from a Grandmother he had never known.

When totalled up he found that he was worth just under three quarters of a million pounds. He was astounded. Money, it was true, had never been important to him but how could he not know that he was worth this kind of amount? There was well over three times what he had expected and the house had been paid off too. He wondered why he had stayed so long in a job he had come to loathe. He had financial freedom. He need never do another day's work in his life if he chose not to do so.

He munched pensively on a Gypsy Cream and thought that he might take a holiday to permit him time as well as space to help plan for the future. He knew, that above all, he desired to try to make the world a

Better place for honest, decent people. But how? - He had certainly improved the world last Friday night!

If he were to take a cruise or something exotic he would maybe invite Mandy to accompany him. Yes, Mandy. Was he putting too much into the dirty weekend they had both enjoyed? Did they have anything in common? She had mentioned an abiding love for discos and going out clubbing. In his view, clubbing baby seals in Canada might be marginally preferable to such forms of entertainment. But she knew enough to get him arrested for murder. There was no way he could 'dump' her even if they were not suited. Don't say that he was going to find himself trapped by a woman yet again. Still. Things were going exceedingly well at the moment and after all 'sufficient unto the day is the evil thereof'. Then he stopped to ponder the quote and was less than certain what it actually meant.

He would give the girl a good time *his* way with theatres and restaurants and maybe the odd weekend in London to catch a show or two.

Ultimately, she would have to dump *him*. Perhaps one thing he could do was to mention other lady friends and make a remark assuming that she was seeing other men. It all depended on whether she was seeking just fun or some kind of relationship. That would need to be handled with care.

The more he thought about it however, the less he could see any future for them both. She was infinitely too young for him, clearly too fast and loose and being honest, too much of a looker for a rapidly aging fart like himself. All these things taken into account, it was the lack of things in common which had to prove the most destructive. He was not adjusted to the concept of casual relationships.

The encounter had fired him up, nonetheless. Miriam had been gone eighteen months and there had been no sex for three years or more before that and a humdrum exchange of bodily secretions on extremely rare occasions from their marriage up until Jenny's birth and an even poorer sex life from Jenny's arrival until her tragic passing. No. He had to admit that he had a great need for feminine company and Mandy had done him the favour of acting like a catalyst in this matter.

He liked the girl. She was sweet, charming and as far as his rather limited experiences could vouch, extraordinarily sexy. He had been off the market for too long. He knew that he was certainly no babe magnet but he was confident that most of his attributes might be seen as positive by many members of the opposite sex. So he would be on the lookout. Perhaps his problem was that he was just too ordinary.

Now. What was it that the Pastor had said? "Vengeance" or was it "revenge"? No matter. They were more or less the same thing.

"Vengeance is essentially selfish." That was it.

So, logically speaking, the killing of Malone must have been a *selfish* attitude on his behalf. He had killed Malone in order to exorcise his own demons rather than to perform a social service. Nor had he taken into account what Jenny might have wanted. She may well not have wanted Malone dead but she would surely have been horrified that he would ever be released from prison, let alone in such a very short time. Difficult.

Some things *were* beginning to make sense! It was not the killing of Malone but *who* did it and for what motives. These were the things which were the spiritual issues.

In his R.S. lessons, teaching about Capital Punishment, he had never had a problem explaining that the Old Testament concentrated on Society's rules for life and the New on how the individual was meant to live within those rules.

Society delivers 'retribution' but the individual brings 'forgiveness'. That was how the system was meant to work. There was no abolition of punishment but an emphasis on taking the personal, vengeful element out of the procedure. Part of *The Sermon on The Mount*.

He had never seen it so clearly before. But! What if Society was not exercising its proper function? What then?

Certainly, he knew the verse in Genesis 9 which said something about the executioner not being a murderer, although he could not remember the precise words used.

He was excited. He was onto something here. The Pastor was right. Killing Malone had been selfish, so in God's eyes he was wrong. But what if it had been another man's retribution he was exacting? If he was just doing it for 'right to overcome wrong' that would not merely be 'right' but entirely praiseworthy. Wouldn't it?

Somebody emotionally uninvolved should have killed Malone and he should have killed somebody different. Hitchcock's *Strangers on a Train?* Not really the same thing.

For the first time in many years he prayed for forgiveness. He half-heartedly asked God to forgive him for taking the life of Jez Malone and he tried to repent. The 'Miriam issue' was a real poser.

He was trying not just to be 'sorry' but profoundly 'regretful' of what he had done. Would that be enough? Did that define as 'repentance'? He was not quite sure what he should do or say about the fornication but decided to take matters a single step at a time.

Euphoria struck him in the afternoon as heavily as the misery had that same morning.

He was able to live comfortably, he was not going to be arrested, he had a delicious girlfriend - however temporary that turned out to be - and what was more, he was beginning to make some sense of the Christian Faith after all these years.

All things taken into account, it had been a pretty good day. He went out, bought flowers at the Asda and returned to visit his daughter's grave and spent a considerable time arranging them as he thought she might have liked them. They were carnations - his particular favourite -and he felt guilty that he did not know whether or not his daughter had her own favourite bloom.

He stayed for well over half an hour and provided he did not look at the name Miriam, he felt some sense of peace.

He bought a copy of 'The Sheffield Star' on his way home attracted by the headlines of a major murder trial which had gone 'belly-up' in the local Crown Court. Some rather dubious character had been released after the Judge directed the jury to acquit on what the paper was calling 'a minor technicality' in its angry editorial.

Anyway, today would be a turning point. There would be no more depression. He was, after all, his own man.

He walked slowly home and turned on the TV while he was preparing scrambled eggs on toast.

Reports came through on the TV News of yet another lynching. The body of a known rapist had been found hanging from a tree in Queen's Park in Chesterfield.

He really hoped that the perpetrators of the act had had no *personal* grievance with the man.

CHAPTER SEVEN

Errol Chapawi was a happy man indeed. He sat at the dilapidated desk in his pokey office looking forward to a week of adding to his already not inconsiderable fortune.

The office was actually located in Attercliffe although the vast majority of his connections and moneymaking were in the more populous area of Darnall.

Attercliffe had been the quarter of Sheffield where the infamous gangs of the 1920s and 30s had principally operated until a tough, no-nonsense policeman called Superintendent Percy Sillitoe, later to be a noted Chief Constable and at this period often called 'Captain', had arrived in 1926 and had used tough, brutal and occasionally unsavoury methods to break the gangs; the Mooneys and the Garvins had been particular targets.

A number of the heavily guilty men had departed to the 'execution sheds' although not always necessarily guilty of the *specific* charges levelled against them.

His name was anathema to liberal opinion for decades to come but the brutal effectiveness of Sillitoe and his team had been welcomed by all the locals, with the rather obvious exception of those either in the criminal world or on its fringes. Such tactics, as employed in both Sheffield and later Glasgow to cure a major, social problem, would never again be used by the authorities anywhere in the UK. This was irrespective of their ultimate success and the fact that living became significantly improved for decent, honest people whose lives had been tyrannised by gang members who bore exceptionally little in common with the principles of that other famed yet noble Yorkshire outlaw, Robin Hood.

Sillitoe went on to become the boss of MI5 and prior to that was given much unmerited credit for the formation of the Flying Squad. Viewers of 'The Sweeney' with John Thaw would be surprised to know that one of Sillitoe's heavy duty officers in Sheffield had also borne the name of Jack Regan, but he did not move on to greater glory but rather ended his working life as a well-liked cleaner in Mablethorpe Police Station where he had a more interesting than usual fund of stories to tell about 'the good old days' than did the average ex-copper.

Chapawi, a relatively recent arrival from Nigeria, had no inkling of the historical tradition into which he was fitting so admirably.

His English being rather better than that of the average Nigerian crook, he had been able to use multi-tasking skills as soon as he had arrived in Sheffield five years earlier, where his career had blossomed.

The tiny Nigerian community proved his first targets as he worked as a strong-arm man for some rather objectionable gentlemen he had met in one of the more seedy night clubs in the heart of Sheffield 9.

He combined this with some of the traditional money laundering so beloved of the dishonest Nigerian expatriates in the city.

It had not taken long for him to achieve a foothold in the drugs trade but, although he made money quickly, he realised that there were just too many people out there doing the same thing and prison would be a distinct possibility. He considered himself too intelligent to take such risks over a sustained period.

The drug money funded his loan shark organisation and got it off the ground surprisingly quickly. Starting with various hapless Nigerians, he found that he was soon lending to a large number of the local Pakistanis whose culture was strongly opposed to such activities. The more desperate were only too happy to go outside their own community in order to secure a loan as the chances were that this would remain a secret with Errol and Errol always liked desperate people.

His interest rates were amongst the worst ever imposed in a city noted for Shylockian tactics. He was reasonable when people could not pay - for a maximum period of seven days and even then the financial penalties could be horrific.

He employed a pair of goons from the low-life sector to explain precisely how much was owed by his terrified clients. Bill and Ben, as they were known in the district, were seriously tough but did not always meet his exacting demands, as their ruthlessness was tempered with a distant hint of almost-forgotten but still recoverable, humanity.

Whenever this began to get in his way, Errol was not afraid to accompany his employees to show them precisely how things would be done in the back streets of Abuja.

Breaking fingers was quite common as a means of explaining Errol's point of view and he clearly possessed a vicious streak which exceeded the given needs of any situation. As a fully paid-up psychopath, he derived pleasure from these occasional forays onto Main Road or Staniforth Road in Darnall where he threw himself with enthusiasm into any situation where it was considered necessary to *encourager les autres.*

He had not been afraid to use a cut-throat razor and his reputation was staggering for the most extreme violence known in the city in many years.

Most people displayed wisdom and paid up and his list of bad debtors was impressively small for such an organisation. It was over two years into his reign before the local Police had even heard his name - one of the perks of being *truly* feared.

The principle reason Errol was so happy today, was that it was just one week since he had been acquitted on a murder charge at Sheffield Crown Court and he retained a feeling of euphoria for having beaten the system.

He had used his much-loved, antique, Sheffield-made razor rather too successfully on the throat of his victim. He pondered whether the Police could be forced to return the weapon which was very dear to his heart.

His arrest and subsequent charging had come about as a result of him having lost his cool with a respectable Pakistani lady who, after keeping her debt hidden from her husband, had found that a simple £100 had grown to over £2,000 and she simply could not find even a fraction of the money he claimed she owed.

He had no regrets for her blood-curdling slaughter, only that he had got several unsightly splashes of gore from an opened jugular onto his new, designer jacket. He thoroughly expected to get away with it. Initially, the idea of being arrested was ludicrous to him. Bill and Ben, however, had unexpectedly and willingly turned Queen's Evidence on advice from their solicitor as they were desperate to avoid being classed as accomplices and, rather unjustly, lost a portion of the credit for this when Chapawi failed to be convicted.

Ironically, this had meant that they had received significant jail time whilst he walked free. Another 'victory' for the legal system.

An attempt by third parties, funded by him to bribe and threaten jurors, had failed. In consequence, Errol had finally accepted the inevitability of a Life Sentence. It did not worry him as much as might be expected, because being street-wise, he knew that the chances of him remaining in prison for even seven years were quite low and there was a very healthy 'pension' awaiting him when released. Occupational hazards.

The sob story for The Parole Board was already being prepared for him by Counsel.

To his utter disbelief his acquittal had come about from a very minor technicality. Even his own Barrister 'had not seen that one coming' and there was severe disquiet amongst the Police investigating team who yearned for the 'good old days under Percy'. Certain comments were made which had suggested that the Judge must have 'taken a bung' and although Errol would have happily attempted to do that if he thought it would have done any good, it was simply no more than one of the many vagaries of the system.

True, the case had given him unwanted publicity but he had much to be self-satisfied about. Bill and Ben would have to pay, of course. Being in prison would be no protection.

The office door opened and a man with a large moustache and closely cropped head came in; a customer reaching out to shake his hand. Errol was pleased and started to reciprocate when a stiletto appeared from where it had been simply concealed under a baseball cap and which was then whipped into the centre of his chest. His death was instantaneous.

The man slipped the knife into a plastic bag and dropped it into his pocket. He put the baseball cap that he had been wearing earlier and which had concealed the knife, back onto his head. On his way out, he wiped the door handle with a large handkerchief.

Having checked carefully that there were no obvious signs of blood on his clothing, he set off to walk the couple of miles back to Bramley. The washing machine would do its job and this time he would *lose* the trainers.

The body remained undiscovered for over five hours.

CHAPTER EIGHT

Another weekend with interesting prospects had come round and he was looking forward to spending it with Mandy. They had enjoyed really good times over a couple of months and neither seemed to have any expectations of the other. In fact, he had even felt sufficiently sure of her to discuss the kind of lady he would like to meet with a view to the future. She had made helpful suggestions and he had been impertinent enough to suggest the kind of man she should be seeking.

Sex apart, they were still friends. They were able to relax in each other's company although she never again raised the issue of the circumstances on the night they had first met; it stayed like 'an elephant in the room' but he knew he would be able to talk about it if ever the need arose.

His only line of demarcation was that he would never talk about Jenny but she had never once asked him to, for which he was grateful. That would never be easy.

So good were they together that there were occasions when he asked himself whether they might, just possibly, have a future but the relationship had the stamp of impermanence across it, so he dismissed the thought.

He would be sad when things reached their conclusion but he was actually more concerned that they should maintain a friendship which was increasingly important for his ease of mind.

It was true to say that he had never been happier in his entire life and the time had come when he felt able to discuss his marriage. He was unsure how the topic had arisen but that was not important and there was a ghost which needed to be exorcised.

"So what was she really like?" Mandy enquired, less out of curiosity than interest in his welfare. It made him feel alive.

He paused and chose his words with care:-

"She was the most unutterable cow ever to be born outside a field. I pray that she was mentally unbalanced because if that was her real personality she must have been the personification of evil.

I was mentally weaker when a young man and she homed in on me with a proprietary gleam in her eye. She was manipulative, self-absorbed and never failed to get whatever she wanted. For reasons known only to her, it was me that she did want."

Mandy shifted uncomfortably in the armchair, a little bemused - but she had asked.

"She rationed sex and managed to make it a duty; occasional, mechanical and joyless. I do not think she possessed any sexual desires and certainly didn't give a toss as to how I felt. If she did have a libido, she was capable of suppressing it in order to get at me. It wouldn't surprise me. She knew that I was permanently frustrated, day following onto

44

loveless day, and seemed to revel in it. I think the only reason we ever had sex at all was because she wanted to remind me of what I was missing most of the time. Sex was desperately infrequent but whatever we did, I always felt worse afterwards. She knew that. She engineered it.

She would only ever communicate on a banal or trivial level. It was as if she was not prepared to expose what she was like inside. If she refused to give herself mentally, then how could she be expected to give herself sexually? As for 'bonding' or 'being as one', with another human being, she was simply incapable. It is just possible, I suppose, that she would have been able to do so but had made a conscious decision not to on that level as well.

You know, she seemed to feed on my personality at the same time as she wrecked me. You would have thought that it would lead to divorce but Jenny's birth changed it all. I had a reason to stay in the marriage and something peculiar happened. For Jenny, she was able to dredge up some kind of maternal love; a love that I had never seen in her.

I am an honest enough man. I asked myself constantly if there was anything I could do .... but it was always a total non-starter. She did not like me and a miserable sex life was simply an accurate reflection of that; my punishment for unknown and unrecognised slights.

But now we had something in common at last and although she kept on treating me like an especially inferior kind of shit, we were able to be united in Jenny's best interests. It saved the marriage at that point, but our sex life swung between disastrous and non-existent. It wouldn't have been so bad if we'd been people who got along. Her interest in anything I did, said or thought was of no consequence to her at all.

She had a trio of equally appalling friends whom she educated into despising me as much as she did. I called them 'The Opening Scene from Macbeth' but not in their hearing - I valued life too much.

They were rabid feminists; man-haters and I suspect that there was something of a lesbian nature going on between two of them - or all three for all I knew.

What got me so badly was the pure hatred they generated and they were totally intolerant of any opinions outside their own narrow world-view."

Mandy interrupted to ask how he felt towards her now. 'Joyless sex' was not a principle she could easily grasp.

"I detested her. True. I half wanted her to fall under the wheels of a passing Supertram and yet I pitied her at the same time. How could you not if somebody was as sick and unhappy inside as she was? And for nine years Jenny saw us survive and somehow I doubt that she was ever able to detect our mutual loathing. We put on a good show. Now? Pity and hatred combined in equal measure. I think. I don't really know.

And.... and when we ... when we.....lost Jenny..... the hounds of hell were unleashed.

She sought to blame *me*. Sex was effectively abandoned unless it could be used as a weapon. By then, sex with her was a distinctly non-appetising prospect in any case.

She used to do multitudes of petty things to upset me, like adding triple amounts of salt to my food or hiding things. It doesn't sound much but it was incessant; an ongoing war of attrition. She never admitted it was deliberate but gloated all the same. Still. You only have my word for it - *she* would have put an entirely different slant on everything, I suppose, but I promise you, I am telling you one hundred per cent truth. I'm somebody who finds it easy to get on with people. I compromise easily and make concessions. I sometimes wonder if that was the problem. Maybe she actually needed somebody to stand up to her all the time. But once you embark on a particular path...... The truth is, I never even liked her before we wed. I must have been crackers - oh - and pre-marital sex was not too bad at all! That proves something, although I am not quite sure what."

Mandy listened intently.

"For a long time I did not want to leave her. I wanted to help her, believe it or not. She was damaged goods and for a long time I tried to repair her but she just became more and more withdrawn.

Sandra, Tara and Tamsin virtually camped out here until I took the message and repaired to the pub every time the 'Weird Sisters' hoved into view. You will never know how much I hated those bitches........perhaps Miriam was salvageable, I don't know, but with the input from the terrible trio there was no hope. Happily I've never seen them since the funeral."

He sighed and paused. Mandy said nothing and waited for him to continue.

"As soon as I mentioned divorce she cynically planned how best to punish me. She couldn't bear the thought of losing her psychic punch bag.

It was a Friday afternoon and I had been to the solicitors with the view to finding out if I could rescue anything tangible and financial from the ashes of our relationship.

The solicitor was a nice lady - invited us to a meeting the next week to talk it all through.

No meeting, just a callously planned assault on my conscience.

She was hanging from the banister. Dangling. Mocking me, purple-faced, as I came through the door.

She had been hurting because of Jenny's death, of course she had, but all that had done was to bring her character flaws into sharper relief. They already existed and that just made 'horrible' into 'the same but multiplied'.

Her suicide was designed to bring her own unhappiness to a premature end sure, but that could not be enough. She had to do it in a particular way - and believe me, she did nothing without pre-planning.

She knew her face would be pointing at me as I came through that door. It was an attempt to provoke guilt in me but you know, it almost had an opposite effect. I never have nightmares about what I *did* see in front of my face - only what I didn't with what had happened to Jenny."

Mandy came across and comforted him as the tears began to well up in his eyes. If only he had met somebody a bit like her all those years before.

The only problem which assailed him with this kind of thinking was that without Miriam, there could have been no Jenny.

He almost asked himself if his daughter had been 'cursed' in some way because of what her mother had been, but as that implied a hand of fate, he had to admit that he was much less happy with that as a concept than the more intellectually-fired challenges of the Christian Faith.

He wondered if he might have had other different but equally wonderful children with a wife more balanced than Miriam.

He wondered too if he would have wanted Jenny to have been born at all if he had known beforehand what her 'fate' would ultimately be. Pointless speculation, yes, but admirably designed to keep a grieving parent miserable for lengthy periods of time.

He had referred to Miriam as 'damaged'. He was not easily able to assess if he himself were 'damaged' or simply 'hurt'. If forced to choose between the two, he would probably have been obliged to opt for the latter.

The trouble was that Jenny had been the only person he had ever loved unconditionally. Of course, he had loved his parents and in some small way he 'loved' Mandy but with her it was more a kind of souped-up friendship with sex as an added bonus.

CHAPTER NINE

Mel finally attended Church one Sunday, a number of weeks later. The Pastor was as good a preacher as he had been a listener. He enjoyed the meeting; the warmth, the life, the vitality. The singing was bright and cheerful with an emphasis on choruses. He did not mind but was a little regretful that there were no traditional hymns at all.

The sermon was well delivered by the Pastor and interesting but not especially relevant to him as it targeted some rather obscure portions of The Old Testament, starting in Lamentations and finishing in Job.

He was made to feel welcome. People wanted to talk to him and were particularly interested to hear that he sometimes taught examination classes in Religious Studies.

There was an assumption that this made him a Christian. He did not want to disabuse any of them of that notion so he said as little as he felt he could get away with. Even so, he did stay for a coffee afterwards and was dumbfounded to find that evangelicals had other interests; a small group engaged in animated conversation about a recent match at Bramall Lane. Perhaps they got a worse press than they deserved. Certainly, the sinister undertones detected in such places by some of his erstwhile leftwing colleagues were clearly a nonsense.

The Pastor tracked him down and they engaged in general chitchat which he enjoyed. He fully expected an invitation to... well ...something or other religious and was not disappointed when he found himself under no undue pressure whatsoever.

It had not been like any service he had ever attended before in Saint Mary's at Handsworth or in the Wesleyan Reform in Richmond but then, Miriam had been an avowed atheist and made every attempt to torpedo any efforts on his part to have 'anything to do with all that religious mumbo jumbo' as she kindly put it, even though he had seldom shown any interest or inclination worthy of the mention.

The fact that she had actively prevented their daughter from attending Sunday School locally was something which had disturbed him, however and more deeply than most of her tricks. He felt it important that children should have enough input so they could make a rational and informed choice for themselves.

For that very reason, the R.E. courses he had to teach filled him with little less than horror. They began with the right on assumption that all religions were equally valuable but in effect they denied them all validity by lumping them all together. He liked logic and it was never logical to claim that 'all religions lead to God'. You might just as well declare that 'all roads lead to Rome'. The fact that opposites should lead to the same destination was patently absurd. The true logic had to be that either all religions were false or just one was correct.

The whole thing smacked of the prizes-for-all philosophies which he found simply risible and abhorred.

He was surprised just how het up he had become on the issue. It evidently mattered more to him than he would normally be willing to admit.

He decided to walk home after the meeting. He guessed it would be about four miles and he needed to think, almost as much as he was in desperate need of the exercise. It was a mild and balmy evening and he thought he might drop in at Handsworth Social Club for a late evening pint. He would need a drink after covering that sort of distance when unprepared.

The moon bathed him in an eerie glow and wisps of cloud scuttled across a rich and mottled sky. Again he felt happy; alive.

He was not quite sure how you reconciled killing people on an 'I don't have an axe to grind with you' basis - and if you could, how might it fit into any directly Christian context?

His earlier attempt having failed, big-style, he decided to try forgiveness again. He said:- "Malone, I forgive you. Miriam I forgive you" but he knew in his heart of hearts that he did not mean a word. Still, there was nobody *alive* against whom he harboured any ill feelings. That had to be a start. The whole 'revenge thing' just wasn't an issue any more.

As for acting as 'the instrument of justice' he was pretty sure that he was on a right track with his thinking - or at the least - not on a particularly wrong one.

Where a government had abandoned its side of the social bargain then what he had done to Chapawi was no more, no less than a social service.

Maybe he was the new Charles Bronson or Clint Eastwood? - Well, hardly.

The problem remaining was that he was acting like the vigilantes all over the newspapers. Of course he was. He *was* a vigilante. The thought took him rather by surprise but he could not gainsay it. He began to wonder if the people involved as vigilantes were as self-analytical in their actions as he was.

'The Sheffield Star' had postulated that his two killings might be connected but nobody saw them being 'vigilante action' and the Police were getting nowhere.

The issue was rather, whether he should continue his mission or not.

Yes, 'mission' was maybe the right way of describing it. What other purpose did he have in life? After all, Mandy would not be a permanent fixture in it. He had accepted that but he did want things to continue.

He felt so much more relaxed. It was interesting how having a sex life was able to make a person feel so much more at ease; less pressured. The thought of losing that was actually quite disturbing. He had never believed all that nonsense about men 'thinking about sex every X number of seconds' but he knew how much it was now at the forefront of *his* mind.

If he were to continue, on what basis would he select his future targets? How long could he expect to escape arrest. How would he cope with prison?

The thoughts of what possible sex lives there would be on offer inside, made him shudder.

CHAPTER TEN

The VOC meetings took place every two months unless there was a special event and these tended to be three or four times a year.

He had missed the last meeting and wasn't sure if that meant that there would have been quite a large turnover - as sometimes happened - and that could mean that he would now know very few people.

The turnout was phenomenal. He had never seen more than about fifteen people and tonight there was more that double that.

He exchanged greetings with a few familiar faces and took his seat as the special speaker was announced, a certain DI Kemp.

He was surprised how coolly he reacted and he even managed to give the star turn a brief nod of encouragement.

Kemp appeared not to be the greatest speaker he had ever heard, at least not as he warmed up, but he made a valiant attempt to convince a mildly hostile audience that the Police could not be doing any more. There was an absence in these meetings of the well-meaning; do-gooders and simpering social workers. Had any such attended, Mel could recognise a host of those present who would simply not have bothered to come. Few were interested in 'managing their pain' or undergoing bereavement counselling. These were good, salt-of-the-earth, Sheffield folk who did not fall easily into embracing trendy social or psychological concepts.

Mel cast an eye around the room and spotted two separate parents who had lost children to drunk drivers, a woman who had lost her husband to a drugged up, fifteen year old scumbag driving along Staniforth Road at a 110mph in a stolen Daimler. There were rape victims and a man with a fist-sized hole in the left side of his skull who had dared to challenge a young burglar who was carrying a lump hammer so as to be able to 'protect himself'. At least three besides himself had lost family members to murderers and one young man had lost his penis when attacked 'for a birov a larf' in a public toilet by some verminous souls carrying Stanley Knives who had made him watch in his agony as they flushed it down a toilet.

He was angry. Embittered even and joined in the general hostility aimed at the hapless Kemp who acquitted himself well enough against odds which were badly stacked against him.

As the complaints built up about what the Police were doing he eventually lost it completely and said in his hoarse, rasping voice:-

-"Listen, will you? I don't care if it costs me my pension but I *will* tell you the truth, the *whole* bloody truth! We *have* lost the streets because at any minute of the day three quarters of the Police on duty are filling in fucking forms, sat on their arses in front of computer screens and learning politically correct jargon to con people like you with, in meetings just like this one.

We could put three times the coppers out on the streets if we dumped targets; crap-useless statistics and political correctness.

Please be assured that upsetting toe-rags must not happen, however! Heaven forfend that we damage the feelings of criminals.

Us coppers have *no* chance!

Blame the poxy CPS, if you will, for losing files and refusing to prosecute open and shut cases.

Have any of you ever seen the 'guidelines' your very own community representatives - the Magistrates operate to? - You'd go ape-shit if you knew.

The Judges operate to guidelines too. It's all from our beloved political leaders who won't build sufficient prisons to house the scum we've got.

And there's too many judges who wouldn't recognise the real world if it jumped up and bit 'em.

You wonder why we have problems with prisoners 'having their human rights infringed' because they can't get their hands on hard porn? Worth compensation that - courtesy of the good ole EU, of course.

I'm a liberal, I am. I'd hang, birch and ensure that prisons stop being hotels for unfortunates.

I effing hate them. We are in a war and our side doesn't even *want* to win.

I've done the tour of Doncaster Prison - I promise you - pools, gyms, computer classes. The only thing I wouldn't enjoy would be the company. The food is brilliant, you'll all undoubtedly be pleased to know.

Don't blame the Police. Don't blame the Magistrates too much either. With the judges it's 'swings and roundabouts' a bit. You never quite know what the scum will get from them.

Blame the adversarial system where lawyers do their utmost to con juries into acquittals.

Blame the system which was changed from property owners as jurors to the more equitable 'anybody and his cat'. No coincidence that 'not guilty verdicts' shot up. Undemocratic, am I? Do you think I care?

All I want is to see the removal of vermin to where they can't hurt people; ordinary, honest Sheffield folk. I wonder how many of *you* were damaged by people who should have already been locked up?

Rehabilitation? - Don't make me laugh coz that's what *they* do. They laugh at the rest of us because they thrive on our weakness like the truest of parasites. ASBOs can only work if *every* breach results in a prison sentence. Nowt less!

They are a noxious scab on the face of society. I'm investigating two murders currently and I think the killers must be more socially aware than our politicians because they have done more good for this city than any twenty Probation Officers or assorted Social Workers. They have removed a couple of lowlifes from the map and I for one am not sorry.

Well I'll get off now. All those wanting to complain about this little burst of honesty, please address complaints to: The Chief Constable of South Yorkshire, c/o West Bar Police Station.

If any of you are feeling antagonistic and want me sacked, please drop a line to 'The Star' or one of the nationals. It will work. I personally guarantee it!"

He was eventually to learn that nobody had chosen to report him.

* * *

The meeting broke up and Mel was anxious not to leave in too much of a hurry as if trying to avoid speaking to the Inspector. He need not have concerned himself with this as Kemp received a call on his mobile and promptly disappeared.

He had a word with one or two more people and Kemp's outburst had left everybody slightly stunned. There was no other topic of conversation.

Jim Martin, who organised the group, suggested a pre-emptive letter to the Chief Constable just in case anybody did try to get the man sacked and there were nods of approval from half a dozen of those present.

"I think I shall refer to his 'dynamic and refreshingly enthusiastic approach to Law and Order'. What do you think?"

There were more nods and so Mel wandered off to get a drink. He remembered that it was possible to get real coffee here and he fancied one.

He bought the coffee at the counter. There were only six small tables and all were occupied. He must have been looking lost as a lady spoke to him:- "You can sit here if you like. There's nobody else to come."

He thanked her and sat at the table, managing to spill some coffee into the saucer as he did so.

She grinned at him as he carefully drained the coffee back into the cup.

"Mustn't waste any. It's far too good," he declared.

"I wish I could say the same for this. I think it's tea," was the reply.

He liked her voice. It was clear and enunciated words, beautifully pronounced without ever having that sound which he called 'artificial posh'.

He looked up into the clearest pair of china-blue eyes he could ever remember seeing and it suddenly became essential to assess the rest of this lady.

He could not determine her age. She would have to be at least twenty eight but could just as easily have been a well preserved forty two.

Her ash blonde hair was elegantly coiffed, achieving a simplicity which he liked. She was slim and as far as he could see, shapely. She had not overused makeup which pleased him.

She had again achieved simplicity in the way she dressed. A simple peasant blouse and matching skirt in powder blue gained his interest.

The final part of the assessment came as he gave her breasts a surreptitious glance and was only slightly disappointed not to find the kind of fullness possessed by a Mandy.

Ah yes. Mandy. What would she think at first view? He recognised that he might be interested in this woman and Mandy's opinion would matter to him. He had no sense that he was initiating a process to betray her - theirs was just not that kind of understanding.

Well. There were two things then. He needed to find out if this woman might be available and he had to work out if she was as agreeable to this going a step further, as their extended conversations might have indicated.

He was confident in himself. He had Mandy to thank for that. She had been a marvellous catalyst in his life. He had no idea why he felt this surge of optimism nor why this woman seemed so right on a mere invite to sit on a spare chair. He was fooling himself. He had to be. Still he had better engage her in conversation. But now there had been this awkward gap. It would be harder to start speaking after a lengthy delay.

His mind was deceiving him. The whole process had taken less than two seconds and if he had spoken any sooner it would have seemed that he was blurting out his opening words.

"Have you been to the 'Victims of Crime' meeting?"

Yes. That was safe. A 'yes' and the conversation would run; a 'no' and he would have to think again. The venue was, in fact, a Leisure Centre. For all he knew she could have been working out or playing squash. Who knew?

What would his second question be? He didn't look as if he was coming on to her too strongly, did he? He recalled the gaffes he had made so unintentionally the night he had met Mandy but then, he hadn't been trying to 'pull' her and he did rather have other things on his mind. No. Perhaps the conversation would run naturally or perhaps some hulking athletic type would come to collect her.

He glanced down and was relieved to see no rings on her left hand. But what did that mean, these days?

A second ago he had been convincing himself that he possessed confidence. Oh! He was just so 'uncool' as his former pupils would have called him. For pity's sake he was acting like a silly school-kid but then how much experience of the female of the species did he actually possess? She was going to be cross if a relationship developed and she found out that he killed people in order to 'find himself.' 'Cross', that was hardly the word. Was he being fair to her?

"Yes. Refreshing wasn't it?"

"That is precisely the word Jim Martin used. I couldn't agree more. We are in a war, you know."

"Well, I have not seen anything in recent years to suggest that as a nation, we haven't surrendered. What brings you here? - Oh, I'm Lucy, by the way."

"Mel."

He half stood up, leaned across the table, shook her hand and considered the ice well and truly broken.

"I've been coming here intermittently for about four years or so. I don't recall seeing you here, though."

"No. It's only my second time. My son went off to Uni' last September and I am on my own now."

So. That answered one question pretty comprehensively. She might be available. Was she deliberately telling him that fact? But why would she find *him* attractive? After all in a setting like this he could easily be very 'damaged goods'. Indeed, perhaps he was. But that also begged the question as to her motives for being there. Everybody at these meetings was either 'damaged' or 'hurting' - that was their nature.

'Son at Uni'? So that made her older than twenty eight. Could be forty, then. Possibly a bit less. Didn't really look forty. Check the neck. The skin was tight. He felt ashamed for looking at her like a piece of livestock. So she was possibly a few years older than him. So what?

"I come if I have nothing else to do. I've met some terrific people here."

Yes. And I think I'm looking at one now, he thought.

"Everybody I've seen has been pleasant but there seem to be a number who are withdrawn and not very communicative but I suppose that they are hurting inside. They are all victims, after all. I wouldn't expect people here to be full of beans."

"Exactly so. There are some who seem to have lost the ability to communicate."

It would be two months before another meeting. He had to make a move now.

"Look. I've not eaten. Would you like to grab a bite?"

Oh no! What if she'd eaten already? Even if she wanted to go out it was hardly likely that she would want to do so enough to have a second evening meal.

"Or just a drink and a snack perhaps?"

That was better. If she turned him down now it was either because she either could not or did not want to come. Which? If 'could not' should he ask her out in the future? Nothing to be lost by it.

"Great idea! I'm ravenous. Do you know anywhere?"

Fantastic! But that was tricky. Just how far afield should they go? What about 'The White Rose'? - I do hope she's not a veggie. Better find out where she lives.

"Whereabouts do you live?"

"I'm in Harthill."

Harthill. That was about six or seven miles out from Bramley. He could suggest 'The Beehive' over there but he wasn't sure if a booking was required or not.

"Do you know 'The White Rose'? I go there from time to time."

"No, but I've driven past it a lot. You do mean in Handsworth?"

"That's right. Are you in a car?"

"Yes. I expect they'll still be serving at this time?"

"I expect so. I usually go there around tea time. If not we'll just have to think again."

He drove excitedly to 'The White Rose' and could not explain how she had got there first. Her car, an ageing, deep red Audi, would surely have burned him off the road in any duel but what route could she have taken? She left the car park after he did. He would have noticed. Odd.

Still, he had a bigger problem when he saw that 'The White Rose' had just stopped serving food. She was waiting in the main doorway.

"I think we could get a takeaway and go round to my place to eat it," he suggested, hoping that he was not sounding too much like some predatory beast.

"Pizza then. I fancy pizza," she said.

They went to the 'Pizza Pronto' on the top road, bought more than they could eat and she followed him back to his house.

This had not been expected. He prayed the house wasn't too much of a tip and to be fair, for a single man living alone, it was well above acceptable levels. He was essentially tidy by nature. The most important thing was that he had put out a Glade air freshener only the day before so the house did not smell too unpleasant - something of a relief.

They went in to the kitchen and opened pizzas, garlic bread and chicken kebab with onions, mushrooms and peppers all over the kitchen table.

He opened a Chardonnay and regretted not having asked her preference.

"You mustn't have more than two glasses when you're driving," he said.

Good. He had said 'when' and not 'if'. 'If' would have been a serious mistake and may have sounded totally presumptuous. No Lothario, he!

She was obviously not somebody who would respond to a brash come-on.

He spotted a letter with an Australian postmark on the floor under the letterbox and opened it curiously, trying to decide whether he needed to remove anything from under next door's shed in a hurry.

He need not have worried. The house was to be sold as Bill Silver was going to live in Papua New Guinea. He was asked to keep an eye on the place and of course, was only too happy to do so.

He put the letter on the work unit to find that Lucy had already filled a plate and was waiting for him.

"Get stuck in ," he told her. "I'll only be a moment."

Within a minute he had joined her and the food was top notch but just not hot enough.

"Mmm. Microwave?" he suggested and they both gave their plates a forty second burst which transformed the meal. The Chardonnay was insipid. He apologised and stood up to look for something better in spite of her protestations.

He discovered a bottle of his favourite Chablis which he promptly opened and left on the table for her to help herself.

"That should be better."

She looked at him with a wry smile and enquired if there was a lady of the house. It had not occurred to him that the question he had wanted answered earlier was one that she might want to know about him.

"No. My wife died a couple of years ago - nearly. I'm a widower, I suppose."

She appeared content with the reply but still probed.

"What, no girlfriends?"

This was tricky. He could really put his foot in it here if he wasn't exceptionally careful and yet he had to be honest with her. She had an honest look about her. Actually, what was an honest look? Maybe it was the same as having a killer's look. Did he have one such? If he did, she was being very brave.

Mind you he had to answer the question. It had been a pregnant pause. The best thing he could do was to take a long intake of breath and get precise. Yes, precise. But would that look like he was prevaricating? Second breath in. Must speak now. Say something!

"Well, yes and no." Oh crap. Could he have dug a bigger hole by trying? Must explain and hope it sounds genuine.

"I have been seeing a younger lady for several months but it's more a friendship, really."

Aaagh! Double crap. Potential lady friends do *not* want to hear about friendships with other women. And younger, too! How stupid could he get?

"So not.....not a physical relationship, then?" she asked pertinently with a hint of mischief.

Ensnared! Abandon ship! This is not a drill! Crap. Crap. Crap.

Be honest!

"I did not say that," he said hurriedly, "It's just that...well.....the relationship is grinding - (oh no. what a choice of word) - to a halt. We have nothing in common at all but we do like each other - a lot, in fact - hence the friendship thing. We have both accepted that there can be no future because frankly, we come from different eras and our attitudes on everything from music to films are just incompatible. Her name is Mandy and I do really like her but it's going nowhere and fast." Did he dare say "You'd like her.?" - Perhaps not. No. Definitely not. "Former pupil?" - No way!

He thought he had rescued it tolerably well, but he was unable to guess how she'd react. Give it back. Now!

"And what about you?" Good. Smooth. Natural. Good. A diversion that didn't look that way. Good.

"Well. My husband died around five years ago." A violent or unnatural death he would wager, after all look where he had met her.

"So I'm a widow. No Mandy equivalent. I've not as much as had a date in all of that time. Things had been ......bad and I just couldn't face it."

Pounce! Now! This was it! The moment! She likes you. Why else would she be here?

"I do hope you will allow me take you out on a proper date?" Good. Voice pitched perfectly. She will agree.

"I'd like that very much."

"*Very* much?" That was over and above what she needed to say. He was excited. This woman had an air about her which got to him. He had never actually felt such feelings. Miriam? - Never! Mandy? - No. That was something else. What *that* was he couldn't say.

It was approaching midnight. Where had the time gone? She looked at the clock and he detected the glance.

Finish it. Close down. *You* suggest it.

"It *is* getting rather late. Are you free Friday? We could go up to Meadowhall Multiplex or whatever they call it and catch a film and get something to eat and have a really good chat."

She was quick to agree so they arranged for her to come to his house and pick him up rather than take two cars.

"If we start early it may give us more options," he suggested, desperate to spend every extra possible minute with her.

And so it was.

CHAPTER ELEVEN

Mandy was delighted for him. They had met up in the city and he was pretty sure that she would be pleased with his news.

They went for a coffee in a venue neither of them knew and were better pleased with the excellent Kenyan blend than with the service.

They were happy to chat and she gave him every encouragement and then she said it!

"Just how do you think she's going to take to ....well, your secrets? Do you plan to tell her?"

His first reaction was to wonder why 'secret' was plural. He had never discussed anything else. How did she know? But no matter, she seemed singularly untroubled by his secret life.

"I don't know. I shall just have to play it all by ear," he remarked.

The subject was allowed to drop and he could not understand the ease they both apparently felt with each other. He was a most fortunate man but then, he had paid the price in his marriage and perhaps deserved one or two breaks in his new life.

Mandy said that she would expect to stay clear of Lucy and was anxious not to lose his friendship but she suggested that 'it might be wise to call off their *physical* relationship, at least until they knew where things were going with Lucy'. He could have cheered.

* * *

Lucy was on time for their date at Meadowhall whereas he endeavoured to get stuck in Friday evening traffic. He was most apologetic and felt a great discomfort as he was never, and never had been, lacking in punctuality - 'the courtesy of Kings' - it was said.

Lucy appeared not to have noticed - the 'courtesy of a good woman', he thought.

They went to the Oasis, the central portion of Meadowhall and laughingly tried to decide which junk food to try. KFC won hands down and so, piled with chicken, fries and large Cokes they settled down to enjoy each other's company, leaning their elbows on the less than stable tables and sinking buttocks into less-than-comfortable, metal chairs.

They did not notice the discomfort, so absorbed were they in each other. Already the relationship was developing, ... well .... into a relationship. Nor did they notice a Mr and Mrs Kemp who walked past their table each enjoying a large Bradley's 99.

It was not until they stood up almost four hours later that they discovered how truly uncomfortable they had become with both feeling as stiff as boards.

Mel introduced the meeting with Mandy earlier in the day into the conversation and Lucy was pleased with the outcome. She really must trust him. She was correct to do so but he was perturbed that this could have been problematical for her had his intentions towards her *not* been as 'honourable' as they certainly were.

* * *

It was only as they were deciding to leave they realised that they had 'failed going to the cinema'. He had learned much about her in compensation: musical tastes - reasonably congruent to his own, religious beliefs - vaguely tended towards Christianity without quite knowing why. Family - both parents still alive - indeed a ninety four year old grandmother as well.

In fact she had a sister in London. They only met up infrequently as they liked each other but had nothing whatsoever in common.

Politics? - She was a convert to being an arch Tory which would have offended many of his former colleagues but as he was feeling increasingly fed up with leftwing do-gooders, the right was looking ever more attractive. There had indeed been one 'shameful' time when he had voted Conservative but he'd given up voting altogether because he despised the cosy consensus of the main three parties on the EU, which he considered to be anti-democracy, hideously expensive, corrupt and deleterious to voters.

In his view, the EU was the single, most important issue as it underpinned every other major policy and none could be implemented without reference to Brussels. She accepted his point readily.

He had noted that UKIP had stood in Sheffield constituencies and was more or less decided to give them a vote to show his disgust. He did not think that she and he were going to fall out too much on party politics although she did seem to think that UKIP were right of centre and he was able to inform her that they were in fact an extremely broad church. If he did vote for them he would be representing the 'intellectual right' within that church. Mind you, that did sound somewhat pretentious.

They returned to his house where he produced a superior Beaujolais. He invited her to stay over so being over the limit wouldn't be a point at issue and said hurriedly:

"I'm not asking to sleep with you. I don't want that at this stage. In just a few meetings you have become very important to me and maybe, a little way down the line it could be right - but not yet. I must be honest. I really want this to work and I don't want to jeopardise anything by moving too fast."

In reply, she leaned over, kissed him gently, nodded and booked the spare bedroom for the night.

There would be time tonight to have a few drinks and to start the exciting process of courtship.

This evening they would talk and by the time sleep brought an end to proceedings they would surely know a great deal more about each other.

The potential was growing. Love was in the air and he thought that she was willing to reciprocate. What she saw in him, he just could not begin to imagine.

* * *

She opened up to him and told the story of how crime had wrecked her life. She was tearful and for the first time, he saw the anger in her.

Her husband Larry had been a success in HSBC and had become the youngest Branch Manager since the days of the long departed Midland Bank.

They had married young while still at university in the city and son Jack had arrived within a year of the marriage. She had settled down into the old fashioned role of housewife and they had struggled in the early years to survive financially but the promotions came thick and fast for the talented Larry.

They moved into a five bedroom, detached house in the tranquil village of Harthill nicely before house prices began to soar. Larry's earnings were healthy and Lucy had no need to seek work to supplement the family budget.

Her degree being in French, it was difficult to see what work she would have been qualified to do without considerable training, so she had abandoned the idea of having a career and they decided that she should devote herself to 'making the world a better place to live in.'

She had joined The Liberal Democrats and worked through their Sheffield campaign to win the local Council. The triumph was crowed throughout the nation as they took control for the first time. She despised Labour's tendencies to reward: bad behaviour, the work-shy, *illegal* immigrants, criminals, irresponsibility and fecklessness.

She was delighted to be part of a movement which would tackle these things at the same time as running the locality in a more equitable way.

The doubts began to set in when she recognised a certain nastiness; malice even, which was immediately levelled at any dissenting voice or the hint of any statement not deemed to be politically correct. She felt the intolerance of a group which 'knew it was right' - always.

She became troubled on discovering that her initial assumption, that the party was in between Labour and Conservatives, was badly awry. Labour was criticised, it was true, but the derision and outpourings of hatred towards anything fractionally to the right of centre shocked her.

She had always supported PR and so the Lib Dems had seemed a natural home. Over a period of time she told Larry that she wasn't sure that she wanted these people to have any power at all. She did not trust them and she was disturbed that they didn't seem to want equality for homosexuals but rather, special privileges. She could not stomach their attitudes to drugs which she considered to be 'supping with the devil - no heroin-cooking spoon provided'.

She was unable to understand why they seemed more leftwing than Labour and then realised it was because they were.

She resigned her membership and switched to the Conservatives - not to be horrified by their policies but more by the lethargy which ran through a local party always guaranteed to see huge Labour majorities in local constituencies. She did some work for them but became disillusioned herself with the apparent pointlessness of it all.

She transferred her efforts into local charities and did three half days a week in an Oxfam Shop. She felt that this helped make life worthwhile and she helped out various churches and assorted good causes in money raising - becoming quite an expert at finding the best ways to raise an extra tenner here or there.

As a toddler, Jack had accompanied her when she went out money raising, an activity which pre-dated her spell as a political activist. After he went to school she had more time to devote to worthy activities.

"He went to the Handsworth Christian School, you know? See. My Handsworth connections pre-date you!" She said teasingly and went on to run through Jack's career to date.

"He got outstanding results there. It's a four to sixteen school, you may know," and her pride in the young man shone through. "He left at fifteen, then onto the Sixth Form at Wales village - next village from Harthill. Four top Grades at 'A' Level then off to Oxford last Autumn. He's doing History and hopes to go on to complete a doctorate."

His ears pricked up when she said 'History' and she spotted it.

"You'll have to meet."

"Indeed we shall," he said "but I think you will have to tell me about Larry, if you can. I'll tell you about Miriam. As for Jenny, I'll get there. I've never spoken about her to anybody before. I may need a little time. It's all so painful." He began to sob but felt slightly embarrassed and wiped his eyes dry on a large red handkerchief, which was apparently multi-purpose. She comforted him with a warm arm around his shoulder and said: "I am alright to talk. You just tell me about Miriam and we'll talk of Jenny when you feel you want to."

He knew he loved her and looked into her eyes and gave her a chaste kiss on the forehead.

CHAPTER TWELVE

She told him about her 'perfect life'. Larry and she had met as students and had fallen head-over-heels in love in next to no time.

They had each found their perfect soul mate and there really was nothing missing in the relationship. The only problem they had to overcome were the incredibly long hours he had to work in order to guarantee his unrelenting, ambitious climb upwards and onwards.

The positive side effects were that his salary kept climbing upwards and onwards also, resulting in a series of spectacular holidays worldwide.

He spent every spare minute with his wife and child and was a tremendous parent.

He had been a considerate partner, a good lover, an excellent provider. He was not particularly handsome but had a warm, infectious personality and a terrific sense of humour. Jack had loved his father as much as she had.

The nightmare had begun at around 11pm one March evening. There had been an urgent knock on the front door and when she answered, three masked men had burst in and after waving a gun in their faces, they produced two sets of handcuffs. Speech was minimal and the only mistake any made that night was to call one of the others 'Shane'. It would be enough.

One stayed behind with Lucy and checks were made to ascertain whether Jack was asleep or not. He was.

Threats were made and Larry was told that he was going to take them to his branch and let them in. He was then to open the safe. If he failed to do this a mobile phone would be employed and he would be able to listen in as Lucy was raped and tortured - eventually to be killed - then it would be time to wake up Jack for his turn.

Lucy was terrified to the point where she could no longer physically speak as her husband was led out to a vehicle where she had later learned that a fourth man was waiting. He left calmly and kissed her on the cheek as he walked out and said, "Don't worry. I'll co-operate," and he left like a jailbird between a pair of burly prison officers.

She found herself in limbo. Panic enveloped her and she sat shivering on the sofa and this developed into a shake.

After an hour and a quarter, which she knew from having been seated in direct line with their Grandmother Clock, the mobile rang. There was a burst of sudden, animated whispering and the two men ripped the phone connection from the wall, reminded her not to move for two hours or Larry would be killed and they disappeared into the night closing the door with a soft click.

Her first reaction was to run to the toilet for a triple body-emptying exercise and she eventually sat on the toilet seat pathetically wondering what to do.

Phoning the Police was no problem there was a phone in the study and another in their bedroom. But should she? She tested her voice and although squeaky, it worked.

It had to be over. Otherwise why the call? If she rang now the trail would be hot. Where could Larry be? Tied up in the bank had to be favourite. Surely he was alright. First, she checked that the twelve year old Jack was still asleep and fortunately, he was.

She rang and the Police were at the bank in under three minutes, as she later discovered. It seemed that it couldn't have been much longer for them getting to her house but logic dictated that it would have taken them at least twenty minutes.

There was no news from the bank for nearly an hour and she was distraught. When the news did come, she was unable to grasp it. There had been an entry. Alarms were going off. There was no money missing and no sign of Larry - at least that meant that he would not come under the usual suspicion in such cases of it being an 'inside job'. That was something. Pray he turned up unharmed. She was not subject to asthma but had a sudden attack necessitating the calling out of a Doctor. Through her gasps she was still sufficiently aware to wonder how the Police could get a Doctor out so quickly. Certainly, most ordinary folk could not.

He gave her a mild tranquilliser and a Ventolin inhaler. The attack quickly passed but the panic remained.

It was to be five days before Larry's body was discovered. Five days of gradually ebbing hope. Nightmares. Turmoil, mixed with positive feelings that, after twelve hours, you felt inside were futile and after twenty four, you were certain and yet still you hoped.

When the Police Sergeant arrived, amongst all the coming and going, toing and froing, she knew. It was not a possibility, it was over. There was no longer *any* hope.

His body had been found, bound and gagged in a field behind a hedge, in a ditch near Catcliffe. He had a massive wound on the side of his head and the Post Mortem revealed that he had probably suffocated after his interrupted breathing was affected by the pressure of the skull fracture on the wrong part of his brain while face down in wet earth. At least that was the best way she could explain it and she cried as she told Mel that his death had been hastened by exposure. Even then, he had clearly taken many hours to die.

The name 'Shane' had hastened the arrests. All pleaded guilty to kidnapping, attempted robbery and in one case, manslaughter.

The one who had actually killed Larry had not been charged with murder.

A twenty year old called Wayne Marner received a Life Sentence as his colleagues in crime gained effectively longer sentences of fifteen, seventeen and eighteen year respectively.

She had no understanding of why there had been no murder charge. Detective Sergeant Kemp had told her that it was the CPS who felt it was safer 'to take a guilty plea on manslaughter than risk Marner getting away with it'.

"You *know* Kemp?" he was startled but there was no real reason why he should have been surprised. Another thing they had in common! And she *had* been at the meeting.

"I was there in Sheffield Crown Court the day they were all sentenced and as regards the three, things were fine. Long sentences for the terror they had caused. But Marner - he just sat and smirked through the proceedings. Mel, I hate him with every fibre of my being. Oh. And by the way, do you know how long a Life Sentence is?" He could empathise with the bitterness in her voice, "A Life Sentence is three years and ten months," He grimaced, "You seem a bit surprised?"

"Quite the opposite! There are about three and a half thousand lifers locked up at any one time in the UK. When you find out the high hundreds of Life Sentences allocated annually and divide, then you begin to grasp it. That is just *not* unusual. It can't be!"

"Well I want to kill him. The state should have put him down. It is just so wrong that Larry's life is worth so little. And let me tell you what the 'little charmer' has been doing for the last ten months. He is driving a bright yellow Audi all over Scunthorpe dealing drugs with a full quota of school children as his clients. How do I know? - A friend's brother-in-law in the Police knew him and has seen him several times over there recently. If he were standing in front of me right now and I had a gun I'd blast his head off his shoulders. We still don't really know what happened at the bank and afterwards. From what one of them said - and only one of the four - it seems that the main safe was on some kind of timelock. Larry was told to override it and just didn't have the expertise. So. There you are."

He sighed, encouraged her to end her account - he had the gist.

It was his turn to make them both feel extra rotten. He told her all about Miriam.

CHAPTER THIRTEEN

Lucinda Saddleworth filled his every thought; his every waking moment and their burgeoning love was something he had not sought out because he had not realised that such circumstances existed. Surely, people were not actually happy in their lives? Surely, all they did was to muddle through with a handful of high points to break the tedium; the sheer ordinariness of life. Was that not the reality? Perhaps Mandy had shown him some indications that joy really was possible.

Well, now he knew better. Life *could* be special and worth living. There were dreadful problems however, which had to be resolved. They would end happiness in his life for all time. He was a criminal; a murderer in the eyes of the Law, moreover he felt a sense of 'mission' which meant that his inner prompting urged him to continue. He wanted to do what The Law could not. He wanted to see society purged and criminals, not decent people, being the ones in fear. He could help that happen. It was a duty.

As is so often the case, duty and self interest do not always complement each other. If he discontinued his 'private execution service', there was a chance - perhaps a small one, but a chance nonetheless - that he might just get away with what he had accomplished so far and be able to build a life with Lucy. The temptation was enormous. In addition, he still had the complication of clarifying, what Christianity was, and if real, to determine how this fitted into his framework. That was an area for serious investigation. His soul was troubled.

Prison was a distinct probability and on one, rather cerebral level, the reality of that was understood. In his heart and soul it simply did not register.

What was registering was that Lucy would have to be abandoned - and cruelly - for her own sake. He cursed himself for not extricating himself from the situation; for not recognising what was happening; for believing that there could be optimism. All this relationship could do was to bring her grief and heartache and he loved her too much to hurt her. He knew he should have backtracked sooner and she was going to be hurt because she loved him, at least a little.

He was angry with himself for their blighted involvement. Even if he were to stop right now, what was to say that forensic advances wouldn't see him arrested years down the line? What would that do to somebody as vulnerable as she had to be?

Were he to continue, the arrest would simply become inevitable.

If he broke it off, he might have to tell her why. He would have to. That might be the least cruel. She would surely be horrified but would find that easier, maybe seeing herself as 'well rid'.

The trouble was that it would mean yet another person knowing his secrets. She seemed quite socially-minded and so there was every chance that she would tell the Police. That was a risk which would have to be taken and he would respect her decision.

He would make a point of not seeing her for a few days but there was a gift he wanted to give her before terminating the relationship.

CHAPTER FOURTEEN

The Prime Minister was 'button-holed' in the lobby of the House of Commons by an earnest-sounding, middle-aged woman MP whom he recognised as one of the original 'Blair's babes' from way back in 1997. She had not worn particularly well and makeup had been slapped into every nook, cranny and crevice so that, from a distance, she looked glamorous but from closer up she looked a little too much like some elderly slapper who refused to grow older with a little grace and acceptance.

As he searched desperately through his memory banks for the name of this low-profile backbencher her face reminded him of the singer in the recruitment scene from the old film of 'Oh What a Lovely War' - glamorous to win over young men's hearts when recruiting but on closer scrutiny, a face in a highly symbolic state of advanced decay.

In this he was most unfair because there was little false about Harriet Meadows other than the obvious, facial disguise. She may have been a rather deluded, do-gooding, jump-onto-every-bandwagon kind of a feminist MP but although her Ivory Tower unreality and disconnection from the working class voters - who loyally returned her to Westminster at four yearly intervals - were pronounced - she was filled with an integrity unknown in this opportunistic, principle-free man in front of her.

He wondered how he had managed to get trapped in this way. He really would have to be more careful. In future, whenever he was wandering about the corridors he would have a secretary with him whom he could pretend was receiving a vital briefing. Yes, that would do it and once he got inside The Chamber itself he would normally be absorbed into a bloc of ministerial colleagues where he could be relatively safe. He would give The Chief Whip a bit of an ear-bashing when he saw her.

The good thing about ministerial 'toadies' was that they depended on him for their advancement in a way unknown to carefree, career-free backbenchers and so they could be relied upon not to hassle him. Backbenchers with ambition could also be relied upon not to rock the boat. Resignations from Cabinet on grounds of principle, as opposed to machinations disguised as principle, were rare in the extreme.

"Ah Harriet. Lovely to see you. I can't remember the last time we talked. Anyway you're looking well. What can I do for you?" A solicitous tone. That was perfect!

"Prime Minister. I understand that this island thing of yours is getting under way."

'Of yours' ? That indicated blame and the finger-pointing at him. This was not going to be good.

"I've just heard that these are all-of-life sentences with no possibility of parole. Where on earth does it mention this in the act that the Whips were so eager to get us all voting for? Where?" - She was almost shouting at him.

That was do-gooders for you. They were always so over the top whenever their liberal sensitivities were offended.

"Well, Harriet, that is just not true. There is provision for The Secretary of State to consider release at seventy and it can be guaranteed at seventy five. Do remember that these are the most dangerous of all the criminals in the country and there would be little prospect of release for them in the mainstream. We are anticipating that there will be fifty to a hundred added each year. The island is big enough to take quite high numbers. Surely, you knew all this when you voted for this."

"We were deceived, Prime Minister. 'Transportation for life' was never mentioned either in The Commons, at Committee or in The Lords. I can't find it anywhere in the small print"

"Harriet. I think what you should be examining are the precise powers of The Secretary of State - because that is the nub of the issue. The Act set out the parameters and he deals with the detail and outworkings. I am happy with the way it is being handled and it is massively popular with voters."

"And thirty eight people have already been shipped out to that hellhole, I hear," she almost shrieked.

"A little balance, Harriet. There are good - no, excellent facilities - and on their side of the island, convicts can live their own lives. Subsidised visiting three times a year is possible, even. It is hardly the Gulag you seem to be envisioning. Visit it if you must, with my blessing, then comment. I'm sorry, I have an urgent meeting with the Canadian Ambassador. Excuse me."

He stomped off, determined to keep out of her way in the future but concerned, as he knew she had the ear of many of the 'Champagne Socialist set' on the back benches.

He set his mind to considering Press attitudes to the vigilante killings and he scoured all the papers with even greater urgency than before.

The tabloids simply got excited whilst both 'The Guardian' and 'The Independent' had made vain attempts to prove that at least some of the targets were 'innocent citizens'. A searing article in 'The Mail' uncovered different facts and so both had then resorted to 'appeals for calm' and saying "this country has a proud tradition of having abolished Capital Punishment - we do not want it back on a private basis."

CHAPTER FIFTEEN

The entrance to Scunthorpe from the M180, via the impossibly short and severely curved M181, looks little different to the beginning of any other conurbation.

Travellers arrive from the West at a large roundabout having already spotted the unbelievable, unwashed, urinal-green-ugliness of Keadby Bridge, about a mile and a half to the left across the flood plain of the Trent Valley. Prior to that, from the M180 itself, newcomers will have noted the modernistic unsightliness of the reconstructed Keadby Power Station on the far side of the Trent which despoils the raw beauty of the inevitably flat, Lincolnshire countryside.

Driving along the M180 from Sheffield, had one been knowledgeable about the history of the region, perhaps it was possible to spot those signs of the controversial draining of the marshes by that odious Dutchman, Vermuijden, who had conspired to dry out what was then the Isle of Axholme and surrounding areas, way back in the Seventeenth Century. Indeed it still bears that now inaccurate name, right to the present day.

To the right, just before the roundabout, rises the first of the new breed of football grounds to be built; Glanford Park, so named to gain sponsorship from the then Council - and strangely, with the name intact many years after the Council had reneged on the deal. The stadium had replaced the Old Show Ground about a mile further up the Doncaster Road.

The entrance to Glanford Park comes up, still on the right - as would be expected - when turning right off the roundabout and heading towards the town itself. Doing this, drivers become aware of how, at busy times, the planners have seemingly engineered the potential for bottlenecks and traffic chaos with entrances to Tescos, B&Q and hosts of other large stores, complicated by the sizeable Trent Valley Garden Centre on the opposite side.

No matter. The second roundabout is equally a drivers' nightmare with five exits but as one follows the Doncaster Road up the hill, the town shows itself at its best with a thoughtfully planned series of well-cropped grass, shrubs and imaginatively chosen trees. Prodigious amounts of bulbs, well spaced across an area of possibly twenty acres, maybe more, leave a sense of well-being, especially in Spring and colourful leaves enrich every Autumn, after the horrors of the conglomeration of shops and stores which greet a first entry to the town.

In times gone by, the second roundabout, The Berkeley Circle, had been the first impression when Lord Quibell, that great patron of the people, had been working for the betterment of an ugly snatch of five villages grown into a filthy and radically unhealthy steel town.

The town needed a more agreeable face and this verdant welcome had helped to achieve that aim.

Had Mel known of Lord Quibell's efforts on behalf of Scunthorpe, or even of Sir Berkeley Sheffield after whom the 'Circle' was named, he would have made the assumption that these ennobled gentlemen were today, spinning in their graves.

Mel did not know anything about this industrial garden town, apart from the fact that it was a steel producing area. Indeed, the fact that it was built on millions, possibly billions of tons of iron ore, hence the nickname of their worthy football team; The Iron - better recognised as 'The *Mighty Iron*'.

Steel production had only started to build up a head of steam at the end of the nineteenth century and at the beginning of the twentieth when John Lysaght, assorted entrepreneurs and other men of vision had transformed the town into a vibrant centre for a steel which could rival and beat anything produced in Sheffield or Rotherham for quality.

The town buzzed and grew rapidly. Rail links were added, not just to transport out the finished steel but to establish direct links to Yorkshire pits to supply the ever-hungry furnaces.

Nationalised, steel had flourished briefly, and then began to wither away as the usual failures of governments being incapable-of-running-a whelk-stall came into play and taxpayers' money was used and overused to shore up gross inefficiency.

The unpalatable truth had to be admitted that Scunthorpe steel was just too expensive on world markets and the industry went into the kind of decline that would lead inexorably to the whole lot having to shut down - the only question being when.

Joining the Common Market in 1973 was close to the 'final nail in the steel coffin'. Our trading partners used illegal subsidies to prop up their own, similarly moribund steel industries and the British Government showed itself too scared of 'Our Masters in Brussels' to do likewise and so Scunny steel became increasingly uncompetitive.

Over-manning was rife and the trade unions were incapable or more probably, unwilling to see the larger picture. Moderate men were bullied, harried and intimidated at union meetings as Marxist trade unionists, with an agenda only peripherally connected to the best interests of their memberships, held sway. They excelled at frightening away many decent steelworkers and, just in case there were problems, they held 'meetings before meetings' when the real decisions were taken.

1979 brought the election to power of the ruthless Margaret Thatcher who was determined to end the drain of nationalised industries on the public purse.

The town trembled in anticipation for the falling of an axe which would bring to an end the town's proud history of steel production and indeed it did fall but only to remove the 'dead wood' and the inefficient. Redundancies were made, many families suffered but the new, leaner industry was once again competitive. The town breathed again.

Nowadays, the industry has Dutch connections and was owned by Corus. The Normanby side of the town which had housed the Lysaghts steelworks no longer showed any evidence of where the huge blast furnaces had proudly stood in all their steaming unsightliness. The area had been well landscaped to eradicate the horrors always found in the hinterland to steel mills.

Today, the site buzzes once more with a host of light industries.

Steel survives to this day on the Appleby-Frodingham and Anchor sites more to the East. So there, to the East of Brigg Road, lies the unpleasant, industrial face of the town but even so, some twenty times cleaner than forty five years earlier.

The people are generally extremely friendly and nobody visiting the town can fail to be astonished by the broadness of an accent which is truly different to that found in any other part of the country. True, it owes a little to North Lincolnshire but still manages to be magnificently individualistic.

So, it was to Scunthorpe that Mel came and he planned to go a-hunting.

He carried his own steel and it had not been made in Scunthorpe or Sheffield but came from northern Italy. It was a gift and souvenir from a long dead uncle's visit to Milan before the days you would get mugged by security staff at airports for carrying a pair of tweezers at the same time as they totally ignored the heavy, glass bottles of airline booze which some unreasonable people thought might have made a rather better weapon for those intending to hijack an aircraft.

The greatest problems facing Scunthorpe on the Friday of Mel's arrival were the proliferation of drugs and the consequent crime.

Mel hoped that his time in the town might help to improve that situation somewhat. He came offering solutions - well one at least which he was convinced would help.

CHAPTER SIXTEEN

Opinion polls were regularly showing a 78% popularity rating for the 'Muckle Voe Project' and even this was slightly misleading because a further 11% were only against it because they considered that it was too lenient, considering the nature of the criminals who were being shipped there.

Under way for three weeks and there was already a small dip in the figures for serious crime as far as the statisticians at The Home Office were able to work out on scant, and at this stage, rather incomplete data.

What did not really make sense was that the incidence of vigilante action had plummeted. He could have understood that this might have happened after a period of time but it was difficult to see why it should have happened so suddenly. Statistics however, will always contain blips.

There was an enormous temptation to make extravagant claims but as these could easily bite back if there were to be a spate of further lynchings, he decided to hang fire in order to avoid the risks and hopefully, the tabloid editors would do the job for him.

He felt just a little bit smug. With a General Election perhaps now sixteen months away, a major victory was possible if he were deemed to have had a palpable success in Law and Order matters. It had real vote-winning potential.

Indeed. It was beginning to look extremely promising. There was a skip in his step and a ready smile on his lips; the kind of smile which, being genuine and heartfelt, was something of a rarity these days.

The total number of felons who had been 'transported' had risen to eighty. Long-term lifers who had little prospect of release were given a 'once and only offer' to leave their Category 'A' Prisons for the wild beauty of Muckle Voe and acceptance rates had been quite high; a point which the PM was quick to use against surly and troublesome backbenchers like Harriet.

The policy for the future was to be that the only transportees were to be those of recent conviction.

Yes. Things were progressing nicely.

CHAPTER SEVENTEEN

He went into a newsagent's shop at the top of Doncaster Road and bought a map of the town.

It was early afternoon and he had just completed a passable three course lunch on The High Street. He had taken note of the way traffic movement was difficult and had walked down towards The Market where he spotted some fine looking smoked bacon at 'Bacon Charlies' and was tempted to buy quite a lot - so nice did it look - but he settled for a pound and a half.

He wandered past specialised biscuit stalls and cake stalls offering lip-smacking Lincolnshire Plum Breads and had been amazed to see one butcher's stall covering an entire side of the internal Market Hall.

He thought that he might prefer a smaller outlet though he could give himself no reason for the prejudice.

He came to a stall labelled 'Judges' and bought a pound of best, thick Lincolnshire sausage and, as he was walking away, almost burst out laughing as he wondered where to get the more intelligent ones.

No. This was hardly a time for levity.

He needed to find his man. He had searched through the Internet, through the files of newspapers and had eventually tracked down a photo of his target. Now he knew what he would be looking for.

He wandered back to his car parked on Oswald Road, well out from the centre and put his purchases in the boot - even serial killers have to eat and he had long wanted to try some authentic Lincolnshire sausage. He had even been given advice - not to cook them straight away but to keep them a week in the fridge first and then to oven-cook and very slowly. He really did not know what to expect and thought he would invite Lucy over for toad-in-the-hole. He hoped she wouldn't think him guilty of some sort of crude come on. Then it struck him that he was planning to ditch this super lady. Tears welled up in his eyes - because serial killers have feelings too.

'A serial killer. Eh?' - He would have wagered that he fitted no known profile. Would that make him more difficult to catch? He did not quite fit the definition yet, anyway. He needed one more hit before meeting the criteria - at least as defined on American Cop Shows.

Would that mean he could keep the delightful Lucy? - No. Hardly. - But what if he confessed to her? - Then at least, it would be *her* choice.

What if he did stop after this one? If he weren't caught quickly, perhaps he may escape detection altogether. What of that? Unlikely.

He could not afford to do anything too hastily. Besides, he had other business that required his urgent attention. So then, where would Marner be found? - 'Schools', he had been told.

He decided to have a drive round past John Leggott, South Leys and Foxhills. He messed up his routes and Frederick Gough was only achieved a long time after even the staff had departed. He was grateful to have found a more useful niche in life than what he imagined these teachers were now doing.

By taking out two scumbags he felt that he had accomplished more than in all his years of trying to swim against the tide in a run-of-the-mill comprehensive. What he was doing now, mattered. 'Crowd control of adolescents' had a value which was strictly limited.

There was not even the slightest hint of a yellow car by the time he had driven twelve miles by criss-crossing the town and trying to formulate some kind of grid-search system.

The schools had all drawn a blank although there were others to try if he had to return the following week and the one after that and so on, for he had no desire to leave this task unaccomplished.

It was just gone twenty past five and he was well into rush hour traffic. He decided to give it another three quarters of an hour of just driving and then he would take a break for some tea.

What he would then do was to hunt around all the pub car parks and try to check them all once in the early evening and a second time later on. It just could not be much more hit and miss and he wondered.....

A flash of yellow! He was onto it like a bat out of hell and driving ten yards behind in just a few seconds. His disappointment was almost physical as he spotted an elderly lady in an ancient VW, which on closer inspection, looked to have been hand painted.

He nearly gave up there and then. It suddenly occurred that it might be worthwhile checking car parks so this he did in between pub visits.

He was surprised, firstly by the fact that he had now covered nearly thirty miles in and around the town and secondly, by the speed with which he had familiarised himself with the town's layout.

He wondered whether his meat would be coming to any harm being so long un-refrigerated and decided that he might have more important matters to consider. Even so, it *was* pork and you do need to be careful but then it was seasoned which gave the sausages a better chance and as for the bacon it had been cured. So, why worry? - Be happy.

He felt a slight sense of losing the plot as he headed for 'The Cocked Hat' pub but as he was about to turn left out of Frodingham Road, he thought he might have possibly seen a touch of yellow just going out of view to the far right. He swung the vehicle violently in the opposite direction and cut up a silver Mazda as he did so. He hared off in the direction where the glimpse of yellow had been and came to a small roundabout. Then he saw it!

About a third of a mile to his left was a yellow car heading in the direction of somewhere called Normanby. The first shades of evening were beginning to close in. Without recognising any of the area at all, he put his foot down and was hard pressed even to keep in contact with the speeding yellow car which his inner antenna told him *was* an Audi.

He passed sections of light industry, mainly to his left and the yellow car slowed down for a large roundabout as they seemed to be emerging into countryside. It got gradually darker by the minute.

There was a series of sharp, narrow bends and he lost sight of it momentarily.

A sign to the left indicated Flixborough and his mind said "disaster". He didn't get it.

"Flixborough disaster". There had been some major tragedy there, he was sure, but it was days later before the name NYPRO came into his mind and he learned from the Internet details of a tragic chemical explosion which had devastated the whole of the area he was driving through at this point. That had been way back in June 1974. It was quite amazing that an explosion could devastate such enormous distances. He put his sidelights on.

He could see the yellow car again. The road was not designed for seventy and that was what they were both doing. The yellow vehicle took a sharp right bend and disappeared from view once again. As he negotiated the same bend, he saw Normanby village just seconds away and the quarry was taking a left at a tiny roundabout opposite the gates of some posh mansion or other which he later established as being Normanby Hall.

The yellow car was definitely slower through the village and he was now sufficiently close to read the number plate - which he memorised, just in case.

The Audi gathered speed around the double bend at the end of this village - surely better called a hamlet - it drove at tremendous pace along the road up to Burton Upon Stather, which enjoyed a pleasing avenue of trees. Just as the car was on the point of entering the village, without any indication, the driver took a sharp right past the darkness-enshrouded ,local soccer pitches which were now on his right.

Mel seemed to lose him but the Audi slowed for girl on a cycle as they progressed along a narrowish road through a fairly modern estate of houses and bungalows. After about a quarter of a mile or so from the turning, he was right behind it again and was even anxious to hang back a little so as to suggest he was not following.

The Audi turned into Huntingdon Crescent and some instinct told Mel to drive past the road end. He could see the car parked forty or so yards down on the left and the driver was going into a house. Mel had no problem seeing which one. By now it was just about dark and importantly, he could see no lights on in the house, so he parked up precisely where he was. Checking pocket for knife, he got out of the car and walked down towards the Audi pulling an England Rugby Union baseball-type cap down to cover the top third of his face.

He cursed as he realised that he had forgotten the moustache. This really was being attempted on 'a wing and a prayer'. He felt emboldened as he thought of what this man had done to poor Larry and his family. This man had paid no debt to society or anybody else for that matter. He marched to the back door of the house and could now see lights on within.

The baseball cap was not needed to hide his face so he removed it, concealing the stiletto inside.

He rapped sharply on the door and took a firm grip of the weapon. It was answered almost immediately and he recognised Marner instantly.

"A message from Larry," he said lunging with the stiletto at his victim's chest. He was unprepared for the speed at which Marner moved in the same millisecond that he heard his victim's name. Evidently, he was speedy of thought and quick in reaction.

The stiletto drove into his chest but was no death blow and did no more than puncture a lung. With a strength that Mel could not believe after the depth the knife had entered his body, Marner thrust his fist into Mel's face breaking his nose. He then slumped to his knees and Mel stuck the knife into his neck. He refused to cooperate by dying easily and Mel drove the knife directly into the heart. As he did so, Mel was conscious of his own heartbeat and how slow and steady it was. He really was not all that flustered by what he had just done.

The pain from the nose, however, was significant; Mel was desperate not to bleed onto the step. He was pretty certain that he had not done so thus far.

He considered dragging the body out of sight and mind, into the house, but this would only mean leaving more forensic evidence and the possibility that the DNA from his now increasing nosebleed might even convict him. No. There was no merit in it. Neighbours would not easily spot the body because of the way fences were lined up. No. He could stay there. Every chance Mel would be home by the time..... NO! What about Marner's fist? Shit!

He dragged the body into the house one handed, nearly wrecking a disc in the process. There was a tea towel on the kitchen drainer which he wrapped around the tap one-handed. His spare hand staunched the bloodflow from his aching nose. Once the tap was on, he left it, soaked the tea towel and used it to put a squirt of Fairy Liquid onto the drainer, dipped the cloth in the soap and then washed Marner's right fist. Returning to the cupboard above the sink he found a litre of Domestos "Destroys all known DNA," he said rather too loudly and poured it over all of the body, not just the fist.

He saved about a quarter for the area around the step. Making certain that he touched nothing, he retreated into the garden and was startled by a low-flying bat.

His heartbeat wasn't quite so regular now. He took the tea towel with him for disposal.

He drove quickly but not recklessly the opposite way through the village, so as to avoid drawing attention to his vehicle by doing a three point turn and eventually found he was coming back on himself along Darby Road. He kept bearing left, which his sense of direction told him would bring him back to where he needed to be and he followed around a couple of tight bends before spotting an imposing looking pub called 'The Sheffield Arms' on his right, standing proudly at the head of Burton's High Street.

He continued through the village until connecting up with the original avenue of trees where he had come in. He headed for Rotherham; a journey of some thirty five or forty minutes. He knew where to look and found an isolated, industrial-sized dustbin, away from housing, behind a parade of shops in Canklow. Using a duster from the car, he opened a rather loose waste sack and emptied out half the rubbish. He put in his top clothes, cap and trainers and re-covered them with the rubbish, handful by handful through the duster. He placed the tea towel at the bottom of a different bag.

He found driving in socks very difficult. He really must never attempt such a foolish thing again and then he saw a Police Car which caused an unwarranted surge of panic. The driver was clearly in a hurry to get back for his tea-break.

Returning to Bramley, on went the washing machine immediately. He laundered the remainder of his clothes with the stiletto still in the pocket, loose.

He took a very long shower and attempted holding a cold compress onto his poor nose but the hot water of the shower made this problematical.

He went downstairs and waited for the washing cycle to be completed and darted next door in his slippers with the knife and the unused moustache.

Had he got away with it? He thought he probably had. It was *just* credible that somebody had registered where his car had been parked but why would anybody have taken the number?

He would stop now. Tonight had been hairy. Yes. Stop now and get away with it at least give himself the chance. Play it cool with Lucy or tell her? Tough call. Be honest. Yes, he *would* confess and throw himself on her mercy. That way he might just get to keep her. Unlikely - but you never know.

Good. *That* was decided.

Blast and botheration! He had left the meat in the car.

CHAPTER EIGHTEEN

Saturday was to be spent at Lucy's house in Harthill. Most of their meetings to date had been at his house for reasons never explained.

She had suggested a leisurely day and allowed time in the afternoon for him to catch the televised England versus Scotland game from Murrayfield.

The second he saw her, he realised that there was more chance of him growing wings and dive-bombing Harthill than there was of him jettisoning her.

It was obvious that he was being awfully selfish and it was not a feeling he was accustomed to. He had always been somebody who never hurt others - it was important to him. It was part of that 'decency' which he had always had drilled into him by his loving parents, both of whom had died within months of each other shortly after he went to University.

He looked at her long and lovingly. She was wearing the same peasant blouse as on the evening they first met. He had told her how much he liked it the last time they had got together and now she was wearing it just for him.

They kissed as he entered the house and it lingered more than any previous one had done. No. It was impossible. He could not give her up but his natural fairness meant that he would have to give her the choice.

He didn't even know if she knew that Malone was dead - he had not mentioned the matter.

"Look. I've got something *very* serious to tell you and it may well affect our relationship. Can we sit down and talk?"

She insisted on pouring them both a coffee from the machine which was merrily flubbing away on the kitchen work unit and they went into the lounge and sat side by side on the sofa. She looked at him, her eyes filled with apprehension.

He didn't know where to put his cup so he held on tightly to the handle, took a deep breath and began:

"Last night I killed Wayne Marner," he paused and her face took on a sense of total misunderstanding. "I killed Malone, too and also the gangster Errol Chapawi who was all over the news. I thought I had to tell you." She did not answer and appeared to be incapable of speech, then:

"For me? ...Marner.........Was it for me?"

It was an obvious question but he had not anticipated her asking it.

"Yes, but he deserved it anyway."

"But you'll get caught. You're bound to."

This was good. She hadn't said 'that's immoral' or perhaps 'wrong'.

She maybe didn't mind that he had killed people - she just seemed worried that he would be caught. This was excellent.

She grabbed the coffee from his hand and put it down on the small coffee table in front of the nearest armchair alongside her own.

She grabbed his head and French kissed him with an unconcealed passion whilst grabbing at his clothing to such an extent that his sweatshirt simply disintegrated. She ripped his remaining clothes off and straddled him. He was about to be subsumed into the most passionate moments of his newly- discovered sex life.

They climaxed together in a couple of minutes and fell apart, laughing and gasping onto the floor where he put an arm around her and said:

"I do hope my coffee hasn't gone cold," whereupon she hit him on his upper arm and it *hurt*. His nose was already throbbing madly but she did not seem to have spotted the bruising. Kissing had proved painful as anybody who has attempted to kiss passionately with a broken nose will readily confirm.

They sat and hugged each other without saying another word for a very long time. After the burst of passion, it was now time to make love which they did for most of the rest of the morning. He was forced to tell her that he had 'knocked his nose' and asked her to take care with it.

He had never made love with Miriam. He only thought he had with Mandy - this *was* the real thing. This was it. It was his first time!

Now he understood why sex was considered so special that it should only be indulged within a marriage. The Christians weren't far wrong on that!

"I would have asked for your hand in matrimony," he said with mock pomposity, "but I think our future has a few potential problems."

"I want to talk about Jenny before we talk about ......well ....the rest. How do you feel about that? I need to understand you better."

It was nearly lunchtime so they decided to go out for a walk and finish up in 'The Beehive' for lunch, which she had recommended but before they went out, she had to find him one of Jack's sweatshirts which was a full size too small and horribly uncomfortable.

The countryside made it easier to empty his soul although he was unable to say why.

Suddenly, absurdly and with neither warning nor explanation, the sausages came to the forefront of his mind.

"Come to my house for a late lunch tomorrow," he said "I'm cooking toad-in-the-hole but it'll be late as I'm going to Church in the morning."

The incongruity of it all struck her hard but she offered to join him.

Their rural walk was simply beautiful. The late morning was fresh but mild and the air seemed breathable. They walked hand in hand like love-smitten teenagers but he was all too aware that his happiness was so likely to be interrupted.

Never having talked about what had happened to Jenny, he was not even sure that he could.

He thought 'If I make a start, we'll see how it goes' and a wave of sadness cut through the euphoria of what had been the best day of his life. Funny. Where had the hours gone? Who had won the rugby?

CHAPTER NINETEEN

Saturday morning. July. Cloudless, blue skies. Weather hot and gentle winds pulsating across the most perfect morning of the year. Butterflies. And surely, in a city, that could not have been a distant lark?

The air was balmy and the pollens a little too high to allow sensitive hay fever sufferers a day of even limited comfort.

Jenny Roberts went for a bicycle ride from which she would never return.

The girls, Jenny and family friend Marianne, who being four years older was considered 'more responsible', had gone out for a ride along the canal towpath close to Marianne's home.

There had been laughter and girlish squealing as they rode, rather too fast for good control, along the pathway. These were joys of a childhood which knew no darkening. Their lungs filled with God's good air - no - His best air.

Careless, carefree; they rushed and scurried; pedalled and braked; laughed, joked and Jenny shrieked in envious anticipation of growing to Marianne's age when she too might have a *proper* boyfriend - one who even visited the house and took her smiling to the Multiplex on *proper* dates.

Growing older would be an adventure as she developed into early womanhood; what a time to look forward to. She was pleased for Marianne but still more than a little jealous. Mind you, she could not see her Mum wanting her to bring a boyfriend home - ever.

At nearly ten, she knew she would have to wait another three years, probably, and her inbuilt sense of reality told her that Mum would do all in her power to put a stop to *any* boyfriend. She was old enough to recognise what Mum would say - "You are too young. You have school and career to think about first."

Mum was never fun. Dad would understand and would be protective in a different, more laidback kind of way. He would talk about schoolwork too, but would be more interested in the qualities - or otherwise - of any potential boyfriend.

Mum was okay but she lacked Dad's warmth, sense of fun and good humour.

If asked, she would have declared enthusiastically how she loved Dad. If asked the same about Mum, she would have said "Of course I do," but young as she was, something inside; something hidden within the depths of her very soul, would have told her that she was just being dutiful.

She had no worries on this splendid day. Why couldn't every day be just like this one?

Marianne was showing off, as was her custom, and sped off pedalling furiously.

Smaller bike, smaller wheels and less developed muscles, the younger girl had no chance of keeping up. In just a couple of minutes Marianne was almost out of sight.

As the young, fiercely good-looking, well-dressed, longhaired man emerged from behind a hawthorn, she had to attempt to work the cycle carefully around him as he gave no ground in the centre of the path. This accomplished, she stood up on the pedals and prepared to win back some of the ground lost to Marianne by putting on a real spurt. Marianne had turned off to the right.

He threw an arm across her chest knocking her off the bike and she landed heavily on the path. Nobody was in view as he dragged her skirt up and tore her underclothes from her body. Already crying, she began to scream as he attempted to rape her. He punched her in the face with such power that she lapsed into semi-consciousness.

Marianne had expected Jenny to catch her up fairly quickly and came back, somewhat puzzled, to see where Jenny had got to. As she turned back onto the towpath she immediately spotted the attack and displaying an indisputable courage, with no thoughts whatsoever for her own safety, she screamed at the man later to be identified as Malone, who looked up as the gap between them shortened. She pedalled as nobody has ever tried to pedal in the entire history of the bicycle.

Malone leapt to his feet having tried and failed to penetrate the pretty little girl who lay limply and awkwardly like a discarded soft toy.

To stall pursuit, he picked her up and cast her scornfully into the dank and dirty waters of the canal. As an afterthought, he threw the bicycle on top of the widening ripples, turned and fled.

Marianne returned, sobbing. There was no sign of Jenny. Not even the merest disturbance of the surface of the filthy water.

She rode home at speed to tell her parents and took the emergency services back to the precise spot. She gave a highly accurate account, only failing to mention how much distance there had been between the two girls when Malone had first pounced.

She had seen the man from close up as she rode past the hawthorn and again from distance. Her description was not much but it was enough.

Malone was arrested and charged with murder even before Jenny's body was recovered later that day but the charge was later reduced to manslaughter. Forensic evidence survived the waters of The Sheffield Canal and he was convicted and given a Life Sentence.

Malone served three years and eleven months. Lucy and Mel had much in common.

CHAPTER TWENTY

Lucinda Saddleworth lay back in her bath under an excessive quantity of soap bubbles and reviewed her day. She was probably tougher than Mel thought. In the last five years she had had to learn to cope with impossible horrors and their consequences which were ongoing and would never entirely leave her. How could they? Very often, crime victims are affected for the remainder of their lives and she would be one such.

She felt happy now, even so. She loved Mel. She was delighted that he had trusted her with his secrets and was filled with the beautiful, malicious joy of that dish best served cold - revenge.

He had played a most unlikely knight in shining armour. It was hard to believe that what he had told her was true but the steel in his account, the satisfaction in his eye and what local Ceefax had just told her, proved the point.

But he was so gentle, so mild-mannered; a mild-mannered Nemesis, in fact.

The sex had been wonderful. She had not realised how much she missed and needed physical contact.

"Shit!" Doesn't sex have a possible side effect called pregnancy? She wasn't a silly schoolgirl, after all. She was worse!

She got out of the bath and dried off. In her towelling robe, she walked barefoot to the phone, leafed through the phonebook and looked for a twenty-four hour Chemists. She thought there was one on The Wicker in Sheffield.

She found it eventually, Associated Chemists, and phoned to establish that she could come to collect a morning after pill.

She dressed and drove immediately into the city, waded past wall-to-wall druggies collecting their methadone and picked up the two tablets, to be taken twelve hours apart.

She was not over happy about this as a moral course of action but knew that she would never permit herself the indignity of an abortion; would never allow any living, part-formed child of hers to be ripped out of her body. Unlike the vast majority of people who did have terminations - oh, how she hated that euphemism - she had seen 'The Silent Scream' and associated feature programmes on video. From that day she had become a vociferous opponent of 'abortion on demand' - more reason still to have abandoned The Lib Dems.

She did feel very slightly hypocritical as the morning after pill could, by some, easily be construed as being 'just a very early abortion'. She refused to dwell on the issue and made a mental note to get an early appointment at the clinic so as to go back on the pill as soon as possible - after all, who knew how many sessions more she and her lover would be allowed together? She sighed.

Returning home she went back to her bath but this time with a stiff vodka and tonic laden with ice and lemon - it would help her relax after the excitement. She wouldn't bother Mel with details of the incident. When she had thinking to do she preferred to feel relaxed and that was what she had intended when first starting this interrupted bath.

Step by step, then.

Right. Was she in love with this man? - Yes.

Did it bother her that he killed people? - Knowing the circumstances, no.

Did it bother her that he might be arrested? - Very much.

Would she still love and support him even in prison? - Indubitably.

Did she approve of his 'mission'? - Tricky. Yes, in theory, but no if it meant that she would lose him.

What was her attitude to the killing of Marner? - A love token!

There was nothing more to be said, really. They were each a foil for the other. She allowed her mind to drift over the things they shared together. How strangely similar they were. How could an accidental meeting in a cafe pitch two people together who were so well suited? - Providence?

She relished the novels of the nineteenth century, especially Dickens and Hardy. He quite liked both but his tastes were wider. She could introduce him to Balzac - her speciality at University.

She liked Dylan, Leonard Cohen and all sorts of Folk Music. They were delighted to think that they could visit Folk Clubs together. The one at 'The Beehive' met seven or eight times a year. There were others in Chapeltown, Wickersley and Wentworth.

They both enjoyed wine but her range was limited, his extensive.

They both liked TV sitcoms with her preferring 'Ally McBeal.' He, on the other hand, liked most, provided that they were not in the 'Terry and June' mould.

Both disliked soaps but were just about prepared to make an exception for 'Coronation Street' as this was 'not a soap but an institution' as they laughingly declared to each other.

He adored the 'Law and Order' series. She had never seen it.

She loved Italian food and he was decidedly lukewarm on that preferring almost all other ethnic cuisines.

They had a great deal which brought them together and so little to separate them. Prison would separate them like nothing else short of death could.

What if Mel were to be caught? Would they send him to that 'Mucky Vole' place in Scotland? How would she visit? One thing was certain - visit she would.

Loyalty was one of her abiding qualities and she knew he would be loyal to her.

One thing that troubled her was that this Mandy knew so much. Too much. Apparently, she held Mel's fate in her hands. Could *she* be trusted? - At least, Mel seemed to be of that opinion.

She was not sure why he had left so early. She had expected that he would stay the night but after the contraceptive slip up, it was as well that he had gone.

She would be seeing him tomorrow. Church? Why had she agreed? She was not especially religious. But then, she hadn't agreed, *she* had suggested it. Still, all new experiences had merit. It was a long time since she had been to Church and that was at the traditional Anglican in Harthill. But with Mel, it would be tremendous. *He* was tremendous.

* * *

She moved onto the moral side of the matter. At what point was a citizen entitled to take the Law into his own hands? After all, she had been brought up to respect the Law and she did understand how the Law was the cement which held a society together; preventing anarchy.

The problem was clearly that there had been a breakdown of the system and the vigilante action over the last year was, in her view, an inevitable social consequence.

So what caused that breakdown? - The answer was complex with strand weaved within strand. She went through the list of reasons which had been put forward when she was a Lib Dem; drug laws were too harsh - decriminalise and see crime to fund habits decrease; not enough for youngsters to do; insufficient emphasis on rehabilitation.

She tried hard and struggled to come up with any others and then remembered that they were seemingly committed to more Police 'on the beat'.

She was unambiguously opposed to the liberalisation of drug laws knowing that the places where this had been tried had all had to backtrack and even if it reduced crime, there would be different social problems caused by the foreseeable increase in the number of druggies.

Had the chemists tonight not shown the downside to the argument? - Sad, pathetic, empty shells of what used to be people; unable to smile but many with an off-putting, inbuilt snarl contorting their facial features.

Neither had she forgotten the big headline in 'The Sheffield Star' some years before which had informed the readership that at that time, more druggies were dying from methadone than from heroin. Surely this should not be allowed. Even a cursory appraisal revealed that this was just another vague idea floated as a panacea. No chance!

More Police could help but the Youth Club argument always seemed to forget how the streetwise kids tended to trash them or intimidate the decent or fringe youngsters, so these so often turned into no more than a gang headquarters. Ironically, it was some Lib Dem members who were Youth Workers who had explained to her how the system worked in reality.

Her best friend, Georgina, was a former Magistrate and had dismayed her when she elaborated on what was revealed in the criminal records she had so often studied. Undoubtedly, the average criminal did not respond to Community Penalties designed to promote rehabilitation. The problem was that the 'do-gooders' as she put it, failed to take into account that most criminals came from an entirely different culture; one which did not require them to become useful members of society. Do-gooders always sincerely believed that 'behind every persistent offender, there was a valuable citizen desperate to get out' - and they were wrong. Dangerously so.

Indeed, why would anybody on benefits, doing a few odd jobs in the black economy, trading in the occasional twenty or thirty cartons of illegally-imported cigarettes, doing a little selling of goods fallen from the back of a lorry, some indulging in petty crime and earning handsomely from low level drug dealing, ever seek honest employment?

The consequences were: a dramatic fall in living standards, having to take orders, needing to get up in mornings rather than afternoons, minimum-wage as maximum potential and the expenditure of large amounts of effort.

Against this backcloth, it was little wonder that so many accepted court disposals as one of those inevitable outcomes or merely occupational hazards , which were no more than minor inconveniences to them getting on with their ingrained dishonesty.

George, as she called her, stated that prison was only marginally more useful and insisted, that having visited three local prisons, she had stayed in worse hotels - and with reference to Doncaster Prison, she had said it with more than a trace of rancour in her voice.

"Fear! This amoral underclass has nothing whatsoever in the system to scare them," she had announced the day she quit The Rotherham Bench; seething with rage and a muted frustration for 'a useless and impotent system'. Lucy never did find out what the final straw had been for George.

She turned on the hot tap as the water had grown cold without her noticing and brought the bathwater up to a more comfortable temperature.

If this was how it was with minor crimes, what about major ones? Well, her own experiences of the system had weighed the system in the balance and discovered that it was extremely wanting. Her two trips to VOC meetings had opened her eyes - not least with what DI Kemp had had to say. Then there was Mel's case........

Fear *was* the key. She was sure of that. George wasn't wrong. All else was peripheral.

What had Marner had to fear? - Precious little. He had not known that Mel would appear from nowhere like a rider on a pale horse.

Perhaps these vigilantes were doing something positive. If they could put the 'fear of God' into perverts, drug dealers, men of violence, con artists preying on the elderly and burglars, maybe it was a good thing.

She wondered if the vigilante acts across the country really were co-ordinated. It made sense.

Stranger too, that if that were the case, then Mel had entered the scene totally independently.

Was there some 'social law of inevitability' that weakness on crime would have such outcomes?

She turned on the hot tap again so as to give the matter further thought.

Justice. That was the key word. The people of every nation craved it. All that most people in the world wanted was the entitlement to be able to live their lives uninterrupted by: bad neighbours, governments, petty officialdom and above all, criminals.

Why was it that there were so many out of touch people who seemed to care more about the needs and even the bloody *feelings* of the criminal classes than they ever did about the needs and feelings of their victims and families?

She could not grasp the picture. It made no sense. Society had given her a few thousand, measly pounds from The Criminal Injuries Compensation Board for her loss - and that was it!

Society was prepared to bend over backwards to help and attempt to rehabilitate people like Wayne Marner - fat load of good it had done - and it all seemed so acceptable to this powerful, liberal elite. Was it because they were largely taken from the upper and middle classes who were usually able to escape contact with social vermin? - If it did not directly affect them - then small surprise how *their* opinions became more important than the actual lives of ordinary people who have to suffer the consequences of such people's finer feelings. She was angry now. Was it all part of that leftwing - possibly even Trotskyite - agenda to make the western democracies collapse in on themselves by erosion of social standards?

In what way had Marner paid for his heinous behaviour? In what way had he repaid this debt to society as the do-gooders were always going on about? - Well, he hadn't - at least not until Mel - lovely, lovely Mel - had entered the situation.

Had justice now been done? - Of course it had. Marner had ultimately paid an equitable penalty for the level of crime committed but in a proper society, no individual should ever have to make their own justice. That was what was wrong.

She realised that justice could not possibly exist when the punishment failed to measure up to the crime committed.

She was fed up of excuses. The classics were: unhappy childhood, abuse (usually unproven yet virtually always claimed), no sense of right and wrong. Well it was garbage. Purest bullshit. The vast majority of crime was committed because of an amoral - occasionally immoral - selfishness. Had Larry died because Marner was anything other than a self-obsessed, greedy, sadistic piece of scum? - Not at all!

Mel had once told her that of the several thousand pupils he had taught, he had met only a few who could not distinguish between right and wrong although he was certain that all of these did know what was *expected* of them - and that was enough. What more did you need?

She recalled the American law enforcement agent who had said:- "Define a liberal on crime - a hardliner who hasn't been mugged yet!"

So true.

The strangest thing was how in Labour strongholds like Sheffield, the constituents tended to want a very heavy line on crime yet they continued to elect total wets without a murmur just because they were Labour. She knew that the Conservatives had little to boast about in this field either, as for Lib Dems, she prayed they would never see power - the situation was maybe bad, but not so bad that they couldn't make it substantially worse.

There was something morally wrong that a detached elite should be able to have their liberal opinions foisted upon a populace who had to pay the price for their social hypothesising. Were we all to be guinea pigs in their bizarre, social experimenting?

She was angrier still, now, and twisted the tap for enough hot water to give her another ten minutes. Bath-time was always 'think time' for Lucy.

Obviously, Mel was absolutely right and if she had had sufficient guts, she might just have suggested carrying on - with her helping. But he was right. Every killing brought arrest a notch closer.

She got out of the bath and put on her robe again and rang him. It was a short call just to explain that she would act as an alibi for the last two killings - 'he had been at her house'.

He pointed out the flaws in this. If a connection were to be made between them and if the hits were linked by the Police, she was actually the *worst* person to be providing an alibi. Better to have been 'home alone with the TV'. Still, he was glad to hear her voice and the 'short conversation' took an hour and a quarter and he did say how unwise it might be for their relationship to become too widely known. What if Kemp found out? That man was no fool.

He made a mental note to pop into ASDA on the way to Church in order to purchase some ready-made Yorkshire puddings - his own attempts to develop this essential, culinary skill had thus far, eluded him. Indeed, his attempts had more than once, ended in abject failure.

Undoubtedly, the noble and compassionate Aunt Bessie would come to his gastronomic rescue.

CHAPTER TWENTY ONE

Pastor Brian Patten was on good form. He led the service, was bright, sincere and amusing. He made it clear that Trevor Witton, who was the visiting preacher on that day, was 'a bit of a catch' as he ran a Church in the USA with over two thousand members.

Mel's heart plummeted earthwards. He had seen enough brash American preachers on TV and had been less than impressed with the God Channel's selection of speakers and some of the other religious Sky Channels turned his stomach. He had abandoned them. 'Emotionalism in an American accent' was the last thing he needed. He contemplated giving Lucy a nudge and making a bolt for the door but they would have had to have walked across the front of the Church in front of about a hundred and twenty pairs of eyes and he was rather too timid to face up to such a psychological ordeal. He remained in his seat, teeth gritted.

The service was lively and he found himself enjoying it, in spite of himself; a rising tide of emotion which never turned into emotionalism. 'That must be a difficult balance to achieve,' he pondered. Surely it was right. Religion should not be a distant, intellectual thing. If it were, how could it appeal to those of lower intellect? Thinking along this line made him realise how well the Church was pitching its lesson to a 'mixed-ability' congregation. (Schoolteacher-think!)

At this point he was surprised to spot former colleague, Kev Marriott, nodding to him. That shook him. Seeing Kev there proved two points: you never really know people and if masterbrains like him could be in Church, there was clearly even more to it than he had ever really believed.

If this surprised him, it was nothing to the astonishment he experienced a moment or two later when he spotted Kev with arms raised on high and clearly lost in worship. He looked around and glimpsed dozens more. He tried to analyse his feelings and was quite unable to do so. Lucy seemed to have fewer reservations and was thoroughly moved - or so it appeared.

If these people were being motivated at some deeper level, it was not something he could quite identify with. He was not sure that he even wanted to. He knew that his leftwing, former colleagues would have dismissed that kind of behaviour as 'intellectual suicide' but then, Kev was the intellectual superior of any of them. Mel was pretty sure that he had gained a first from Oxbridge in Geology - he couldn't recall precisely which college.

Coming here always seemed to give him food for thought and bountifully so. He would have to return to first principles.

Was there a God? If no, then it just didn't matter a jot. If they were living in an amoral, survival-of-the-fittest, mechanistic universe devoid of absolutes, then there was no point in worrying about the morality of his actions. Yes. That *was* clear. What he was doing was a perfect example of improving the species. Evolution would be very proud of him. Irrefutable!

He had already dismissed 'multi-faith' as nonsense because it was so intellectually puerile. So, that was also clear.

The trouble was that if there were a God, then by definition He had to be the most important thing in the universe; there had to be a total commitment and agnosticism was a dangerous practice. Vague deism was hardly an improvement.

He had been told by Bri on his last visit that C.S.Lewis was a good starting point for the intellectual basis of why God had to exist. What was that book he'd recommended? Something Christianity. 'Foundation'? No. 'Basic'? No. 'Mere'? That sounded right. Possibly. Would have to go to some shop called CLC - also recommended. Now, er, that was apparently on Division Street, wasn't it? No. Yes. Or was it West Street? Not sure. Shall definitely go tomorrow.

Bri introduced the speaker. Mel was dazzled. The man was funny, profound, informative and the congregation loved him. Some shouted out 'amen' as a sign of approval when he made a particularly telling point. How off-putting - but then it was just a scriptural sign of agreement, 'so be it' if he remembered correctly. It did seem odd, however - way beyond his life experience.

The text was Mark Chapter Sixteen - 'The Great Commission'. "Go into all the world and preach the Good News to all creation. Whoever believes and is baptised will be saved but whoever does not believe will be condemned."

A clear division. No mincing of words. No arguments. Christians had a duty to share their faith because 'all of mankind was lost and heading for a Godless eternity known as hell'.

The 'Good News' or 'Gospel' revealed that there was a way to avoid this catastrophic outcome. Belief that Jesus had died personally for you and overcome death itself. Repentance and commitment should then be followed by baptism - and that meant a *total* immersion in water. 'Salvation', in other words was what the package amounted to. Hmm. Mel knew all this. Knew it. So why was it a surprise? Why did he continue to have the feeling that if there were a God, all you had to do was to ensure good deeds cancelled out the bad ones? He knew that wasn't Christianity. So what was it then?

Jesus. Son of God. More! God the Son paying the price for the sins for all of mankind, for all time. Why? - Love! Some love that God should sacrifice himself. Wow!

Pastor Witton explained that 'believe' implied that the 'repentance' and 'giving one's life to the Jesus who had conquered death, who was still alive and who could live in our hearts' could be experienced as a reality.

No more opinions, then. Mel *liked* opinions.

He was not ready for this and by the look of Lucy she had been affected on some level but neither was she ready for such an enormous step.

"Remember, you are not promised tomorrow. Now is the accepted time. Now is the day for your salvation."

This was heavy, indeed. But it felt disturbingly right. Lucy proffered a thin smile.

The visiting minister sat down. Bri rose to his feet and challenged the congregation to respond by coming out to the front and 'giving their life to Jesus'.

Five people, seemingly representing ages from five different decades, came forward and two even fell to their knees. Mel had never seen anything like it but he understood, or at least thought he might be beginning to.

He was stunned and was desperate to leave at the earliest opportunity at the end, but he and Lucy were unable to get past his erstwhile colleague without a friendly but fairly innocuous chat.

He wondered if Lucy was as inspired as he had been. Again, he needed to think. Too much in a single dose. Heavy. Really heavy. But where could it be criticised? - Not easy.

They made good their escape but he was still concerned about being seen publicly with the love of his life. In her Audi, on the way home, he gave thought and attention to these matters.

He would suggest that they perhaps continued to come here, stopped the VOC meetings and should avoid all other public places in and around Sheffield.

. When they wanted to go out, what they could perhaps do was to go a little further afield to Chesterfield, Barnsley or even Scunthorpe - he had liked the town. At the first opportunity, after reading up on the NYPRO catastrophe, he had looked up Normanby on the Internet and found Normanby Hall it sounded interesting and he had suggested that they might spend an afternoon there the following Saturday.

Lunch now became the priority as they arrived at his house but not before he had had the thought that a further visit from Kemp, with the two together, could prove a disaster. He told her to park the car around the corner and they began to learn the art of being furtive. He also told her that he thought it would be a good idea for her to disappear upstairs whenever anybody came to the door.

There could be merit in them leaving the area and finding somewhere different to live - he had the money and even living abroad became a possibility. Spain? La Mata had that kind of slightly past-its-best feel which he had found attractive about Withernsea on the East Coast and singularly depressing about Rhyl in North Wales.

Miriam and he had holidayed in Torrevieja when Jenny was about seven or eight and they spent a day in nearby La Mata. Miriam had hated the place so this made him concentrate all the more on its unpretentious merits - because if Miriam disliked it then there just had to be some. It was something for discussion. He already felt that Lucy and he had engaged in more discussions in a matter of weeks than Miriam and he had done in a whole engagement and marriage combined.

The matter in hand was now lunch. They both stayed in the kitchen. He refused her offers of help and oven cooked the sausages slowly whilst preparing the vegetables.

He asked her whether she preferred his special mash or sauteed potatoes and she opted for the latter. He was mildly disappointed because he was especially proud of the former but busied himself with all the preparations. Working quickly, he had everything done in fifteen minutes. She had spoken little during this period and he could see she was lost in thought.

"I suggest we indulge ourselves in a glass of my best Chablis for now and a Beaujolais for with the meal. *Red* wine with toad-in-the-hole as all the best chefs will tell you," he said with a hint of amusement in his voice.

He had about half an hour before he needed to do anything of significance in the kitchen so they repaired to the lounge and sat so they could face each other.

"Comments on the service?" he asked.

"Well. I was flabbergasted, to be quite honest," she avowed. "I had always thought those sort of meetings were heavy on manipulation, psychological pressure, working on emotionalism. In other words aiming to establish control .... but it was not like that at all, was it?"

"No, but I'm not exactly an expert, though. I've always despised those, usually American Churches, with exaggerated voices of money-obsessed preachers. I'll confess that I was perturbed that the speaker was from the USA. My heart sank, I can tell you for free."

"I suppose it could have been subtle - subliminal even - but I really don't think that was it. What it probably is, is that you are required to make a decision for or against. That's what gets up some noses - probably *always* in the cases of those who reject. But I've been thinking about this. If somebody, out of the goodness of their heart, gives a warning of danger - isn't there a tendency to disbelieve at best and to shoot the messenger at worst?

Even then that isn't the issue. The issue is whether they are telling the truth."

"Not quite. What if they *think* they are?" he said provocatively.

"But that was one of the main points," she argued. "Brian Thingy said earlier in the meeting that it was all about a *personal* search. That nobody could hope to find God for anybody else. They were just pointing the way and it was up to us to institute our own search. Not so?"

He thought about this for several moments and asked whether she thought there might not be people who fooled themselves that they were 'living a personal relationship with Jesus - God the Son'.

"Of course there are. There has to be but that invalidates no argument. If your political party has some nutter in it, does that cancel out all other rational belief?"

He decided to check the sausages. She argued well and he needed a few seconds to clear his mind. It was so good to be able to chat and debate.

He acted rashly and didn't think of the consequences as he turned on his heel, went back into the lounge and said: "If we hadn't been in all this mess, I'd have asked you to marry me by now. It all feels so unfair - we are so good together. Real happiness, a second time around would have been possible for us. Not now, and I *do* love you."

Her response was immediate and she sprang to her feet and kissed him delicately.

"I *will* marry you. I am all too aware of reality- that you could be snatched away from me- but as long as you live, there can be no other man for me."

He burst into tears and the two hugged tightly and in total silence for what was probably an eternity. Suddenly he remembered the food and detached himself from her with a swift kiss on the cheek. He squeezed her hand and headed back into the kitchen to heat up the oil for the potatoes which he had inadvertently forgotten to parboil. He turned the oven even lower.

Lunch would be further delayed but inside he felt that his heart was about to burst. He was incapable of articulating either thoughts or feelings as wave followed wave of overwhelming happiness.

Having put lunch back on course he returned to the lounge and they sipped ice-cold Chablis in an atmosphere where words were just no longer needed. This time they sat together and hugged with the difficulties customarily experienced by two people in close contact who are trying not to spill the contents of glasses of quality white wine.

* * *

He put the finishing touches to Sunday Lunch and their plates were piled so high that he thought that he would probably fall asleep as soon as he had finished eating. He had some Hibaldstow-made Sargents' Ice cream in the freezer - the highest quality dairy ice on the planet - which he had intended to serve up as a dessert with a liqueur on top. It seemed highly unlikely that it would be required and he doubted that his bottle of Taylors' Port would be called into play as a *digestif* but these things were there if needed.

The coffee pot was poised to perform its single function, with a jar of Viennese containing fig seasoning standing alongside it - that indeed *would* be required, he was sure.

He tried the sausage and felt transported. He had never tasted anything even vaguely similar. Sage. Strong flavour. The way it blended in with the Yorkshire Puddings which he had covered in his very own, rich onion gravy was a gastronomic wonder. How could simple food have such quality? Lucy felt much the same but was less impressed with the Yorkshire Pudding and told him she could do better - and next time - she would.

* * *

The meal was half completed when the doorbell rang. He glanced at Lucy and she slipped silently upstairs.

Somehow, he was not entirely surprised to find DI Kemp standing there and indicating by body language that he wanted to come in.

He stood to one side and the detective came into the hall but did not walk into the lounge as expected but into the dining-kitchen, attracted by the smell of the food. He spotted the half finished lunches. When he first opened his mouth it was to say:-

"Could you call Mrs Saddleworth down? I'd prefer to speak to the two of you together."

His legs turned to jelly but Kemp seemed to be alone. He would not have come to arrest a triple killer without four or five uniformed men alongside. Maybe the situation was merely bad and not desperate.

He called Lucy to join them in the kitchen and said nothing to Kemp.

She did not have a great deal to say to him. Kemp had been around when her life had first been wrecked and here he was again to ensure that she could not rebuild it. What a bird of ill portent he was, however little blame could be attached to him personally.

"Sit down and finish your meals," said their own particular example of Sheffield's Finest.

They took their places without complaint but for reasons unexplained, neither really felt any vestigial pangs of hunger. They could not think of anything to say and so said nothing as Kemp pulled a chair up to join them. It was a relatively small table and with the three sat around it, there was an incongruous sense of cosiness.

Kemp reached into a deep pocket and placed an FN Herstal - 9mm Hi-Power Browning on the table, covered in a handkerchief. He let the gun slip onto the table and still using the handkerchief, he returned to the pocket and removed a 12 centimetre long, cylindrical metal tube which he attached onto the barrel, again using the handkerchief. Mel assumed it was some sort of silencer. For one second, Mel entertained the perverse thought that Kemp intended to kill them. Then he considered that Kemp was just mirroring what he had done with Malone and the knife. He wondered what Lucy was thinking but she could not have even answered that question herself.

Kemp went back into the pocket and produced a box containing some twenty or so bullets, still using the handkerchief.

"There, now. That's for you. That's all the ammunition I've got."

Mel could only stutter and nothing coherent emerged beyond "Erm, erm, well...................."

Kemp said, "I know what has happened. And, Mel, I know who did what and why. *You* killed Malone, for reasons too obvious to mention. *You* killed the Nigerian because he was scum and *you* killed Marner because he too was scum and his death would be appreciated by the delightful Mrs Saddleworth. All very reasonable in my view. Had there been a Death Penalty, I would have strongly objected to your conduct, Mel. It would have been totally unacceptable but as the only Capital Punishment we have at the moment in this country is that administered by criminals - usually but not exclusively - against decent and honest people, how can any reasonable human being object? The anti-social elements are winning and I want to change all that.

You see I am anti-criminal - but you knew that. You were both at my rather injudicious talk to the VOC, weren't you?"

Mel was not only listening but he also remembered the VOC meeting and how Kemp had spoken there. A crazy, surrealistic thought surged through his brain. "He is going to let me go. He is the only one to know and he's not telling."

Lucy was unable to think. Her mind was in as much of a turmoil as it had been when Larry went missing.

"I'm on your side, Mel. I'm here today to help you."

Was it a trick? Was he angling for a confession? Surely, not. He hadn't been issued a caution, Kemp was alone, Kemp was offering a gun and where was the voice recorder? Surely he wasn't 'wired up' as they said in 'Law and Order', was he? - No. It only made sense if Kemp were telling the truth.

"You are correct Mr Kemp, but Lucy had nothing to do with all of this."

"Of course she didn't," said Kemp supportively.

"How did you find out?"

"I saw you together at Meadowhall. It didn't take a Holmes to work this one out. I haven't allowed the connection to be known to my colleagues, hence today's conversation. You will have problems if - no - when the connection is made between Malone and Marner and possibly the VOC, and especially with your relationship.

The real problem is that with you two being something of an item, if you are seen in public by any colleague of mine, you will end up both being arrested.

I am trying to ensure that we are investigating two *separate* crimes here in Sheffield and the link is detached from the Scunthorpe killing. At the moment, people have only connected these tenuously because of the similarity of the deaths. All stabbed with a thin bladed instrument; stiletto is the forensic guess. If all three are linked – there *are* only three?" Mel nodded. "Well then, I shall try to separate out the Nigerian as there is no motive for you to have done him. But I know you, Mel. You have a sense of justice. Motive enough for me - but not for the CPS, perhaps."

Lucy said her first words, "We are so grateful, Mr Kemp."

"I think we are friends united here," he said, unfazed by the not-so-hidden reference, "Call me Jerome, or better, Jerry."

"Lucy," she whispered.

Mel shook his hand and whispered a thankyou. The three of them entered an instant yet perfect understanding with each other. They did not *feel* that they could trust each other; they enjoyed an absolute certainty.

DI Kemp said: "Let's summarise, shall we? There are no fingerprints, there's no DNA, no witnesses to place you in the vicinity. No cameras to have picked you up in Scunthorpe in your car - that would have been very bad - and no motive in one of the three. You cannot be convicted unless you say something stupid onto tape - and you are not going to. You have shown a good grasp of forensics. CSI?" he postulated.

Mel nodded, "Being a couch potato has its up side."

"Now," said Kemp seriously, "there is nothing there to convict but plenty of room for suspicion. However, when you do the next one with a gun, that is going to throw all the investigations right out of kilter - and we'll pick a total lowlife you could never be connected to."

Neither he nor Lucy were surprised by this announcement. The handing over of the gun had tacitly stated where they went from here. Lucy did not entertain a single moral qualm about the fact they were casually plotting an unknown human being's death. Nor was she aware of any incongruities when comparing what was occurring now to her feelings from the Church Service earlier in the day. What panicked her was only the possibility of losing Mel. She was well aware that she could end up charged as an accomplice to murder and it just didn't matter.

As if on cue, Mel repeated, rather too emphatically, "Lucy must *not* be connected to any of this."

"We'll have to ensure she isn't," murmured Kemp. "Now, I suggest that I have you in for an official interview, with another officer present. It would look odd if we didn't and with the right approach, I think we might be able to throw the hounds off scent a bit. You are rather too obvious to be ignored. Your relationship with Lucy should not be known if you can manage it. If I can spot you, so can others. Low profiles are essential at this point."

It was agreed that he would go to the Police Station at West Bar to be interviewed. "It also helps justify my visit here today if it's been spotted," said Jerry. "Make it Wednesday. Can't do Monday, I'm in court and Tuesday I've a hospital appointment. Wednesday at 2pm?" he asked after a consultation with his diary.

"Fine", said Mel, "My days are my own these days."

"Right," said Jerry. "We now need for you to know how to cope with two things: first, how to deal with this or any other interview when not under arrest and secondly, how to act if arrested or charged or convicted - the tactics don't alter much then.

He spent a further hour with them and drilled into their receptive minds everything that would have to be done depending on which particular scenario emerged. It wasn't that what he had to say lasted more than about ten minutes but he was extremely thorough - covering every angle or quirk and then returning to the main points, thus testing them both to the utmost.

Suddenly and with no warning he stood up, grinned broadly, and made it clear that he was satisfied both with his pupils and that it was time to leave them alone to finish their stone-cold, half-eaten lunches.

Mel asked, "Why are you doing this?"

The reply was what he expected: "I am on the side of victims; ordinary people; the decent; the hardworking; - you two. I just do not want to bother with the unredeemable; those who society cannot salvage but it refuses to recognise the fact. I'm on the side of the angels."

Mel was pricked by the remark and wondered if Brian would agree.

Just as he was on the point of leaving, he asked, "You don't know anywhere we could meet on, say, Saturday? I'd prefer not to be coming here or Harthill."

Mel thought about Normanby Hall and Park and put it forward as a suggestion. "We could meet up at the main doors of the Hall at eleven, if that suits. A nice social outing."

"Yes. Good. And a tactical planning meeting too," said Jerry as he walked out after shaking hands warmly with them both.

"Food for thought!" said Lucy as they heard his car pull away. "Now I've got my appetite back, will the lunch microwave?"

The answer to her question was 'sort of' as she discovered the state into which Yorkshire Pudding can deteriorate under certain conditions but the sausages were even better and no other parts of the meal had suffered.

The Sargents' ice cream was required and was set off by a measure of 'Triple Sec'. The coffee was exquisite with creamy milk, well pre-heated, again using the microwave.

Both had a great deal to think about and for once conversation between them was minimal. They basked in each others company whilst holding a comforting glass of good port.

CHAPTER TWENTY TWO

Monday was a day for quiet reflection. Lucy had agreed to spend the day with George and so she and Mel would not see each other and would be forced to rely on a pair of short phone-calls - an hour and forty minutes and an hour, as it turned out, - one first thing and the other in the mid evening.

'I must buy her flowers,' he thought, never having done so, as he caught the First Mainline bus into the city. He saw Rebekah again and so he waved across the bus to her.

He tracked down the coffee house where he had gone before his first visit to the Church and settled down with a cup of Mocha and 'The Times', which was more for show than anything else, as he did not want to look like a saddo with nowhere else to go and nothing to do.

He turned his thoughts to Lucy, and as was always the case now, became extremely pessimistic for their future - funny - whenever they were together, the pessimism disappeared. What he was now thinking was totally rational. What he had realised days earlier was the *true* reality. He could not hope to escape capture if he continued - even with Jerry's help.

What would Jerry do if he chose to retire? - Nothing, was his best guess. If he were to give up this dangerous existence, the time to do so was now. For Lucy's sake, that was what he ought to do.

His eyes glanced down and the lead story was that of the vicious murder of a young woman near Derby. Her body had been mutilated and there were pictures which clearly captured the anguish of her parents.

It was a defining moment for him but he would have been the first to admit that such moments were an all too regular and inconsistent occurrence, these days.

He vowed that his own wants and needs would have to become secondary and he *would* continue what he was doing. It was for the good of mankind that it be purged of this vermin. His heart went out to the victim's family and he was able to empathise. With Jerry's gun, he would be able to avoid messy encounters like that with Marner. What was it Julius Caesar had said? "The die is cast." That was it. It applied to him. He had a duty and he promised that he would acquit himself honourably in his 'self-appointed task'.

He had no sense that such an appointment had any divine hand upon it, indeed the only doubt to assail him was the lingering niggle which suggested that this might *not* be within the 'will of God' - but then, *he* wasn't 'in the will of God', in the first place.

He found CLC without difficulty, located on West Street. He went in and bought ' Mere Christianity' by C.S.Lewis and also 'Surprised by Joy'. He spotted a boxed set of 'The Narnia Chronicles' and bought that too.

He went to The Haymarket and caught a 52 back to Handsworth Road.

He crossed the road and went into the florists called 'Stems', where he bought a mighty bouquet of flowers with the assurance that they would keep a long time and would certainly be at their best the next day when he was delivering them to Harthill.

* * *

He walked home carrying the flowers, and so that he did not forget their welfare, was quick to put them into a bowl with about an inch of water in the bottom.

Overwhelmed by an urge for egg and chips, he found some frozen chips in the freezer and had a meal ready in under a quarter of an hour. Plenty of salt and vinegar and two glasses of leftover wine to wash it down, meant the meal really hit the spot.

He was not especially accustomed to eating at lunchtime on a working day and would inevitably succumb to weariness during the afternoon, he knew, but he was no longer a wage slave. He could please himself - and would.

A bout of extreme tiredness hit him as the noontime alcohol charged through his veins. He went into the lounge and lay down on the sofa. He was just drifting away when he sat up abruptly in an acute panic as his deadening brain tried to convince him that the gun was still in the house and he was in mortal danger.

Rational memories returned equally rapidly and, in his mind, he retraced every step taken when he had concealed the weapon in the customary hidey-hole.

He found his heart was pounding and he was unable to determine whether this was as a result of the shock or the alcohol. Physically, he felt a fear which had been so unexpectedly absent as he had executed those three egregious individuals.

He fell back into a light, troubled, REM sleep. The nightmare followed promptly.

Malone and Marner were holding Lucy. She was wearing a loose and flowing, pure-white dress which billowed and rippled in a stiff breeze. She was tied to an enormous tree in the precise centre of a large, rectangular field and a scimitar was held by Marner to her throat. Marner changed his facial features and became Kemp for several seconds before turning back into the features of Malone.

The characteristics of a classic nightmare began to take shape as he ran across the field to her rescue, the distance between them steadily increasing the faster and more desperately he ran. Legs took on the consistency of jelly and feet waded through invisible treacle.

The gap increased quickly and she began to fade into an increasingly hazy distance. So he took out the gun and pulled impotently on the trigger. It would not work and he threw it to the floor in tearful frustration. Distant as she was, he could hear the sounds of her screaming and he added his frantic voice to the din. Distraught, he screamed her name. It was no longer a dream world. The scream was real. It had woken him up.

He found himself shaking in terror. His breathing was rapid and shallow; his heart pumped at over a hundred and fifty beats per minute and he recognised that his blood pressure must be off the scale. The sheer, primeval panic that had engulfed him was slow to settle and he felt distinctly uncomfortable for half an hour or more and had a palpable feeling of unease for the remainder of the day, to such an extent he was late to bed for fear that the dream might be repeated. He did not mention the dream to Lucy when she called.

* * *

Lucy and Mel were minds and bodies in tandem but perhaps it was mere coincidence that they both had nightmares that day. Certainly, they did not occur at the same time. His occurred during the afternoon but hers began shortly after going to bed.

His had been vivid and detailed; hers were wispy and inhabited by 'the monsters which emerge from the sleep of reason' as Goya would have put it. Indeed, the Master Artist would have easily understood the world she restlessly inhabited and would have felt more than comfortable sketching the terrors which plundered and pillaged through her fear-filled, semi-conscious mind.

With Lucy, the interpretation needed little elucidation. The key to her dreams lay in the repeated theme of seeing an ethereal Mel dragged away to their lairs by the most sinister of her mental creations.

Eventually, the fact that she was in a relatively shallow sleep and had the power to intervene and force herself awake, half penetrated her tortured brain. She grasped the opportunity and made herself wake up.

It was astonishing how physically wrecked one can feel after a bad dream. She checked the illuminated alarm clock and found it was twenty three minutes past two.

Exhausted as she was, she decided to get up, make herself a cocoa and read the bestseller she had bought the previous week. The book was amazingly tedious, for which she was infinitely grateful. Once able to concentrate, she found that the combination of the chocolate drink and having her mind follow a different line, had the desired effect. She was able to return to bed before three and slept peacefully until ten a.m.

On Wednesday afternoon, Mel's official interview with Kemp was short and totally without interest or incident. DC Calver felt that she could have done the job rather better than her boss.

CHAPTER TWENTY THREE

Both of them liked Brenda Kemp within minutes of their meeting. At first, Mel was unsure what he was able to say in front of her but it soon became clear that she was fully apprised of the situation.

"Just how many bloody people know?" he muttered to himself, under his breath.

He was however, quite happy when he thought about who each one was and realised that he was more than happy to trust all of them.

They had travelled separately to Normanby Hall, the rather compact stately home which was owned by the Sheffields, a family with links to the Dukedom of Buckingham. It was they who had leased it to the Scunthorpe Council many decades before.

Having parked up, the two couples enjoyed a superb walk through the magnificently kept grounds and were only disappointed not to have brought bread to feed a vast array of ducks and geese inhabiting a cheerful duck-pond surrounded by a riot of foliage. The Park had a feeling of tranquility. They simply walked and chatted as if they were friends of many years standing. Mel was truly at peace - which was usually the case when with Lucy anyway, but this charming setting and good company only enhanced the feeling. He noticed that Jerry had a nasty cough which he had been trying to shake and which former WPC Brenda said it would not get better until he reduced his stress levels.

"What do you think I'm doing today? he asked her. But she only smiled.

She was bordering petite, had tinted her hair with a very similar colouring to that used by Lucy, and although her hair was just a little windswept, it seemed natural and complemented her personality. She was a good ten years younger than Jerry and had a sense of fun which added to what was already an excellent day. There was something else about her which Lucy could not quite put her finger on. Her personality had a steeliness; a kind of determination about it. Lucy struggled to describe Brenda but speculated that she was a most determined lady; the sort of person always welcome in the midst of a crisis. She wondered if this might have had any roots in the obvious childlessness of this impressive couple.

Independently, Lucy and Mel had been most impressed by her and could see the development of a friends-for-life scenario.

Mel thought further about this and realised how absurd this idea might be. She was a policeman's wife; he a multiple murderer. Even so, the fact that he, a killer, was spending the day with the Police Officer investigating his own case had no ironies which escaped him.

They paid and went into the Hall itself. In many ways it was typical of its type, with a mix of furnishings from different eras.

Lucy was quite taken by a gadget which, at the turn of a wheel, administered electrical shocks as a medical aid but was unwilling to try it out as the curator invited her to do. It wasn't a Van der Graaf generator was it? Certainly, something like one. Similar principle.

Mel and Jerry were both thrilled by one of the death masks of Napoleon which was proudly displayed.

Twenty-five minutes inside and Brenda had had enough and suggested that Jerry would do better to get some fresh air, so they returned to the park and finished off checking out many an interesting nook and cranny.

It was twenty past twelve and the intention had been to go to a pub for lunch. There was one on the opposite side of Scunthorpe in a place called Scotter which was pretty much the start of the alternative route back to Sheffield via Gainsborough, Bawtry and Maltby, before rejoining the M18 quite close to England's fourth city. The Scotter pub was called 'The Gamekeeper' or some such, and came recommended, but Mel had a stroke of inspiration and suggested 'The Sheffield Arms' in Burton upon Stather. It was only a mile away.

Jerry gave him an old fashioned look but did not disagree.

For reasons they were unable to perceive, they could not get a meal in the restaurant - it did not seem full - but fortunately an excellent selection of sandwiches were conjured up and they enjoyed chatting about everything from politics to Sheffield United over no more than a single alcoholic drink for the men followed by cokes, whilst the ladies knocked back four glasses of white wine each. Lucy was showing signs of wear but Brenda looked the same as ever.

Mel caught Jerry's eye and looked sideways towards Lucy and indicated 'away' with his eyes. This was greeted by an almost imperceptible nod from Jerry. The exchange was missed by the ladies and Brenda was quite surprised when Mel stood up, saying that they needed to leave.

Lucy got to her feet and followed him to the car-park at the rear but not before they had both expressed heartfelt pleasure at having met Mrs Kemp.

"I'll keep in touch," said Jerry as they went through the door.

* * *

Jerry rang Mel the next evening from a public phone and gave Mel directions to a spot near the tiny village of Ulley where they would be able to park up independently.

"Don't forget the 'equipment' I gave you," he said unnecessarily.

They arrived within five minutes of each other and walked into undergrowth.

"Right then. That tree is only ten feet away. You must never fire from greater distance - you haven't the expertise. Besides, the gun is awkward to handle. The silencer destroys all balance," said Jerry.

He explained the workings of the weapon: how to reload, safety catch, what happens as you pull the trigger.

"The main thing you need is the *feel* of the gun. With that homemade silencer, it is incredibly heavy. You must always use two hands - none of this film-gangster rubbish where they wave guns about as if they are made of plastic. They'd have no control....No. Support it - with it cradling in the left hand. Yes. Comfy? .... Put a round into the tree."

There was a hiss; a gentle click from the gun and a thud from the tree at approximately the point where Mel had been aiming.

Jerry coughed loudly and Mel wondered if he was trying to disguise the sounds but it was just the remnants of his chest infection.

"Two more," said Jerry as Mel stared at the beautifully crafted, Belgian-made weapon.

"Do two shots really fast into that discoloured knot in the wood."

Mel held the gun at his side pointing at piles of leaf mould. He brought the gun up by ninety degrees, slipped his left hand under the barrel and fired twice. Both shots missed by about an inch and a half and left deep marks in the bark.

"Good enough," said Jerry. You should shoot from about four feet. Work out where the heart is and go for it automatically. Use two shots in quick succession and only if necessary finish with a head shot - but from distance or you may get blood spatter on you."

Jerry went across to inspect the three holes and to determine whether or not to dig out the slugs. For whatever reason, he did not seem to find this necessary.

"That's it."

"Where did the gun come from?"

"Ah. It was handed in by some colonel type during an amnesty. He gave it to me and I 'forgot' to book it in. I made the silencer myself. I've got a lathe in the workshop in my garage," he said with pride. "I'm not sure I can get more bullets as they are of low-velocity, which is required for 'silenced' shooting - well, I can - but not without risk, so use sparingly. You have seventeen there."

The two men shook hands. Mel returned home and the gun went under the shed, but not before he had made certain that there was no remaining sweat or bodily remnants on it - these days you couldn't just rely on wiping off fingerprints.

As he went back inside, Jerry rang - again from a public phone.

"Sorry! I forgot to tell you about GSR."

"GSR?"

"Gunshot residue. After firing it, remember not to allow it in contact with clothing and for pity's sake take a shower and wash all clothing immediately."

Mel thanked him and Jerry hung up.

He felt that it would not be long before the weapon was brought into use.

He thought he could do with a nice iced bun and a cup of Lapsang Souchong would make a rare treat. "Yes, excellent," he said out loud in a voice not too unreminiscent of Montgomery Burns.

CHAPTER TWENTY FOUR

The car was positioned in a side street in Wincobank. It would attract no attention from any passer-by unless they chose to leave the established pavement and walk across the wasteland to the right where the path came to an abrupt end.

From this vantage point, the car was overlooked by no window within a couple of hundred yards. The vehicle was as anonymous as its owner desired it to be.

He had considered the dangers of using his own car but as he had driven through the area three evenings previously, he could foresee few problems.

The car was parked alongside the side wall of a house built in the 1970s which had no window at all on that side. He was concealed in plain view.

In the darkness of a fresh night where a gibbous moon revealed itself only occasionally from behind extensive cloud cover, he had a partial view of Millie Smart's back door.

He watched intently and even dared to have the car stereo playing a little bit of Dire Straits at what was an inappropriately low level for Knopfler's extravagant, indeed, occasionally musically self-indulgent, skills.

* * *

He and Jerry had met up at a pub called 'The Green Tree' on the old A18 to the East of Doncaster. Mel had bought them each a pint. They sat down out of earshot of other patrons.

"This guy Tony Preston is the truest of scum," said Jerry. "He kills for fun. We have linked him to three murders and have absolutely no evidence. We have grasses who bring us his name over and over again. Mr. Teflon - nothing sticks. He laughs in our faces, refuses to talk to us when brought in for questioning but taunts us and threatens us personally. The last time we had him in, he whispered "Brenda" to me and smirked. I am at my wits end.

His main stock-in-trade is crack cocaine. He runs the largest network in South Yorkshire and is removed from the danger of arrest by always having at least two, and usually three, levels of dealers between him and the drugs themselves.

We've arrested him three or four times and can't get close. We put a barrow-load of evidence in front of the CPS and they said that it just wouldn't lead to conviction - and they were right, I'm afraid.

The only way to get him is to infiltrate his organisation or get one of his own to set him up. There is no way to infiltrate and as for anybody giving evidence against him - well - a body might just as well commit suicide. This man is powerful. So, if I can show you an easy way of dealing with him - what do you think?"

"Fine by me," said Mel.

* * *

So that was why he was now sitting in a car, in Wincobank, outside the house of Preston's girlfriend at twelve forty in the early hours. The gun rested on the seat beside him. The distance to the gate was no more than fifteen feet.

When Preston emerged, he would be able to slip out of the car, round the back and hide himself alongside the wall. He would be able to stand right up to the corner only five feet from the gate.

If Millie stayed to watch him leave until he got into his Mercedes, parked on the opposite side of the road, the mission would have to be aborted.

He waited and wondered how accurate Jerry's information was. This was apparently the only time when Preston could be found not surrounded by a group of toughs. Millie's husband was in Doncatraz serving eight months for 'Possession with intent to supply' and it was more than possible that Preston did not want this liaison made public.

He lived in a seven bedroomed house in Dore which was surrounded by an eight foot high stone wall. The reason he would not stay the night with Millie was that Mrs Preston, a brassy and artificially created lady - both in terms of class and cosmetic surgery - would be less than tolerant and even major drug dealers must fear wives who can 'take them to the cleaners' via the Divorce Courts.

According to Jerry, he tended to leave in the early hours and lock the door behind him with his own key.

Mel picked up the gun and weighed it - the balance was appalling but better to have the silencer than not.

He had memorised the face of his intended victim from a photo Jerry had shown him. The man was unusually tall and thin, almost to the point of being gaunt. It would be difficult to shoot the wrong person. All he had to do was be patient. The likelihood of anybody coming near his car was small. He patted the large, empty plastic bag on the passenger seat to confirm it was still in place.

A light went off in the upper part of the house and to the rear. He had to stretch to see. It seemed possible that something was about to happen. Mel changed the plan and alighted from the vehicle not closing the door but merely pushing it to so that the internal light went off. Yes. This was better. He was able to stretch his legs and make himself ready. He pulled on his gloves; plastic and thin, courtesy of a local Shell Garage. The trouble was that if Preston did not choose to leave within a moment or two, he would be exposed - not to a dangerous extent - but more than had previously been the case. And it was cold.

Movement from within. The door began to open, a figure came through. Mel ensured that he was invisible behind the corner of the house.

The thought occurred to him how much more difficult this would have been had this not been the end house. The set-up was perfect. He checked the gun. Safety catch off. He held it in his right hand and cradled with his left, as taught. A frisson of excitement made him shudder or perhaps it was just the crisp evening air.

He clearly heard the key in the door. Steps on the short path. Time to move. One, two three, four paces and he faced Preston just as he emerged through the side gate of the tiny rear garden.

Without thought or anxiety he pointed at his centre chest, avoided the look of panic in Preston's eyes - in truth, he was oblivious to the fact - and fired into the centre of his torso. The amount of recoil surprised him. Surely there had not been that much in the woods. He was also surprised that Preston had seemed nailed to the spot as he first glimpsed his slayer.

One half second later, he aimed the second shot into the already slumping body. Preston made no sound. Mel considered how the soft 'click' of his pistol seemed to echo in the chill air. It was unnatural as sounds go but the noise was incapable of carrying any distance, he decided, as he looked at the dying man who had endeavoured to fall half across the small gate and was lying slumped. Mel thought he was dead but was unsure how to confirm this, so from about eight feet, he shot again. There was no twitch nor reaction from what had to be a corpse.

Back unhurriedly to the car. Gloves and gun into bag and out of sight in case he got turned over as a possible drunk driver by the Police. Engine on. Drive away steadily. So much better than in socks!

Smooth! He was a professional now. The thought jolted him a little as he drove downwards in the direction of Meadowhall.

Would God really employ a hit-man? It certainly *seemed* incongruous.

CHAPTER TWENTY FIVE

The Prime Minister was not especially worried. There had been several lynchings, it was true, one in Worcester another in Totnes and there had been assorted severe beatings in Peterborough, Stockport and Glossop.

Frankly, on a personal level, he did not really 'give a damn' - provided they did not select the wrong person and even then, there was a shed-load of political capital to be made if they did. It was true that some of those targeted did not have actual criminal records but their true histories being so well accredited and often documented in the various local communities, there was little to be gained by pretending that targets were any less abominable than they truly were. Indeed, it almost seemed that they had been chosen because the Legal System had missed them somehow.

He reasoned that, in spite of this having the clear smack of mob rule, the Government was no longer getting quite as much blame for having lost the streets. The anti-Government press made some telling points but his private pollsters indicated that the public was well satisfied with what was going on with the Government's apparently tougher attitude towards crime.

He had come in for severe criticism in a series of editorials in The 'Guardian' which had deeply upset the luvvie brigade within the Government but he almost took criticism, from such sources, as a badge of honour. There were few votes to be lost in Middle England from upsetting cloud-cuckoo land 'Guardian' readers and much to be gained elsewhere. It just crossed his mind that the Lib Dems could benefit but since Blair's Iraq fiasco, the haemorrhaging of votes to that unscrupulous crew had probably reached some sort of saturation point.

Of course, there were murmurs of disapproval within the Parliamentary Labour Party itself but large leads in opinion polls were always a wonderful way of stemming criticism from troublesome backbenchers.

This latest killing in Sheffield had been established as some kind of internecine dispute between gangsters and emphatically not a lynching. The Deputy PM had spoken directly to the Detective Inspector in charge of the investigation and had been assured that this was not to be seen as part of what had occurred in Worcestershire and Devon.

Muckle Voe now had over one hundred and twenty residents and had attracted worldwide interest as a 'new, radical and even humane way' of dealing with prisoners who could never be released or rehabilitated.

It did just cross his mind that there would be a real row the first time that a prisoner was shot dead by Naval Personnel whilst trying to escape, or the first time a Naval missile had to bring down an aircraft trying to spirit away one of these misunderstood souls - but then, that may well never happen.

He would worry about details like that when he had to and not before. The plan - no, *his* plan was going remarkably well.

Perhaps Prime Minister could be a job for life. Obviously, he was very good at it.

CHAPTER TWENTY SIX

He kissed Lucy long and hard as she came into the house. He loved the way she always seemed to want to be in physical contact with him. There was seldom a time period of more than a couple of minutes passed without her touching his hand, stroking his hair or grasping his arm. She loved him and this was a simple demonstration of that love.

Miriam had sought to avoid physical contact. She had been wholly unwilling ever to kiss him or display affection. She had remained cold, aloof and distant at all times. Mel eventually had to give up as any efforts from him inevitably felt as if they were no more than an imposition. Even on those rare occasions when there had been a five-minute, joyless coupling, he had merely been expected to clamber on top of her and perform to nobody's very great satisfaction.

There had never been any afterglow; never had there been nights nor even sessions nor even single hours devoted to what might have passed for lovemaking. As for experimentation - forget it! He actually felt diminished as a human being every time they copulated.

With Lucy the contrast could not have been greater. With her, he was enriched and their genuine lovemaking was simply a natural extension of their deepening relationship.

Sometimes he felt like crying because the course he had chosen; 'his mission', meant that they could never spend the life together their love and abiding passion deserved.

He was well aware that in relationships, the initial excitement eventually and tragically, gives way to something more humdrum. Often it is caused by long working hours, diverging interests or the needs of children. They had none of these distractions and he knew that their love was only at its beginning and that their feelings for each other would only deepen further and their physical life would only get better still as it was so entwined into the unit; the oneness they had become.

"I have been naughty," she said, so he gave her a playful slap on the backside. "No, wait - I do hope you aren't going to be cross with me." She handed him two pieces of paper; a Marriage Licence and a confirmation of a date three weeks hence at The Sheffield Registry Office. "And I've been to see Brian, that minister, and he is going to perform a blessing in the Church immediately after the ceremony. I know I should have consulted you but I want this so much."

He stared into her eyes, and this time did burst into tears and hugged her. He said nothing. He was incapable of saying anything but it did not really matter. How could she have done something so perfect?

"Let's go for a walk," he said. They went out, hand in hand, and at this point, he did not care who saw them. He led her up the steep hill which forms the top end of Richmond Road up to Handsworth Road where the traffic was appalling. The building of the new ASDA store some years before had been a planning disaster. The concentrations of traffic a third of a mile along Handsworth Top were truly horrific. The supermarket had been built right on the roundabout which led onto the Sheffield Parkway - the main link road between the city centre and the M1. No proper consideration had been given to the inevitable congestion. Pathetic.

Mel and Lucy walked past a line of quietly seething drivers who were moving forwards slowly and then only occasionally. It struck him how silly it was that environmentalists were always talking about getting people out of their cars yet never seemed to complain about artificially created traffic jams which resulted in the worst of pollution. Taking 10% of these drivers off the road and out of the equation would help but little. Car emissions would be a fraction of this level if the traffic management systems just allowed them to move freely.

He was all too aware that The Handsworth Forum had received information that this road was bathed in more pollution than anywhere else in the area. He felt cross, but feeling Lucy's hand in his, the feeling rapidly melted away. They walked down the hill passing St Mary's Church and 'The Old Crown Pub' and managed to cross the road further down.

He took her towards Orgreave - site of several bloody clashes between Scargill's miners and hundreds of Police at the time of The Coal Strike. 1984 was it? - No. Earlier, he thought. But the pit had long since disappeared and the area had been landscaped but the tunnels from the mine still snaked their way under most of Handsworth and there had even been compensation claims for subsidence to properties long after attempts to bring inexpensive coal from beneath earth had been abandoned. They appeared, at first, to be heading towards where the former ASDA store had been more sensibly located. He led her into the Cemetery and somehow, although she had not consciously realised where they were going, she was unsurprised by their destination.

She was sorry that they had not brought flowers but was delighted to see a fresh bunch of carnations had been placed in the metal vase below a small but superbly crafted, white, marble headstone with gold inlay in the lettering and she realised that he must have probably visited the previous day.

"It's beautiful," she said simply and a wave of regret hit her that she had had Larry cremated. Funny that. It had never been something she had given thought to previously.

She recognised that this was a sacred moment; a pivotal point in their relationship. There were now no doubts. He was giving her the final thing he could give. Everything he had and was had become hers. She wondered if there was anything that personal which she could dedicate to him and felt a tinge of guilt that there appeared to be nothing.

"This is Lucy, Jen," he said and took her hand. "I love her and she is my future. You would have adored her." His tone was clipped and to the point. Somehow, this meant that the introduction seemed neither mawkish nor macabre. He ignored Miriam. Knowing as she did, Lucy understood.

They stood before the grave in silence for about a minute, whereupon he squeezed her hand and they turned away to return to his house. How wise and sensitive he could be. He had judged the short time they should spend there, to perfection.

* * *

She made the coffee even though he thought that he usually made better coffee and that tea was really her area of expertise.

It was good. They sat in the lounge and enjoyed it with a shortbread.

"Radio Sheffield mentioned a shooting........?

"Yes. It was arranged by Jerry and went very smoothly."

He did not want to say much more as if this could distance her from what he was doing and ensure that she could never be accused of complicity.

She understood this and settled for reading all the details on Ceefax and in 'The Sheffield Star' later in the day.

The more she read, the more she accepted that this had been entirely justifiable. The man had been vermin and the city was a slightly better place overall for his demise.

A wave of pride struck her. Her man was a hero. He was utterly selfless. She knew how much he loved and wanted her and yet he would put what he saw as duty ahead of his personal well-being. This man was special and her heart ached because she understood that in the coming weeks or months - she must lose him. Could it stretch into a year? She seriously doubted it.

She would make absolutely certain that she would do everything in her power to make him happy in the limited time they had. He would certainly have some interesting, erotic memories to take away with him!

He was preparing food in the kitchen and she shouted through to him: "Leave that. I have a better idea!" – and it was true. She had had an idea that was much better than banal matters such as food and drink.

CHAPTER TWENTY SEVEN

"I'm not sure if you'll want this one," said Jerry, "but before we talk this through, I want to go through my checklist. What do you do if arrested?"

"I say nothing," said Mel.

"Correct. What do you offer?"

"I..... er ... I offer a prepared statement as a sign of my willingness to assist."

"Correct. I'll go through it with you at some point. Now, what else?"

"I must deny and keep on denying without offering any information whatsoever. They have to prove my guilt - not me, my innocence, isn't that it?"

"Correct. What if they tell you they want you to go to the Police Station to help with enquiries?"

"I refuse and offer to let them give me a list of pre-prepared questions in my own home. I must insist on seeing the questions in advance and I shall prepare answers. I say I am willing to help in any way but it will be done at my convenience and under my terms only. Right? Oh, and I put a time limit on any interview of, say, half an hour?"

"Correct. But why are you acting like this?"

"I am resentful, that as a victim, I seem to be being targeted by the Police and although I want to help, I am not going to play any games which may be used to unfairly persecute me. I refer to the P.A.C.E. caution, if necessary. I do not ask for a solicitor and say that I shall not as I do not need one."

"And if evidence is offered against you?"

"I say that it is a police fit up and refuse to discuss it on those grounds. But why no solicitor?"

"The reason for that is that usually, most Police Officers consider that it is an admission of guilt and particularly if it is the very first thing you say. You can ask for one after being semi-cooperative after arrest. Not sooner. If you can get officers believing in you - it can rather help on occasions.

One small point, if I see an arrest on the horizon, *I'll* arrest you and that will mean *I* will conduct the interview. Now. If you are charged, keep denying and cry 'fit up'. Somebody will believe you. There's always somebody simple to believe that. It's the norm. It helps if your solicitor believes you, as well - so, give nothing away. I suggest you get Dawkins from Snell and Ackroyd. He is clever, cunning and has a fantastic knowledge of how the system works. He is utterly odious and has no interest in justice. All he wants is acquittals. They are his bread and butter. His reputation amongst the criminal classes is rightly second to none. If anybody can stop a case going to Crown Court, he can."

"Got it. What if I *am* convicted?"

"Then I shall get you out. It will take a while but I *can* do it. Promise. You will need to be patient because these things move slowly. Just never, *never* admit guilt and I shall be able to do it eventually."

Mel looked at him in utter bewilderment but Kemp was giving nothing away and he wore a small, confident smile.

"Trust me," said his friend and mentor and the matter was closed.

"Right. Let's see if you like the principle behind this one," said Jerry, "There's an Islamic preacher of terror and hatred who is urging young Muslim lads in the Darnall area to become suicide bombers. Just think of the London bombings of July the seventh, 2005.

We have had complaints from a number of their parents and we have even managed to get recordings of him doing this. The trouble is that, in this day and age, nobody at CPS has the guts to prosecute him because of politically correct thinking. There aren't sufficient grounds to deport him apparently and it looks as if he is being successful. Last week two sets of Muslim parents came to see us because their seventeen year olds have disappeared and are thought to be training for martyrdom in Yemen.

This man has, to our knowledge, killed nobody himself and seems to be looking after his own safety while sending others out to die. It is a tricky issue because killing him will automatically bring a great deal of moderate Muslim opinion behind him.

I've had one thought. It's not brilliant but could just work. Remember the drugs you left when you killed Malone? Clever. It might just work here. Shoot him. Place a load of drugs on him and we must make sure the body is found by Police or somebody who is not likely to want to conceal them. There may be suspicions but if somebody had rung the Police anonymously with a drugs tip off ....corrupting young lads..... maybe if we had turned him over fairly publicly in a drugs search beforehand........ who knows? The event may not blow up out of proportion but more importantly, the bullets would be forensically linked to the killing of Preston; a known dealer. Get it?

Still. I know the man is no murderer .....yet......but he is at least the equivalent. Actually, worse in my book. What do you think?"

"No problem. I'll need details of where and when and I would want to wait for an opportunity as propitious as the Preston thing, which worked out well. No point in taking unnecessary risks. Drugs?"

Jerry passed over nine small bags of crack cocaine which Mel immediately tucked inside his handkerchief and hurriedly concealed with the thought that this would make the hole under the shed rather crowded.

"Forensically identical to Preston's stuff," he said with a smile.

"What an organised, calculating, unethical, ruthless man," said Mel.

"Why, thank you pal," said Jerry appreciatively, wearing his broadest grin.

CHAPTER TWENTY EIGHT

Mel settled down to do some reading. When at work he had generally been too tired to read more than the occasional chapter. Now, as a gentleman of leisure he was able to concentrate on one of his favourite occupations.

He was half way through 'Surprised by Joy' and found it expertly crafted. There was something distinctly familiar about it and it was slow to dawn on him that this was the origin of the film 'Shadowlands'. He could not understand why he had not made the connection sooner. Joss Ackland had played Lewis. The Christian element had been neatly excised from the film version and the book was quite fascinating; much more profound and stimulating than what had been a most agreeable and moving film. He recalled how Miriam had poured scorn on it with a venom he still found difficult to understand.

He decided to make a coffee before starting as he suspected that he would not want to put the book down until he either finished it or at least, completed a sizeable chunk.

As he poured the best Mocha his newly found wealth could afford, he heard the noise of mail being forced through the letterbox. He peered through the curtains but was unable to see anybody.

There was just one item in an A4 manila envelope. He knew instantly that this was the information on his next hit. Funny how becoming a serial killer altered your vocabulary.

He took coffee and envelope into the lounge, settled into his favourite chair and tore the thin package open. A photo fell out of an extremely handsome man in his early thirties. He was clearly Asian in origin and had a skin colour to match the recently poured coffee. He wore a long beard but what struck him most was a face contorted with the purest hatred - the like of which he himself had not even felt towards Malone.

He read Jerry's instructions and details:

Read then destroy everything.

There is nothing forensic to compromise me here destroy it and there is no link to you either!

Hassan Abdul Jomahl. Probably an alias. Saudi connections. Address: 45, Larch Terrace, Darnall. No job. No official Moslem position. Trained in the Sudan by a group with Bin Laden funding.

Minor role in 9/11 in finding and posting flight details on the Net. Under investigation by MI5 and Special Branch.

Speaks at The Rowan Lane Mosque most Friday evenings. Walks home alone. That is the only opportunity. There is so little traffic, especially late evenings in that area that you would be pretty safe to attempt a drive-by - American street gang style.

Regards. A friend.

Mel memorised everything and set fire to the envelope and contents in the sink. It is more difficult to make sure that everything is consumed than one might think. He paused briefly and wondered if he should keep the photo.

He pondered this for several moments and was certain that there was no possibility he could ever forget those twisted features. He was also sure that he would recognise the face when in a more relaxed mode - he had always been good with faces as a teacher. It was a small skill which gave you an edge when teaching a new class if you picked up names and faces quickly.

He left his book and went out to drive the route from the Mosque in daylight. As he worked his way through intense traffic on Staniforth Road, he wondered if his two, closest Muslim friends would think less of him for this 'hit' when it all became public. Still, no matter. When it all came out he did not expect to have any friends left other than those who already knew what he was up to. He had totally neglected all of his friends in recent months. Perhaps that was as well.

He found the Mosque easily enough and worked out how to get to the Larch estate. He saw the most obvious route his target might take and could see over wasteland across to the magnificent Don Valley stadium. So he was unlikely to be seen from about half of the area. It was no use. He would have to return at night to get the right feel for what was happening. In fact, the best would be to go on the next Friday evening and just watch. He would learn the likely route, how many cars to expect, where houses were, what windows might overlook the site he chose.

"Should I take the gun along, just in case?" he murmured to himself. It would certainly be a shame to let a gilt edged opportunity escape if it presented itself.

He drove back up Staniforth Road and turned off to go to Lloyds TSB to get some cash from the machine. He crossed the road and bought a fresh scone to have with his next coffee. He liked Darnall and was not quite able to say why. It was perhaps just that some places have a personality of their own; a genuine character when too many others are simply sterile.

Was he taking dangerous risks by using his own car in these jaunts? - It was hard to say for sure. It occurred to him that he might leave GSR on the car window or around the edges of the driver's window by firing through. No point in making forensics easy for the investigators.

Right, then, the gun would have to go all the way through the window and he would have to go to the ARC Carwash on Main Road first thing the following morning.

He stopped to consider just how easy it had been to kill four people. Writers always said it was difficult yet only Marner had been a problem thus far.

He must not get arrogant and besides he needed to put his mind around this 'revenge thing' again. "I will repay saith The Lord." That was Romans 12 verse 19.

How did this fit with his hypothesis that if society let the forgiving man down then different rules applied?

The point was that forgiving was easy in the pure Biblical context where society does its duty for its citizens. The *Lex Talionis,* 'eye for eye' idea was not a scriptural principle cancelled out because Jesus had said to 'love our enemies'. Society as opposed to the individual again.

In Matthew he had read that Jesus emphasised that 'He had not come to abolish The Law' but what was the next bit? - 'To bring New Law' - was that it?

It sounded to him as if everything remained the same but with extras added on - such as the requirements on the individual to forgive. "As we forgive them who sin against us." The Lord's Prayer. That was personal.

Wasn't Jesus' teaching that, just because somebody was rightfully to receive a punishment, it did not give the victim the right to be vengeful?

If what he was doing fell outside these parameters, would it be some kind of situation ethics coming into play? Did God approve of such?

What if what he was doing made the world a better place? Good overcoming evil? Rooting it out? After all, his motives were pure. He was 'loving his neighbours' by protecting them from the predations of social vermin.

But should he not be loving social vermin? At least, legitimately instituted Capital Punishment gave people a chance to repent which his sudden death-dealing most assuredly did not. This was the only argument of significance he could level against what he was doing. It wasn't enough. It was the fault of those who had broken the bargain by removing hanging.

What too of the families of his targets? What about compassion for them? That too was a peripheral issue but he knew that some of these people would be missed. Grieved over, even. He could empathise - to an extent.

He examined his conscience. He accepted that he had been wrong being vengeful over Malone but that was not the current issue.

Christians often spoke of 'that still small voice' which he had always equated to conscience kicking in.

What was there within him? - Satisfaction? - Well that was not appropriate. He really should not enjoy such a calling, - if indeed a calling it were, which, to be frank, he really did not think it was.

What of 'conscience? - No. None. Was that evidence that he was right or just that he was not a born-again believer and so there could be no voice from God's Holy Spirit to lead him?

He still had to establish God's reality or otherwise. He never ceased to be astonished that so many people just did not bother with God - did not bother to investigate.

If God existed, what could possibly be more important? - Money, power, television, Sheffield Wednesday - or United for that matter? Just how shallow people had become, concentrating on the unimportant and the unmitigatedly trivial.

115

He was pretty sure that Brian and his fellows were correct and he recognised that they possessed something he simply did not have. He realised this was a commitment issue and he was holding back from that true 'leap of faith'. He asked himself if he thought his attitudes to the mission would change if he made that leap. He was unsure.

His thoughts turned to Lucy and he tried to ascertain precisely where she stood spiritually. It would have to be a topic for future discussion but not before he had finished more of his reading.

He returned home and took his now buttered scone into the lounge with a coffee to resume 'Surprised by Joy' only to be surprised that he fancied the idea of reading 'The Narnia Chronicles'. Now what was the order? He had been warned that some people were misled on what was the best. Now: *The Magician's Nephew, The Lion The Witch and The Wardrobe, The Horse and His Boy, Prince Caspian, The Voyage of The Dawn Treader, The Silver Chair* and, obviously enough, *The Last Battle.* Good.

He wondered how much time he would have for reading in prison or in wildest Scotland. He guessed that there would be time in abundance but without the quality of coffee he was now sipping being much in evidence.

He turned to the opening of 'The Magician's Nephew' and settled back.

The phone rang and he said a rude word, quite loudly.

When he heard Lucy's voice, however, a surge of delight encompassed mind and body alike.

They had nothing to say to each other so they spent a happy ninety minutes not saying anything of any great import. However, a certain visitor gave her some cause for possible discomfort.

When he had put the phone down, he was disappointed that he would not be able to see Lucy that night as Jack had rung to say he was coming home unexpectedly and would arrive later that afternoon.

Lucy said that she had already told him about the wedding plans and he wanted to come up and give Mel 'a once over'. There would be a meeting to be arranged the next day and she said she would either ring late evening or call first thing the next day.

My. My. It looked like it was again time for a tasty coffee which he made patiently and settled down in the lounge to find out how Lewis had portrayed the creation of Narnia.

The one fact he was able to deduce as he greedily consumed the book was that this may have been written for children but as an adult volume went, - well - it ran very deep indeed.

How was it possible to write on so many levels at the same time? - Ah, well. That was Professors for you! It contained considerably more depth than Tolkein's 'Lord of the Rings'. Interestingly, Lewis and Tolkein had been close personal friends.

When he came to where Digory brought 'original sin' into a brand new world, he was startled. But when the issue of 'The Deplorable Word' was raised he gasped in amazement at Lewis's didactic inventiveness.

By early evening, he was towards the end of 'The Lion, The Witch and The Wardrobe'. He had read the book as a child and was vaguely cognisant of the connections between Aslan, the Great Lion and Jesus - even as a ten year old he had made the link - surely that was some proof of Lewis's genius?

As he read the sacrifice scene at The Stone Table, he remembered Aslan's words in the earlier book which suggested he would take the punishment for all Narnians. It explained the Crucifixion and Resurrection in such terms that all might understand the principle of Redemption.

By mid-evening he was well into 'The Horse and His Boy' constantly marvelling at the expertise of the writer.

The phone rang at nine thirty just as he was finishing this latest prod to his awakening spirit. It was Lucy suggesting he came to Harthill at about ten the next day. He agreed willingly and wished her a contented 'good night'.

Something was not quite right. For a moment or two he was slow recognising that he had eaten nothing since the scone. He made the decision to pop into Sanam's in Darnall for a kebab and he could always kill two birds with a single stone by checking out the same route he had followed around the back streets when it had been daylight.

Research and forward planning would always pay dividends.

* * *

The following morning found him driving past 'The Beehive Pub' on his right and the Church on his left as he entered Harthill village. A tall, thin man dressed as a Morris Dancer, carrying a fiddle by its neck in his left hand, walked purposefully past the pub with a jingle of bells.

He drove nervously on and turned into the finely block-paved drive of Lucy's house. He was glad that it had that kind of wet-look to it, as that kind of paving seemed to attract fewer weeds and did not look worn out after four years.

He was astonished to find that he felt more nervous at the prospect of meeting Jack than ever he had on one of his sorties.

He did not need to ring at the door as it opened for him just as he was about to.

A young man, agreeable in feature, gave him a warm smile accompanied by a handshake. He felt welcome and walked into the house he had come to know as a lover and which he had expected to enter this morning as a stranger and was glad to find it as familiar as ever.

"Hi. I'm Mel. Delighted to meet you."

"The same. I never thought Mum would find anybody daft enough to take her on," he said loudly enough for Lucy to hear, and to show that it was meant in jest, he wore an enormous grin from earlobe to earlobe. He forgot to introduce himself but Mel thought he could probably guess who it was.

"I only come here as an act of charity," he said, joining in Jack's little game and in turn, ensuring that Lucy heard. She came through from the kitchen with a mock scowl.

"Well, you historians, I'll make a coffee and I've got some warm Belgian Buns just out of the oven. I'll let you get all the boring stuff about which modules who studied and why, well out of the way before I join you."

"You have Belgian buns in the ...." started Jack in mock horror.

"Don't you dare!" she said, cutting him off. "He thinks he's funny," and she retired to the kitchen.

* * *

The morning went superbly well and he could detect no animosity whatsoever from Jack towards his future stepfather, in fact the talented student seemed delighted that Lucy had found somebody he could so easily approve of.

It seemed that they would be friends, at least until...........well...... there was just no point in dwelling on the negative aspects.

They went for a walk around the village and had a light lunch at 'The Beehive'.

With the weekend beckoning, he returned home aware that he would see little of Lucy, if anything at all, until the following Monday.

He settled down for a weekend of serious attention to Clive Staples Lewis although there could well be a distraction on the Friday evening. It was all in the lap of the gods - or perhaps that was not quite right.

CHAPTER TWENTY NINE

As it worked out, there was no hit the following Friday. He found his man at about 9-45 easily enough. He was able to recognise him as he drove past and in the opposite direction but the terrorist was in urgent conversation with a smart, English-looking man for most of the way back to the Larch Estate. Mel found the liaison sinister but did not know why. He turned the car round and followed them from more than a hundred yards away.

By the time the mysterious friend had gone off in a different direction, the street was surrounded by houses and he did not want to risk being exposed. Mission aborted.

Mel was surprised how patient he was being at the missed opportunity. With Malone, he had had to stalk his quarry. With this man it was the same. The only difference was that if he delayed too long with this target it could be the difference between an airliner plummeting out of the sky into the centre of Westminster, or not. Maybe he was overstating his point. Who could know?

He did not want to delay any more than necessary.

* * *

The next Friday and just a week before his wedding, he picked up his man again at precisely 9-45. He was alone and followed the expected route. It was a moonless evening. He had to rely largely on the residual glow of street lighting.

Unfortunately, the target had chosen to walk on the opposite pavement to the previous week, meaning that he was on the nearside of the car. This would mean that he could approach from behind but would have to have the passenger window open and would need to shoot through that. He was not happy.

Under some pretext, he would attract his attention and shoot through the driver's window from a shorter distance. He would also have the choice of whether to raise or lower the weapon which would be more difficult through the passenger side. The length and awkwardness of Jerry's gun would just have to be overcome.

He drove past the man at normal speed and travelled almost half a mile before turning around. He rested the gun on his lap and drove back. Body language suggested that Jomahl had no suspicions about the car.

The road being empty, he pulled across to the opposite side, with his window already down and pulled alongside his man.

"Excuse me! Do you know......?" and he raised the weapon and fired more or less one-handed. He was trying to support it with his free hand but all he managed to do was ensure that it did not dip below the level of the open window. It was certainly awkward to avoid the barrel catching the door or window frame as it was so long but he had practised the manoeuvre and it had sort of worked. He knew where to aim for the heart but missed by at least ten inches catching him in the Adam's apple - that was one-handed shots for you - and the discharge threw him backwards with a spontaneous effusion of blood.

He got out of the car and fired a second bullet to where the heart would be if this man had one. The shot was wasted because the condemned man had already been dead for several seconds.

Satisfied, he got back into the car and put it into gear. Suddenly he had a thought.

"Shit!" he said out loud and got out of the car to force the bag of drugs given by Kemp, under Jomahl's body, with the usual precautions, as the moon, freshly emerged from behind a cloud, caused a disconcerting gleam in the corpse's widely-staring eyes.

Headlights appeared from behind his vehicle. That was the trouble when you were as early as the 9-48 in the evening indicated by the LCD display of his car clock.

He was up and gone rapidly but was thinking quickly enough to realise that he must not leave rubber on the road. He travelled the first five yards steadily then accelerated away in second and then a racing change into third.

He checked the mirror after six or seven seconds and was clearly pulling well away from what was evidently a slow-moving van or small lorry. He could not tell. It would certainly never catch him. He felt safe and noted that the van had stopped. He could not tell but thought it was maybe alongside the body.

By the time a call was made he would be half a mile away and that would be probably well over a mile by the time a Police Car received the message, even if very sharp indeed. They could not even know that they should be looking for this vehicle.

He was fairly confident that he was well clear. The road had been dry - no possibility of tyre marks. That was something that he had considered in his planning.

As he pulled up Main Road hill, past the carwash, his certainty that he had escaped the scene was complete.

* * *

He read up on the slaying in 'The Star' the following day and was concerned not to see "and a number of suspicious substances were removed from the scene for analysis." Could the van driver have nicked the drugs? - It was possible but not really his concern.

This information did appear however in the paper the following day. There was no unrest.

Having completed 'The Narnia Chronicles' and having been staggered by 'The Last Battle' - and so much more -'Surprised by Joy' finished, he turned attentions to the more intellectual 'Mere Christianity'.

CHAPTER THIRTY

Mel had told Lucy all about Jomahl but only because she had asked. His determination to keep her well distanced from events was failing miserably but the choice had ultimately been hers.

She had taken Jack to the station that morning so that he could attend some important lectures over the following days and he was to return on the morning of the wedding, when he would act as Best Man and be one of the witnesses. George was to be invited to act as the other. Mel wondered how Lucy would explain to her friend why the two of them would be continuing to live in separate houses. Clearly, there would be no publicity for the nuptials in 'The Star' or anywhere else. Lucy's parents would attend on the day but Grandma was too fragile to travel.

Lucy would continue to be known to the public at large, as Mrs Saddleworth.

She had only just got back when Mel arrived at her house. She had asked about Friday night and he told her succinctly and without detail.

They made coffee and love before settling down for an important chat to which each brought rather different questions.

"Well. What did you think of my young man?" she asked with no little anxiety.

"He liked me apparently, which makes it very easy. We talked freely, we laughed, we got on. I *really* liked him," he replied emphatically.

There was an almost audible sigh of relief and she relaxed. Obviously, it had been preying on her mind. He reviewed his earlier question as to how Jack would react when he found out the truth about Mel and dismissed it. There really was no point in bringing the matter up with Lucy. It would only add to her concerns.

"I have a suggestion......." he began.

"What again?" she said mischievously and Mel began to realise how like his mother Jack was and that was one reason why he had found him so easy to like.

"I think we should both sell up and move away. We do have connections here; links which are important but I think we could sever those without too much difficulty. I love you so much, I am beginning to think I should try to avoid capture so we can live together happily ever after. I plan to tell Jerry that I shall do two more and then finish. One maybe. To be done quickly, in the next couple of weeks and then close down. I've already accepted that I must eventually be caught, as you know, but I keep thinking - What if there *is* a tiny chance of avoiding capture? Will I not owe it to my new wife to be there for her if I possibly can? I feel that what I have done has social value. It may not be much in the big picture but I do so feel that I have improved the world by executing justice. But I should retire. I owe it to you."

"I know. I understand," she said, "and whatever you decide I respect it. We both know that violent criminals are a scourge on us all. We know that successive governments have betrayed the people but that doesn't necessarily mean that you have to sort out the whole mess yourself. Why not think in World War Two terms – that you have done your bit?"

"Jerry has been terrific. I'll speak to him about it and he can have up to two more. I wonder if he thinks there are any absolute musts out there?

Now, let's think wedding. We haven't discussed a honeymoon."

"There will be time enough after and yes, I do agree that we should leave here. Shall we put both houses up for sale - it will take an eternity to lose both and in the interim we could share the unsold one? I know it has dangers but I want to be with you night and day."

"That makes it even more urgent that we move to where we are not known. I know a place on the Costa Blanca where we could get a nice flat as a bit of a bolt-hole and then try somewhere in the south, over here as our main base. Still, we'll have bags of time to sort out details while the houses are selling. Now is the time to start seeing which items are of sentimental value and must go with us. Pretty exciting all this, isn't it? But remember; let's not get into a fool's paradise it probably won't work out."

* * *

The wedding was as dull as the majority of Civil Marriages are. Mel thought that it was not the best of starts and was unsurprised that a greater percentage of Registry Office marriages would fail than those completed in a church - even when there was no faith issue involved.

It was sterile but he had to admit that his Church Wedding to Miriam had not been a resounding success.

He was nervous at being seen on public display in Sheffield with Lucy and rather wished that the wedding could have taken place somewhere......somewhere.... less risky but that was not an appropriate thought and he immersed himself in the occasion.

There was one good thing however, and that was his bride who was resplendent in a beige outfit set off with a yellow carnation inset with threads of red and pink; a quite remarkable flower; and sporting a simple hairdo which showed off her magnificently sculpted features needing only the tiniest trace of makeup to add the finishing touch. It was just not possible for man to be more in love.

Mandy attended. She was truly happy for him and wisely kept a very low profile.

As Lucy met Mandy for the first time so did he make his first acquaintance with George and Lucy's Mum and Dad. Everybody seemed to get along swimmingly.

* * *

The blessing attracted one of the Church Elders, a cleaner and a member of the congregation who had 'just popped in'.

Even with just eleven present, three of whom were strangers to Lucy and Mel, there was an atmosphere. It was tangible. It was right. And yes - it *was* kind of, well, spiritual.

Whatever it was, it formed their main topic of conversation that evening but then, remembering that it was their wedding night, they felt that they could legitimately put such considerations on hold for twenty four hours, at least.

CHAPTER THIRTY ONE

The following Friday, Mel and Lucy, Jerry and Brenda again met up in the Sheffield Arms in Burton upon Stather. It was Jerry's rest day. Mel felt considerably more comfortable than being seen with either Lucy or Jerry in the city. Mel and Jerry had bought Pay-as-you-go mobiles to be able to keep in touch more easily.

"Do remember that these two phones must never be connected to each other. If a problem arises - drop it into a river - and Lucy, same thing if Mel is arrested. Only ever use to contact me," said Jerry.

Jerry did not know about the wedding and both he and Brenda congratulated the ecstatically happy couple and were sad not to have been allowed to attend. The four really were old friends.

They also explained their intentions to put the houses up for sale which Jerry who had a secret he was not over willing to share, was only too happy to hear.

Police Constable Ronnie Sayers, who worked the Handsworth patch, had spotted a familiar-looking woman going into Handsworth Cemetery with a man he thought he might also recognise.

The woman was a certain Lucy Saddleworth whom he had got to know by sight during the investigation into her husband's murder five or six years earlier. The man, he thought, was somebody who had lost a daughter to a foul killer called Malone - a man killed in a not-too-distant pub. He checked up to find the name and came up with a certain Mel Roberts. The death of Malone was under major investigation. Putting events together, he thought CID ought to be aware of the link.

This was standard police work and PC Sayers was a standard officer who worked largely to the rules, was thoughtful, good at juxtaposing events and had an excellent detection record in the context of the rather meagre detection rates found in South Yorkshire.

He did not quite know who to tell but as fortune had it, he bumped into Jerry Kemp, who was 'most interested' in the information and said that it was probably 'just one of those things' and 'a lot of victims got to know each other well at the VOC' but he said it was 'worthy of a look and he would do so discreetly, below the radar as it were, because he did not want to upset victims more than necessary'. He also suggested that Sayers keep it 'under his hat' and congratulated him on 'excellent observation and police work'.

If Mel and Lucy were planning to leave, so much the better but a warning was necessary even if he did not choose to upset them with the information about Mel's local 'Beat Bobby'.

"I am not sure you should be seen together at all. It is potentially very dangerous. The wedding was a tremendous risk. Yes. Get out of the city as soon as you can. It improves your chances".

Jerry and Mel had separated from the ladies and both pairs engaged in intense conversations on rather different matters.

Brenda was fascinated to hear the details of the wedding and obviously regretted having been unable to attend. She had a host of questions to ask. The two chatted merrily over white wine spritzers .

In the meantime, Mel was explaining his thinking to Jerry over a pint.

"Two more, tops. Then I *must* stop. I know my chances of escape are minimal but I owe it to Lucy; to my wife. With your help and a bit of common sense I must give myself the possibility of getting away with it - however minute that chance may be. I love Lucy."

As he said it, his heart sank as he remembered the appalling, American pap of the late fifties which had passed for comedy and he determined to be more careful with his choices of words in the future.

"I do agree," said Jerry, "connections will be made. Being connected to one of the dead puts you in the frame but of course, the more unconnected killings there are, the better your chances. It sort of dilutes the only thing against you, which is motive.

We did nearly have a connection made with you and Lucy, therefore Marner too, but I am sure I've headed it off. The details don't really matter.

The point is that as soon as your name pops out of the system by good police work or a link by computer, we have problems but these aren't insurmountable. Suspecting you did it or even being certain is no substitute for evidence and there is none. Remember and keep repeating to yourself all the advice I gave you because it could save you, even when it's looking pretty dire. Trouble is, once one of my *compadres* gets a grip on you, they will never let up and that is real pressure - and for life. You can only convict yourself, unless very unlucky.

"Are there any more in the pipeline? asked Mel, "I now want to draw matters to as rapid a conclusion as I can."

"Then why *any* more?" asked his mentor.

"I had planned to just go on and on but now I've something to live for I'm looking at things rather differently. But now that plan is in operation I feel I need to tail off a bit rather than stop. It's not easy to explain and I feel I owe you."

"You owe me *nothing*!" was the sharp retort from his friend and Mel had to pacify him somewhat.

"I don't mean it ....it's not obligation so much, it's more a question of, well, following through to a natural finish. Are there any more?"

"There are," he stated. "There's a man and woman, a couple, working a sauna and massage parlour, the 'Fruits of Hawaii', down in Attercliffe. They import girls, apparently some as young as twelve, from Russia, The Philippines and of course, Thailand.

After a while these girls disappear and possibly have just moved on or so we thought, right until a body turned up near Leeds. She was a Russian aged eighteen and positively identified as one of theirs although they denied it all and when we raided, you would have thought it was an upper class poodle parlour. Zilch.

This girl had literally been tortured to death and grossly sexually abused - I shan't tell you details, it would put you off your food.

The turnover of these kind of girls is always high but from what we can gather, theirs is abnormal.

So we sit and sweat it, when all of a sudden a local Labour Councillor comes to see one of my colleagues with a bit of a confession. It must have been serious for this 'happily married bloke', with literally everything to lose, to come to us to admit that he's big, so to speak, in the world of sado-masochism. He's been promised that we shall keep it all hush hush and we shall. It's doubtful, and anyway unprovable, that he has done anything wrong.

He told us that on one of his visits he heard desperate screams that suddenly stopped. He said he was truly terrified by it and this is a man who knows and understands 'the world of pain' but that same week, he was apparently offered a 'special' at £4,500. Two days of genuine torture to his heart's content at a secret location. Methinks they misjudged his tastes and so he came to us.

But it gets worse. Our pervy politician asked what would happen if the girl accidentally died and they said, "It hasn't been a problem so far."

Now we know that's all a bit ambiguous but we firmly believe that that is what happened to the Russian lass.

We can't even find the younger girls and we know for a fact that they do exist.

So that is your mission should you choose to accept it. Take out the bloke Michael Tensing and Tulip Frost, his bit of stuff, may well pack it in, but who knows?"

"No absolute proof of murder but they abuse children?" he asked.

"Not the shadow of a doubt about it. They make Malone look up for beatification."

"That's no problem, then. I shall need the details but the answer is a yes."

"There is one problem, their outward appearance is just honest pimps and there won't necessarily be anything other than newspaper hatred aimed at the perpetrator."

"You assume I care," said Mel.

* * *

Lunch in 'The Sheffield Arms' had been booked under Brenda's maiden name and was excellent. They enjoyed each others company for another couple of hours before going their separate ways.

Mel was anxious to go into Scunthorpe Market which was quite busy for a Friday and parking was no fun at all. Eventually they managed to get into the Market Hall where Mel quickly bought in a healthy supply of smoked bacon and a mound of Lincolnshire's own sausages. As an afterthought he bought an expensive but delicious looking Lincolnshire plum bread from a cake stall.

CHAPTER THIRTY TWO

Toby Meredith could be described as darkly handsome; extremely so, in fact.

His attraction to members of both sexes was legendary on the Manor Estate in Sheffield; a district noted for its criminals and low-lifes. At a young age he had left a trail of pregnancies behind him and simply did not care. Although the vast majority of the people of that area tend to be either decent or generally law-abiding, there was and always has been, a significant element who have tended to monopolise the timetables in the Magistrates Courts in the city and no small percentage of these who are promoted to the city's own Crown Court. Because of this, many people have a less favourable opinion of The Manor than the area and its people actually merit.

This being understood, amongst that underbelly of social detritus; amongst that social underclass dedicated to being: anti-authority, parasitical, dishonest, violent, destructive, often racist and generally perverse, he managed to stand head and shoulders above the rest.

This was no small talent for one who had yet to reach his sixteenth birthday.

His childhood had not been particularly helpful as the spawn of a somewhat feckless and less-than-honest, effectively single mother, who specialised in shoplifting and who had lost all control of him before he had reached his sixth birthday and of a ne'er do well father who spent remarkably little time in their council house as he had better things to do; namely, the smoking of copious amounts of high grade 'skunk' which he was given in exchange for tasks of minor dishonesty performed for a local dealer.

Toby had no sense of right and wrong, in the accepted sense, although he had learned two of the important, moral lessons of life; never to 'grass up yer mates' and 'might is right'.

He had a well developed understanding of what society had as expectations of him but had learned years before that 'might' was lacking in the way society dealt with him and so therefore, those expectations were a total irrelevance; weakness no less.

There were many brought up on the Manor in much worse home circumstances who did not turn into that feral nightmare which was Toby Meredith. He was a one youth crime-wave who spread misery in his wake like some trainee Genghis Khan.

From five years old he had discovered the delights of breaking glass to the chagrin of every neighbour. Complaints to his mother would result in the targeting and terrorising of the complainant's house for years into the future and his neighbours were quick to learn to keep their heads below the parapet. It was not the local culture to call the Police but it was difficult to see what difference this could have made, where Toby was concerned, and was a gesture which may well have earned the opprobium of many other neighbours who were not particular fans of any kind of authority.

This attitude fuelled his actions as the better read locals wondered how Toby might have fitted into the island colony in Golding's 'Lord of the Flies'.

To say that the local comprehensive had failed to control or educate him in any way, was only accurate up to a point. True, they had made little impact on his behaviour because a number of hardworking and well-intentioned members of staff had made the fundamentally-flawed assumption that he had some sort of conscience or 'better nature' as they called it, which they could appeal to. Even so, the reason the blame was not really theirs was that he attended school so irregularly from the age of nine, some staff were hard pressed to recognise him.

His mother was threatened with court on frequent occasions for not sending him to school but somehow, it all seemed to fizzle out if she ever forced him to go for three successive weeks at a time, which she managed to do, on average, twice a year until he reached twelve when this reduced to just once.

He had learned to read and write and bully as young as five and had added exceptional arithmetical skills to his achievements before the age of seven. When his IQ came back showing a level of 152 none of his early teachers was surprised.

When high intelligence is added to low cunning and these are combined with an amoral approach to life and when you fail to control that individual - the result is a monster.

On the two occasions when desperately worried teachers had inveigled him into the presence of a bemused psychologist, unsurprisingly, he failed to cooperate and maintained a sullen silence punctuated only by bouts of the most extreme foul language.

This hapless professional had then made the most risible misdiagnosis in the history of all assessments of human behaviour:

"He is clearly suffering from low self-esteem," he had declared when Toby was ten. This misjudgement was confirmed a year later.

In practice, Toby had a *superiority complex*, if anything at all, and no other hints of mental illness at that juncture. The fact that he was what is often called a 'sociopath' by the layman, tended not to take into account the perfectly logical position he held. He did as he wanted simply because he was allowed to. It is difficult to see why this should have been perceived as any sort of *mental* aberration.

Indeed, if people take a Darwinian approach to psychology, it is difficult to see his behaviour as being anything less than fully normal. His greed, nastiness, violence and ability to beget fear were surely advanced virtues in a non-spiritually-based world where the-survival-of -the-fittest is held in such theoretical awe. His physical assets only underpinned this idea as he was big for his age and used this advantage to mesmerise and terrify youngsters as much as two years his senior and sometimes even older.

He had learned that sending out others to do his dirty work made life simpler and he would take a very reasonable 75% from their breaking and entering, drug dealing and shoplifting in exchange for the exciting and often necessary privilege of being in with him.

At a very early stage, he learned that the Courts had no powers to check him and they were viewed by him with no less than total contempt. As his arrests and convictions grew, they did so at a much slower rate than those of less intelligent thugs and so it was only the honest people in his neighbourhood and, of course, the local Police, who recognised just how appalling he really was.

Nonetheless, in a discussion at the CPS, Cecil Fawcett, one of the 'leading lights', had named Toby and said that in his opinion, there were over a hundred similar youngsters in the once proud City of Sheffield, even if not all were quite as advanced in evil as he. It was hard to imagine the social damage this collection was accomplishing. Targeting him had not worked especially well, and no Youth Court was willing to lock him up when they did not jail people with much longer records.

Getting the ASBO in place had cost thousands of pounds and was quite limited in its scope. Just after his fifteenth birthday, it kicked in. He simply chose to ignore it and still nobody seemed eager to give society a rest by locking him up. The main reason for this was that the Bench he appeared before had two members on it who thought that doing so would be to condemn the 'poor young man' to a studentship in a University of Crime. What they had signally failed to grasp was that, in reality, he was one of the potential lecturers.

The catalogue of his misdeeds ran into thousands. No day went by without a significant handful of egregious incidents; mostly criminal, some merely anti-social. He was genuinely amused by his powers to annoy, anger and upset.

Were one to seek redeeming features, it could be said with honesty that he did have some positive feelings towards his mother but this did not prevent him treating her like a *skivvy* and her house like some cross between a brothel and a drugs den.

He groped any girl he fancied, underage or not, and bullied them into having sex. Not one had the courage to prevent him. Knowing his predilections for violence, the families of such victims refused to complain to the Police and were probably wise to take that line.

Several Police raids had failed to amass evidence against him but one had resulted in him seeing his mother convicted for illegal possession of drugs which had been found imaginatively concealed under the sofa in the lounge.

She took the blame and gained a lengthy and rigid community punishment.

At the hearing, her solicitor, the genial Mr. Dawkins, argued convincingly to the Bench that she was a loving mother who could not be jailed as her son, who was an 'easily led sort of boy' could so easily 'go off the rails if that course of action were to be taken and besides that, this was her first drugs conviction.'

The stranger suspected of being his father moved out of the house altogether but whether this was from a pure fear of his offspring or because he had found a new lady friend was unclear.

* * *

What had angered the man in the hood and for him had proved the final straw, was a report that Toby had broken all four legs of a kitten and had left it in the back garden to die slowly. If the source were to be believed (and she *was* usually reliable) Toby apparently paid the cat a visit every hour or two to watch its agony. Perhaps *this* gave evidence of some form of incipient, psychopathic tendency. It came from the same stable as "Power corrupts and absolute power corrupts absolutely." So maybe he was just drunk with power.

The man carried a broad, heavy walking stick, the centre of which he had drilled out himself. He had melted a couple of pounds of scrap lead - no easy process in a single garage made of corrugated iron - and poured it with studied care into the centre of the stick with the fumes from the process clogging his throat and making him cough throughout.

Once complete, he weighed the stick and found it came to over four pounds on his ancient scales and was much more heavily weighted at one end than the other. Perfect.

He had mounted a surveillance on the house - something which he did secretively and well even in the most difficult of circumstances - and had gathered that Toby took orders for cannabis at the back door between ten and eleven every evening. There was a secret knock consisting of three consecutive raps, a pause and followed by three more.

The average number of visitors would be six or seven. On this particular night, by ten fifty, there had been nine. Mum was of course, at the pub. Thinking that there may well be no more clients, he approached the door and gave the knock. The door opened instantly and he was ushered in without comment and no apparent disquiet because of the pulled down hood.

Only when the stick broke his right arm did he look at the face of his attacker. It was not there. Shielded under the hood was a ski mask only showing very plain, ordinary blue eyes of no particular distinction.

Initially, Toby was more angry than frightened. He should have been frightened as he was now about to receive the beating of a lifetime.

The man swung the stick hard and smashed his left kneecap with the heavy end of the club and on the backswing broke his right shin.

He avoided the head but belaboured him about the ribs and shoulder.

Blood began to spurt about the room and as he crumpled into a whining heap, in a false voice; a kind of mock growl, "That was for the kitten and now you are going to behave to everybody. You are going to learn to be nice. You are going to learn honesty and treating all people and neighbours with respect. I am watching you. I shall be back and on your case every couple of months if necessary. Do you understand? Well?

Do you?" and he raised the stick, whereupon Toby did something he had never done before in his life, he made a promise to behave - and more than that - he meant it.

Somebody had finally explained to him properly- in a way that he could understand - why he should conform and as this man had proved to be such an effective teacher, he had *definitely* understood.

His rehabilitation was completed even without the man explaining to him that on one future occasion he or his friends would visit and any further bad behaviour could well cost him his life.

The final explanation really had not been necessary. This was one community punishment which had, most assuredly, been more successful than prison could ever have been.

CHAPTER THIRTY THREE

"I think Michael Tensing can be the last for you," said Jerry and paused because the cough was still troubling him. "There was another essential but I made arrangements and got it sorted myself, without extreme prejudice, shall we say?

Tensing is now the worst in Sheffield - South Yorkshire, even. You can start to make plans for your and Lucy's future and I have a feeling you won't be seeing the inside of a prison. No guarantees, of course, but it's looking good. You are just one rather inconsequential name on a long list of possible suspects. We have no actual suspects. I do sometimes regret that Police time, that could be better employed, is taken up on this - but then, some things just can't be helped," he remarked

The two men had met up in a pub called 'The Dolphin' on the old A18 at a place called Gunness - again not too far from Scunthorpe. Mel regretted that it was a Thursday and therefore not a market day in the town which occurred on Fridays and Saturdays. The plum bread had been a resounding success.

It may have seemed extreme travelling independently some thirty five miles to meet up for a chat, but 'better safe than sorry' thought Jerry. He could not afford to have his connection to Mel be known. Police work is often simply about links and connections. If these cannot be made in a large investigation then the chances for an arrest plummet. Besides, they were friends and deserved to have a relaxed chinwag about more general things.

They had a shared interest in rugby and both men wanted to talk about their wives of whom they were inordinately proud. Their politics proved congruent and Jerry was astonished by the machinations of the EU, which he truly hated. Mel had always been heavily opposed to it but was surprised to discover that Jerry was able to say, "There are only two things I truly hate: one - obviously enough - is serious criminals, but the EU with all its sickening corruption is for me on precisely the same level. I don't get it!" he reasoned. "It's corrupt from top to bottom. Impossibly expensive. Dictatorial. A bureaucracy factory and it churns out nearly 80% of our laws. All three main parties support the fucking thing. We can't do what *we* want. This isn't The Common Market I voted for in '75 when the late Ted Heath told us it was 'a trading agreement' and nothing but."

'A man of strong opinions,' thought Mel, but agreed with every word all the same.

They talked of their respective childhoods, their education, their musical tastes. Mel was quite surprised that Jerry was a Pink Floyd fan. That had seemed incongruous but he too was rather fond of their work and had actually been to one of their concerts back in his university days.

Jerry was also deeply into classical music whereas Mel simply enjoyed listening to the classical charts programme on Classic FM on many a Saturday morning.

Both men adored test cricket: "The highest art form known to man," said Jerry. Mel struggled to disagree. They had a sandwich and a pint each but were careful not to have a second alcoholic drink when driving - Mel did not abuse alcohol - he was far too socially responsible and he certainly did not need a Policeman present to remind him of the Breathalyser Laws.

Their chatting went on through lunchtime and well into the afternoon.

By the time Mel drove away, he was in possession of a number of valuable and well researched pieces of information about the sinister Tensing and he thought what a pity it was that this man should so abuse the name of that most worthy Sherpa who had guided Hillary and Hunt in the first successful assault on Everest.

His only concern was that killing Tensing might not do too much good if he were part of a larger, mafia-style organisation but he reasoned that at the very minimum, there would be some justice for the abused young women and it would stall the development of any larger group's plans.

He had mentioned this concern to Jerry who agreed that there was a possibility but that there was no obvious evidence that this was the case and Jerry had said to him: "If the odious Petunia, or whatever they call her, gets in your way - kill her but only if it is unavoidable. Scare her very wits out of her but I'm not expecting you to run into anybody other than Tensing."

* * *

And so it was that Mel had caught the last bus down into Attercliffe. He was wearing smart-casual clothing and his false moustache. He carried an Asda carrier bag which contained a brand new 'hoodie' and the ubiquitous baseball cap. The ski mask was in there too along with the Browning complete with silencer. He had put a second carrier around the first so that there was no danger of the silencer protruding through the side of the bag. As an afterthought, he had put a third bag around the previous two. It would not be good to be turned over by some over-ambitious young copper - but any risk was small.

Being a hit man had been easier than you might have expected. It was a thought that he had had many times before and he could only conclude that it was because his work had always tended to be so well researched, either by Jerry or for himself. Killing Marner had been the least professional and that was the job where it had come nearest to going wrong but then, arguably, the elimination of Malone had been even worse. He would have approached it differently now.

He wondered if this one would be as easy and felt a nervousness and adrenaline rush which he had not felt since the death of Malone and if he thought about it, that had been afterwards. Perhaps this was because he was on the finishing strait and for some reason he could only think disturbingly about Crisp in 'The Grand National', pipped at the post by the worthy Red Rum. Had he even been born when that had happened?

The plan was for him to put on the hoodie after getting off the bus until behind the rear of the premises, knock on the back door at about midnight and Tensing would come to answer. He had no photo and needed to establish identity. Once done he would shoot him through the hoodie which would, by now, be folded over his arm concealing the gun. Simple was always best. He had a rough description of Tensing and so not everybody answering to the name of Michael would have problems.

He knocked on the door on the stroke of the witching hour and as predicted by Jerry, a man fitting the description answered it.

"Michael?" asked Mel conspiratorially.

"Yes. Are you loo......."

The man disintegrated in front of him as the first bullet struck his heart. No point in being concerned about the number of bullets if this was the last one. He put a second into the dead man's chest and stood back, steadied the clumsy, over-long weapon and put a third between the eyes.

"Michael!" shouted a woman's voice with no particular urgency from within. So Mel stuffed everything in the carrier and made himself scarce.

He walked down to the old Banners Building - a former department store with a long defunct Jacksons' Supermarket in the basement - and turned off behind it, heading towards the Super Tram stop, keeping well clear of the CCTV cameras he knew marked the approach route. He adored the Super Tram but had to admit that it had been something of a white elephant. He checked as one stopped and went past. Nobody got off and this was no surprise as few people lived in the heart of Attercliffe.

Once the tram had gone he walked past the mini station and turned off right towards Darnall. After about a quarter of a mile he concealed the bag in a prepared spot on wasteland, knowing that he would return to collect it in his car at dawn.

Jerry had assured him that the Police would not begin a search that far out for some considerable time and he could not afford to be caught with the bag. More co-ordination here as Jerry knew that he would be the first CID officer to be called out to this and he would make sure that all early enquiries took place around the sauna itself.

Mel would have had to have been very unlucky to have been noticed with the bag but if he was, he would be wearing a bright, white baseball cap. The cap had to be left in the carrier so that if he were spotted walking home through Darnall, the chances were that no connection would be made.

He would be back in Handsworth in just over twenty-five minutes from dropping the bag and there was precious little chance that a patrol car would pick him up and the Police helicopter was largely irrelevant. The crime could easily remain unreported for quarter of an hour or more.

Mel had been three different people from any witnesses' point of view.

The plan was simple. It worked as Jerry had predicted. Nonetheless, he did not relax until able to collect the bag in his car some seven hours later and he went through his customary, safety procedures.

Mr Silver's house was still unsold and the two together had matching Heppenstall Estate Agent boards out front. There was no hurry to dispose of the weapons and he needed to discuss these with Jerry in any case, so back under Silver's shed they went.

It was over. Life could perhaps begin again. With Jerry's assistance in the Police investigation there was every chance he could put this all behind him. He was now retired. It was truly over.

Let the 'new life' commence.

CHAPTER THIRTY FOUR

He relaxed into his favourite chair and savoured a feeling of true freedom.

It was a well known fact that serial killers always went on until they were caught. Well, *he* had stopped and the chances were really not all that bad for him escaping justice. 'Justice'?

Was it not he who had been the 'dealer of Justice'? Did the executioner have to pay a price too? Certainly, that was out of line with Genesis Nine.

Was he expected to be official for that to apply? It all came back, as it inevitably did, to what happened when a government was failing its electorate and exacerbated by the fact that several generations had grown up blithely oblivious to the fact. The violent world they inhabited was all they had ever known. It was only older people and those like Mel; true social victims, who were able to see that Life had not always been like this.

The revenge element had been entirely expunged, of course, so he was now more somebody who was - no *had been* - dedicating himself to his country's welfare.

His problem was that what he had been attempting was so out of the box. There really were no precedents for what he had been doing - or at least, not any that he could think of. But it was so strange that what he was doing, at least in part, reflected the actions of the vigilante groups.

His 'State of Grace', as some of the Christians would have put it, was still most open to question. He was most assuredly not a Christian. He and Lucy had attended Church on a regular basis and it seemed that Lucy was ahead of him in the spiritual investigation stakes, a fact which he resented slightly because was it not he who had been investigating first; reading up on C.S.Lewis? Competition in such matters? - No that was just ridiculous.

The relief of his second retirement produced feelings which were quite tangible. He had not really spotted how much pressure he had been putting himself under in recent months. It was the falling in love with Lucy which had undoubtedly brought that pressure, as prior to that, his life had been quite worthless; simply nothing to lose. He supposed that medal-winning heroes were mostly taken from the ranks of the not-much-to-live-for brigade. He could not see himself as a hero. He preferred to consider that he was just somebody performing a service for the common good. Still, it was all over now. Lucy and he would have to book a holiday and build a life.

It occurred to him that apart from marriage and making a success of that, he had precious little idea what he would be doing with the remainder of that life. He would have to have a project; plans to try to build a better world with rather different methods to those he had been employing latterly.

He really cared about the disabled so perhaps he could work for a charity. It had worked for Lucy and she was putting a great deal of effort into some of her former causes and seemed happy, although in the depths of many a night he heard her issue deep sighs as she suffered bouts of insomnia which sapped her energies. He knew it may have been what had happened to Larry which troubled her but was sure that it was worry about losing him too which was causing the greatest of her distress.

He wondered about politics. Would he want to work for the Tories? He was not happy with the prospect. Greens? - Former Marxists in sandals? - He could not really see it, besides he was far from convinced that their policies were ultimately beneficial. Certainly, their thoughts on how to solve crime were puerile in the extreme, even their environmental policies were based more on opinions than established facts.

Labour then? - Hardly. The Blair Government had cured him of his family tradition of always voting Labour. - No. No and thrice no!

He had always thought The Lib Dems in between the Tories and Labour until Lucy disabused him of that misconception. He would not vote for a party of the theoretical left.

B.N.P. - No way! Respect? - Same reasoning - extremes. No!

He realised why he had been attracted to UKIP. They were anti-EU with a large raft of policies which looked good to him. But surely it was a wasted vote? - But if everybody thought like that, nothing would or could ever change and they *could* be relied on to get votes and seats under PR in EU Elections. He wondered how many votes they might achieve under PR in National elections - quite a few, he guessed. Scoring well under PR in EU Elections was one of life's little ironies.

But did he want to work for a minority party? - Probably not. Maybe a bit for EU Elections then and he would give them a vote any time they stood. There was quite a lively group of UKIPites in Handsworth who worked tirelessly for the cause.

No. Charity work it would be. He had always tended to give heavily to a variety of charities as his sympathies were firmly behind those less fortunate than himself. Miriam had always bleated at the size of some of his donations but when a person has a social conscience it is difficult to act otherwise. He had never really worked for charities before although he had often helped out with various fund-raisers and thought this might be a suitable avenue to explore. If Lucy were involved - then all the more reason to muck in and help.

* * *

He was expecting Lucy to stay over at his house that night. In the few short weeks since the wedding, they had become quite lax about the issue of not being seen together. He would have to give up his house, perhaps. Harthill was more off track than Bramley. Definitely, as soon as one house sold they would leave Sheffield.

He fancied Burton upon Stather. He adored the village and liked the scenery. The views over the Trent Valley could be amazing and there was a wide variety of good walks. It may be necessary to buy a dog. It would be quite expensive to buy a quality house with a panoramic view, but as Lucy apparently had even more money than he had, and he had more than he could spend, that just did not matter. She agreed tentatively but said that her approval was entirely dependent on the right house with the right view. She was happy enough to move to that village. She liked the semi-rural life of Harthill and the change of style would not be too demanding.

She was happy to buy a seaside flat in La Mata as he had suggested - even without seeing it first - but would insist on three bedrooms, two bathrooms, community pool, balcony and sea view. She was surprised how little this could be bought for, even in days of inflated Spanish property markets.

CHAPTER THIRTY FIVE

Agreement had been made to sell Lucy's house to a property developer from Thurcroft. She was pleasantly surprised that he wanted the house so desperately that he had offered an extra two and a half percent in order to secure the purchase, then and there. He was looking to completion in just six weeks and with this pressure on them they spent a full Saturday, house hunting around Burton and discovered a veritable plethora of small villages in the vicinity which enjoyed the kind of views they were both seeking; Flixborough, Whitton, Alkborough and so on - all along the Trent itself.

The thought of finding the perfect house on their first excursion seemed an unlikely possibility but when you are not really limited by price these things are generally easier.

They found it in Burton itself - a four bedroomed, ranch-style bungalow with more features than you could shake a stick at and precisely the quality of view which was the principal object of their search.

They offered the asking price and stated that they were not prepared to enter a bidding war and that the offer would be withdrawn once and for all should one commence.

Mr Stubbs, who had just won a contract in Bahrein for his pipe-laying enterprise and had to leave the country shortly, agreed with alacrity. Much had happened in a very short time for all concerned.

* * *

Church the following day saw an appeal at the end of the Evening Service after Brian had finished preaching on 'Jesus scattering the tables in the Temple.'

Not to his great surprise, Lucy went forward a seeker and returned a born again believer. At first he was troubled. What if his beloved Lucy became less the Lucy she was and .... well.... somebody ....different? Would she report him to the police? - No! Don't be absurd! She was his wife. They were in love and nothing would ever alter that.

He knew her commitment was real and had been brewing throughout the weeks since the wedding. He tried to be happy for her and to his surprise - he found it easy to do so. This may have pressured him to follow the same path but he found himself wholly unable to follow her.

It was not lost on him that Lucy was the name of the protagonist in 'The Narnia Chronicles'. She was a character who had delighted him and he enjoyed the coincidence that his love bore the same name. That Lucy became a highly developed spiritual person and he knew that *his* Lucy was bound to be the same as she had depths that he could only begin to guess at.

She returned to her seat, eyes glistening with unconcealed joy. The *reality* of Christianity had never struck him so forcibly. He now accepted it was the Truth, indeed - the 'Only Truth'. The solitary problem was that he did not feel able to take the step she had taken and in spite of all his searching, he was not sure he ever would.

He was glad for Lucy, however. She deserved the best.

The next day Lucy disappeared early to begin the packing of all her worldly goods.

Mel walked up to the top of Handsworth and bought flowers. The only thing causing him anxiety was the distance between Burton and the grave to which he had such ease of access at the moment.

He sat down beside the headstone and talked to his daughter.

"I shall still come, you know. Just because we are moving to Lincolnshire doesn't mean that you will be forgotten. Nothing could be further from the truth. I shall always come," and a pang struck him as he realised that the keeping of such a promise was not necessarily always going to be within his powers or control.

"I shall always try," he said, amending the promise ever so slightly.

He walked home happy that he had told Jenny so much. He was happy to have told her that Lucy had become a Christian; happy because he had a wonderful wife; happy for their new house; happy for their new life. It was all going to work out now. He was absolutely certain of it.

As he walked into the house, the phone in his pocket rang. He did not recognise the tone. It did not feel quite right. He realised it was Jerry making the first contact on their mobiles. He had almost forgotten about that.

"Hello!" he said cheerily.

"Raid.Imminent! Remember *everything* I told you!" said a disembodied, anxious voice before ringing off.

Must lose the phone. He went out the back and hurled it into Mr. Silver's rhubarb patch. He would throw it away properly later.

The front doorbell was ringing by the time he re-entered the house. He opened it and CID Detective Constable Calver thrust a warrant into his face.

"Search of house," she announced and four further Police Officers trailed in behind her.

Mel made all the protests that Jerry had advised then went off to make a coffee. His offer to the searching policemen to make them one was rejected - but the gesture seemed to go down well with them all, except of course with DC Calver, who seemed to intensely dislike him. He was unsure why this was the case. Perhaps she thought a gruff attitude represented professionalism.

The search continued through house and garden for nearly three hours before they gave up; defeated.

They had found a clipping of Malone's death from 'The Sheffield Star' but realised that there was nothing unnatural about this and left it on the kitchen table without comment.

Mel simply sulked. He did it rather well and occasionally muttered: "This is what you get in this crappy country for being a victim. I suppose I've clicked a speed camera somewhere, have I?"

They ignored him and when the search was completed they left politely enough but it was clear that Ms Calver was far from pleased. Indeed, it had seemingly become her turn to sulk.

* * *

At eight o clock the morning after, he heard noises at the front of the house. Good job the phone was now at the bottom of the River Rother. There were four Police cars parked along the road and they were taking apart the house next door.

He knew that it was all up for him if they searched the garden.

They searched the garden. He wondered why as he looked out of his window. Why search next door? And as he looked at the two sale boards, virtually side by side, he realised he was the victim of some intelligent lateral thinking by DC Calver, who seemed to be wielding more power than any junior officer should be entitled to have. Clearly, on the visit the previous day, she had registered that the house next door was empty and had concluded that it would make an excellent hiding place. The delay was to allow for gaining a second warrant. No Jerry.

He was glad that Lucy had stayed over in Harthill and decided to make a cup of good coffee. After all, who knew when he might get another. He could not understand why he felt so calm.

As the search progressed he allowed himself a brief touch of optimism but deep inside, he knew the Police would find the weapons. If he had finished his mission, why oh why had he not disposed of them? Part of the problem had been that he had not wanted to jettison Jerry's gun. It wasn't his to throw away. Silly!

He had been going to discuss it at his next meeting with Jerry but it was too late now.

The ring eventually came and he answered the door. DC Calver invited him to come to the Police Station to 'answer a few questions' and he refused.

He was promptly arrested, cautioned, handcuffed and led out to a car. He had no real feelings. He was cold inside but was concerned about his wife. How would she find out? Jerry would tell her, of course. He would be able to ring her legitimately. No worries about that, then. However, he did not give out any hope for improvements in her insomnia.

Where was Jerry? - Perhaps he wasn't on duty. He certainly had not managed to warn him of the second raid.

By the time he had been taken to West Bar Police Station and processed in the Custody Suite, it was already late morning.

He was scheduled to be interviewed at 12-20. He refused on the grounds that he had not had any breakfast and would not be prepared to discuss anything until after he had eaten.

Whilst they pondered this, he cast his mind back and wondered why they were only interested in the murder of Tensing. Why that one? Why not one of the others? Perhaps it was a tactic. Was it what they called a 'holding charge'?

He recalled Tom Sharpe's Wilt being interviewed by the Police and hoped he would be able to cause as much confusion as poor Henry Wilt had done but there was nothing particularly amusing about *this* situation.

He decided that he would enjoy it. Why ever not? It was a new experience and even with what they had, the Police would still struggle to convict him. Perhaps he would be able to write a book about his varied experiences. Sometimes life was about scoring a series of minor victories - that was how the prisoners in Colditz, Stalag Luft Three and similar had kept their sanity. Could he not do the same? He had already put them on the back foot with his insistence on having a meal. Perhaps he could regard it as a little game of some kind.

He wondered how long they could keep him. It stuck in his mind that he had seventy two hours before they had to produce him before Magistrates but was unsure. He wondered if Lucy knew what had happened - all her nightmares come true. What would happen about the house? Would she be able to go ahead with the sale and purchase? He did not know.

One of the troubles of being here was the not knowing. The Custody Sergeant had given him some card or other with his rights on it but he was unable to concentrate sufficiently to read it.

An officer appeared with an adequate cooked meal consisting of meat pie and three vegetables which was accompanied by a cup of tepid tea and a packet of three digestive biscuits.

When he returned to collect the tray, he tried to foist the Duty Solicitor onto the prisoner who simply said, "Dawkins." The PC scowled and relayed the unsavoury message to The Custody Sergeant who was less than thrilled with the news.

"Heaven knows how long it will take to track down *that* oily turd," he stated warmly.

"I saw him in the Magistrates Court.... er........ Court Two about an hour ago. He looked as though he was set up for the day," said the PC.

"Fetch!" said the sergeant curtly, "He'll drop what he is doing like a hot spud if he knows he has a serial killer to defend."

In the meantime Mel stared at his cell wall and waited patiently. Was prayer appropriate? - Maybe so, but he was unable to offer any.

He retired into his mind and dwelled on pleasant thoughts; his wife, his new home and hopefully, his new life.

A trial could be a year or more away and so even if not convicted he could expect a lengthy, forced stay at H.M. Government's expense.

He wondered if there was even the slightest possibility of bail and correctly thought it impossible.

Would he be allowed reading matter? Perhaps he should refuse to cooperate if he were not allowed any. He was, after all, an innocent man - at least until somebody could prove otherwise.

It came to him suddenly that if he gave evidence in Court on his own behalf, he would have to take the oath. He was not prepared to lie under oath. What if he chose to affirm? - Well, he was not sure it made a great deal of difference to his conscience. He would choose not to testify. Tell the Court it was some kind of protest at having been locked up, perhaps.

What about lying in the interview, then? - He was flummoxed for a while and determined to say little and be as truthful as he dared but he would deny all charges. He hated lying and was unable to remember the last time he had told a lie. Lies were the tools of the shifty, the brazen, the foolish and the dishonest. Liars were low-lifes. He did *not* want to join their ranks.

He demanded something to read so the PC who had been to tell Dawkins of his latest misfortune decided to have a bit of fun at Mel's expense and he produced acomplete, Gideons NIV Bible. "There you go pal. Plenty of reading in that!"

Mel was delighted. He had always intended to read the Bible from cover to cover and as somebody unqualified and largely press-ganged into teaching R.E., he had always promised to learn more about the subject and this was top of the list.

He was encouraged and began straight away. Genesis One, Verse One.

"In the beginning, God created......" Five words and he was already plunged into a new sphere of existence.

Was it literal? Was God more of a 'motivating factor'? Did evolution happen? If so, who or what was behind it? Could blind chance create people through lines of literally billions of beneficial mutations when mutations were always or virtually always damaging? Why were there not billions of transitional forms in the fossil record if evolution were true? Would billions even be enough?

Why did famous evolutionary scientists run from public debate with creationist scientists if they were so sure?

Aliens?

What of the simplified version of evolution? - "Hydrogen is a colourless, odourless gas, which given sufficient time turns into people." Was that not the height of absurdity? Easier to accept the 'God version'. Possibly. Probably.

What of 'The Big Bang Theory'? - "In the beginning there was nothing which then exploded!" - Illogical. He may not have been a Christian, least of all a creationist, but he was rapidly falling out with the 'Evolutionary Hypothesis'.

Life in prison would give time for deep thought, philosophical exploration, a broadening of his reading and self-education. Perhaps he could even do another degree. A doctorate maybe? Had it not been for his enforced separation from Lucy, he could have quite looked forward to it.

He did suppose that the other inmates would leave something to be desired but that was a bridge he would cross when he came to it.

They had taken his watch and he had no concept of time but as he meditated on the opening of Genesis it did not seem to matter a great deal. It was almost as if a concealed tension within him had been suddenly and irrevocably removed.

He was pretty sure that the interview planned for 12-20 had been put back. They were most likely having a problem locating Mr Dawkins. Mel was quite looking forward to meeting this interesting sounding chap. He expected that the feeling would be reciprocated as mass murderers are always noteworthy.

What about Jerry? Would he have found out by now? - He was senior to Calver and so *must* have been informed. Would he be on the interview? He had promised that if convicted, it would still work out in the end for him. How did that work?

The cell door opened and Algie Dawkins was ushered in.

"I understand you have a problem," said a dapper, diminutive, dark-haired man with an extravagant moustache which was just too extravagant to be gay. 'That would have drawn attention if I'd tried disguising myself with one like that', he thought.

"I just don't get it. They came to my home months ago and sort of asked me some pointed questions, then I had to go to the Police Station for a chat with Inspector Kemp. Yesterday, they raided my house and today they searched my neighbour's house and promptly arrested me. They are apparently charging me with the murder of somebody called Tensey or something like that. Who is he? Why me? All I am is a man who has had his daughter butchered and his wife driven to suicide. I expect they also kick cripples."

"No worries," said his new protector. "You haven't said anything to them have you. Discussed your case?"

"I have no case to discuss. Do you know why they've arrested me?"

"I do. One of them said to me that they have you 'bang to rights' to use the jargon. They found a gun and a knife concealed under the shed of the house next door to you. We shall have to wait for forensics but they are pretty sure that they have been used in five murders."

"Five?" asked Mel, his surprise because of the low number which had been interpreted as a surprise by Dawkins because it was so high.

He rightly speculated that it would be Marner they had missed. It may actually help him if that one were included as it did not fit a pattern.

"Oh shit. Of *course* it did!" It was the killer of his wife's former husband. A rather overwhelming connection. How could he possibly forget, even for a moment?

"What motive could I possibly have? I know that scumbag Malone was murdered and I'm glad. But they, I mean Kemp, told me it was a *drugs* killing. Where do I possibly get a motive from to kill four other people? Who are these people? Are they Malone's family and the triple cursed midwife who helped drag that vermin into the world? If not, I just don't get it. And how do they find weapons in somebody else's property and blame me? What if they are the real murder weapons? DNA will clear me, won't it? Finger prints? Has that cow Calver planted weapons nearby? She was pretty pissed off yesterday that she failed to get me?

Is that it?" He thought he had been quite convincing but who could tell if Dawkins believed him? He saw a great many 'innocent' people locked in Police cells. Did it matter what he believed? Jerry thought so, apparently.

"Listen. Say nothing at interview and sulk because you are innocent. They can't make you talk. Offer to look at a list of questions and tell them you will give them prepared answers. That way you have cooperated but have not capitulated to their bullying tactics. Okay?"

Dawkins was telling him almost exactly what Jerry had advised.

* * *

The planning, which had almost been tinged with a kind of euphoria, came to an abrupt and utterly unforeseen end and was replaced by wave after wave of a profound depression the like of which he had not even experienced in the darkest days following Jenny's death. Why? Had Dawkins acted as a catalyst of some sort? Collision with reality?

He now understood why it had begun. It was losing Lucy. He had been offered the chance of happiness and he had not grabbed it with both hands.

Why ever not? It was all too clear. He was to blame. Why had he let society become so important to him? Was God punishing him for God's work? Was God punishing him for being presumptuous?

He could no longer talk to Dawkins. He felt as if he were losing his grasp on reality.

"Lucy.................. house sale.....buy.......... arrest ......prison ....more.............prison.............long............................Lincolnshire sausages no more..............no more coffee.......................no more Lucy..........................Jenny. Can't see... ....Jenny..............................Dawkins............Genes is...................Brian. Wedding.......................no more............. sex....................... Chablis. Jerry........................ Gone!"

Dawkins was stunned. "From lucid to loony", as he put it later. Mel had not even realised that he was saying all of this out loud. He slumped onto the table between them and became totally incoherent.

Dawkins was immediately thinking 'insanity defence'. It was a simple but nonetheless devastating mental breakdown. The pressure had got through and by the end of the afternoon, Mel was in a prison hospital wing with a cocktail of drugs pulsating through his veins.

He relaxed and the pressure was gone. He was able to recognise that he had had a breakdown. He could see why it had happened. He had been under stressful pressures for years and the arrest had been the catalyst, not Dawkins.

He relaxed. He slept eighteen hours a day and over a couple of weeks he got better.

Lucy had visited. Several times, he thought. Perhaps more. A sea of happiness overtook him but he was unable to talk.

DI Kemp came and felt guilty at pushing Mel, but he had to get him to keep silent. He thought he had probably got through but nevertheless contacted Lucy to advise her to tell him not to talk, too.

After three weeks he was conversing normally and the drugs were allowed to taper off. He did not say anything inappropriate The legal procedures were under way again and he was now charged with all six killings which he refused to call murders.

CHAPTER THIRTY SIX

The trial at Sheffield Crown Court must have been about somebody else, it certainly did not seem to be about him. It was accepted that he was 'fit to plead', with his breakdown seen as being of small consequence.

It was difficult to equate all of this to the killings in any way. When they were discussed, they were almost unrecognisable as the scenes he had lived through. He had never seen a real trial before and found the proceedings quite bewildering. The red robes and wig of the Judge, Mr. Justice Harcourt, were quite off-putting. Wigs on barristers - disconcerting. Why did everything move so incredibly slowly - trials on TV were always sharp and fast-moving?

Witness followed witness. Who were all these people? Why was it necessary to have so many giving evidence on oath to confirm that a forensic bag had been opened in a particular way? It was all quite absurd. If he was finding it so difficult to follow, what would it be like for those of below average intelligence, or worse? Normally so good at concentrating, there were extended periods when he became so bored that he was unable to get the gist of what was going on. It was all about his life and yet, on occasions it became too monotonous for him to bother following the trivial intricacies.

What about the jury? What were they thinking? It was impossible to read their faces. At one time he had avidly consumed works by Grisham and knew that in the USA there were professionals who spent their whole lives studying jurors and their reactions. How could that possibly work? Fortunately, there were no horrific machinations in jury selection in *this* country. But what were they thinking? A line of inscrutable faces peered at him, seemingly devoid of emotion.

What on earth were all these 'legal submissions' which managed to clear the court periodically?

Interviews. Agreed statements. Forensics thrust at him. Exhibits. Yes, exhibits. The gun and the stiletto were both produced. Forensics had determined that the 9mm had been used in three murders. How he objected to that word. No. It *should* be 'killings'. But where was the connection? Got them there! There *was* no DNA to be found, no fingerprints and no GSR to link to him. Terrific. This meant that all the evidence was, in effect, circumstantial. How could they convict? - They couldn't! Maybe the weaknesses of the system would see this 'guilty' man walk free from court as so many others do. It was going well.

Dawkins. Dawkins with Counsel, Mr. Braintree. Court appearances, literally by the dozen. Witnesses by the score. Police. More experts. DC Calver.

Month following tedious month. Finally an end was in sight.

Mr. Braintree rose imperiously to his feet and launched into his assault which was genuinely the only hint of excitement in the many, many tortuous weeks:

"This is the clearest case on record of a man being accused on the basis of planted evidence by Police out to make a name for themselves. My client will not testify. Why should he? The Crown has to prove its case *and* 'beyond reasonable doubt!" Well, I ask you. Has it done that? What have they put before you? - Motive in just *one* case, I grant you. *Possible* motive in another. And *none* at all in four more. So are you, members of the Jury, going to convict a man because he happens to live *near* the tangible evidence and has the equivalent of less than one third of a motive? An intelligent man, too stupid to hide these so-called tools of his trade properly, is that what you really think?

Are *you* going to be responsible for allowing the real guilty parties to escape justice by convicting an entirely blameless victim of the most heinous crime of all - I think not!"

The Judge did his summing up fairly, pointing out the strengths and weaknesses on both sides.

Mr. Braintree was proved wrong. Three hours and a quarter later the Jury returned with guilty verdicts on all charges.

To be honest, Mel was more than a little surprised and Braintree was cross.

Mel was in complete charge of his mental faculties as the Judge pronounced six life sentences to run concurrently but with a recommendation that Mel never be released as he was 'too dangerous a man ever to be set loose onto the public again'. It made him think. If *he* were 'so dangerous', then why had Malone and Marner not been viewed in that way too? It hardly seemed balanced.

Mel waved to Lucy and she waved back. Kemp looked serious but dared to launch the slightest of smiles and nodded almost imperceptibly in his direction as Mel was led back to the cells. Never, never confess!

Mel wondered if he would now get past the first five words of Genesis as he began his 'new life'.

CHAPTER THIRTY SEVEN

Prison was quite uneventful, initially. He remained in Doncatraz as they wondered what to do with him and he caught up with his general reading.

By the start of his second month he had read everything theological C.S.Lewis had ever written along with some light theology from David Pawson and a number of other authors brought in for him by Lucy who visited at every opportunity. On the one occasion she was too ill to attend because of flu, she had allowed Mandy to take her place. What a gracious lady Lucy was. Her trust was absolute and he would never betray it. He wasn't going to be getting too many opportunities to do so, in any case.

It was the first time he had seen her since the wedding almost ten months earlier. It was good and made him the envy of many an inmate - particularly those who had seen Lucy as well. Chatting with a friend was so good.

He was surprised how sympathetic she was to his cause and she remained one of the very few to know for certain that he was guilty.

"You only got rid of trash. Don't be guilty about it."

"But I'm innocent, remember?" he said with a knowing wink.

"I've always known you were innocent," she said with a wink too, "and I've never understood why the Police never got back to me over your original alibi. *And* why didn't you call me as a witness?"

"There were reasons," he declared. "One, it was a trial tactic and we couldn't risk you under cross examination - you see, as my girlfriend who would have believed you? Two, we didn't want to risk you being done for perjury and three, I can't tell you at this stage," he said anxious to say nothing about behind the scenes influences from Jerry.

The visit was a success and she promised to write every week provided Lucy did not mind.

It was as he returned to his cell that the unpleasantness began. He was kicked behind the knee and ended up in the hospital with serious but fortunately not long-lasting damage.

The assailant was a vicious moron by the name of Shipley Applebaum who was enjoying making the lives of any who came into contact with him as miserable as possible. As far as anybody knew, he was the only homosexual rapist in that wing but a highly successful one.

A rather pathetic youth called Rowson had tipped Mel off as soon as he arrived. He had been the first of Applebaum's victims and since that time three months earlier, there had been a further seven who had fallen prey. Apparently, he was considerably worse the day after mainlining his occasional heroin. The low after the high tended to add to his natural viciousness. The rumours that the prison was awash with drugs had proved unfounded but that did not mean that they were entirely absent and there were occasions when he was able to shoot up although nobody seemed to know who his supplier was.

Mel was less than delighted on getting back to his cell to find that he was now sharing with the aforementioned addict.

To put it simply, he was terrified. Shipley, as the muscle-bound ogre had warmly told Mel to call him, was friendly and remained so until precisely the moment when he launched an attack on Mel in the very instant that the lights were doused.

Mel shrieked in terror and a Prison Officer appeared demanding to know what was going on. "A touch of cramp in my calf. I got a knock behind my knee today. I've been to the infirmary - please check. It's right", he avowed.

The officer wandered off showing no further interest.

"I'll make you pay for that," said Applebaum.

"What the fuck have I done?" said Mel having learned to join in polite conversations in the local vernacular. "I saved you. I could have grassed you up - and I didn't. You owe *me*!"

If it was an attempt to win by psychological domination it failed miserably but the lovely Shipley decided to leave matters for one night at least, since the officer had clearly been alerted.

He went off to sleep issuing a variety of threats; some of them quite rude and anatomically threatening.

* * *

The following day, Applebaum drove a toe end into the area behind the other of Mel's knees as they walked to breakfast. It was vicious, but although an extremely effective weapon, his timing was not quite as good as the previous day so the hospital trip was avoided.

That day Rowson was raped again and he suffered in silence because although Applebaum terrified them all, it was more than any two people's lives were worth to grass him up. As an honour code it left a great deal to be desired or so Mel thought and he began to turn his mind to dealing with the problem.

Where brain meets brawn, if the brains can avoid the physical dangers for a short while, they should always overcome the brawn in the longer game.

Mel was imaginative and his chance was closer than he could possibly have expected.

Lights were extinguished as usual and immediately, Shipley produced a syringe from who-knows-where, found a vein in the crook of his arm and filled what passed for a brain with pure, pure white peace.

He lapsed into semi-consciousness and Mel wondered how best to kill him.

It was not easy. Killing the ape was a doddle but it might interfere with Jerry's plans to get him released if he were to gain a murder conviction whilst inside. Had to think. Suffocation might work but they would have to be certain that it was a real accident. Accidents do happen to druggies.

He looked at this apology for humanity and could see no possible redemption for this particular specimen. Death would be doing everybody a good turn. Where was the moral dilemma?

His eyes focused on the syringe and an idea occurred. He went across and knelt alongside his would-be violator and picked up the syringe. He searched for the spot on the arm where Shipley had injected himself.

It was difficult to see so he stole one of Shipley's matches to illuminate the spot. With the match in his left hand and syringe in his right, he put the tip of the needle on top of the exact, same spot and injected air. The air bubble would enter his veins and eventually induce cardiac arrest. He was not sure it had worked so he did it again and was as sure as he could be that it would look to the forensics people as if Shipley had jabbed all around the small puncture wound himself whilst trying to angle the needle.

He rushed to the sink and washed the whole of the syringe thoroughly in plain water, gripped it through his handkerchief - now where had he done that before? - He worked Shipley's now dead fingers all around the implement's barrel, particularly on the top of the plunger where he organised a thumb print from the opposite hand.

He allowed it to drop naturally. It fell onto the floor just below the bed.

Nice work. He wondered if he would be required to give evidence at the Inquest. He would refuse on principle; as a 'wrongly convicted man' he would refuse to assist the wicked authorities who had engineered such a massive miscarriage of justice against him.

* * *

His appeal was fast-tracked in four months and his trip to The Court of Appeal in London was a pleasant couple of weeks out but failed to overturn the "entirely reasonable verdicts" as it was stated.

It seemed the authorities might have entertained unreasonable suspicions that he had been behind Applebaum's sad demise and were wanting to transfer him out of the way to Muckle Voe at the earliest opportunity.

And so it was. Mel began to prepare for another 'new life'.

PART TWO

CHAPTER ONE

A young herring gull blended its raucous voice with the sporadic cries of a rowdy gang of black-headed gulls. The sounds mocked the arriving prisoners who found the noises something between slightly eerie and profoundly sinister. For those townies, who were in the majority and who were unaccustomed to tiny, Scottish, coastal towns, the shrieks seemed veritable harbingers of their anticipated doom.

It had once been a fishing village and there was evidence that some small craft plied as much of their dismantled trade as was permitted under the terms of the locally despised Common Fisheries Policy.

Mel was aware that UKIP was not well represented in Scotland but he correctly assumed that this would be a pocket of support. He was unable to ascertain the name of the village and was unwilling to ask any of the rather stern-looking Prison Officers, so he remained in perfect ignorance.

His fellow jailbirds showed no interest in the quaint and truly picturesque, little parish whose houses, better called crofts, he incorrectly supposed, were hewn out of a greyish, local stone which he thought might be granite.

Gentle waves lapped against the sturdy harbour wall and an equally gentle breeze wafted agreeably through ones hair. The sky was a deep, June-blue and clouds were as rare as cuckoos in December.

The influence of The Gulf Stream made this potentially dour spot a haven for half the year but was unable to weigh in with sufficient strength to ameliorate the effects of some hugely devastating winter weathers.

A motley set of schoolchildren lined up along the quayside to stare silently and piercingly at this set of mainly English transportees who were going to be shipped out to an island just eight miles away across the water.

One brave young madam decided to wave to the group of fifteen men and fourteen pairs of eyes turned away or made pretence of not having spotted her.

Mel noted this pretty, mop-headed urchin-child who was at more or less the same age as Jenny had reached but from which his gem had progressed no further. This girl would undoubtedly live to enjoy a purposeful future. He wondered whether she would be one of those to stay or if she would join that endless stream of expatriates from isolated communities such as this one and he waved enthusiastically back to her as his handcuffed companions glowered at him.

The wave created a ripple; a frisson amongst the assembled youngsters. It was a high point in many young lives to be waved to by a murderer because they all assumed that Mel was waving personally to them. So as they all now waved, Mel ignored his scowling companions and waved vigorously to the whole line and a current of contentment ran through the younger group.

A current of malaise ran through the prisoners. He needed to be careful and as he knew none of the men alongside him, he decided to lower his profile somewhat.

It was well known that he was a serial killer but fortunately, nobody had twigged the rationale behind his actions as that would surely have been a death sentence from this collection of angry, embittered, spiteful and malevolent felons, all of whom were killers in their turn. It was generally assumed that he was a professional hit-man and this was not an opinion he wanted to see dislodged from their minds. He grunted and puckered his eyebrows a great deal and would occasionally stare into their eyes whilst half closing his own left eye in a threatening gesture, developed De Niro-style, in front of his shaving mirror. This tended to induce a certain amount of fear whenever he did so.

It was quite fun, really. He iced the cake by 'effing and blinding' even more than they did. He may not have been as physically strong as some but he had been working out; trying to develop his fitness for whatever the future would bring but his intelligence was already helping enormously in his bid to survive.

The chances were that he would spend well over thirty three years on this island if Jerry was unable to come through with his mysterious plan. So Mel had long since decided that he could not afford to rely on that at all and he assumed that it was just Jerry trying to give him some encouragement.

What he did determine was, that if it were humanly possible, he would be the first to escape and if not, he would make a satisfactory life there for himself.

The effects of his breakdown had disappeared and for reasons that were not entirely clear, he seemed to be stronger mentally than at any time since before he had met Miriam. It was perhaps that all the pressures on him had been removed and the only regrets he had were in not being able to visit Jenny, not being able to see Jerry, Mandy and Brenda again - they had all become friends more special to him than any he had ever made previously.

It was not being able to cuddle up to Lucy and build that life together which hurt most of all. He wondered too how Jack felt about him now even though Lucy had written to say that it was apparently 'cool' and he had become a kind of celebrity in his Hall of Residence, something which he referred to as 'basking in reflected infamy'.

What he was suffering from at this point did not produce stress as much as it created a dreadful ache in the depths of his being.

There had been no day since his arrest when he had not questioned himself as to whether it had all been worthwhile. The answer depended on many things: how he was feeling on a given day, whether he had got a letter, whether the sun was shining.

What he always accepted entirely, was that he had been socially valuable but was never quite sure that he should have been prepared to risk all to achieve his goals.

In that, it was a little like his views on the Iraq War, when P.M. Blair had helped to invade Saddam Hussein's fiefdom; hanging onto the coat tails of the American President.

He had thought that there might possibly have been a case to invade but he could not approve of the way Phony Tony had thrown British lives into the equation on what had evidently been a gung-ho quest for unmerited, second-hand glory.

Mel, at least, had never sought honour and glory for himself. No hypocrite, he.

There was no particular need to put his mind into gear. He was convinced that his mental faculties would not let him down again and he began to plan what he would do on Muckle Voe.

He thought he might possibly lead a Bible Study - if anybody needed God, these people did. It would help him shed light on some of his own opinions and who was to say that it would not do some good to a portion of these convicts who stood, rather bemused, on the sun-baked quayside waiting for a ferry to cart them off to their unasked for new life.

This was not entirely true for all of them because four had been due to serve lengthy sentences but had volunteered for Muckle Voe as they had no friends or relatives worthy of mention, being fed up of gaol they were prepared to try something else - anything else. Clearly, they had been accepted.

The prisoners sat down on the burning concrete of the dockside and waited patiently. It was so pleasant a day, late afternoon now and everybody was a little more relaxed.

A seedy little man shouted to the Prison Officers, "Why can't we go to the pub and wait?"

The reply was disheartening, "Pub? Pub? There's no such animal within twelve miles. This village is far too small to be able to support one. Anyway. Not to worry. You'll probably be able to go out to your own local soon enough. Thirty five to forty years is my best guess. I'm glad *we* aren't staying!"

This did put something of a damper on proceedings until one of the others, a tall, thin, black man with the remains of what had no doubt been fine dreadlocks asked, "They say them lot don't come to our side of the island, innit?"

"True, pal! So I've heard. They seem to have the brochures, we weren't given any. You should really have had them on the way up."

"Brochures?" asked the seedy individual in puzzled fashion. "He don't mean it. He can't."

"It'll be some instruction book with all the rules in it," said Mel, forgetting his low profile for a moment and also forgetting his growl.

Several men grunted and the conversation came to an end as abruptly as it had broken out.

Some lay down to sunbathe then one of the ten officers shouted, somewhat incongruously, "Thar she blows," and indeed a medium-sized steamer hove into view and they could see the round paddles to either side of the boat, its single funnel resplendent with a shiny coat of fresh, bright-red paint with a black hoop near the top of the stack.

"That's the *Mary O' Shea*," shouted an officer with a pair of binoculars and indeed within a couple of minutes they could all read the name of the refurbished paddle steamer in crisp, new lettering along the port side as she docked.

"Doesn't sound very Scottish," grumbled one innocuous captive.

The gangplank was lowered and all the prisoners were ushered onto what they were told was a car deck but that seemed unlikely as it could only have taken a maximum of four vehicles, or so Mel thought.

They had travelled to this point by 'luxury coach' - or that was what it proclaimed on the side - unfortunately, the luxury did not extend to having air-conditioning that worked properly. It came on only when the thing was doing more than sixty miles per hour, which was not frequent. It had been a hot, stuffy and seriously disagreeable journey.

This had not stopped a number of prisoners trying to hatch a plot to overcome all their guards and throttle them to death with the handcuffs they were wearing. It was maybe the four patrol cars and two motorcycle outriders, all armed, which had dissuaded them from the attempt. Mel was not really surprised by it all but it did give him the message that the company on this trip had nothing to lose, no sense of moral conduct and were all, or certainly most, incredibly dangerous people. For the first time he realised how difficult surviving could turn out to be, particularly if the Naval Guards rarely ventured onto the prisoners' side of the island.

It was early evening as the ferry pulled out. The coach had left at seven in the morning and had stopped off at a variety of prisons en route to collect the transportees. They had all been given a substantial packed lunch the effects of which had long disappeared. In short, they were all very hungry. The relaxed feelings began to diminish and as these departed, many now felt a touch mutinous.

The armed Police who had seemingly vanished into thin air when the coach arrived in the village had made a rapid reappearance as the ferry had prepared to leave and these ten men boarded the boat at the last moment; their weapons obvious in holsters at their sides. There would be no ferry hijacking on this trip. They were greeted by a contingent of men dressed in light blue casual uniforms who were also armed.

The prisoners were allowed to wander around the ferry but only with both hands cuffed in front of them. Some kind soul had propped the toilet door open and so they had, with some minor difficulty, been able to relieve themselves. There were no other passengers on the boat which was no great surprise.

The trip took over an hour and had some added interest when they saw a number of smaller, Royal Navy craft on exercise.

One of the Police nodded at these and said, "I hope you gents weren't planning to swim back to the mainland. Her Majesty's Navy is around all the time to make sure you can't. They have all the hi-tech gear to detect human movement and have been told they can shoot escapers if they feel it necessary. Make yourselves at home when you arrive. Most of you will die there so wave goodbye to the mainland while you still can." He did not say this to be especially unkind but more to be informative to the new influx.

The destination was clear after only thirty minutes travel. One of the guards in light blue pointed and said simply, "Muckle Voe." By the time the island appeared to be just a hundred yards away, the mainland could no longer properly be seen.

To the left were some beautiful homes; new, detached and as far as they could tell, quite luxurious.

Directly ahead was a huge building, steel-coated, which clearly extended a very long way across the apparent centre of the isle.

To their right, they could see a small town with a series of rows of tiny, single storey bungalows which they would later discover were all prefabs and were each eighteen feet by fourteen across their base. They appeared to be completely identical.

As they got closer they could see that each house was fenced off with a small garden to front and rear. The distance between them, side wall to side wall, was less than ten feet.

Mel did a quick estimate and thought that there had to be about three hundred. It was only after landing that he realised that there were at least seven hundred and the space had been used exceptionally well.

Of these, he would discover, only a quarter or so were occupied and the others were 'mothballed', awaiting their first occupants. There was a central heating system, centrally controlled, which allowed minute amounts of heat into the unoccupied properties to keep them aired until occupation.

The efficient infrastructure on the prisoners' side of water, heating, drainage, sewage and electricity had been put into place at the remarkably low price of twelve million pounds by a local contractor. Economies of scale.

The basic prefabs had cost less than eleven thousand each, fully fitted and operational. It was efficient.

To one side was a tall, imposing wooden-clad building which carried the words 'Leisure Centre'. To the other remained the wild beauty of Muckle Voe which presumably extended to the very end of the island and on the side with better quality houses, there was what looked like an even finer run of scenery to the opposite extreme of the island.

They were marched off the ferry and the Police who had accompanied them sighed and relaxed for the return trip to where the winds always blew free.

They entered the vast building, which was at the head of the small harbour, under the command of men in blue uniforms, armed with the L85A2 assault rifle, more famously known as the SA80. This vast edifice had cost considerably more to produce than all the prefabs put together - and then some. They entered a type of hall with high windows and were taken into what appeared to be a kind of a sparsely-furnished lecture room.

They were told to sit and, as if on cue, a uniformed, Senior Naval Officer with an air of authority entered the room. Mel was unable to guess his rank.

"All right you lot. You are now in the Neutral Zone - 'Star Trek' fans can laugh at this point." Nobody was in a laughing mood. "You will live here for tonight and two full days after that and you will undergo an induction to prepare you for life on Muckle Voe before release into Convictville - imaginative, isn't it? The other side of the island is for Naval Personnel only and you will have noted that my uniform is Her Majesty's Royal Navy because that is who guards this delightful place, both on the island and in the waters around here. You cannot escape, so get used to life here. Apart from women - absence of - and that can have some advantages too - you can make a decent life for yourselves here, believe it or not.

Now we have some supper for you. Then off to the dormitory for 'Lights Out' at ten on the dot. You will arrive here for your first talk at seven thirty in the morning after breakfast and shower. Understood? There are clothes on beds for you to change into - you'll have to agree sizes between you. The general alarm will sound at six thirty. I also have your brochures. Read tonight and I shall answer any questions in the morning." Whereupon he turned on his heel and exited leaving the prisoners with more than a dozen aggressive-looking armed Naval recruits.

CHAPTER TWO

Mel read the brochure from cover to cover and in fairness, it *was* a brochure.

The first thing he learned was that the part of the island they were on was only just over one third of a mile wide, hence its name 'The Neck'. The Neutral Zone stretched fully across this and prisoners, or residents as they were euphemistically called, in line with a somewhat incongruous political correctness, would rarely step inside this area and when they did, they would all be constantly monitored by armed guards.

Hospital, dental and general medical care took place here and the guards would always outnumber the prisoners in the Neutral Zone.

This was where they would meet visitors. They were now allowed one visitor per month but a single travel warrant was only granted every three rather than the four originally suggested. The arrangements for the ferry were not made clear as this was more the concern of visitors than of the 'residents'.

This was the area to which they would come to collect shopping orders which could be achieved without actually entering 'The Neutral Zone' itself. Goods were passed through a heavily guarded window in the wall.

Each 'resident' had a grant of £148-56 monthly, out of which they had to purchase all their needs. They were required to fill in a form for orders and they never saw the money which only existed in the form of credits. Electricity usage was measured centrally in The Zone and deducted from their allowances.

Nobody would ever be allowed to overdraw their account. Savings were permitted to be made towards acquiring luxury items which generally took a month to deliver rather than the customary week. Every resident was given a price list and descriptions called 'The Catalogue' from which to choose their purchases.

Surprisingly, there were no hard-line restrictions on what visitors could bring with them. Drugs, alcohol and weaponry were the obvious exclusions although the guards maintained the right to refuse any item considered deleterious to the smooth running of the colony.

Residents were permitted to have goods delivered by visitors up to a value of £200 per visit and in the case of computers, this limit was waived. Nobody ever heard of the rule being enforced.

The guards did not put the prisoners' orders together. This was a lucrative business for the enterprising local firm which had the franchise for keeping the system operating. To be fair to the unlikely named 'MacTavish and Sons, Ltd', prices were fair. It was the sheer volume of custom which made their healthy profits and they performed a similar function for the Naval Personnel.

In order to ensure that the whole project would work smoothly, the ferry had been purchased by the Navy and it actually operated to a small profit for the work it did for local people both on the mainland and for isolated communities on other islands.

All locals, whether island or mainland based, were instructed that boats would risk being sunk if they came within three miles of Muckle Voe but after negotiation with local Councillors, this was reduced to a mile and a quarter. Emergency guidelines were put in place for in the eventuality of vessels in distress or at risk in severe weather which allowed landing on the island but with the assurance that they 'would be sunk' if they then attempted to leave before a full search and they would then be escorted away. The locals found the terms acceptable.

From the brochure and the crisp, efficient lectures delivered by a Petty Officer through a Powerpoint presentation, the residents began to learn a great deal about their new home.

There were forty cells in The Zone and these would be used for any serious abuses of the living rights of others, attempts to escape and attacks on officers. At a pinch, they could each house two prisoners. The display showed a picture of one of these dungeon-like abodes and pointed out that it was possible to spend an entire life sentence in one such. It was a chilling prospect and they were all told 'different rules apply here'.

Currently, these cells were all empty and had been so since the opening. It was not until later that, that Mel would discover that the phrase 'living rights of others' was a concept ignored by all on both sides of The Neck.

Apparently, the Prime Minister had made a sudden visit by helicopter about five weeks earlier. He had toured both sides of the island and had thoroughly explored the Neutral Zone before pronouncing that this was a 'new way in criminology, penology and public protection'. The plan was announced as cost-effective and a 'roaring success' - perfect forward-planning for an election almost certainly just four months away and which would be half way through the final year of his term. Late.

The P.M. was less concerned about the project as a working model than he was at the prospect of being seen as 'Mr Tough' - the man who had turned back the tide of serious lawlessness. This was how he was portrayed in 'The Mirror' although his pet 'Guardian' had still managed to put together a flurry of letters and articles from liberal readers and columnists which denounced everything as 'barbaric', 'returning to eighteenth century values' and 'utterly ineffective'.

The latter at least, may have been wide of the mark as there had been a small but significant drop in the murder rate.

'The Mail' was horrified that vile killers were being given so much freedom, were living in hotel-standard luxury and were cavorting in a more agreeable environment for the commission of the worst of murders than the relatively decent people convicted of mere manslaughter.

Mel was quite *au fait* with the national picture and how Muckle Voe fitted in. As a neutral in these matters, somebody capable of standing back and being objective, he was yet to make up his mind how he felt about the project. If the truth be told, he suspected that it was a gimmick, no more no less, and it would ultimately be ineffective as it was lacking that vital ingredient in dealing with almost all profoundly anti-social individuals - genuine fear.

The people with him were not afraid. They were just apprehensive and this would pass as soon as they became accustomed to the new life. Mel knew enough to recognise that the apparently liberal regime would soon be made public and thus any deterrent effect would evaporate rapidly.

The question he asked himself was whether there would be some residual fear in the process simply because the tariffs were effectively 'full-life'. This could make a slight difference he supposed. This island was definitely nothing which could have induced Henri Charriere, Papillon, to paddle to South America from Devil's Island and this left no job vacancy for any budding Steve McQueen. But then, how was he able to judge properly when he hadn't even been into Convictville yet?

CHAPTER THREE

By the time Mel was escorted to Domicile 177 forty eight hours later his mind was in utter turmoil. It was due to a surfeit of information - some of which had seemed to contradict what was written in the brochure.

So, by the time he entered his new home it was with an abiding sense of relief. He carried a bag of personal effects with which he would commence his new life.

The house was smart although being emulsioned internally in magnolia and with woodwork being painted in a 'turd-brown' which he would not have recognised as being the imaginatively called 'Conker', the colour scheme was not much to his taste.

There was a three quarter size bed in one corner piled high with linen, two duvets and covers, with a bedside cabinet alongside, as well as a plain table in the centre of the room with four solid wooden chairs. The furniture was completed with a sturdy, plain three piece suite with the sofa a two-seater. To one side, a shower room with toilet had been installed. To the left of this was a wide broom cupboard with a folding chair and small stool inside. There was also an electric heater and an angle-poise lamp. To the left of this storage space, completing the length of one wall, was a good-sized wardrobe containing a set of clothes, all in his sizes, which explained why he had been required to fill in a form with relevant details immediately after the failure of his appeal.

On the opposite side of the room there was a well-equipped kitchenette with electric cooker and a broad work unit with a fridge, sink and basic washing machine underneath. The cupboards and fridge had been stocked with a fortnight's worth of provisions and there was a box containing toilet rolls, cleaning materials and all basic essentials.

Drawers and the single lower cupboard beside the fridge contained cutlery, pots, pans and crockery. The only timepiece was the cooker clock.

As a student he could never have dreamed of living in such accommodation - it would have been considered palatial and certainly, never had there been such views.

From one window, above the work unit, all he could see was the other domiciles and he determined to keep the cream-coloured Venetian blinds permanently half closed - just sufficient to allow a portion of natural light into his home.

To the rear, over the twenty five square yards of garden, which was South West-facing, the view across the sea was positively magnificent. Four large paving slabs had been placed under the rear window - just enough for two chairs. There was no paved or metalled path to the small back gate. There was the opportunity to grow a few vegetables and still have space for a dwarf fruit tree and a single shrub. It would require very careful planning.

A plain, three bar, creosoted fence separated his garden from those of neighbours to both left and right.

He knew that the 'seedy little man' lived on one side and had learned that he was called Rich'. He had had no contact with him during the induction and so he was an unknown quantity. On the other side was the black guy with the failed dreadlocks. He was called Lewis and had seemed personable enough. They had chatted a couple of times during breaks between lectures.

To the North East side he could view a portion of the sea on the other side of the island and breathtaking panoramas of heather-filled, heart-wrenching, natural beauty.

On a perfect June morning, it was possible to feel suffused with optimism. The keys he had been given worked on both front and back doors. The locks seemed secure. He checked the windows and found them all to be double-glazed, something which would be essential when winter came.

He put his Bible down on the table; it was one with a concordance which Lucy had bought him. He reached into his travel bag and took out assorted photos and put Lucy's and Jenny's in pride of place.

He had about thirty photos and determined to request some Blue-Tack on his first order because the allowance for the month had already been credited as a concession which had been made to give people a start. This meant that the starter provisions were, in effect, a bonus.

With Blue-Tack he would cover the walls in pictures.

In his pack he had a notebook and a packet of three biros which he had been given that morning so he began his list. All of a sudden, he put it down, locked the house and went out for the first walk life had afforded him in over a year.

He was anxious to get away from the occupied houses and it was only a matter of two minutes brisk walking for this to be achieved. He passed five or six other residents at intervals, all of whom seemed to be pleased to be out in the warm sunshine but none of whom seemed keen to communicate, for which he was quite grateful. There was an aggressive, threatening surliness about them.

There was something which resembled a path which he followed but it looked as if it had had little use. He was surprised to see nobody else enjoying the untamed landscape as the walk was truly superb. He could see the sea to left and further over to the right and within ten minutes it was to be distinguished ahead of him as well.

The grasses, gorse, broom and variegated heathers concealed a multitude of birdlife and he was astonished to hear what he took to be a curlew's cry, mingle with the incessant clattering and shrieking of gulls, which, in the manner of cock blackbirds, managed to sound permanently cross.

A seemingly endless stream of small birds flittered, fluttered and rapidly withdrew into the undergrowth at his approach.

He had lived long in a part of Sheffield where magpies; those corvine gangsters, had pillaged and wrecked the local songbird population, aided and abetted by those nest-robbing tree rats, otherwise known as 'the grey squirrel'. Combined; their uncontrolled damage had been immense and probably permanent.

Although a townie himself, he was angry that so many people in his position adopted so sentimental an attitude to wild life. Grey squirrels may appear cute but he knew them to be an alien and mindlessly introduced species which needed to see numbers reduced to a fraction of current levels by some serious culling. As a member of the RSPB he had eventually resigned in resentment that, in his view, they did not help birds by their weak approach to the 'magpie threat'. The most attractive of all crows, they plunder nests of small songbirds taking both eggs and nestlings alike; with a single pair in the nesting season being responsible for the loss of literally hundreds of other birds. Clearly, a massive cull of these wretched, ever-proliferating creatures would help literally scores of less offensive species. He wondered if there was some hidden principle here.

As for urban foxes, he stuttered in rank disbelief at the antics of supposedly intelligent people who encouraged such vermin; some even putting out food to encourage them. Once again, people with little or no knowledge of wildlife became so easily wooed by the extremely superficial attractions of such 'devils in disguise'. He wondered why these same people did not try to attract and feed rats and cockroaches. Ah, not so pretty! Superficial or what?

How such people would so easily be able to rejoice in enormous varieties of birds if only these cursed creatures were decimated or even removed. He was not a man often driven to anger but this was a topic which infuriated him and he directed much of this fury at so many members of allegedly green organisations which seemed to miss the point and thought that all creatures could dwell contentedly, side by side, in perfect harmony, if only man did not interfere. The part of the equation which they failed to grasp was that this was a kind of damage already largely caused by mankind in the first place and only man was in a position to remedy this ongoing harm. In the wilds, Nature had some opportunities to be self-correcting in a way which was simply not possible on the fringes of urban existence.

Yes. It *was* difficult not to make a link between such thought-deficient individuals and those who had been responsible for astronomical increases in crime over half a century.

He really did not understand how do-gooders could not and would not admit to the failures of their experiments. That their policies had been tried and failed was one thing; that they were not prepared to be honest about the consequences was proof that the ideal itself was non-negotiable; irrespective of consequences. Positively frightening.

It was crystal clear that being nice to criminals would - indeed could - only ever work with a small percentage; it was psychologically indefensible to believe that all carrot and no stick could work. It defied all logic.

He had never been one to believe that the lack of stern punishments alone was responsible for the desperate state of society when: poor parenting, lack of ethical guidance, amoral broadcasting and 'summat for nowt' and 'survival of the fittest' philosophies all made their unholy contributions. Still. Such serious thinking did not sit well with the treat that this walk was turning into.

He was delighted that there were so many types of bird which he was unable to recognise. He would ask Lucy for some sort of bird book to aid recognition but he knew that she was already planning to bring him a laptop, a TV with Combi VCR and DVD, some books, a Walkman, CDs and DVDs. How could she possibly carry all of that in one go?

He walked to the very end of the island and estimated that it must have been well over a mile and a half. He was unable to calculate with any degree of accuracy. All he knew was that he was alone, communing with nature on a lovely, nay perfect, day. The weather would not always be so wonderful. He wondered for the first time if he would be allowed a dog - unquestionably, it would make for absolute delight on every walk.

He reached the end of the isle where three directions of water effectively merged into a single vista.

The beach had some rough sand, bits of what looked like half dead gorse and a hint of shingle. Most of the rest had the appearance of baked mud and a scattering of dry boulders which made him suppose that this beach was not tidal. The island being so low-lying, he wondered if there was ever any serious danger of flooding. It was not something that had been mentioned at his induction.

He remained there for more than two hours in what seemed remarkably like freedom. As somebody who always spent most of his life exercising his mind, this was a time to relax; to blend; to forget; to allow the warmth of the sun and the softest of sea breezes to caress his face. He felt an overwhelming desire to remove all of his clothing and let the gentle elements caress the whole of his body but to what might possibly have been the relief of a rather prudish-looking herring gull, which was eyeing him suspiciously from a nearby rock, he resisted the immense temptation.

Brian had once remarked on something he thought was probably in Romans which stated something like 'creation declares the existence of God so we have no excuse not to believe'.

It was in those numinous moments, or even hours like these, when that teaching had a particularly developed ring of truth. It was like that thing about 'being nearer to God in a garden...' but he could not remember where that came from - he was pretty sure that it was not in the Bible.

There he was - thinking again. Better go back now and find out what makes the place tick. He was also quite hungry. He had paid little attention to the food in the house and it now seemed rather important. Perhaps when Lucy had delivered hardware she could bring him some real coffee and a filter. That would be marvellous. There were definite plus points to being here provided that the residents were all prepared to indulge in a little give and take. Would these outcasts rise to the challenge?

He enjoyed the return almost as much as the outgoing journey and changed his mind on the issue of trying to escape. There was no point in risking the 'dungeons' as the cells were known.

As he walked back into the cluster of housing it was to be greeted with the sight of four men violently beating, belabouring and sticking the boot into a figure lying prone on the floor. So much for 'rising to challenges!' Mel walked past without comment but registered the faces of all five in his memory. He would not forget them. The incident had been an introduction to the stark realities of life here.

He opened his door and went inside. There was an immediate knock on the same door and a pug-ugly character with a broken nose and multiple scars across the face pushed into the doorway and said menacingly,

"Your salmon."

"No I'm not", he said in a Wilt-like attempt to confuse.

"You ain't what? asked the thug in anger.

"I'm not a salmon. I'm sorry but I don't know what you mean."

The thug, who thought he might have detected an extractor of urine, retorted viciously, "You have a tin of red salmon."

"If you say so," said Mel contemptuously "I haven't looked."

"Get it for me and I shan't wipe your face across the floor."

"Fuck off!" said Mel emphatically, "and I shan't kill you. If you don't know who I am, ask around before you threaten me, twat!" and as the man began to look both menacing and slightly confused, Mel caught him off balance with a shoulder charge and as he was only one step inside the house, it carried him straight outside with a double stagger and Mel slammed the door shut. He really did not enjoy the swearing as much as he thought he was going to but he knew he had a role to live up to.

Perhaps the psychological tricks would work for a while. He *must* induce fear if he wanted to survive. All the agreeable feelings he had enjoyed were now replaced, in just a few moments, with the anxiety of an animal constantly trying to avoid the cunning, local predator. The real problem would arise when some of these came to see him mob-handed because there was no way that he would permit himself to join some clique or be able or willing to form his own gang.

The alternative would be to pay these people off with whatever they asked for. Yield to extortion? That would be simply unthinkable.

The first step would have to be to let his reputation precede him, so the question was just how this could best be achieved.

He made a pot of tea, found a box of milk in the fridge, some sugar, a packet of biscuits and three mugs.

He then went to the houses on either side of his, knocked on their doors and asked both round to share a cuppa.. They locked up and came round to sample his tea-making skills.

Mel decided to go straight onto the attack and asked if the scarred man had paid them a visit.

"Yeah. I gave him a can of salmon from my provisions to get rid," said Rich', and both Mel and Lewis began to explain how this would only mean that he would keep coming back.

"They really shouldn't mess with me - people like - well, him. I *kill* people who annoy me," declared Mel speaking in a mere whisper so as not to be thought boastful, "and he's now number one on my list."

"Say," said Lewis, "You are that 'hitman', yeah? Six hits innit?"

"That's what *they* think," Mel pronounced. "Twenty-eight, if the truth be told. Death is my business and I am not very tolerant of bad behaviour. If he or anybody connected comes to see me and threatens, they will die - and quickly. But not necessarily painlessly," he declared.

"By the way, I'm thinking of setting up a Bible Study Group. You guys interested?"

Lewis agreed with alacrity as he came from a black Pentecostal background and was more than a little ashamed to have burnt both his wife and mother-in-law to death when it was only the spiteful older woman he had intended to dispose of. Mel was convinced that he *wanted* to come and he was not displaying caution in the presence of a 'very dangerous man' such as himself.

Rich' however, was not interested and seemed afraid to say so.

"No obligation," said Mel kindly.

"I think I'll leave it 'til I'm more settled if you don't mind, Mel?"

"Okay with me. Your choice." and he ushered him to the door as he seemed anxious to leave.

Mel watched through the window as Rich' trotted off to a house about a dozen doors down and smiled as his plan was clearly working. The news about Mel should be around the site within a matter of hours. Rich' made his flesh creep.

"Not much chance of him joining you," said Lewis nodding and pointing at the teapot asking with signs for permission to pour a second cup, "He's a satanist, him. He was up for killing two teenagers in some blood ritual. It was all over Winson Green. We were there together at the same time. Bible study? I think not," he said with a little laugh.

Mel decided that he liked this lofty, ebony-coloured, jovial young man and would enjoy some study time together.

They chatted about this and that and Mel felt guilty for lying to him when he explained that he had swapped teaching for the lucrative life of dealing death. It sounded silly if not downright ridiculous when he said it but he had been consigned to Muckle Voe and so there had to be some compelling reason for this - or so he hoped others would think.

Lewis departed and Mel was quite sure that he could pick up a pile of Gideons' New Testaments for free through the shop.

He would attempt to set that up on the following day. He went out again and found the part of the site where the builders had last worked. A large piece of four ply wood about two feet square was his trophy. It was clean, on one side at least. He took it inside and washed it as best as he could. Hunting through the bag of belongings he had brought with him, he pulled out a black bingo marker which he used to write: *Bible Study, every day at six thirty. All welcome!* in the largest and boldest lettering the failing, writing implement would allow.

He was unable to fix it up anywhere at the front of the house where many, if not most, would spot it on their way to the shop, so he propped it up on his front sill where it caused him to lose a great deal of light through the venetian blind - in a physical sense, at least.

He was not just doing this because he desired company but because he thought that some of these men might respond to proffered help in the mounting of a 'spiritual quest'. He had never said that he thought that rehabilitation and reform never occurred. Besides, it would make him seem a bit brazen; possibly eccentric and this combined with his reputation as a killer might just serve him well. He would be deemed as potentially deadly because he was some 'God-bothering, do-gooding hit-man'. It really was an impossibly incongruous amalgamation of ideas for the average levels of intellects to be found on the island. They may well shy away from what they could not comprehend.

This being happily sorted, he made some sort of meal and settled down to plan out the routines of his new life. He would need mental and physical stimulation. The latter would be accomplished by walking to the end of the island as many days as weather would allow and he would begin every day with a training regime of sit-ups, press-ups and weight training although Heaven alone knew where he would find appropriate weights - maybe he would have to carry back some of those rocks from the beach, it was far from ideal but would accomplish his aims.

For his mind, he would read The Bible daily and become an expert. He thought he would read three chapters from the Old Testament and one from the New. He would spend parts of the day committing the more incisive verses and passages to memory - that would make Lucy very happy as her Christian life was advancing at breakneck pace and she was currently acting as a Sunday School Teacher to a collection of excitable seven year olds. He was immensely proud of her.

He would be able to use these scriptures as a basis for meditation but he remained unable to offer any full commitment to God to replace his half-hearted attempts to do so which now seemed so long ago; lost in a dim and distant past.

There was also a need to organise his days and The Bible Study would go ahead daily whether well attended or not attended by anyone but himself. This would help provide a kind of foundation to his days which did promise to be long and tedious if he were not careful.

Above all of this, he had determined to be happy; content in all he did; to abandon pessimism as a worthless part of life; to put on a brave and positive face for every minute of every day.

For what seemed like the umpteenth time in the last couple of years, he was embarking on a new adventure called 'life'.

CHAPTER FOUR

Lucy caught the ferry with a gigantic carrier bag in one hand and a positively huge shopping trolley dragging reluctantly behind her, pulled by the other.

Her car had been left on the dockside. There seemed to be no parking restrictions anywhere. The drive from the small, country hotel where she had stayed overnight had taken only twenty five minutes.

She had pre-booked on the Internet what had turned out to be a high class, family-run establishment. The drive up had taken over nine hours, including stops, the day before and she wanted to look attractive for her husband, hence the overnight stay which allowed her to look her very best this morning.

Her looks attracted approving glances from the ferry operators and the Naval Personnel who were returning to the island after a night on the town - although it might be hard to imagine how they had located a town to have a night on.

Lucy enjoyed the trip and correctly divined that it would often be an horrendous journey in the depths of winter. The view of the village - she had not been able to see any sign indicating its name - was remarkably picturesque from the boat. She was enjoying herself which she would not have done if this had been at the end of a seemingly interminable drive and best of all, she would not only be seeing Mel but helping to make his life a little better.

There were no phones in Convictville and so no Internet access easily available. She had brought him a mobile packed with credit but was right to assume that getting a signal could be difficult, if not totally impossible.

The boat docked and she was ushered up to the giant, heavily guarded main door of The Zone where she was searched - with perhaps a little *too* much enthusiasm - by a rather small Wren who then ran a practiced eye over the goods she had brought.

She entered the main hall and was surprised to see some fifteen, fully armed guards when there were only five residents having visitors. She was puzzled as to where the visitors had been on the ferry as she had only spotted one of the other four.

No such thoughts mattered as she spotted Mel and gave him a cheery wave and big smile. They hugged and kissed and before sitting down, she asked to use the toilet.

"I'll show you," he said with a grin the breadth of the Mablethorpe Promenade. "They are over here. Unisex."

The reason for the grin became apparent as he joined her in one of the wide, well-equipped and beautifully finished cubicles with only one thought on his mind. She was exceptionally slow. It took her a full quarter of a second to latch onto his line of thought.

"The guards know, so I'm told, but nobody objects," he announced as he gave her a passionate, lingering kiss.

This was not the most romantic, ideal or comfortable of environments but nothing would prevent them consummating their love - and nothing did.

* * *

Lucy handed over the goods she had brought which had remained unsupervised in the hall area during their tryst. Fortunately, nobody had interfered with any of them and Mel was able to give her a list for her July visit which would hopefully weigh considerably less than what she had brought on this occasion.

They talked for most of the remainder of the two and a half hours she was allowed before the boat was due to depart. She did not realise that by the time she rejoined it, the ferry would have completed a round trip taking in five other islands. The proud little vessel certainly earned its keep.

"Both houses are now sold as you know, but I need signatures on a whole sheaf of papers," she said. "I finished moving in at Burton - I've brought you some photos. With this excellent summer, the village is so appealing; so pretty. Oh, and Jack has finished his degree and should soon know what he got in his Finals."

Mel told her little about what was going on in Convictville, preferring not to worry her but in any case, chose to describe his domicile in glowing terms and to let her know how excited he was by the beauty of the island. He could not wait to tell her of his Bible Study Group which now had three other members, all of whom were quite enthusiastic.

The time passed at the speed of light and a quarter of an hour before she had to depart, Lucy pointed out that it would be necessary for her to use the toilet as a precaution. Mel kindly showed her the way in case she had forgotten its location during the previous two hours.

* * *

She left the trolley for him as he would not have been able to move all the things she had brought without it. It was almost a ten minute walk to his house but this was doubled by the amounts he had to carry and drag. He walked through the heavily-guarded door and back into Convictville where his load attracted considerable interest from onlookers.

He doubted that he would be able to get any TV reception at all but the set would act as a video and DVD player, at least.

He could not wait to get his hands on the tiny laptop - he had requested the smallest available as this would be easier to conceal - he had few illusions as to the likelihood of it remaining un-stolen if he let anybody know of its existence; the TV however, he was unable to hide from prying eyes. He decided that he would have to be very careful disposing of packaging from the computer.

Rubbish had to be taken every Tuesday morning to the entrance to the Zone and deposited in bin liners where it was collected by a team of twenty guards bristling with a variety of weaponry. The packaging was pushed to the bottom of the black bag beyond where any dishonest parties might see it.

As he returned to the house, it was to find the back door off its hinges and the TV already departed. He rushed to check the bed and found the laptop where he had left it under the pillow. He was seething with anger and bitterness for the rest of the day until he brought himself under control and he set to finding a better place to hide the computer.

As an afterthought he checked the food cupboard and found that his single tin of salmon was missing. He was being tested to the limit and this could not be allowed to continue or he would be regarded as weak - a death sentence if ever there was one.

The salmon-loving visitor was a forty year old recidivist called Georgie Ford who lived in number 155.

He placed a rock which he had been using in his weight training and put it into the bottom of a sock. He took several practice swings before marching to 155 and tapping gently on the door. A score of pairs of eyes were watching him from behind curtains and from idlers just hanging around in their front gardens. They knew what had happened as people in these situations invariably do and were interested, in a detached kind of way, to see how professional killers operate.

The door opened and he swung the sock with all the force he could muster and crashed the rock into Ford's temple. He collapsed. Mel dragged Ford inside and beat the unconscious body as hard as he could, trying not to break bones or hit vital organs, with the nose he made an exception as he smashed a fist into it, breaking it with ease - this would act as a permanent reminder to all others to show what he was capable of.

As he collected his TV, his can of salmon and a second one to pay for his trouble, the thought came to him that this was an unholy act; he had wanted to avenge himself and there was precious little evidence of him having 'turned the other cheek'. On the other hand, his very life was under threat and that would only reduce if he were prepared to show just how tough he was. Situation Ethics again.

He walked past the fascinated spectators with a cheery smile and a nod to all those he recognised. He was not to know it but this was the final thing he had needed to do in order to establish a reputation as being 'extremely dangerous'.

The message had been received and understood by everybody and it rapidly did the rounds 'Don't mess with that religious freak, Mel Roberts'.

What was especially surprising was that the following day, Mel had a visitor; the bruised and damaged Georgie Ford.

"Just came to say sorry," he mumbled. He was a man who did not want a second round. "They say you're a teacher. I figured you was soft."

"Forget it," said Mel and went to fetch the second can of salmon to give back to Ford. "I am a very quiet and peaceful man if people leave me alone. You should get to know me better. Bible Study at six thirty. It's not for boring poofters - it's dead interesting. Come. We'll make you welcome."

Whether from fear or interest Ford became a regular, even repairing the door and the two men, having got to understand each other, became somewhat unlikely friends. Mel began to feel that this was somebody he could trust - to a degree, anyway.

The other members of the group were Lewis, an ex-Anglican priest called Tiberias who had suffocated his homosexual lover in a fit of pique and the 'King of the Post Office Raiders' a man called Craig who had managed to gun down and kill two people during his final raid. "It all just went wrong," he said, "I never hurt anybody before and it was my last raid - I'd made enough to retire in luxury after seventeen successful raids. It just went tits up. Somebody grabbed my arm and it made me fire this Uzi in every direction. I just lost control and it just sprayed bullets. I didn't intend to fire it. It only had bullets in coz I never took them out when I bought it. It wasn't what you could really call an accident but nor was it intended. I killed two innocent people and it is making me sick with guilt."

Craig and Lewis were repentant. Tiberias seemed filled with hatred and Georgie was just confused. It should prove to be an interesting group.

CHAPTER FIVE

July came and went and Mel had managed to rig up a small aerial, carried over by Lucy, which allowed him to watch all major channels on his TV. The reception was appalling which was proved when contrasted to the high quality he gained from his collection of DVDs. He wondered about digital.

Lucy had bought eight or ten which she thought he might like and had then gone to a market stall and bought an armload, second hand, which she had taken from their plastic cases and placed into polythene sleeves to cut the weight.

She had also brought him a small radio/CD player and many of his CDs, again abandoning the heavy plastic boxes.

The main weight for her was made up with carrying large amounts of books but she would never again have the weight problems of her first visit.

She had now made several visits and the routines were established. They were able to make love and swap information. She brought him luxuries and he gave her lists. It occurred to him that it was increasingly like the olden days when visitors either kept you going in the Fleet, the Marshalsea, Newgate and such like, or you faced possible starvation.

He had got his coffee filter and two kilos of his favourite roast on her second visit. It was quite amazing how this one small thing improved his life so markedly.

His wife was even more thoughtful and delighted him with four pounds of Judges' sausage and two of smoked bacon on the third trip to Muckle Voe.

She was spending her time working on a huge variety of good causes and putting ever more time into work at the Church whenever she visited Sheffield. Life was quite fulfilling but she missed Mel.

Jack had gained an Upper Second in his degree, just missing a First, and was considering doing a Phd.

Mandy had sent him a friendly card and was now engaged to a man who worked for the local Council.

Lucy had met up with Brenda and Jerry at the new house. They all considered that there were no risks to such an event. She had made them a slap-up meal and they had enjoyed a wonderful evening of good company. Nothing had been said about 'Jerry's plan' and she thought it better not to ask. She did say that Jerry was looking overworked and rather drawn. Brenda confirmed that he was working far too hard and hours which were too long.

In the meantime, his routine was now established and he was all too happy to tell Lucy about it.

He got up at seven each day and did some weight training and a variety of exercises. This was followed by a lukewarm shower and he made himself breakfast. He would read his Bible for twenty five minutes or so, after which he went out and walked to the end of the island. He had not, as yet, had any weather sufficiently severe to prevent him taking this morning constitutional.

He would then return and listen to music, read old newspapers and prepare a light lunch. Lucy brought a whole months' worth of newspapers but to cut the weight she would select only the ten or a dozen pages from each and cut out anything worth reading. It was messy but he appreciated it.

During the afternoons, he committed himself to reading, preparing Bible Studies and writing a series of articles on various facets of life on Muckle Voe.

In the early evenings he tended to do the walk again, usually carrying the pocket bird book which Lucy had brought on her second visit.

He had spotted eighteen different species so far and thought this could easily double with the movement of the seasons, as well of course, as the ones he had as yet failed to see.

Just because he had spotted eighteen did not mean that he had identified all of them; three had apparently not been seen before by the authors of his book. He assumed that it might well be different plumage for different seasons which was impeding his quest for greater avian knowledge. It was also possible that these were occasional summer visitors.

It was extremely rare for him to meet anybody else on the path and he was amazed that his fellow residents seemed to have no appreciation whatsoever for the natural beauty which reached into his very soul.

He was struck by the comparison to the scene in C.S.Lewis's 'The Last Battle' where the small-minded, renegade dwarves were awaiting disposal in a kind of pre-heaven/pre-hell environment. They were given a magnificent banquet; a veritable feast but could not recognise it for what it was and thought they were eating 'old turnips and stable litter'.

He wondered if hell and Heaven could be the same venue but becoming one or the other depending on one's attitudes to that place. He dismissed the thought on theological grounds but felt that on earth, good old C.S. had got it about right.

One of the books he had recently read had been on the life of that remarkable Pastor, Richard Wurmbrand, who had spent fourteen years, oft times tortured, in a brutal, communist prison in Rumania. Imprisoned for his faith he turned an earthly hell into a spiritual Heaven by focusing so completely on God that some years after the end of his ordeal, he was able to declare that if he were invited to live his life over again, he would not have wanted to have lost that time in prison - so valuable had it been. Remarkable.

He was no nearer being able to make any commitment now than before. This too was remarkable as he was utterly convinced that all the claims of Christianity held water. They were surely valid.

He had spent considerable time on that one idea which could disprove all the claims of the world's greatest religion. "If Christ be not risen, your faith is in vain." The Bible gave you the clue for disproving itself.

Jesus had to have risen from the dead or the whole lot was just hot air.

The Resurrection was the pivotal point. It was quite reasonable to assume Jesus to be God as he claimed, if he could beat death - and if he could not - then he was just one more preacher with an ego.

He was impressed that there were four different Gospels not just one. He had examined the question of 'what happened to the crucified corpse?' and concluded that if the Jews or Romans had removed it (and why would they want to?) they would have soon produced it when the news of Christ's Resurrection became an embarrassment. But they could not. Significant? - Highly so.

If the disciples had removed the body and then preached 'Resurrection', they would have been liars and deceivers which was always a possibility *but* that then created a further, major problem. If these men *were* liars, how come they were prepared then to go out and die for what they knew was untruth and with no personal gain? It was psychologically impossible. Their very success was an indicator, although no more, that there had been a 'Divine Hand' guiding their path. Men would die for truth, yes, or even perhaps for what they *perceived* to be truth. But for a lie in which they had all conspired? Impossible!

All the Gospels presented these men as wimps and failures yet they went on to carry the 'Message' to the ends of the known world; virtually all perishing violently and separately in the process.

Surely, only the Resurrection was an event big enough to have transformed these wasters into world-beaters.

The facts of the Christ appeared in all sorts of other ancient writings but what had struck Mel hardest, was the 'feel of truth' when he read the Scriptures. There was never any attempt to brush anything unsavoury under the carpet. If biblical heroes were flawed - it said so: Jacob, Abraham, David, Solomon, Peter. The list was endless. The temptation for writers to make all of them into supermen was something Bible writers resisted in a way that writers of other 'holy books' are always unable to avoid. He called this 'a smack of reality'.

In spite of all of this he could not release himself and accept that The Christ had died for *him*. No. That wasn't true. He *did* believe. It was more that he was unable to *apply* it to himself and he was unable to see what was causing the blockage.

He knew that 'belief does not bring salvation' if that were the case there was a problem in that 'all the demons in hell believed'. No, belief was only a step. He had proved that quite conclusively.

What had Lucy been able to do which he had not? He was troubled because he half wanted to commit; wanted to take that step.

Arriving home he worked on his Bible Study, happy in the knowledge that his friend Lewis at least, had become a Christian. Another of life's little coincidences was that his friend's Christian name was the same as his favourite author's surname. This Lewis had taken the full step. He was a changed man and began to display a keen, spiritual insight which far exceeded Mel's interesting but more academic approach to opening up the Scriptures.

As it had been back in Brian's Church, there was an assumption made that *he* was a Christian. He wondered how members would have viewed him after his trial. He was sure that Brian was one who had not previously thought him to be one of the 'elect'.

Here, he did not feel sufficiently able to share such deep thoughts with his fellows but was lifted by several long and encouraging letters from the caring Pastor - some of these thoughts he passed onto the group.

Now, today he would look at the 'Rich young man' - or 'Ruler' as he was called in some translations. There would be plenty for them to get their teeth into and even Georgie was now prepared to throw ideas into the ring as he yearned to understand.

Tiberias was a different matter. Mel got no sense of a practising Christian from their meetings. Indeed, he seemed to prefer sneering and casting doubts - not out of genuine conviction but rather to present himself as objectionable. Mel wondered how he could ever have been ordained and more to the point, why he bothered coming daily to these meetings. In the end, he concluded that he merely wanted to show off his knowledge.

To the man's chagrin, it was Lewis who began to take control of the meetings with his astute observations and perceptive comments. Mel did not mind. Leadership was not something that interested him - besides, Lewis was doing an *excellent* job.

It was after that night's meeting that Lewis met privately with Georgie and he guided the long-time criminal into 'giving his life to Jesus' which he did with an enthusiasm which, over coming weeks, was mocked unrelentingly by Tiberias but the faith held firm.

He later explained as part of his testimony that it was the fact that 'The rich young man' had left Jesus disappointed as his wealth had been allowed to become a spiritual barrier. Georgie did not want to be 'disappointed' in The Saviour.

The group began a weekly meeting in the Chapel section of The Centre and although they advertised widely, week on week, until September they were unable to persuade any others to join them. At least, they were left alone so there seemed to be some sort of respect - or maybe it was Mel's unwarranted reputation as a hard man which kept them at bay.

By September the bird-life was beginning to change and Mel thought he had observed more than twenty seven kinds - sometimes he got confused as to whether a male and female were or were not of the same species. The weather from the memorable, balmy summer held up into the autumn although the mornings wore a fresh, sharp coldness which offered the initial warnings of oncoming winter.

The seas were higher than previously and the winds, although intermittent, were building gradually as each week went by. The colours on the island were changing and taking on autumnal hues.

It was predictable that the winter weather might prove to be quite severe.

CHAPTER SIX

It was only as Mel entered his fourth month as a resident that he began to grasp fully what was going on across the island.

The Guards made very few sorties into Convictville and these were only for essentials. One man had collapsed from a heart attack. Somebody went to the Zone and informed them. Within an incredibly short time, an efficient team, as heavily armed as ever, had entered their side and removed the man. The whole process was completed in eight minutes and the man was taken into the tiny Hospital Wing of The Zone to receive the best treatment the Navy could offer.

Such forays were a rarity and the men were simply left to get on with their lives.

Mel began to realise that he was outside a 'tribalist culture' which had grown up as leaders and gangs began to emerge and jockey for positions of power.

He had witnessed firsthand the extreme brutality of four onto one, just the once but as the weeks went by, he began to recognise that this level of violence, which he had started by assuming to be unusual, was in fact endemic. No day went by without a handful of beatings, some more public than others.

The sheer, ugly nastiness of the place began to appall him. There was so little evidence of people being prepared to work together. Clearly, nobody was prepared to do anything which did not contain a significant element of self-interest. Greed reigned supreme and sexual frustrations gave way to a whole series of homosexual, gang rapes which proved to Mel that sexual deprivation leads to many outcomes and rather undermined the case that homosexual behaviour is largely genetically programmed. A huge percentage, at the very least, had to be caused by environmental factors.

He was horrified to learn that Tiberias had joined in at least one such incident and was not prepared to allow him to return to the Bible Study Group. Lewis questioned this but Mel said that unless he showed genuine repentance, there was no point. At this, Lewis agreed.

Ten of the nearest fourteen properties to his house were broken into. Extortion was rife. Threats were made to take the choicest foods from anybody weaker and the weaker sought out those even weaker than themselves to bully and rob. The very weakest set traps to catch out the ones they could not defeat face to face. Making cakes containing ground glass then allowing them to be stolen became a particularly vengeful and effective art form for a while.

Electrical goods, CDs and DVDs were all particular targets. Many people would take a delivery from a family member only to be mugged, beaten and relieved of their bounty even before they could get it home.

It seemed that Rich' had started a 'satanic group' in opposition to the Bible Study and they made the point of trying to catch small animals and birds which were then ritually sacrificed. Few were untainted by the proceedings as the numbers in Convictville rose to over two hundred.

Somehow, drugs began to find their way in and this closed society sank even further into the deepest of depravity.

The first murders began to take place and when it was revealed that even these would not be investigated by the authorities, it actually led to numbers dipping to below the two hundred mark.

Bodies began to appear in the streets and a sense of terror ran through the town. It seemed that every single person outside The Bible Study was involved in horrendous activities as behaviour began to plummet to lower levels than those ever seen outside a Nazi Concentration Camp or a Stalinist Gulag. The only difference was that on this island, it was a group of social lepers who were turning inwards on themselves.

'Lord of the Flies' was about the inherent, primeval behaviour to be found in children - but this was amongst adults who really should have known better.

Mel was especially horrified because this really had been a new start; a great opportunity to build a positive life. If ever the failings of liberal attitudes towards crime were to be exemplified then that would be on Muckle Voe. The residents could never be re-integrated into any form of normal society. The vast majority; virtually all of these people were beyond any type of rehabilitation. It was of no interest to them. His group had tried to give them a chance for something better on a spiritual plane but they had cast this aside without as much as a thought. They were base and animal-like in their approach to life. Man had not progressed one iota in the years of so-called civilisation - if anything he had regressed. Civilisation was a veneer and one which did not run too deep.

He understood the Christian concept of sin like never before. One did not even have to be murdering scum to be soiled; to be unable to live a proper life.

The Gospel had it that you should 'Love God' and 'Your neighbour as yourself'. It was the key. There really was no alternative.

These were people trying to exist in a spiritual vacuum and in succeeding with that aim they were creating a society which was beyond degenerate.

Litter piled up in the streets as residents could no longer be bothered to keep their home looking respectable. The houses, which were under fifteen months old, began to take on a seedy and dilapidated look and gardens began to look as if they had been subjected to a flying visit by the very worst elements amongst Diddicoy.

Plants, trees and shrubs were broken, wrecked and destroyed. Walls of many houses were sprayed with graffiti. Mel wondered why it had not seemed so bad when he first arrived. What catalyst had brought about this degradation of humankind? - He could not answer. He simply did not know but something inside him convinced him that the outcome had been predictable even inevitable as the scheme had not budgeted for the inherent evil in the heart of man. And - just who would waste their allowance on cans of spray paint or have them delivered by visitors?

He was unable to grasp why absolutely none of this was making the news. In his old papers there was no mention of the nightmare that was Muckle Voe; no references in TV news programmes.

Did bodies on the streets not constitute news? How could a secret of such magnitude possibly be kept when so many men had visitors every month?

What about the families of the men who were dead, did they not mind?

He began to suspect a conspiracy; a cover-up at the very least. Did the Navy not come and remove the bodies?

Were there not Post Mortems and Inquests? If not, why not? Who ultimately gave the orders? Just *where* did the buck stop?

CHAPTER SEVEN

The Prime Minister was worried. Not only had there been five deaths reported on the quiet to him from Muckle Voe in the space of a fortnight but the vigilante acts were on the increase again. Indeed, they were now at the highest level since that curse had begun. There was just no pattern.

One man had been hanged in Barnsley; some sort of pervert who had thrust a bottle into a little girl and ruined any future chance of her being able to conceive.

"Deserves all he got, the bastard," he thought to himself before correcting his ignoble and politically incorrect thoughts.

There had been three lynchings of Lifers who were out on parole and suspected of all sorts of horrific, additional crimes. Nottingham, Mansfield and Bognor Regis.

The P.M. knew that over thirty Lifers a year killed again after release. That was a stat he liked to keep to himself and well away from the Great British Public. Fortunately, the media were in no hurry to publish the fact either as it could give rise to renewed calls for a referendum on Capital Punishment. That major thing apart, governments do not like the risks attached to a referendum. Besides he wanted to keep it quiet that the UK Government no longer possessed the powers to re-introduce the Death Penalty even if desired by 99.9% of the voters. Former P.M. Blair had sold out on that one to the EU! Better left alone.

It did not really balance up if you took it as unacceptable that one innocent person might be executed per decade - if that, what with DNA and all the wonders of modern science. 'Roughly three hundred innocent lives to one, on those rough stats," he mused.

Just for a tiny moment he wondered if the Death Penalty.................. Then no. He had to get real. No Labour P.M. could possibly advocate that route.

As for the lynchings and a couple of dozen vicious beatings, all he could do was to get the best Police onto them and hope for a breakthrough.

There had been a disappointing number of objectively innocent people attacked or lynched. He needed it to happen to the entirely guiltless for public opinion to turn truly anti-vigilante but if it did - then the Government would be in for piles more blame, anyway.

What was happening on Muckle Voe was horrendous and all he could do was to pull in favours. Many contributors to the newspapers were wound up by the newshound editors - many of whom actively disliked him. How was that possible? How could people be so obtuse?

It seemed likely that somebody would break the story soon. No. Inevitable. Then what?

He was well aware that the countdown to the General Election had begun. It was already far later than he had been hoping. The clock was ticking and the Press were already speculating uncomfortably over possible dates in October. He could not leave it until the last minute.

He was always so shocked how the papers always seemed to work out the date with such ease.

Maybe this time he should try to wrong-foot them by going a week earlier or later. No point in always doing the 'bleeding obvious'.

* * *

He was entirely devoid of sympathy for any of the dead, whether on Muckle Voe or in some park in Daventry. Perhaps he was closer to being a man of the people than was generally thought or maybe he did not care too much about the genuinely innocent which was what some of his detractors might unreasonably have claimed.

CHAPTER EIGHT

"If it is a 'woman's prerogative to change her mind', then being non-sexist, it means I can too," reasoned Mel.

He had settled down to life on Muckle Voe but within a matter of two months the place had descended into such pandemonium that he was now as eager to leave as he had previously prepared himself to settle in. There were times when 'Dante's Inferno' might have seemed preferable.

He watched as the place became more of a hell-hole week on week. He wondered if the signs had been as obvious when he first arrived. Maybe he had simply been unable to read the subtext.

The latest abominations had kicked in when the residents had discovered that making alcohol is not all that difficult and so to add to the general loutishness was the opportunity to: assault any person who crossed your drunken path, the fun of vomiting onto window panes and the hilarious merriment of urinating in everybody's doorways and the best of all, urinating onto the comatose bodies of other drunks lying on paths. Hilarious.

To escape would take imagination but it was beginning to look more appealing than the alternatives.

A boat? - Chances were that he would not make it the eight miles and where would he possibly find the materials to construct one in secret.

Swim? - Ridiculous.

Through the Zone and onto the ferry? - Sounded good but seemed impossible. Disguise? - Too unreliable and they would discover he was missing and institute searches. Better to be thought dead?

Swim round to the ferry when it was docked? - Would be spotted. They had already made plans to stop residents swimming to the Naval personnel side of the island. Underwater barbed wire. Besides, how would he clamber aboard a vessel without being spotted?

By air? - Would probably get shot down by a naval missile and who could he possibly try to hire? Who would take the risks?

This was going to prove a toughie. What was more, he did not really want to escape and have people know that he was gone. They would only search for him. Tricky. Seriously tricky.

* * *

There had been a notice in the Centre advertising a comedian putting on a short show one lunchtime, so thinking he would enjoy a laugh, Mel wandered across and was pleased to see that his reputation was still intact proved by the way so many people seemed anxious to avoid him. Perhaps it was just because he was a noted 'Bible-basher' and people did not want to become infected.

Maximilian Martin was a multiple murderer; one who had wiped out a family of five, without provocation. There was evidence of torture and seriously deviant practices whilst they were bound. Fascinatingly, he still seemed to find his killings a source of amusement. This was the main thread of a show which made Roy 'Chubby' Brown seem like the turn at an elderly ladies' tea party.

Mel could not see it through. He experienced utter revulsion at the raucous guffawing of the audience. They really were subhuman. He managed to conceal his disgust and exited the Centre in desperate need of some fresh air and grunted angrily on seeing one of the posters offering a full, sordid evening with Maxie several weeks down the line. Nasty.

He walked around the back and parked himself alongside a giant generator and the huge fifty thousand gallon, petrol tank which operated all the generators which ran the heating system for the Centre which would have overloaded the general, domestic structure. He stood a while and put his mind to serious thoughts.

He walked slowly back into the Centre and mooched purposefully through every inch of the immense building. He even climbed up to a precarious gantry above the stage and could still see Max Martin, as foul as ever, receiving ribald, tumultuous and appreciative applause some fifty feet below.

He descended and entered every side room. Then he went into the basement which seemed totally deserted and more or less abandoned. It consisted of a warren of small, under-used rooms with windows on ground level. On his way out, he noticed a different, hand-written sign offering a full, evening gig from Max Martin for a Friday in the following month.

An idea began to take shape and he trekked all around the island until he found a spot where his mobile could pick up a signal. He phoned Lucy and asked her to bring him certain 'extras' on her visit the next week. The call was of poor quality but he managed to get his message across by shouting. He returned home, put on some 'Best of Bach' before settling down to work on his plan which he did until it was time for Bible Study.

* * *

"I think the study needs to be later when the nights start drawing in," he suggested, "I like to go out for a walk before dark whenever possible. Okay with you men? Eight perhaps?" The clocks would soon be going back. Darkness can be a friend; it is not always sinister.

It was fine with the others. First step accomplished.

The study was based on the Disciples responding to the 'call' of Jesus and by the end of the session Craig had 'given himself to the Lord'. The others were not aware but this had the irony of leaving Mel the only one of the four who was not 'born again'. Even so, he felt delighted for Craig and genuinely rejoiced as much as Lewis and Georgie.

The situation would have left him embarrassed had Lewis not been growing as a leader. In just a few short weeks, he seemed to have taken on a kind of spirituality which reminded him of Brian. His personality gained a certain depth and wisdom was never far from his lips. It seemed a pity that one who had so much to give was condemned never to be released.

The whole situation gave rise to a sad, stark contrast between these three men who were beginning to exercise their potential as human beings and those many out there who had all been granted an opportunity at worst, to embrace a positive attitude and at best to be able to develop themselves spiritually in the way that had happened with Lewis, Craig and Georgie - and yet they had so rapidly reverted to type, becoming: vile, bestial, uncontrolled, unprincipled, insatiable and savage. Had they been dogs they would have been put down.

They had been granted the most wonderful of opportunities and had simply treated it with utter contempt. What right, what entitlement did these people have to the bounty offered to them? - and still it was not enough?

How different to those original transportees who had perhaps committed some minor misdemeanour often out of the direst of necessity and the most absolute poverty and starvation; men and women who had gone on to build a new nation and were not afraid to graft for their personal betterment and who were profoundly thankful whenever a genuine opportunity arose, as was frequently the case. Such people he could readily admire even if the stories had undoubtedly had a certain embellishment from Aussie historians.

He wondered if the Victorians had been right to have adopted a moral imperative which distinguished between the 'deserving' and the 'undeserving' poor. Maybe Society had to take *all* the tough decisions which today, most politicians did not even admit existed as problems. A run-away-from-every-problem set of politicians paved the way for social disaster. The reasons why crime was off-the-scale were indeed many.

He could have wept for the state of mankind - and in times past, he had. He wished that the countless idealists responsible for the degeneration of society could come and live as he was now obliged to.

What would they see?

Would there be a pretence, attempting to 'find a basic goodness, common to all humanity'?

Would they embrace optimism against all the evidence of their eyes and of experience? Or would they shrug shoulders and say limply, "Well. What can you do?"

Would they still insist that rehabilitation was possible in spite of the daily horrors they would witness?

Would they believe that 'evil' was a false concept and if it existed at all, could only truly exist in limited forms such as 'racism' or in 'Nazi Politics' (Using only their own preferred definition?)

Was human nature to be exalted above all else?

Would they fail to see that their self-described, free-thinking rejection of absolutes left mankind as no more than a pitiful example of a fetid species controlled purely by its DNA - with no true free-will - battered and buffeted by the agents of pure chance in a dark and terrifyingly mechanistic Universe?

Would they still believe that this island was populated with sufferers - people who were not to blame for their actions; those who were principally victims of a combination of capitalism on the one hand and of their 'deprived childhoods' on the other?

Would they continue to fail to see that it was their pernicious, liberal policies which had largely contributed to this sad state? Why is it so hard for people to just admit it when they are proved wrong?

Mel had talked to many prisoners during his remand period and had been anxious to see what he could learn. Virtually all had been quick to blame anybody else for their misfortune. Those who admitted responsibility, in every case started their story with "I know I did wrong **but** ......" That 'but' told its own story. Every one had a 'reason' which proved how their dishonesty was 'actually quite reasonable and always understandable'. Mel was unimpressed with their whining, self-justification - all he had to do was recall how much 'wrong' the average person has to do in the twenty first century in order to get locked up. At that point, he would ask himself how much misery these men had caused to others and secondly, he wondered how it would be if they were your own next-door neighbour.

All were motivated by either greed or power. Those whose offending was drug-related blamed the drugs as if they had no responsibility for having arrogantly started on that path themselves. Hubris. Nobody could deny that the drugs were a mighty negative factor but they also remained the most convenient of excuses.

Many of the residents were druggies and the powers-that-be ensured that all were clean before sending them to Muckle Voe. Even when free, some cravings continued and the small amounts of crack and heroin which found their way onto the island caused disproportionate damage as some became hooked again only for their supplies to dry up and leave them stranded - this helped fuel the rampant anarchy of this paradise-turned-hell-hole.

Mel supposed that an army of social workers would eventually appear to assess the situation and would come, once again, to their customary, muddle-headed conclusions.

He expected acres of pity for these 'poor creatures who had been driven to misbehaviour by this cruel attempt to demean them and abandon them as if they had no social worth. What else could you expect of humans if you treated them with such contempt?'

Mel laughed out loud as this thought occurred to him and it seemed to him that the Scriptures had a much better grasp of Man's nature - written thousands of years ago - than these who were 'the blind today who would not see'.

If you largely abolish 'evil' as a concept, it leaves an unfillable vacuum in its wake.

He thought it was probably Chesterton who had said that when man ceases to believe in God - it is not that he then believes in nothing but rather that he tends to believe in anything. Well, whoever it had been, they certainly had possessed good insight.

His historian's thoughts turned to the 'optimistic outlook' for the future of Man which had arisen pre-First World War and recalled how this view had even managed to survive that period of butchery; damaged, battered, bruised, yet intact nonetheless in many people. This had been reflected in that title used even more frequently to describe that conflict than 'The Great War' - 'The War to end all Wars' with all of its pathetic, ringing hopefulness.

Laughable had it not been so sad. The idea that Man had 'learned his lesson once and for all' that he had 'moved on'; grasping the need 'to live in harmony', this was an idea somewhat damaged by the Japanese depredations in China, Stalin's Purges, The Spanish Civil War and a minor squabble, a mere twenty years later, called World War Two.

No. Optimists were dangerous characters, especially when allowed to take control, in the context of their hypotheses on the 'disposition of Man'. 'Sin' was a fact. Why could ancients grasp what Modern Man could not?

He had looked at his original, fellow prisoners - few being of the low standards of his present colleagues - and he wondered how many of those would have been locked up at all if they had undergone the strict, but generally reasonable, discipline which had been the social norm in the immediate Post-War Period. And as for the people - if that was what they still were - here on the island, who could gainsay the fact that they too might have been deterred from the terrible depths to which they had descended had they lived in a less limp-wristed society?

Ever one to spot an irony from forty paces, he gave his own situation a thorough examination and reasonably concluded, as he had before, that he was simply the natural and inevitable consequence of five decades of undemocratic success for liberals on crime. This was the kind of society you created by lowering social standards and requirements. This was the kind of society you produce when you tell people they do not have to accept the consequences of their bad behaviour, recklessness or even, downright stupidity.

If the people on this island were victims in any sense, perhaps it was that they had not been granted those 'tight guidelines' with 'firm punishments' during their childhoods and teens, to which they were entitled.

They were not 'lucky to have avoided being punished with a resolute hand' - this was their true 'social deprivation'. It had cost them: their freedom, self-respect, dignity, hope and feelings of self-worth. It had contributed to the creation of a race of sub-humans. This was an objective fact and he wept inwardly for what they had become and cursed those who had contributed. After all, few find self discipline without first having been through a process of discipline. Discipline was not some outmoded concept. It had incalculable value; family, schools, courts, peer pressure, social requirements.

He did not forget however, that even then, these people had still had choices and they had made the wrong ones. Other factors came into play, yes, but they knew what was expected of them and could still have opted for the *right* path.

What it had cost Society was beyond calculation. It had brought: fear, loss of decency, selfishness. It had brought about: crime, yobbish behaviour, graffiti, packs of loud, foul-mouthed youths abusing drugs and alcohol and even something as basic as litter.

Yes. It was surely true that multitudes of young adults - many being nothing less during their teens - became super and socially-minded individuals with the very lightest of disciplinary touches.

As a teacher he had seen hundreds. But there were oh so many who put up two fingers to the system - and why? - because they could!

He was able to think of countless such. There had always been the good and bad. What particularly concerned Mel was the large numbers of 'kids in the middle' who were *led* astray. Youngsters on the fringes of bad or deviant behaviour had often succumbed in the past. One of the problems today was that so many who did not begin 'on the fringes' were also drawn in. Depressing.

He was deeply concerned that these children were also taught that there were no absolutes. He had been part of this system, which he now condemned. He had been all too happy to promote 'moral relativism' and this had to be nearly as damaging as anything that Society had done with its lax attitudes towards anti-social behaviour; something which pricked his conscience.

Cases where householders, for apprehending a young thug could be locked in a Police cell whilst their tormentor was released, uncharged, set his hackles rising. The Law must never favour the wrongdoer over the honest citizen.

If dogs are mistreated and begin to bite they are put down. With a human being you have try harder but when you have tried and failed.......
It was a recurring thought and he wondered how those who referred to Man as 'just being a higher animal' could so often refuse to accept that if that route is taken, it is inconsistent to consider Mankind so special that they should be allowed privileges to opt out from the consequences of their actions in an animal-based world. Were they arguing that human life is sacred? That denotes a God.

He had never come to terms with the fact that so many of the rabid pro-abortionists he knew were so often the most vociferously anti-Death Penalty which they would describe as 'barbaric'.

Just how topsy-turvy could values become? Killing innocent babies - now proved to feel pain - was perfectly acceptable whilst taking the life of the horrifically guilty was 'wrong'.

It defied logic. Those who opposed both, he could understand a little. Those who supported both, yes. But pro-abortion, anti-hanging was unfathomable in terms of consistency.

CHAPTER NINE

Lucy was puzzled by the list of items to be bought: a proper stethoscope, a name badge holder, a printed card with false details and a cut-down photo of Mel to use inside the badge and on the card, a lab coat, a plug-in timer switch designed to turn on domestic appliances, a false moustache and several minor items. None of these would prove a problem at The Zone with the exception of the stethoscope. It would undoubtedly promote curiosity. She thought hard then put a label on the box - 'Theatrical props'.

The ID card was easy, she wrote on the back, 'Love from Gran' and put it in place with 'Prit' using the tiniest dab on each corner and fixed it to the inside page of 'Hard Times' by Dickens. It could effortlessly be detached. The holder would just be one of hers, kept in her handbag.

She now knew for certain that an escape was being actively planned and this was confirmed by Mel's request for her secretly to hire a holiday cottage for two months, with the option of a third. She was to pay in cash and had to ensure that the dwelling was remote and would attract no friendly farmers offering milk direct from the cow or anything similar.

He asked her to ensure that she had their passports, both of which had been updated in the last couple of years and vitally, he had signed a document transferring all his property into her maiden name; he would be unable to get his hands on his own money when he was on the run.

A significant portion of their funds were placed in the Banco de Bilbao for ease of access in Spain. Again Lucy forgot to mention her married status.

She made a check as to where she could hire a car at just a few moments notice and she even did so as practice for what would prove to be her final visit to Muckle Voe for reasons which to her, would prove to be quite unexpected.

What she did not know at this point was that Mel's plan had a single, major flaw. He was making an assumption as to how the authorities would react under a given set of circumstances. He was operating 'on a wing and a prayer' and he had made a reasonable guess, but if he were wrong, the entire plan would die a death with no chance of a second attempt.

* * *

Under instruction, she flew to Alicante and five days later was the proud owner of a medium-sized flat overlooking the Mediterranean in the town of La Mata which her dictionary seemed to translate as 'the killing'. She wondered if Mel was trying to be funny.

She was relieved that Mel had stopped the killings and she did not yet know that he had disposed of one Shipley Applebaum whilst in prison.

Her faith was making it increasingly difficult for her to accept Mel's interpretation of the Scriptures. It was not that he was wrong in any part of what he held to be true - quite the contrary - she was convinced that he was correct in every detail with just the one exception; she was unable to find the text which authorised Mel to become an 'instrument of God'.

He had been called: neither by Angel, nor by God Himself, nor by signs and wonders, nor by prophetic utterance, nor by a 'Word of wisdom', nor by vision, nor by Maid-of-Orleans-type voices, nor by visitation, nor by the call of an Apostle. He had made no claim that he was responding to 'answered prayer'.

Indeed, how could any of the above have applied when he was not even a Christian? It was a matter which troubled Lucy greatly and she spent much time in prayer and meditation and finally wondered if she should talk to Brian on Mel's behalf. She thought about this long and hard until recognising that Mel could well see this as a kind of betrayal. If Bri were to be approached, then it would have to be through Mel himself. She would do nothing that might upset the man she loved.

It was at about this point that she first began to develop a conscience about the death of Larry's killer. She had to accept some of the responsibility, she thought, if her love for Mel had prompted this death. It was not that she believed that Marner had deserved any less, it was more that she was beginning to harbour some - albeit infrequent - doubts as to the principle behind 'a personal execution service'.

These ideas gave her pause for thought as she flew back to The Robin Hood Airport on the Thomsons, afternoon flight.

She had been bowled over by the Spanish landscape thirty thousand feet below her with its preponderance of brown shades, followed by the dull greenery of those parts of France crossed by the aircraft and then it was England with its non-stop, luscious greens.

The flat was everything she thought Mel would want and she just hoped that he would be able to take advantage of it in the not too distant future. It had two bathrooms, three large bedrooms, an extensive lounge, American kitchen and a dramatic, sweeping balcony from where the sun could be seen dragging itself into the form of a great, orange ball out of the sea, morning after morning. It was furnished tastefully and immaculately in the Spanish style and she was extremely pleased with it.

The Wednesday Market was colourful and she had happily bought hand-painted sea scenes for a few euros; clothes; leather shoes and a host of curios.

She had given a great deal of thought to Jerry's promise in her cramped seating position on the airliner and had become uncharacteristically cross when a superfluous and over-priced drinks trolley banged heavily into her elbow.

Jerry? What had he meant? When she had met him and Brenda at Burton - it must be nearly two months ago now - or perhaps it was longer? - she had asked the question and he had reiterated his point and said, "It won't be too long, maybe six months. It *will* happen. I promise."

She found it hard to believe. Obviously, she wanted to, but well, it was ....
sort of ......too unlikely. Mel was probably doing the best thing.

She dismissed the thought but wondered why she had been out of
touch for so long with Brenda and Jerry. It was not from a lack of trying
on her part to contact them. Perhaps something *was* going on. Jerry was
frightfully busy, wasn't he? Just for a moment she asked herself if they
were to be trusted and then instantly dumped the thought as unworthy.

She especially liked the balcony. She had paid fifteen thousand euros
above the average for the corner flat which was sufficiently well sited to
overlook the sea at one side and still have the possibility of gaining more
than a glimpse of the Salt Lakes on the other.

Being eight floors up, the height gave the chance to see the occasional
wandering flock of flamingos wading through the murky waters whilst
making life both dangerous and short for any of the passing shrimps who
were responsible for the rosy tinge in their plumage.

It had to be admitted that the flamingos were at a distance of a good
half mile, and sometimes more, from the flat, which made flamingo-
watching less than straightforward, so Lucy had bought a small but
powerful pair of binoculars which she found difficult to put down.

'Mel would love the place' was her thought as the wheels hit the
tarmac with a mighty screech and several bumps. It was surely one of the
poorest landings she had ever experienced.

As she went through Passport Control and Baggage Collection she
decided to make a couple more trips out there in the next couple of weeks.
She would transfer all things from the house which were important to
Mel. She would be able to carry some twenty kilograms of his stuff. She
assumed he would lose his CD collection which was now in his possession
on Muckle Voe. That would be quite a blow for him.

If he genuinely thought he was about to escape, she wondered what he
would do with all his other important, personal effects on Muckle Voe.
She supposed she could be more than a 'delivery service' maybe she could
be a 'collection agency' as well?

According to one of Mel's rare phone calls - he really did have
immense difficulties detecting a signal - the 'hot spots' seemed to move
around - the escape attempt was getting very close indeed

"Two weeks after your next visit, put yourself on standby," he had said
and she thought how it was all beginning to sound like some kind of
military operation.

She had no idea how he planned to get out of the country, nor how he
planned to live in Spain, in a busy tourist area, without putting himself at
risk of being recognised. After all, wasn't that what was always happening
on 'Crime Watch'?

She was subdued in her excitement - it was a strange combination -
and as she pulled into the drive at Burton upon Stather was disappointed
that she and Mel would never share this lovely place, the risk was just too
great.

She began to busy herself unpacking then went straight back onto the Internet in order to book a couple more trips to Alicante Airport - she would have to take her own personal things as well, but would presumably be able to return periodically.

She wondered if they would have to sell this magnificent - no perfect - house without Mel ever having spent a single night under its roof.

If only the clock could have been turned back......

She planned to make a trip to Church in Sheffield that weekend and noted that she seemed to be commuting a great deal between Burton and Sheffield. Perhaps she would have to find a more local Church - but why bother? She would be out in Spain - well, maybe. And what could be done about a Church out there? She simply did not know and it mattered to her and may well matter to Mel too.

Back to the Internet, she found several English Churches in the area of Torrevieja/La Mata. She heaved a sigh of relief.

With a degree in French she realised that she would have few problems learning some Spanish and wondered how necessary it would be in such a cosmopolitan area. She was angry with herself for her laziness. Of course they would learn the lingo!

She started to worry that she was beginning to assume that Mel's escape would be successful. What possible guarantees could there be?

How would Mel respond if it all 'went pear-shaped'? She smiled as that was one of *his* favourite, slang expressions but was concerned because she had not forgotten the breakdown he had endured after first being arrested. Mel had told her that there would never be a repeat and she believed him.....well, half believed him. She did not realise that her husband was mentally stronger now than he had been at any time in his life and for what he was about to do - he would need to be.

CHAPTER TEN

As she arrived at The Zone, Lucy wondered if this would really be for the last time. It was possible that she could be charged with aiding and abetting Mel's escape attempt but she could not care less. What could be done to ruin her life which had not already happened? The thought crossed her mind that if governments had done their duty to the citizenry, there was every chance that neither of them would be here today. It was not easy to avoid feelings of profound resentment.

Mel must have been confident as he *had* brought a number of personal items for her to take away, mainly photographs but also the CDs which he could not bear to lose. There was nothing to prevent her from returning them if the attempt were to prove futile, of course.

She, in her turn, gave him all the things he had requested plus a later request consisting of: a pair of off-the-peg reading glasses, four large tubs of workman's putty, some Polyfilla, a white baseball cap and a smart, leather, attache case, all of which proved extremely heavy. Nobody had as much as raised an eyebrow at these, making her wonder what other strange goods had passed this way. In truth, she was rather surprised that they had not been searched for drugs - maybe it was because the tubs of putty were so clearly new and had not been interfered with.

They both had a ready answer if asked about the product. It was 'for putting rapid repairs onto windows' for as the authorities knew, glass was being broken with a sad regularity.

She told Mel that there was a General Election in the offing. She had heard it announced on her car radio on the way from the hotel to the ferry.

Mel realised that this meant the vote would be taking place the Thursday following his escape. He was fairly sure that there were several good reasons which might prevent him from being available to cast his vote; something which actually bothered him a great deal as he felt that this was something which every citizen should always do.

He considered Muckle Voe and wondered whether it might have any bearing on the result. The PM had certainly managed to keep secret the horrors of what was occurring on the island. It was possible that an anti-government paper would break the story. Still, nothing at all had happened at this point. Were they saving up the information to use at a particularly effective moment?

Mel was quite aware that his escape would make headlines, one way or another, and successful or not, the papers would not be able to ignore it. Would he, Mel, have an influence on the result? - Who could know?

He did hope that people would turn out and support the democratic process even if that meant casting a vote for some pretty crappy political characters and their sordid parties.

Be that as it may, he had to admit that he quite understood why people refused to vote if they felt they had effectively been disenfranchised by the attitudes of the three main parties. He had heard it argued that by not voting at all, if enough people did it, 'things would have to change'. He could not accept the logic. It meant that responsible people were not voting and this gave party activists a free run. Would they really respect what they saw as weakness? – and, worse still, it was a weakness which aided their self interests. Result? - more of the same. Mind you, what would have to happen to change the face of British Politics in any given circumstances? Disheartening.

He considered his own attitudes towards the EU and recalled that all three main parties tended to sing from the same hymn sheet with the Tories pretending that they could be eurosceptic inside the EU itself. Utter balderdash!

Who could he vote for, then? He had, of course, decided UKIP was the nearest and he remembered his promise to himself to do some work for them when the General Election came around. His present circumstances could make that rather difficult. He correctly assumed residents would not have a vote.

On this occasion he would simply have to stand back and watch from a distance. In truth, he wanted all the major parties to lose but prayed fervently that the BNP would not cash in too heavily on people's frustrations and dismay with the high-handed, arrogant attitudes and fundamental ineptitude of all major parties. He despised them all.

No. If voters refused to turn out, if they did feel effectively disenfranchised on: the EU, Law and Order, Immigration and a host of other major issues, could they really be blamed for not voting for any?

He thought they could, perhaps, if they had a UKIP candidate. But what of those who were simply too idle to turn out? What of those who could not be bothered to find out who best represented their views? - He was prepared to bet that these were the first to complain in the saloon bar down at 'The Mucky Duck' or wherever.

Those upstanding citizens were supplemented by those terminally-sad people who voted for a given party 'because they always do' or marginally worse, 'because their family always has'.

Voting was so important and yet, so many treated it with a carelessness which bordered on disdain.

These thoughts had surged through his mind in just the few seconds after learning of the Election. Nonetheless, he felt guilty at having wasted any valuable time at all in the presence of his beloved.

They chatted about her trips to La Mata and she explained that she had found driving difficult over there but thought she was probably getting quite a lot better. She had taken anything which could be considered as of interest to him and deposited it in the flat.

She showed him a variety of pictures of the flat, both internal and external and he praised her for having done so well. He felt that this would be a temporary step and if they were to move permanently to Spain, he wanted to buy a villa and his preference was probably one overlooking the bay in highly expensive Cabo Roig but he thought he would let Lucy come to her own decisions on that.

Selling the house in Burton would release enough funds to do this and they would have enough between them left to live on for the remainder of their lives or so he thought.

No. Too much forward planning.

A Naval helicopter flew overhead and the noise was phenomenal, curtailing their conversation for a period, whilst it hovered and landed on the Navy side of the island over to their left.

"You get used to it," he remarked and they returned to their chat.

"So. How are you getting away?" she asked suddenly and the question fazed him a little. He had not expected it and felt a fool for not having done so. It was so obvious that she would want to know.

He considered the problem and decided not to tell her. He sensed that there was quite a possibility she might disapprove of his answer and moreover she could be extremely worried and so on balance, he preferred not to give a clear response.

"I don't want to be evasive," he said "but you know, there are still so many things I have to work on. I am assuming that under a given set of circumstances, a certain line of events will occur and if it does, then I think I can make it. If all that does happen, I still have a lot to do for it to work. I think my chances are fairly good. I reckon a fifty to sixty per cent chance if I make no serious mistakes. I shan't go into detail. What I need from you is for you to be anywhere within fifty miles of here on that Friday evening, from eight o clock onwards and to wait for my call. You will pick me up from where I tell you - bring a road map - and then we'll drive to the cottage you've hired. Where is it by the way?"

"I found a place, out in the sticks, almost equidistant between Scarborough and Whitby. There are some fine walks around there and it should be easy to hide up."

"If the plan works properly, they won't be looking for me. I shall 'be dead' and that rather means that searching for me will not have too much of a point." He smiled at her bafflement and gently squeezed her hand.

"Don't worry. It may not work anyway. Don't raise hopes too high. It is a bit complicated and I prefer simple. There are a number of places where it can all go *badly* wrong. But if it does work......then our lives are straight back on track."

They chattered together happily but this was interrupted by her urgent need to use the toilet facilities on two separate occasions.

He told her little about what was taking place on the island, again because he did not want to concern her with all the negatives - she had quite enough on her plate to worry about with being involved in his breakout.

They could not believe how speedily the time passed and the visit was brought to an end with a lengthy kiss which was ignored by the plethora of heavily armed guards who were flanking them.

"You won't take any risks, will you?" she whispered anxiously.

"I promise," he replied as they separated.

Whilst walking back to his house, he kept his eyes peeled but there was nobody there to mug him. A kind of lethargy had descended over the place in the last couple of days and some of the worst horrors did not seem to be occurring as a consequence.

Somebody with a Degree in Sociology might well have concluded that 'man's inherent goodness was indeed starting to show through - and 'with time, this delicate seedling could be nurtured into a fine and exquisitely beautiful plant'. He was rather more pragmatic, not to mention , philosophical.

Mel understood the reality of the situation rather better. Home brewing had developed into home distillation and several recent batches had been of such strength and low quality that they had left a majority of the islanders in a stupor which had in many cases lasted for in excess of three days.

There had been incidences of temporary blindness and two had departed to the Infirmary in the Zone as the deadly hooch burned through their stomach ulcers creating both agony and the life-threatening danger of peritonitis.

Obviously, this meant that the firewater was deemed to have been a resounding success and several parties were planned. As these were likely to degenerate into S & M, homosexual orgies, Mel decided to give them a miss although he had been offered several invitations; one by Tiberias who seemed to be poking fun at him in a particularly malicious and calculated manner.

Living on the island was definitely easier than it had been for several months. The residents emerged with much less frequency than before and life became substantially more bearable although it was increasingly necessary to pick ones way between pools of vomit whenever emerging from any of the more centrally positioned domiciles.

If he took his walk around the island just after daybreak, he could go a full week and never see a single soul on any of his excursions, so he often changed the patterns of his routine to accommodate this. There was joy to be had and he was forced to admit that, as far as Richard Wurmbrand's imprisonment was concerned, he just could not grasp how he had developed so well in the face of equally awful circumstances. 'God's presence,' he surmised. He was also all too aware that his circumstances had numerous compensations which had not been available to the amazing Pastor.

He was certainly fitter than he had ever been before and looking at the rest of the men he guessed that he would be able to beat almost all of them in a fair fight, one to one. He trusted that this would not be necessary.

His weight training equipment was pathetic in appearance but served a purpose. His muscles had extended markedly in the months he had been there. The fresh air of the island was doing his lungs good. He kept to a fairly healthy diet, avoiding stodge and using his allowance to buy in large quantities of fresh fruit and vegetables and good quality meats. As he grew stronger, his fellow residents grew flabby and ever more apathetic.

The morning after Lucy's visit, he walked to the spot where the construction men had strewn, then abandoned their waste over about three quarters of an acre of land. The sun was just rising and it seemed unlikely that anybody would see what he was doing with the two tubs of putty he had brought.

He went up to a string of old buckets which had had their bottoms removed. They had been inserted, one into the next, to make a chute so small waste and rubble from the roof of the Centre could be placed at the top and could then plummet safely downwards and, hopefully, directly into a skip at ground level.

They must have measured about twenty five or perhaps thirty feet in length as a single entity. It consisted of seventeen plastic pails. It was hard to determine whether it had been factory made or just cobbled together. In any case, it would suit his purposes.

Keeping them together was no problem for Mel who dragged this 'Heath Robinson affair' around to the back of the Centre where he could work on them undisturbed and out of all likely view.

He sat on the frost-bitten floor - he hadn't expected so severe a frost this early - and set to work, rubbing the putty around the rims of each bucket to ensure that nothing, however small, could escape whilst descending the chute. His hands ached with cold but he completed the task. It took all four tubs of putty to do an acceptable job which mean that he had to make a return to his house to collect the last two tubs. The process took almost two hours to do a good job. There was enough of the putty but only just. He had to spread it rather thinner than he would have liked.

He would now leave the chute, reasonably confident that it would not be touched by any of the other men. It would have a few weeks in which the putty could dry out and harden a little and he was in no doubt that when he came to use it, the chute would do the job he had in mind with the utmost efficiency.

He was not as handy as somebody like Jerry but was not entirely useless. A shower was now essential to remove the sticky filth and grime. It took days to get his finger nails clean again.

He missed his friend and hoped that they would be able to meet up in Spain. How he would enjoy explaining how this plan had been made. Jerry would be extremely interested, he suspected.

He was concerned that Lucy had found Jerry and Brenda so difficult to contact and could not think of any reason to explain it.

Job completed, he returned home, took his shower, had breakfast and read his Bible. This done he went out again and spent a great deal more time relaxing in the unsullied Autumn air at the end of the island than was normally the case. Only once had he ever seen another inmate up there and he had never chosen to return, as far as he knew.

He wanted to meditate on a couple of scriptural texts. Firstly, he considered how God had been angry with Jonah who hated the people of Nineveh - a bit of solid racism if ever there was one. God had told Jonah to preach 'a message of salvation' to these enemies, whereas Jonah simply wanted God to 'zap' them all.

Eventually, post 'great fish episode', Jonah had had to do as he was told. He preached his message, the Ninevites accepted it and were saved from extinction. Jonah then entered sulk mode.

So even the most wicked of all could repent. Good.

Secondly, he turned his mind to the 'Twin Cities' of Sodom and Gomorrah. They had been given their opportunities, had rejected them and had been wiped from the face of the earth with fire and brimstone for their godlessness.

Mel looked at Muckle Voe and had to admit that this was not Nineveh. The chances for repentance *had* been offered but rejected by all but three of the other residents.

He could not look at all of this as if it were simply *desirable* to deal with the pond-life and to sort out the bottom feeders who were all murderous scum - just on a social level. It was equally important to him to put these feelings against a scriptural backcloth. As a non Christian, he was unable to explain why this was so.

If many people would deem him to be 'just as evil' as the people he had taken out, it was something which did not concern him in the least. Provided he acted with integrity and was true to himself, he was contented.

He would have been more disturbed by the knowledge that Lucy was beginning to entertain some doubts about the validity of his mission. He was not yet aware that she was troubled, not so much by the acts in themselves, but more with the absence of authority which he had for committing them.

He turned his mind to consider the possibility that he might be insane. After all, how many other ordinary people go around wiping out any number of criminals? But then, how many 'ordinary' people had experienced the reality of having an innocent family member butchered by a low-life? Might that not change perspectives somewhat when you have the bitter realities of what the world has turned into, deposited on your very doorstep?

He had suffered a breakdown at one point. Might his activities therefore, be based on a major mental defect? He considered the possibility. He was always prepared to be brutally honest with himself whenever he analysed his emotions and actions. He *believed* he was acting logically - although to be fair, what kind of a proof was that? - Pol Pot and Stalin had undoubtedly believed that they were being 'logical' too.

Well. His thinking was accepted by others of like mind. Hmm. Back to Pol Pot and co but this argument carried more weight because any neutral observer would not detect the obvious signs of insanity in him. That was not conclusive though, as many people were naturally adept at concealing what they were behind a huge facade. He was concealing nothing about himself apart from the seven people he just happened to have killed.

What about the fact that he was so clearly motivated by 'justice'? It was difficult to see how this argument could take him beyond any of the others. Ah. But he was analysing and constantly assessing the validity of his own actions. That was probably the best point he had. If he were some kind of monomaniac, then this process would either not take place at all or its conclusion would be inevitable.

He was now fairly well satisfied that he was sane. But why did he have no conscience about what he had done? Did he value life so little? - No. On the contrary, he maintained that society, by its changed outlook towards the vilest of criminals was in fact where the true undervaluing of life was best seen.

So was life 'holy', then? - Hardly. 'Sacred', perhaps? - More difficult. The two words were not precise synonyms. It was one of the kinds of questions he had been forced to endure when teaching GCSE Religious Studies. It was generally agreed in Christianity that this was in fact, the case. He had never been really all that convinced.

Just because God has created life, would that always mean it has to remain 'sacred' if it had been in the first place?

Surely, if freewill exists then Man must, by his actions - ['sin', if you will] - have the possibility of *becoming* 'non sacred'. If this were not true, when God committed somebody to hell, He was destroying something sacred - but of course, He *had* made the rules.

Man is 'special'. Yes. 'Sacred'? - He could not be sure but he doubted it. If he was wrong then why did God authorise Man to kill in given situations? Was that just a case of 'suspended sacredness'?

There really was a miserable lack of evidence that Christ had 'abolished the earthly death penalty' as liberal Churchmen insisted. It was almost as easy to prove the case in favour in The New Testament as it was in the Old. The attempts to use the case of 'The Woman Taken in Adultery' were laughable. The key to that was the *nature* of the trap set which had frequently been overlooked and misunderstood - often deliberately so. It was simply an issue of whether the Christ would upset the Jews or the Romans. Terrific trap, incidentally.

Was his ability to reason a valid argument for him being sane? - No. But taken in combination with all the other '*nearly* proved arguments' he decided that the circumstantial case for him being 'of sound mind' came as near to being conclusive in proof as one could subjectively reach.

Good. He would enjoy the walk back to his house then.

CHAPTER ELEVEN

The PM was a worried man. The 'Daily Mail' had run the story he had most wanted *not* to see.

"Reports of death and mayhem emerging from Muckle Voe" was the leader which struck him to his very core and within forty eight hours his lead, already reduced over recent weeks to a paltry three percent in the opinion polls had disintegrated as jubilant Tories moved in for the kill - like circling jackals around a moribund, runt antelope.

All other newspapers of whatever hue, now had to join in and it looked as if the damage could prove fatal. There was more than a chance that Labour could lose its overall majority. That prime ministerial hell which is a 'hung parliament' was beginning to beckon worryingly.

Even the 'BBC Bias' organisation, usually so adept at uncovering an incessant stream of complaints, could for once, find little to criticise. The State Broadcasting coverage saw the sharpened knife penetrating deeper and deeper still, as its victim was prepared for probable, total sacrifice.

Harriet Meadows MP had managed to give him the foulest of looks after the final sitting of The House as they all filed out of The Chamber. If looks could kill, he would have been seriously injured, at the very least. Her expression screamed, "I told you so" louder than shouted words could have ever achieved.

He possessed even greater, deeper secrets; politically commissioned reports had revealed that crime had actually started to increase in many areas as Muckle Voe was now regarded as an absurd 'gimmick' by the voting public and criminal classes alike.

This was something which ought not be too difficult to conceal for the week and a half in the run-up to The General Election. What he could not afford to happen was the escape of this sting-in-the-tail piece of information which thus far, only he and the compilers of the report knew.

Interviews and canvassings had been undertaken, statistics had been checked, double-checked, re-checked; polls taken and views canvassed in those areas where the vigilantes had struck and to his horror, local crime figures in these districts had plummeted. The contrast between different areas was nothing less than astonishing.

For a codicil on this report, both members of the public and carefully selected criminal types had been interviewed and it was clear that the vigilante groups had sent a resounding message of fear into the minds of malefactors in the places targeted by the vigilantes..

After all this time, why had there been no arrests? It was just too sinister. Too unlikely.

Even the Cabinet was giving him a really hard time. They could see their jobs dissolving into the thin air and were sufficiently unhappy to ditch all thoughts of loyalty and attack the PM directly. This was new. He had heard of 'lame-duck presidents' in the USA and was now beginning to grasp the concept.

"It was *your* scheme, Prime Minister," muttered Henry Lofthouse, the Minister without Portfolio.

The PM ignored him and swore to himself that *there* was a wretched individual who would definitely not be in his next Cabinet - that was of course, provided that he was in a position to allocate jobs and titles in ten days time.

This was a meeting which had an air of gloom overhanging it like the threat of some weighty Damoclean Sword poised to rend its holding-hair asunder. No member of the Cabinet could suggest a strategy and even Tom MacIntosh, the Prime Minister's 'enforcer' was for once, at a loss for words.

Nobody had previously thought the Election was losable but almost all could now see the distinctly unhealthy prospect of 'no overall majority', meaning that the next Cabinet would probably be awash with Lib Dems. It was not a happy thought.

Still, most of them were confident that the Lib Dems would huff and puff about Proportional Representation as the price of their support, but they would ultimately capitulate in customary fashion on being offered the merest hint of power.

PR really was a non-starter. This was something that was an unspoken consensus in the thinking of the two major parties. At least under 'First Past The Post' both of them were guaranteed to rule periodically.

An absolute 'no'. Why, it could and would bring the likes of UKIP into the political process and, heaven forfend, the BNP and Greens would take seats. The three party, even cosier consensus, that the UK should be sold off piecemeal to the political mandarins of the EU, was of course utterly non-negotiable. The Bilderbergers would be apoplectic.

The PM was beginning to find life hard work. Up to this point, he had been able to cruise through the political scene, always getting his own way, always well supported by most members of the Party; there had been trips and junkets, meetings with 'important' people, globe-trotting, camera calls and hosts of toadying interviewers hanging onto his every utterance as if it were Holy Writ. His opinions on the Pop Charts were the vital stuff of many an interview for lowbrow magazines and afternoon telly.

The thought that all of this; the accoutrements of power and fame, may all be on the point of unravelling, hit his ego especially hard. He was not actually all that politically-minded, it was more that he had enjoyed the game but the perspective was rather different if you weren't winning. He could just as easily have become a Lib Dem himself. He had no sense that any great work to 'carry the nation inexorably forwards' was possibly in danger of being lost. He was not even all that convinced of the extravagant claims made for future benefits which would inevitably accrue from the burgeoning powers of the EU. It *was* the power and he had sufficient vestiges of honesty not to delude himself that his reign had been some sort of moral crusade. *Realpolitik*. Nothing more, nothing less.

Most of his policies were handed to him on a plate by his fellow members of the shadowy Bilderberg Group. That was a place where he was able to wallow in his own self-importance; a place where the excitement of secret meetings fired his child-like sense of adventure.

His Cabinet may not like him. The electorate may reject him, but the Bilderbergers would always love him for the unqualified support he offered them in their quest to create, then dominate The New EU Super State, by any means at their disposal.

He was a man of few ideas; a fact proved by his only original thinking having been the now disintegrating 'Muckle Voe Project'.

With the Bilderbergers it was so much easier. These world financiers and statesmen - there were few women - these politicians and arch europhiles did his thinking for him.

"Around the coast the languid air did swoon," so had written Tennyson of 'The Lotus Eaters' - those who had sampled unwisely and paid a price of permanent, inebriated lethargy. There was no rescuing Odysseus.

These meetings too were heady but he knew he would still be welcome as an adviser even when his tenure as PM came to an end. He would be a 'Statesman' in his own right; a man of profound wisdom. A 'somebody'. One 'who had truly arrived'.

If Mel had known the inner workings of the PM's mind, after his reading of 'The Narnia Chronicles', he would have probably concluded that the man had 'been at the enchanted Turkish Delight'.

* * *

"You must not worry," said The CEO of one of the top three banks in Europe.

"Quite so," agreed the Head of a pan-European retail chain with annual profits into billions of euros.

"We can help - and we shall," said Hans Van Euten the former Prime Minister of Belgium and a nod from the highest ranking Civil Servant in France confirmed the point.

"We cannot have such a 'good European' as yourself out of office. You are the best man in British politics to further the aims of the EU. We shall have a 'few strings pulled' with the media. It should help pull back the lead in the polls which you had until recently. The EU puts funding into the BBC, as you know, so we ought to be able to call in a few favours there. I shall have a 'quiet word' with one or two Newspaper Publishers - in fact isn't that Julius now?" he asked, pointing towards the corpulent figure of a Champagne-toting, newspaper magnate.

This was, of course, not a meeting of The Bilderbergers, as such. It was merely a Champagne reception at Number Ten for eighteen of the PM's personal 'friends' and to tell the truth, they *were* more his friends than anybody he knew in Labour Politics in general.

There was however, a broad 'political mix'; a senior Green with aspirations to become an EU Commissioner, several conservative friends of the ageing Ken Clarke and a wondrous host of euro-socialists and just the one euro-communist.

Only two of the people present were not Bildebergers but both hoped to join the clandestine but highly prestigious organisation, as soon as practicably possible.

One of these was a vociferous left-winger who led a medium-sized trade union. He was lost in conversation with an Italian Government Minister, known universally as an extreme right-winger. They were enjoying their chat; united in their utopian dreams for a 'Brave New Europe'.

"It eez all about power, no?" said the Italian and these two anti-democrats laughed loudly; united in a general political creed and both beginning to feel the effects of that fourth glass of Bollinger.

The PM beamed. He was at home. Downing Street *was* his home. These were the people he knew he could trust. They were working for him because they loved him. No lack of self-esteem, here. They did. They really did. He was firmly ensconced in one of the select groups of power-brokers who run the world. Forget the Freemasons. Forget the so-called Illuminati - this is where it was *real* and he was part of it. His worries about the Election began to evaporate. These were the people who not only knew; but mattered. The fact that huge amounts of the honeyed words directed to him were merely flattery was lost on him completely.

The organisation would protect him from the vagaries of the voting public. What the hell did a dustman know? Or some teacher or unemployable layabout? What *could* they possibly know? It was so much better for the 'people who knew' to run countries.

The democratic process was surely an outmoded concept.

CHAPTER TWELVE

Lucy had thought long and hard about whether or not there would be a problem if she were to stay in her usual hotel. After a great deal of deliberation she could anticipate no particular dangers so she had rung ahead and booked the Thursday night.

The journey up had been especially long and tedious. Her Audi was a good drive but nothing could improve the journey when she found every jam, every set of road-works - and on the country roads - also found herself behind every tractor north of the Border.

She was not sure how life would develop from this point and so had driven down to see Jack for a couple of days the previous weekend and had taken a diversion to visit her parents for another three. She had only been home in Burton for one day before the drive to Scotland.

She was tired out but had found some nameless, small town where she had bought a strong coffee to revive her. Why were there so many towns and villages in Scotland which chose to hide their names?

She went into a small newsagents' where she bought several maps to ensure that there were no problems and checked that her mobile was still charged.

"Oh, no!" she shrieked when, back in the car, she realised that she had forgotten the charger. She wondered if the phone would be alright. It probably would. 'Probably' would not do.

As luck would have it, she was able to buy a car charger from a branch of Halfords to which she had been directed by a pleasant-faced, middle-aged lady. It would plug into the cigar lighter and so she put it on charge immediately.

She could have kicked herself for her stupidity and wondered if she had made any other errors.

She arrived at her hotel at about half past six, exhausted after a very long day's driving and took a soak for three quarters of an hour. Feeling slightly better she went downstairs and dined handsomely in the small restaurant. Half a bottle of Chianti had an effect.

Returning to her room, she fell asleep immediately on top of the duvet before having a chance to get undressed, then slept a solid eleven hours.

On waking up the following day, she read the papers and killed time waiting for the day to pass. She would have quite liked to have gone out and about but decided that it would be better for her not to put herself in sight of any more people than necessary.

Nobody knew that she used this hotel and so why should they check it? She was safe here and so she remained for lunch as the minutes dragged ponderously by.

She chose to pay the bill - in cash of course - and told them that there was a possibility that she might want to stay a second night.

The hotel staff were singularly uncurious and unable to foresee any problem with a late booking for that evening.

In the afternoon she went for a walk wearing a headscarf and wrap-around sunglasses, on the one hand, these were to filter out a watery sun but they also served to prevent any unlikely but possible recognition.

Looking unsuspicious makes you appear very suspicious indeed and although she felt self-conscious, she was unaware that she was looking somewhat sinister. Fortunately, there were few to take an interest in suspicious-looking, late season visitors.

It was highly unlikely that any connection could be made between the 'something' which was to happen that night and a regular guest at this hotel. As luck would have it, nobody thought anything doubtful about a pleasant lady who chose to make short trips to enjoy the panoramic views in one of the finer parts of Scotland.

Driving a new Audi diverts attention rather than attracts it. She had only had the car for about a month and was still getting used to it. Nobody could possibly have made a link between this polished lady and the ne'er-do-wells over at Muckle Voe.

She produced a paperback from her overnight bag and settled into a large, leather chair to kill time during the afternoon.

She wondered if she would dare order a dinner that evening. How could she take a phone call and rush out in the middle of waiting for the main course to arrive without it being thought odd'?

It was probably best to order a sandwich and 'one for later' which would be useful if Mel were successful and needed sustenance. She ordered two unopened bottles of fizzy mineral water for the same reason. There was also chocolate, crisps and an apple or two in the car. She wished that she had brought a thermos with her. Hot coffee might have been very useful later that night. She would go out and buy a flask a little later on.

She put down her book and tried to think of any means by which Mel could possibly escape. She could think of none.

This was the longest and hardest waiting period of her life and she was on edge although she concealed this well.

Why did Mel not know where they would be meeting up? It did not make sense. If he knew so much about his plan, why not something obvious like that?

She waited, worried and wondered.

CHAPTER THIRTEEN

Mel spent the afternoon in preparation. His most important task was to ensure that Georgie, Lewis and Craig would meet that night at 8pm. He confirmed this casually with all three. The meeting was to be at Craig's house which, of the four homes represented, was the furthest from the Centre, at a distance of well over half a mile. This could prove important.

He walked up to the Centre and checked behind it to confirm that the chute was intact but did not touch it. He then went across to view the only piece of truly flat land which was in the immediate vicinity; an area of about a third of an acre located beyond that piece of wasteland where the builders had spectacularly failed to clear away the last of their rubbish. That had to be the spot. He had no doubts that he had judged it correctly. There was simply nowhere else as suitable.

Few residents were stirring. It seemed that some, if not a majority, were now sleeping sixteen hours out of every twenty four. They might just as well have been locked up in 'solitary' for all the benefits gained from living on this superb island - still, the opportunity to imbibe rough alcohol would not have happened in an ordinary gaol. Probably.

Mel went into the Centre through the main entrance and found it deserted. He spotted some crude posters made out of A4 and marker pen advertising Maxie Martin with his performance to begin at 7-30pm. 'BYO booze' was pencilled in for this 'cabaret' which had excited a significant majority of the residents as it would be their 'first proper night out' since arrival. Three men entered the foyer of The Centre discussing something in animated fashion. One then vomited over his friend who gave him a karate chop to the throat and he fell into his own vomit, whimpering. The two others departed cursing as the man sat up and Mel gave him an encouraging nod only to receive a scowl and hear something croaked which sounded rather like "Guk o' , you 'pible fumper."

There had apparently been some excitement over at the Zone where a resident had foolishly attacked a guard who was ending his visit prematurely as his visitor had attempted to smuggle some crack into Convictville.

The guard had been critically injured according to some of the more excitable and extravagant stories, but as more emerged throughout the day, the details were inconsistent. The one indisputable fact appeared to be that the particular resident had become the first person to sample the 'dungeons' beneath The Zone.

"Lucky man!" muttered Mel with no detectable trace of irony and having established that there was nobody watching him he descended into the bowels of the building and turned on every light.

He had managed to find a lump hammer but was desperate to find a sledge hammer if at all possible. It was not. He hid the hammer in a carrier bag to take away and spent half an hour or more making his initial preparations. These included the strategic positioning of eight Glade Air Fresheners; all opened to their maximums. He wedged a couple of side doors firmly shut, leaving four rooms for the execution of his plan and once satisfied that the first stage was complete he left the building and would return as people arrived for the performance - or better - a little before.

He concealed the hammer behind the building and strolled calmly to the end of the island for his final walk. He would miss the isle for its raw splendour. Even if the escape attempt were to fail, as it easily could, it was guaranteed that he would no longer be here in twenty four hours. This really would be his final day.

The walks he would miss. The Bible Studies he would miss and the three Christians too. There was little else because even though his accommodation was so comfortable, it was just not possible to conceive of worse company with which to spend your probably shortened life.

He thought of Lucy and found it hard to believe that he could be back with her and free in just a few hours.

If time was passing slowly for her, for Mel it was moving at the speed of light - which sounded scientifically reasonable.

He returned to his house and read his Bible. He chose to leave it behind tonight as it was something that people knew he would not leave without. It would be a good clue that he would have been unable to retrieve it and therefore aided the fiction he was trying to promote.

He attempted prayer for the umpteenth time and found yet again, that he was unable to do it, so he prepared a substantial meal and napped for an hour as he was desperate to be at his sharpest for whatever the night would bring.

At ten past seven, he packed a carrier bag and walked to the Centre and descended into the basement area. The combined smell of the air fresheners was overpowering but would probably not be enough to hide the odours completely.

When he came to the first of the four rooms, he placed the plug-in timer Lucy had brought him into a power point and twisted a pair of thin wires across, not quite touching and awaiting the spark which would emerge when the device turned itself on at ten past eight.

Confirming that there were no outlets from any of other three basement rooms apart from through the main door of the first, he shut this main door and reached into his carrier for a pot of ready-mixed Polyfilla.

He filled all the cracks around the door, paying particular attention to the section under the door itself and smeared the bottom eighteen inches around the sides with extreme care, by using a broad paint scraper.

Within five minutes it was beginning to dry and after another five, it should produce a watertight seal, although water was far from his mind.

He left the empty tub on the floor to the side and reached again into his bag. He took out a sheet of A4 marked *DANGER! DO NOT ENTER. FUMES!* and then fixed it with Blu-Tack onto the outside of the door.

He walked upstairs into the foyer where a fight had started between rival, drunken gangs and he noticed that the vomit from earlier in the day remained where it had landed. Still, the smell might help the plan.

Nobody paid him the slightest attention as he exited. He was pleased to see that the show seemed to be attracting such a good turnout.

He walked to the back of the centre and in the gathering darkness found the chute and dragged it, more or less into position.

He took out the lump hammer and systematically smashed the window at ground level which led into the cellar area. It was all as deserted as ever. The noise of the breaking glass would not carry too far even on the cool, steady air.

He went up to the petrol tank and smashed the tiny padlock off the tap at the base of the enormous tank using his lump hammer. Unfortunately, the mechanism, which was rather delicate, disintegrated unexpectedly under the assault and petrol began to gush from the broken tap. He dragged the chute to encircle the tap and bound it in place with a roll of twine. This took nearly five minutes to complete with any degree of effectiveness. The majority of the fuel now poured into the chute and spurted away into nowhere in particular at the other end. He was drenched from head to toe but was not unduly worried as he had foreseen that he could hardly expect to complete his task without this occurring. Even so, all he could think about was those Buddhist Monks who had burned themselves to death, using considerably less petrol than this, in their protests over the Vietnam War.

All that remained was to direct the bottom of the chute into the low window which he accomplished at the expense of a further soaking. He rather hoped that nobody would come around the back with a lit cigarette or even a discarded fag end.

It was done and the generator's fuel gushed, spurted and streamed into the cellars. He looked at his watch to find it was twenty one minutes to eight. Good enough.

He headed off to his own house trying to avoid the fairly high numbers of people who, although late, were still heading for the show.

He burst through his front door and fell straight into the shower where he stayed until no smell of petrol remained. He emerged, doused himself in deodorants and aftershave then deposited his clothes into the washing machine and, picking up a different carrier bag, a much larger one, he left the house for what would prove to be the final time. He turned up for his Bible Study slightly late and settled down to await whatever might happen. At nine minutes past eight he checked his watch.

What happened forty seconds later was quite different to anything he could possibly have anticipated.

CHAPTER FOURTEEN

The PM had a rough grasp of what had gone on when a message was passed to him in his private study at Number Ten with the clock showing eight thirty-two.

By eight thirty-six, he realised that six days later, Bilderbergers or no Bilderbergers, not only would he no longer be the Prime Minister of a government with an overall majority, but neither would he be presiding over a government of any description.

Nobody could tell what had happened exactly on Muckle Voe, but it seemed that there had been at least two almighty explosions and the death toll was horrendous.

He would be made to appear an utter incompetent with less than a week to go. It was all over.

Salt would be rubbed into his wounds by the time the Sunday papers appeared as they were all rushing to knock together a late poll on the Saturday in time for publication.

What he did not yet know was how serious this would all become within the next thirty six hours.

The Conservatives were presented as having an average lead of not less than eleven per cent. A landslide beckoned.

The public might be blase about spin, intrigue, corruption, dishonesty, illegal wars and even to a degree; incompetence, but any government made to look like a ring-load of clowns was defeated before a single polling station opened.

The explosions on Muckle Voe had cast a dark pall of smoke over what had once been a government.

CHAPTER FIFTEEN

The first bang was thunderous, puzzling and unworryingly distant. The force of the second explosion which followed it a matter of seconds later, was felt in the hotel rather than heard. Lucy knew automatically that there had to be some sort of connection to Mel's plan. What she could not know at this point was that the first bang represented almost three thousand gallons of petrol, in the enclosed space of the cellars seeing its heavy vapours ignite and pass onto the main body of the fuel. There remained sufficient oxygen to feed a massive eruption. The flames then travelled at lightening speed across to the main petrol tank where around forty thousand more gallons waited, paused and then exploded in a volcanic fury to match Mount St Helens on a particularly fierce day.

As the crow flies, Lucy was a full eighteen miles from Muckle Voe and her fear was that the explosions represented something which had gone desperately wrong with the escape attempt. She was worried sick that Mel could have been injured or even killed. She had not expected this. But then, what had she been expecting?

There was a TV in the bar and so she asked for it to be turned on. There was some appalling reality TV show being inflicted which could only have appealed to the intellect of a retarded mollusc.

Within ten minutes the first newsflash appeared, meaning that the general public now had some inkling of what was going on even before the PM.

A lugubrious newscaster called Geraint Fellows looked gravely into the camera and pronounced:

Reports are coming in of a series of massive explosions on the prison island of Muckle Voe. It is thought that casualty levels are extremely high from reports received from the Naval side of the island. It is believed that the disaster has not affected the personnel guarding Muckle Voe but took place on the prisoners' side of the island to the East of what is called The Neutral Zone – a buffer between the two sides.

It is stated that the prison infirmary is likely to be swamped and rescue services from the mainland have been alerted and are expected to fly out as many casualties as they can to a variety of local A&E departments.

We shall get back to you as soon as we can. Our roving reporter, John Whitehouse, has been on holiday in the area and is meeting up with a local camera crew. We hope to hear more from him before the scheduled end of this programme.

Lucy's blood turned to ice and she was convinced that the plan had turned into a catastrophe.

She tried to pray and found it difficult. A sense of panic ran through her and she knew she had to maintain an appearance of calm.

Fortunately, nobody had spotted the ashen pallor engraved on her face. She did not want to be a widow again. Once had been quite enough.

She ordered a Remy Martin and sat down heavily, staring at the TV.

The next report came rapidly on the heels of the first, by which time the PM had been apprised of the situation. She recognised pictures of the ferry docking point but not the reporter who was pointing behind him to a plume of smoke which looked to be about half a mile high. Flames could still be seen from the eight mile distance and the cameramen were doing their utmost to zoom lenses onto the island where the fires, at least, could not be missed, belching out with spiralling columns of acrid, dense fumes hurtling ever heavenwards.

A third report came in after a further eight minutes when a helicopter carrying cameras flew up to under a mile from the island and was warned off, relatively unconvincingly, from the diminutive control tower on the other side of the island. It backtracked slightly.

A mile was more than sufficient for their purposes and the sheer devastation and mayhem was finally captured. There was little need for infra-red assistance as the fires illuminated the scene with an eerie glow and the pictures were transferred instantly into eight million homes.

Viewers could see a massive building - or rather what had once been a massive building - and dozens, if not scores of small detached houses which had been wiped off the face of the earth and those further away looked like smouldering, skeletal remains.

It appeared that about half the total of houses might be relatively untouched but none had escaped damage and a pair of medical helicopters appeared from the East within a minute or two of each other and landed side by side, some nine hundred yards from the epicentre of the explosions.

Of the petrol container nothing remained apart from the brick base of which a surprising amount was still intact thereby indicating the directions of the explosions. The first of which had taken place beneath the large building, largely destroying it and flames had rapidly shot up the chute and ignited the petrol surging from the broken tank before taking the tank itself as Mel had hoped. It had recently been filled and in total, had anybody had the ability to be precise, over forty two thousand gallons had just gone up.

Forensic experts from the fire service would never establish how this had started. The temperatures had been so fierce that all evidence had been obliterated. They would perhaps find out where it had begun but the 'why' would surely be impossible.

A sense of horror ran through an ever fickle population and huge amounts of somewhat misplaced sympathy were directed towards the residents in inverse proportion to their feelings about the government and especially, the Prime Minister.

CHAPTER SIXTEEN

Mel simply could not believe what had happened. He knew there would be a rather large bang and there was - one which shook the entire island - but he was totally unprepared when the force of the second explosion, six seconds later, tore through Craig's home, blowing out the windows, devastating the interior of the house and knocking all four men to the floor. The blast kept running on blindly through the rear windows of the house and continued on its curious way.

Mel's first thought was one of concern for the Naval Personnel but he need not have worried, there were a few very minor injuries in The Zone and nothing at all on the other side. The Zone Building had stood up well to the power of the explosions and to a large extent had protected the other side of Muckle Voe from much of the force of the blast.

His next thought was to establish what had happened and so he peered through where the window had once been, towards where The Centre had once been. It was noteworthy only because of its absence.

His third thought was a hope that the bird-life on the island would not have been affected too badly.

There were some moans from the floor and he helped the others to their feet. Lewis had been cut in the left cheek by flying glass and Craig appeared to have broken his little finger by falling awkwardly. He felt guilty for not having thought primarily about the welfare of his friends - after all, he was responsible for their discomfort - however inadvertently. He had, of course, ensured that they were away from The Centre and the point of the explosion. He was unable to believe the explosion could have carried so far. It must mean that his own house, which was considerably nearer, must have been wiped off the map. He wished he had brought that Bible with him now.

This was the moment. "You stay here. Look after them," he said to Georgie, "I shall go and take a look. Wish me well! It's dangerous out there."

He plucked his large bag from amongst the debris on the floor and disappeared into the night.

His preparations for this next twenty minutes had been thoughtful and meticulous. A person who knew Mel well would have had to have looked harder than usual in order to recognise him. The changes had been made gradually. It had taken well over three weeks for the goatee beard to appear and earlier that day, he had shaved his head completely, not that this would be effective in the initial stages of his plan.

He was wearing a pair of glasses with the most neutral lenses Lucy had been able to find. He was able to see through them okay but had trained himself to look over the top of them as well. Finding where to change might be difficult.

He wandered through the detritus and pieces of detached wood and masonry. The strength of the fire over to his left was astonishing. The chilly night was actually warmed by it from well over a third of a mile away.

He could hear several minor bangs from time to time and periodically, the flames would increase only to die down again a few moments later.

The conflagration simply kept on gushing flame and the intermittent, pyroclastic eruptions thundered more pollution into the heavens than his mind could take in.

Amazingly, this was the first time that a man who was fundamentally caring about the environment found himself considering the deleterious effects on the surroundings; on the wildlife of the island; on the atmosphere. He felt truly ashamed of himself.

The brightness to his side made his pathway seem darker than it really was and he tripped over rubble on several occasions. He was heading towards the flattened out piece of land alongside where the builders had dumped their rubbish. It had to be the only spot. The only alternative would have been to have landed on the Naval side of the island and transfers of the injured would simply have taken twice the time. It made sense. As if to prove his point, a Naval helicopter landed nicely in tandem with the arrival of four guards carrying two injured men on stretchers. These were loaded on board and the helicopter departed towards the East. The whole process was fast and efficient. The four personnel then disappeared, still bearing their stretchers, in the direction of the remnants of The Centre.

Mel walked up to the last prefab before the helicopter landing point and, noting that the damage was even worse than at Craig's place, he concealed himself in the shadow of the house. There was virtually no movement he could detect from around the houses and this one appeared never to have been occupied. Clearly, it had been a very high audience to enjoy the dubious delights of Max Martin who was now, presumably, no more.

This was a good vantage point and Mel decided that this was the time when he would become a paramedic or Doctor or whatever anybody else determined him to be.

From his large carrier there came a well-made, black leather bag in a style popular with so many doctors. He put on the lab coat and straightened his name badge. He placed the stethoscope around his neck and searched along the ground for some ash. It did not take a great deal of finding. He rubbed some across his face and a handful smeared the fresh whiteness of the lab coat. Perfect.

To finish the effect he took out a white baseball cap which he had been working on, with the utmost care, for the last three days.

Handwritten in red lettering, which was so well done it looked to be printed, was the word *MEDIC*. The effect was complete.

The sheer size of the explosion had obliged him to consider a change of plan. He had intended to try to make good his escape, at the very first opportunity, on the earliest, available civilian helicopter.

Now he was able to think that his disguise might have more authenticity if he did not appear to have come into being from out of the thin air. Perhaps he should attempt to take a later one? There would certainly be a great many in the wake of what had happened here.

The longer he waited, the better the chance that the Navy would begin to succeed in bringing some order and organisation to the island. He was depending on the chaos. Moreover, the longer he waited, the more nervous he would become and more prone to make mistakes.

In the final analysis, it was difficult to say what his best plan might be. He was certainly quite safe from detection where he was now. A decision would have to be made and soon, so he arbitrarily opted to target the second, civilian craft.

It might be the best, it might not. This was where the plan was out of his hands.

He turned over in his mind how, if he were captured in this disguise, immediate suspicion would befall him for the explosions. It simply did not matter. There would not even be a trace of circumstantial evidence.

Anyway, if they were miraculously able to convict, what more could they do to him? He already had a life sentence. There was no death penalty for killers who kept on killing.

It did just cross his mind, and not for the first time, that he might have upset the applecart where Jerry's plan was concerned, but as both Jerry and Brenda had apparently dropped off the radar this could not be a major consideration.

Two helicopters which were clearly not Naval aircraft appeared and swept in to land on the identified site within what seemed only thirty seconds of each other but was actually longer.

As if on cue, the four stretcher bearers reappeared and loaded up the first chopper which took off, hovered for several seconds, then vanished, although its ear-splitting clatter could still be heard above the sound of the idling engine of the second machine.

Time.

He trotted across the waste ground and saw that there was a middle-aged nurse as well as the pilot in the helicopter. He ran up to the machine and clambered in.

"Wa'er," he croaked. "Smook in'alashun." He attempted a broken, guttural, Lowland Scots sound and then gasped convincingly and coughed several times. He pointed at his badge and bravely murmured "John." The deception was complete. Neither nurse nor pilot mistrusted him in any way and it had all been accomplished in less than a minute. What was that which somebody had said about the vital importance of first impressions?

He sat away from two mattress-like bases which were surrounded by drips and medical equipment of every imaginable variety and the nurse offered him her can of Fanta. He coughed convincingly, thanked her with a further croak, and asked, "Which 'ospituh?"

"This one's going to the 'Galbraith'. The others - and there should be about six in all - are spreading the patients around. The number of casualties is very high."

"Yeah," he breathed and coughed desperately. He was trying not to catch her eye full on. "Very. Doan worri abou' me. I'll live. Help them." He spluttered, again underpinning his gallantry as he pointed towards two distant stretchers which were being carried in their direction at speed.

At least ninety seconds too late, a contingent of Royal Marines arrived to guard the 'new heliport' and ensure the safety of the medical teams. Mel was surprised that he had not spotted their rapid approach.

Some twenty, heavily-armed men were ordered into position and swiftly deployed themselves to their various locations. The occupants of the chopper were all grateful for the gesture, not least Mel, who now realised how difficult his task might have been had he waited for a third helicopter.

At this juncture, the two injured he had seen approaching were lifted aboard and the stretcher bearers inevitably thought him one of the medical team. Again, he made sure the peak of his cap was pulled well down and looked nobody in the eye. They had other matters to concern them. From this point on the nurse ignored him. Within a few seconds, the side door was pulled to and the chopper lifted into the air and carried Mel, if not to freedom, then at the very least, in its direction.

He lowered his head and made as if to get up to help but sat down again with a burst of coughing. "This one's dead," she announced and began to work on the other man who was groaning. She gave him some kind of injection and he relaxed. She put him on a drip and began to try to clean him up but was not able to spot where he was injured. There was no danger that the injured man might recognise him. She tried to make the man comfortable and within what seemed only a couple of minutes, the chopper was descending and it landed in a large car park. Had it been an hour earlier, the landing would not have been possible as the parking had been taken up with several hundred visitors' vehicles, now returned from whence they came.

The time was just after ten past nine and he was taken aback at the speed with which his escape had been executed, but all the same, the time scale did not make much sense to him. Where had an hour gone? That was not something to concern him. This was the final hurdle. It was almost as essential that it be kept secret that there had been an escape as it was to escape at all. Ultimately, his success depended on ceasing to exist.

* * *

As a group of doctors and nurses appeared, he simply alighted from the helicopter and was promptly ignored as the team from A&E began their work. He found a side door and went just inside the ancient building. There was nobody about. Off came the lab coat and cap. These were placed, with the stethoscope, into the bag. He remembered the glasses and dropped them into his pocket. From the leather bag he pulled out the large carrier and placed the leather bag inside that.

The change was dramatic and accomplished in under thirty seconds. He was not surprised to hear the helicopter taking off again.

Gratefully spotting a toilet he went inside and washed the ash from his face in front of a cracked mirror. He was sure, looking into the mirror, that neither the nurse nor pilot would recognise him if they walked right into him. Good work.

He reached into his pocket and withdrew his battery shaver and removed the thin goatee using the beard trimming facility and followed this up with the total removal of his rather pronounced eyebrows. The final touch.

* * *

Now all that remained was for him to avoid any CCTV cameras in and around the hospital.

He went back to the side door and was fairly certain that he would be able to avoid direct problems if he took the footpath which bordered the car park. This was deserted and would presumably remain so until the next helicopter load arrived. He wondered why a side door into a major hospital was unlocked and showing no evidence of security staff at this time on a Friday night but he would not look the proverbial 'gift horse' in the mouth.

Back he went into the carrier and he had to fiddle around a few moments in the 'bag within a bag' to extricate a 'hoodie' which he had almost forgotten to put on. Once done, he walked away from the hospital and into both the town and anonymity.

He stopped at a conveniently placed seat for bus travelers, where he rang Lucy. He refused conversation but simply stated where he was and as he could see a 'Red Lion' pub just across the road he told her that he would see her in their car park, as soon as possible.

This done he walked briskly into a small Peace Garden where he was able to remain thoughtful and unobserved until the Audi appeared almost half an hour later. Never was a sight more welcome. He sighed.

* * *

During his wait, there had been two further helicopter deliveries of injured convicts. If there was one thing he was convinced of, it was that nobody would have escapees on their minds on this night. The plan had succeeded with military precision. A sigh of relief was appropriate.

There was every chance that he would be declared dead. His friends would truthfully state that he had gone to find out what was happening and he had presumably been consumed in one of the subsequent explosions. To all intents and purposes, Mel Roberts was dead.

* * *

He crossed the road, kissed Lucy through her car window and went around to the passenger side. She put the vehicle into gear and drove them away into yet another 'new life'.

CHAPTER SEVENTEEN

They had so much to say to each other they could hardly speak. It was almost impossible to know where to start but Lucy obviously wanted to know what had happened and Mel was not prepared to tell her until he had given her a full picture of what life had been like on Muckle Voe. She listened as she drove along her pre-planned route down to Barnston Parva in The Yorkshire Dales.

"I wasn't open with you about what was going on there. I couldn't tell you as you would have worried yourself into an institution. Yes, the accommodation was excellent. Yes, we had all our needs met. Yes, it was a lovely place and arguments that it was like a holiday camp were not too far off the mark.

The facilities were terrific and it could have been all that it had been intended to be. But, you see, what they forgot was that they were dealing with human nature at its very lowest. If you put murderers, the criminally insane - because some were - potential torturers, potential concentration camp staff, the greedy, the selfish, the vain, the vicious and the mean-spirited all in together, all you have is a good pre-view of what hell must be like.

For the first week or two, you don't really see it then as the scales fall from your eyes you recognise that it is no more than a nest of the purest evil. I can't even tell you some of the things I know went on. Let's just say it was brutality and, yes, evil. That's all I can say to describe it and it sucked nearly everybody in. There may have been more who were redeemable - in any sense - but I only discovered three."

"You shouldn't have tried to protect me, you know. I prefer reality," said Lucy pensively.

"Trust me," Mel replied, "However bad you think it was, it was worse. The only reason I survived was because they somehow got the idea that I was a professional killer who had murdered nearly thirty people and I even had to demonstrate violence myself so they would believe I was capable of anything. There have been twelve deaths on the island in the few short months I was there and six, I think, in the last month alone. She looked at him in disbelief.

It has all been hushed up. None of these was natural. It was only a matter of time before they sussed me out and I was killed off. I refused to join any of the power cliques, you see. On your own, it's a death sentence. One side or another will eventually demand you 'pay homage' and kill you when you don't.

If you join one, the others are planning your death and The Navy just left us all alone to get on with it. Genuine freedom, you see? Power plays."

"I didn't realise," she said in a murmur,

"Well. I decided that it had to be dealt with and have spent many an hour planning something which would kill off most of these people, shut

217

down this hell-hole, make the world take notice and embarrass anybody who was involved in setting up this cursed place. The idea that you can create harmony by putting all the worst elements in a society together is just stupidity beyond human sense.

In the War, the Germans made the mistake of putting all the best escapers together in Colditz Castle and they made a rod for their own backs. You should dilute trouble, if you can.

You know, when I was a teacher they came up with the bright idea - politically correct idea - of taking all the kids who were troublemakers and dumping them in the mainstream schools in the name of equality. Idiots! They were wrong with that and never seem to learn anything from their mistakes.

When those youngsters were in Special Schools, experts sometimes, and I *mean* sometimes, were able to help some of them. Instead they were dumped where they would cause the most damage. Muckle Voe was an extreme example of that kind of non-joined-up thinking even if it was the opposite side of that particular coin.

I hate inflicting pain on people but I did what I think had to be done. Yes, *I* created a massive explosion and got away in the chaos. In case you are wondering, I have no conscience about this whatsoever. All I have done is what I was doing before. I've made the world a slightly better place and you will be interested to know, those who repented, those who changed, they were left unharmed. That's about it."

Lucy was a long time silent and then turned on Radio Four. The whole of the programming had been abandoned to what was being called the 'Muckle Voe disaster'.

"No disaster as far as I can see. Those views may change when the truth comes out and it will now!" Mel stated.

The radio reported a minimum of eighty deaths.

"It will be over a hundred at my guess," said Mel in a matter-of-fact kind of way which rather annoyed Lucy.

She was having problems coming to terms with the thought. Her head accepted what Mel was saying but her heart half rejected the idea. She had already been having trouble reconciling serial killing with the Christian faith and it was now mass murder.

There seemed to have been quite an escalation but in all honesty, in logical terms, what was the difference? Either everything Mel had done was wrong or he had been right. It was most difficult to find a half measure.

There was a bag filled with food, fruit, sandwiches, crisps, chocolate and a flask of strong coffee in the back.

He ate hungrily and poured coffee down him, only remembering that it was for Lucy too, at the last minute. She did not mind but really needed to have the final dregs of the coffee to keep her going for the long drive.

Mel offered to share the driving but she was set at this point and was more or less used to the car whilst he was not.

She avoided any roads where they thought they may be spotted by cameras but this was not truly important for two reasons. Mel was convinced that nobody would be looking for him in the first place and they were not heading towards Sheffield, which would make the car considerably more difficult to detect.

Their original plan to hire had been abandoned for these reasons. It might possibly have proved more dangerous to have rented a vehicle. Yet again, it was one of those decisions that could easily go either way. Mel, who was not generally an optimist by nature, was confident that the plan could not have gone any better and was starting to suppose that he was free, once and for all. If they were seeking him, then he would surely be tracked down, eventually, but why should he be caught if they were not looking for him on the obvious grounds that he had perished in the fires?

The only possibility of matters going wrong was if either the pilot or the nurse began to entertain suspicions and fomented an investigation into the identity of their mystery traveller? Why should they? He had only been a 'mystery' from his own point of view. He had not been sufficiently 'injured' for a kindly nurse to want to make enquiries as to his welfare. No. Everything had been pitched perfectly.

What about the cadavers removed from the flames? It seemed improbable that DNA and/or dental records could supply identities for every single set of body parts. If the flames and explosions had been as fierce and destructive as it appeared, it seemed extremely likely that they would not even be able to find all the bodies. Eventually, they would be forced to compile a list of the dead based principally on the names of the missing.

Even if in the worst case scenario they determined that his body was missing, it was unlikely bordering on impossible, that they would conclude that he had indeed escaped. No. It was as near perfect as you could ask.

They chatted a lot but were lost to a degree in their own thoughts and their conversations bordered on the trivial. This suited Lucy as she needed to concentrate. She did not particularly care for night driving at the best of times.

As there was little traffic, progress was good and within four hours she was hurtling down the A19 being careful not to attract the attention of any Police Cars or static, speed cameras. This was not the time to draw any unwanted attention.

The radio droned on with incessant news reports on Muckle Voe. The Prime Minister had exhibited 'shock and horror' and had sent 'heartfelt sympathies' to the relatives of all these 'poor people'.

It seemed that there was no idea of how many had died. At the time of the explosions there had been two hundred and eleven residents. A roll call had found just seventeen uninjured and a further forty eight had either been treated in the infirmary or flown to mainland hospitals.

Police leave in the area had been cancelled to allow the guarding of dangerous prisoners in Scottish hospitals. This was supposed to be temporary as The Navy were still considered to be legally in charge of all residents until the survivors could be shipped back to 'proper' prisons.

Mel was as sure as he could be that his three friends would have escaped the concatenations and was relieved. He loved the fact that, even amongst the worst of humanity, there were on occasions those who could turn and repent. This trio really had been 'born again'. He wished them well and his conscience began to niggle at him that given time, perhaps some of the others might have gone the same route. He conceded that it was unlikely in the extreme, but it *was* indubitably the moral weakness of his plan.

Just like a switch being thrown thrown, he wound down. It was almost as if his adrenaline had turned itself off without a hint of warning. The excitement, the 'rush', the anxiety; they all disappeared as one and were replaced by a surge of extreme weariness.

He was delighted that Lucy had opted to drive - he could have been dangerous. Relief enveloped him and all he wanted to do was hug his wife. He entertained no sexual desire whatsoever but was desperate to be close to her; he was looking forward to sleeping alongside her - he would not cease touching her for the whole of what remained of the night. He was in love and this was a feeling which she shared. Was it possible to be more content than he felt at this moment?

The car cruised on and Lucy turned off towards the East. Their temporary new home was beckoning them. Just five hours after leaving The Red Lion car park, they were in Barnston Parva.

The cottage was attractive he told her.

"It wants to be, the money it cost. We have it 'til the week after Christmas and an option on a further month. They don't get many bookings through winter, I expect."

The car was parked at the side of the house, away from a relatively minor road and the two lovers entered their private haven.

PART THREE

CHAPTER ONE

The word 'idyllic' is not generally used to describe accurately either lifestyle or romance in the real world but in the case of Mel and Lucy the next five or six weeks lived up to that depiction.

They basked in each other's company and: went out for long walks, read widely, made love and talked. As soon as they tired of any one activity they moved onto one of the others, finding it as fresh or new as ever.

They watched with no small interest but with a degree of suspicion as the new Prime Minister took his place as leader of the nation.

"He couldn't be much worse," Lucy observed darkly as she wondered if her husband had single-handedly been responsible for a government lead being reversed into a Tory overall majority of forty two seats.

Mel knew differently. His life experience had proved conclusively, on more than one occasion, that *any* situation could get worse. Even so, he was guardedly optimistic for one usually so lukewarm in his feelings for the Conservative Party and was quite surprised by *her* lack of enthusiasm.

Mel used the Internet to follow up details on Muckle Voe and was delighted to see his name listed amongst the dead. It seemed that at the outset, the list had been 'dead and missing' and after less than a fortnight this was simply referred to as 'those who perished at Muckle Voe'. It made little difference as he was on both lists.

It was also in the second week that Lucy brought up a rather obvious point that had been missed, "Shouldn't I be holding a funeral for you?"

"Oh, shit yes! Of course. How did I miss that? This is a real problem. Clearly I shan't be attending, my name ain't Tom Sawyer!

How can there be a funeral with no body? It'll have to be a memorial service. You must contact the authorities and demand to know why you have been kept in the dark about your husband's death. Say that you have been on tenterhooks waiting for their call. Do they have the address at Burton? Probably not. That's to our advantage, I haven't given it to them. We should be okay with that. So ask why they hadn't found you. Threaten them with your MP. It won't be too bad. Make noises about compensation - that will get them eating out of your hand."

So it was an 'interrupted idyll' as Lucy went home and berated the rather bemused authorities from there with her best, arch telephone manner.

They decided not to have the memorial taken by Brian as they really did not want to deceive him, so Lucy found a tiny Church in the middle of nowhere, in the wilds of North Derbyshire and then advertised the service for a single night in 'The Sheffield Star'. One of the reasons she did not mind the small amount of deception at this Church was because the Minister was clearly a time-server who cared about nothing provided he got his fee and the little bit of kudos from the notoriety of the deceased.

She rarely disliked people but was prepared to make an exception for this abrupt individual who seemed totally lacking in compassion. How glad she was that this 'funeral' was not genuine.

The service was given some publicity in the local rags because Mel had been local himself but the Church was ill-attended which was what Lucy had hoped for. Jack came and she told him the truth. Inevitably, there was a tearful Mandy, Lucy's parents and Georgina. One or two others who may or may not have been former colleagues of Mel came and left without finding a chance to speak to her at the end.

Lucy had written or phoned each of those she knew with the details but of Jerry and Brenda, there was no sign at all. Eventually, she had to send them a letter. It was the only thing to upset her on the run-up to a day which was far worse for the others than for her.

Ten minutes before the service came to a close, Brenda rushed in and sat down at the back, at least three rows behind the main group of mourners.

Lucy sought her out at the end and refused to allow a newspaperman to photograph her. Strangely, he respected the request.

"I just can't stop. Sorry I'm late. Jerry was under the weather and couldn't make it. He sends his apologies. I know it's rude but I've got to go. I'm *so* sorry for you."

As Brenda made to leave, realising how much she trusted her friend, Lucy whispered, "It's a fake. He's not dead. He escaped." But this was all they got the chance to say as they were inconveniently surrounded by the small group of others. The former Police Officer gave her a reassuring and positively ecstatic smile then promptly disappeared.

They went to a local pub for lunch which had not exactly been booked. Lucy had merely enquired as to how many walk-in guests they could cope with on a given lunchtime. It was sufficient.

She spent most of the meal with her parents before Jack drove them the lengthy distance home.

"It's not as bad as it looks, Dad," was all she dared to say to her father who could only give her a disapproving look and she realised how crass the statement must have sounded. She could not tell them too.

"I shall be spending a lot of time in Spain in the future," she said. "You'll have to come out and see us....I mean me." She knew that the ageing couple would be less than willing to travel and promised herself to visit them at least three times a year.

All in all, the messing about and the activities surrounding the service took less than three full days out of all these weeks spent in such perfect company.

Mel investigated on the Internet and could not find the names of Lewis, Craig or Georgie amongst the injured or dead. It seemed impossible to find out which prisons they were in. That was again something which Jerry could do, if only.....

One looming spectre hovered above these 'lovebirds'. They knew how impermanent their stay in the Dales would have to be and so they enjoyed it to the utmost. Lucy went out and found a wine merchants in Thirsk from which she brought back a selection of the very finest reds and some of Mel's much loved Chablis. She would always pay in cash. There was no point in leaving a paper trail behind her. Movements are so easily checked in a modern world.

They did not remain tied to the area around the cottage but toured the region and even managed to find some excellent walks along the coast around Robin Hood's Bay where passers-by were a rarity in what was turning out to be a vicious winter. It was on excursions like these that Mel wondered how his walk would have been on Muckle Voe in these seasonal conditions - 'quite raw', he imagined. It was strange to think that there were things about the place he missed. The absence of Bible Studies had left a hole in his life but he worked hard to gain a better understanding of the Scriptures and on occasion he and Lucy would analyse a passage together.

Lucy knew better than to ask him to pray with her.

Their thoughts turned to the important matter of how to get Mel out of the country. The first plan was simply to catch a ferry or take The Channel Tunnel to France. They were fairly sure that passports were not always checked on outgoing journeys and even if they were, would Mel's passport name raise any eyebrows? He would after all, be 'Melvin' not 'Mel' and 'Roberts' was a common enough surname. In the end it was decided that there was too much of an element of risk involved.

They had to find a way to avoid that possible check and Lucy came up with it. They would hire the services of a pilot to take them from a small airfield so that the passports would only be checked on the other side, if then.

Lucy found such a service from a tiny airport near York and flew to Lille in a four-seater aircraft with a sullen pilot who was happy to take two and a half thousand pounds from her for a private daytrip. As a 'dry run' it was a major success. Her passport was not checked either way and she enjoyed some pre-Christmas shopping in Lille itself.

CHAPTER TWO

Mel was delighted with the flat in La Mata and was quick to congratulate his wife on the excellence of her choice and the quality of her taste. He adored the views and spent as much time with the binoculars watching the antics of the local flamingo population as she did.

The weather was colder than he had anticipated but as it was the first week in January, what else could he expect? It was a good ten degrees Celsius warmer than in the Dales - and some days, more.

Lucy was rather in two minds as to what they should do with the house in Burton upon Stather. She loved it dearly but was not able to foresee any way in which it could get any reasonable use in the future.

Mel maintained his 'new look' without hair or eyebrows. He almost always wore some sort of hat when outside the flat and he had acquired a decent pair of wrap-around sunglasses in the market with the dubious brand name of 'Ray Bands'. He re-grew the goatee as few people from his past would have seen him wearing facial hair. He made a point of always wearing any clothes that he would not have been seen dead in previously. As he was now 'dead', perhaps this was appropriate.

The journey down had been easy. The second flight to Lille had gone smoothly with the 'extra passenger' who had 'stayed behind in France to visit friends' whilst Lucy had returned to the UK to make preparations for their life together by winding down some of the services to the house in Burton. Suspicion had been non-existent or perhaps it was just apathy. In either case, the outcome was in their favour. Her returning also gave her the opportunity to bring more of their effects out from England to Spain. A couple of days after this, she flew out to Alicante from Robin Hood at Finningley.

Mel had caught a train to the Gare du Nord and had spent a happy two days wandering around Paris before heading South from the Gare de Lyons.

He had spent three days exploring in South-West France before crossing the border into Spain at Hendaya without problem. He had then taken a taxi to a major car hire firm which also had a branch in Torrevieja. He had rented a Ford Focus and driven down to find Lucy awaiting him. Smooth.

Perhaps they could now begin yet another new life. They ate out regularly and quickly learned the places where one could dine without being overlooked by fellow customers. The last thing they needed was a nosey, bored client putting them both under intense scrutiny as they awaited the arrival of a meal.

It was surprisingly easy to find a whole variety of eateries where this simple requirement could be met. In others, it could be achieved just by the choice of seating position.

Mel was reluctant to remove the sunglasses but there were sufficiently high numbers of British tourists doing precisely the same thing for this to be considered no way unusual. Lucy began to call him 'Andy' as that was his middle name and she took care never to address him otherwise in public.

They ate well and became accustomed to eating 'Spanish style' and at Spanish times. Mel had thought that indigestion was an inevitable consequence of having the main meal of the day as late as ten o clock in the evening but they encountered few problems with this.

Their diets were excellent with an abundance of fresh fruit, meat, vegetables and fish from a host of local markets not to mention La Mata's wine from its own, local vineyard alongside the salt lake. They both thoroughly enjoyed the rich, deep flavour. They were considerably less impressed with the quality of the fresh produce when purchased directly from the supermarkets which seemed specifically designed to appeal to non choosy, British expatriates.

They supposed that one of the dangers of living in this area was the huge number of British people who had retired to the sun but were quite happy that they were not going to be caught out.

All financial dealings were done by Lucy who always used her maiden name. The fact that her passport had never been updated was frequently useful and helped allow Mel to leave no traces of his existence, so it was only the direct recognition of somebody who knew him that could scupper their peace.

CHAPTER THREE

Detective Superintendent, the freshly-promoted Martha Smythe, had been given a force of a hundred detectives drawn from every Police Force across England. She was based in Birmingham. Her task was quite simple – 'to break the lynchings' which were beginning to grow in number and spread ever more widely across England. There had been no incidents in the other parts of The UK and therefore these were simply to be ignored.

The death toll was now running at forty three and severe beatings exceeded several hundred. Many people had increasingly concluded that what was happening was being centrally coordinated. The sheer efficiency of the attacks had been breathtaking. Evidence was at a premium. Forensic scientists were tearing out their hair. Never had any series of crimes produced less evidence as to the identities of the perpetrators.

The newspapers were beginning to pick up on the fact that in any area where there had been several assaults or killings, crime levels had begun to fall. This would not do!

Thus, if there was a sex offender beaten to a pulp in Ipswich for example, sex crimes were tending to fall dramatically throughout Suffolk. The correlation between 'rough justice' and falling crime rates was now undeniable.

It was almost as if there was a parallel justice system operating. The only difference was that this justice was seemingly arbitrary, often brutal, was astonishingly effective and did not allow for an appeals structure. Nobody targeted was ever able to be portrayed as a 'total innocent'-however hard certain sections of the Press were to try.

It was the expression 'parallel justice' which made several of the more senior investigating officers conclude that there was the possibility of a Police link. Nobody knew where the phrase had originated.

Just why was it that no 'innocent' person had ever been targeted? Why no errors? - Criminals always make errors. All of those who had been 'sorted', as the officers called it, had either been released absurdly early from prison or were well known as those who were said to be 'cocking a snook' at the entire legal system.

It made a great deal of sense that there had to be some Police involvement. Why had no officer on patrol ever stumbled serendipitously onto one of these incidents? Had the incidents been properly checked out by local forces? How did the offenders know so much about not leaving an evidence trail?

Even more pertinently, how did these people know who to target; how and where to find them? Were they perhaps using Police facilities to target their victims? Were some Police indeed spotting the offences and keeping the matters quiet - a little bit of 'noble cause corruption'? What about the knowledge of Forensics? The only way to leave virtually no trace is by thoroughly understanding how Forensics Officers operate.

There had to have been arrests by now and yet if Martha were to be absolutely frank, her team did not even know where to begin.

Initially, she had the team feeding copious amounts of data into specially created computer programmes. There would be no ballsups like there had been in 'The Yorkshire Ripper' enquiries all those years earlier. Her team worked long and fruitless hours which turned into days, then weeks and finally, months.

Experienced officers in droves were utterly incapable of coming up with a direction to go in, let alone finding clues to follow. The quality of the Officers was of the highest but nothing made any difference.

Once all the information was electronically and digitally stored, the ideas ran out. In the end, Martha kept a handful of the loaned detectives working to find links on the computers and she put as many as ninety officers to follow up any attack, preferably a matter of minutes after an act of violence but practically speaking, within a couple of hours.

No tactic made a ha'porth of difference. Bodies were still found periodically hanging from trees or viciously beaten and the crime rates moved inexorably downwards.

More than one officer on her team had commented that if they found the guilty people, the consequence would be that crime rates would rise and they were actually attempting to make the world a safer place for criminals to live in.

Martha had to recognise that a significant percentage of her officers were not really over keen to solve these particular crimes. She even began to ask herself whether some of these officers could actually be involved. No! That was an unworthy thought. The lack of success in her first major investigation was beginning to make her a touch paranoid. It was only on TV where the killer was commonly part of the investigating team - an overworked and silly theme if ever there had been one! Had it ever happened in real life? - She thought not.

But where could she go from here? The politicians were getting on the backs of her superiors, a fact of which she was all too well aware as they passed all their fears and recriminations back in her lonely direction.

The new PM was ringing her immediate boss every week and asking for progress reports and The Home Secretary did so with even greater frequency. The excuses used at the beginning of the investigations were all now more than a little 'threadbare' from overuse. These same excuses were passed onto the Press who began to mock them and began to 'name names'. Martha was an inevitable target of tabloid abuse and her adequacy was brought into question in all the former broadsheets.

Her problem was that she was somebody who had been produced by a system which 'discriminated positively' and she had been promoted according to the Peter, or better, the Petra Principle. Her abilities were actually those of a Sergeant who with time and experience might have made a decent Inspector but so desperate were her Senior Officers to present a politically correct front that they were willing to dish out promotions like dolly mixtures to any female, homosexual or person with an off-white skin (and with the ability to breathe as sole qualification), to furnish proof that they were 'at the forefront of futuristic employment policies'.

No matter that there were perhaps dozens better qualified than she who had committed the heinous offence of 'being male', these would be expected to accept willingly and in silence, the punishment for their dastardly offence *and* were required to curb all resentments as they then watched 'incompetence in action'. Unfairness in such systems is to be ignored, eventually denied and finally, forgotten about by all except its victims.

To be fair to Martha however, the above scenario was only partly true in her case. Yes, she had received help from positive discrimination but she had also contributed in no small way to her own cause by sleeping with a well-chosen Assistant Chief Constable and an equally valuable Deputy Commissioner - both, of course, unknown to each other. It could also be reasonably claimed that no better qualified and substantially more experienced officer could have done better in a case where clues were so pitifully few.

Martha began to fear for career. If there were no breakthrough, sooner rather than later, it was inevitable that she would be replaced by a more experienced officer. The powers that be have to be seen to be doing something. It was the 'football manager syndrome'.

Men were sent out on wild-goose chases to re-interview those who had been beaten. The hoods covering faces of attackers might have had some bearing on their inability to offer either clues or descriptions but whispered promises of death if 'they opened their mouths' were easily as effective at ensuring that no new leads emerged.

One DI explained to Martha about the 'GAL effect' in Spain during the 1980s.

Some sources pronounced the President of Government, Felipe Gonzalez, as being the man who had decided to use a shadowy and sinister organisation called GAL to assassinate ETA terrorists who were causing mayhem, especially with car bombs, throughout the Peninsular. Mr Gonzalez always furiously denied the accusations. The DI thought that Gonzalez had never sued his accusers.

Some two dozen ETA terrorists were bumped off on either side of the Pyrenees - the majority in ETA safe havens on the French side of the border.

The result was that the active, violent members, who had been some three hundred strong, out of the blue, could find many less than two dozen to do their dirty work.

GAL was exposed and disbanded, ETA returned to 'normal' business; murders, kidnappings and car bombs.

Fear had worked with ETA, it was working here.

The point was not lost on Martha and she noted that the letters columns of all newspapers except 'The Guardian' contained at least some letters supportive of what was happening, sometimes out of malice and others out of admiration that targets had been so well chosen.

Letters with 'name and address withheld' also began to appear with tales of how 'this block of flats' or 'that housing estate' had improved beyond all recognition after just a single visit from those who were now being nicknamed 'the Vigilante Kings'.

One would have expected a spate of copycat attacks and there was some evidence that this was happening in isolated pockets but when arrests were made, the perpetrators were so amateurish and these were easily excluded from the main investigations.

Indeed, excitement levels were almost off the scale when a twenty-two year old was arrested for an attack on a well known paedophile in Lincoln.

Martha and her senior officers travelled to Lincoln Police Station en bloc, with an almost unseemly haste in order to make some sort of indentation in this impossible case by interviewing the man at the very earliest opportunity.

That it was a complete waste of time became evident in the first few moments. The man was half drunk and as the father of a four year old girl, was particularly disenchanted at having a 'kiddie fiddler' living within fifty yards of his house.

The attack on the man had been vicious, certainly, but was designed to make him 'just go and live somewhere else'.

Martha's sympathies were with the attacker and all her politically correct Bramshill training slipped, just a little, as she emerged disappointedly from the interview room.

"Sounds to me that the paedophile bastard got what he deserved." She wished she had curbed her tongue but she was unexpectedly seen in a somewhat better light by her less sensitive colleagues who were insufficiently politically correct to have attended Bramshill or even to have the dubious and forlorn hope of doing so.

The fruitless quest continued.

CHAPTER FOUR

It was decided. The house in Burton upon Stather was put on the market. This had necessitated a quick visit to Scunthorpe and on Oswald Road, Lucy had rapidly organised the sale through Bell and Watson, Estate Agents. She took advantage of the trip to visit parents and Jack and was back in Spain with Mel just seventy two hours later.

"Look," said Mel, "If we are selling up at Burton, I think we have funds a plenty and we should perhaps consider buying a villa out here. It would be more private and we *are* looking for a place to live for the rest of our lives. There are some very expensive properties with phenomenal views down the coast at Cabo Roig. We could either sell this flat or rent it out. What do you think?"

Much as she liked the flat in La Mata – as did they both - it did not have the 'ah factor' of the house in Burton and Lucy was unusually downhearted about selling a house she had learned to love. Mel understood, even though he had never spent a single night under its roof.

It was decided that they would try to buy a 'dream home' and would begin their search in and around Cabo Roig.

In just a few days with a phrasebook and a tape, Mel had become quite adept at some rather basic Spanish. Unlike most pupils in a comprehensive, Mel knew that languages could only be acquired with considerable effort on the part of the learner - or perhaps that was the point - the pupils *did* realise.

He put in six or seven solid hours per day and began to make connections to his 'O' Level French classes many years previously. He had taken advantage of Lucy's absence to put in some extra time and was beginning to feel quite pleased with himself.

He would have quite liked to have signed up to one of the multitudes of courses offering 'Beginners' Spanish' in the 'Costa Blanca News' and various 'give away' newspapers in the area, but knew that this could be potential folly.

Lucy was streets ahead in the Spanish learning. She had been working on the language quite intensively for a number of months and had been able to gain much advantage from having a degree in French with a subsidiary in German. The links between the various tongues kicked in and she began to experience a rush and remembered how much she had enjoyed her University degree course.

By the time Mel got under way, Lucy was already beyond 'A' Level in her efforts and was developing the language rapidly by reading novels; preparing them with pencil and dictionary. A typical novel took over forty hours for her to write in the unknown vocabulary. She would then read the book from cover to cover in just a couple of sittings.

British TV and even SKY and the sport channels were cheap and easy to achieve in La Mata and this proved an excellent link to home. Mel was glued to the news channels. Lucy preferred to tune into the Spanish stations as much as possible as she was determined to be genuinely fluent in Castillian in under six months. She set herself a variety of tasks in translation to and from Spanish and was able to offer considerable help to Mel in his more tortuous efforts to become proficient.

They began to visit all the local estate agencies and were unsurprised to learn how little Spanish was required for that particular exercise.

Lucy liked Cabo Roig immediately and thought that there were some of the best views along that coastline. Once again she and Mel were as one. They understood each other and seemed to want the same things.

They saw a goodly number of houses they definitely would have liked to buy but none was for sale. They enjoyed the search and travelled further afield, even going as much as fifteen miles inland but each time they returned to monitor the situation in Cabo Roig. They found the right houses in the wrong locations but no houses on offer in the right ones. It was slightly frustrating, admittedly, but they were not in any particular hurry.

As the weeks went by, there were no offers for the house in Burton and they thought they might struggle financially to buy in Cabo Roig without selling first. Although Lucy's Sheffield solicitor had now managed to have all of the 'deceased' Mel's money and goods put into her name, with three houses – one very expensive and yet to be purchased - ready access to funds was none too easy.

Life simply continued in La Mata and routines began to develop. They kept to Spanish times and even learned to have a winter *siesta* when not entirely necessary.

January was mild and drifted into a February which was crisp and cold in the early mornings but produced a series of mild, sunny days. Mel enjoyed frosty, English mornings but was glad to have escaped a winter which inevitably, would have been dark, dank and what he referred to as 'mucky weather'. Such days were not greatly missed.

When you can keep in touch with British sport, your favourite comedies and BBC documentaries, life has a slightly unreal feeling, particularly when located in the middle of a very foreign country.

There were a great many British, Dutch and Germans living in the vicinity but Lucy and Mel made a conscious decision to keep their distance from anybody with connections to the UK.

They began to make a few Spanish friends and Lucy was happy to chatter away to these and could feel her Spanish developing. Mel made some valiant attempts to keep up. The Spaniards were impressed as so few English people tend to make the effort. The gesture engendered a kind of respect.

Lucy began to fret that Church was not a part of their lives and disappeared many a Sunday morning to an English Church in Torrevieja, hidden away on the Calle Luis. It was a Pentecostal - Assemblies of God to be precise - and was well pastored by a broad-accented man from Leeds called Jessop and his delightful wife.

The congregations were older than Lucy was accustomed to but she found the slightly old fashioned type of services to be very lively, thought-provoking and very much to her personal taste.

Mel would have liked to have accompanied her but was not prepared to put himself into close proximity with English people. The risk was tiny but any risk was more than he was prepared to take.

For the first few weeks, Mel thought that he needed home contact and spent exorbitant amounts on English newspapers but eventually he began to rely more on the local papers designed for expats and when he finally managed to get set up and online, this need ebbed away and finally disappeared.

Mel had never been especially keen on Spanish reds, having always thought that Riojas were a little jammy in flavour but as he emptied the shelves of various supermarkets, he came to the conclusion that Spaniards very cunningly exported their plonk and kept the better quality wines for themselves.

When he decided to pay as much in a Spanish wine merchants as people tend to do for a bottle of plonk in England, he discovered that he was sampling wines of a very high quality indeed. He became very fond of the *tempranillo* grape. Even so it was a long time before he was able to root out any worthy whites. With the vast majority, he was distinctly unimpressed.

Days blended into days. March arrived and brought some beautiful weather along with it and several heavy rainstorms. April followed and a Spanish spring was decidedly inspiring.

Mel and Lucy enjoyed the remarkable sunrises, sunsets and each other.

The house in Burton had attracted little interest, mainly because of the hefty price tag which had not put off Mel and Lucy when they bought.

Towards the end of April they finally spotted a villa in Cabo Roig which met their requirements and which was sufficiently inexpensive that it would not necessitate their own house having to be sold first - or so they thought – although it would be a struggle.

The house had four bedrooms, four bathrooms, two balconies, a garage, plentiful parking space, a walled garden, an orchard, lawns, pool, solarium and a view to die for. This was it. Their offer was accepted. They now had six weeks under Spanish law to put the funds together.

Generally speaking, life was good.

CHAPTER FIVE

The dream was relaxed, slightly surreal and featured Jenny as she had been when four or five. It was strange that her face always seemed a little less clear as time went by, irrespective of whether he was thinking about her when awake or lost, dreaming about her.

The little girl gave him a giant hug and went off to play with a soft toy penguin and this disturbed him slightly as he knew that there had never been any such plaything. He knew he was dreaming - he usually did. Had he wanted to wake up he could have done so but he was enjoying this reverie; he was able to rejoice in the presence of his daughter, however unreal the situation.

If the penguin had troubled him, the doorbell did more so and as it rang a second time, he realised that it was real. He forced himself awake and noticed the clock was saying seven ten as he dragged himself across the room. He was rather surprised that Lucy had not woken up as the slightest thing usually tended to wake her.

He opened the door and was shoved back into the room and four *Guardias Civiles* in their bottle green uniforms knocked him to the floor. One knelt beside him and began to handcuff him behind his back and this was the point where he registered that two of the others were holding handguns and the third a sub machine gun.

The doorbell had not wakened Lucy but the noise of all this had and she glided into the room and stared unbelievingly at the scene where her husband was being dragged back to his feet. She echoed Mel in having nothing to say. What was there to be said? Her heart sank as she saw her life disintegrate before her eyes and her feelings of love towards her husband had never been so intense.

Mel had no similar feelings. He was stunned into a kind of numbness. He had grown so confident that their plan had worked that he had not even considered such a scenario. His mind could simply not get around the situation.

The first emotion to pierce this lack of feeling was a concern for Lucy. The terrible thought occurred to him that she was going to be arrested. After all, she was 'harbouring a fugitive' or whatever it was that they called it over here. He soon established that there was no interest in her and this eased his mind considerably. He then began to worry about her mental state as he felt that this was even worse for her than it was for him.

He was permitted to bring a few clothes and Lucy thrust a small Bible at him for which he was truly grateful.

In less than four minutes from answering the door he was in the back of a white Police car heading north along the N332. There were some excellent sea-views over to his right but they failed to register. They passed flocks of flamingos in the salt pools on both sides of the road but they only seemed to look mockingly in his direction or turn away in apparent disdain.

He correctly assumed that they were going to Alicante. At this point he felt that his Spanish was somewhat superior to GCSE standard and asked himself whether it was a better for him to answer questions in English only, or to let it be known that he spoke Spanish moderately well. This was something which he would ponder. Good tactics were always important. Jerry had always said so.

He was always staggered how superbly he seemed to cope at most times of crisis. He was well aware of the breakdown he had suffered following his last arrest but was quite certain that this would not be repeated.

The *Guardias* had not said a single word to him although they had spoken quietly and frequently amongst themselves. They treated him with a degree of respect. Once the arrest of 'a dangerous criminal' had been accomplished, they felt able to relax somewhat. As an act of kindness, when he showed some discomfort, they re-cuffed him with his hands in front. He was extremely grateful for this small mercy. He would speak in Spanish. It could do little harm. How could his situation possibly get any worse?

He could see more flocks of flamingos, single egrets and cormorants in the salt lakes either side of them as they cruised up the heavily used route. Alicante airport was then glimpsed, shortly after they had passed through a lengthy, well-lit tunnel.

They drove onwards and Alicante was not properly awake as they entered the normally bustling city. The trip across town to a rather grey-looking Police Station took only a matter of minutes.

He was unloaded and taken into a dark, silver-painted cell in the bowels of the building where he was given a cup of moderate coffee and several of the sponges called *bizcochos*. Normally, he was not too keen on these as they always seemed drier than dry but on this occasion he was pleased to get something into his stomach and to be honest, they really weren't all that bad.

Now he had more time to consider his situation, he realised that he would now spend the remainder of his life imprisoned. He would not bother to fight the inevitable request of the British Government for his extradition as there was nothing whatsoever to be gained. He decided that he would not even bother to take on an *abogado* to represent him in Spain. He knew he was heading for a Category 'A' prison and that was all there was to it.

He was able to reflect that, for the umpteenth time, he was facing an entirely new life and definitely not one of his choosing.

He wondered whether they would try to charge him with what had happened at Muckle Voe but thought that this was impossible - no doubt there would be some pretty intensive questioning about both that and how he had managed to escape. He had no intention of giving them any clues at all. The coaching which Jerry had given him about interviews was fresh in his mind and he would give them no help. He would not be facing charges and frankly, the less the authorities knew about him the better.

Prison for ever. Ah, the vicissitudes of life!

His next thought was the problem regarding the house in Cabo Roig. He was sure that there would be a hefty cost for pulling out of the deal. Lucy would have to engage good legal help. He was struck with the irony that she would have a lawyer for a civil matter and he, in his dire situation, would not have one at all.

Maybe she would be forced to carry on with the purchase. He supposed that she would now take the house in Burton off the market. But finances would be gravely stretched. Perhaps it would be possible as they had previously budgeted to buy without selling first. She could always sell up in La Mata? The flat wasn't worth a tremendous amount but it would probably be enough to keep her afloat into the foreseeable future. This accorded roughly with past planning.

He guessed correctly that the flat in La Mata would now be seen by her as 'tainted' following his arrest there. In this he showed how well he understood his better half.

He sat back against the cold, cell wall and found sufficient light to read his Bible. His original plan to study the whole of the Scriptures by reading a single chapter of The New Testament and three from The Old, on a daily basis, had succeeded - indeed he had exceeded the minimum on most days. He was now a member of that tiny band who had read The Bible in its entirety. He would not do that again. He would continue to study the single, New Testament chapter a day, in sequence, but he would now delve into various sections as and when they appealed or seemed particularly significant in his life.

For reasons not entirely clear, he returned to the story of the Prophet Jonah. He visited this quite frequently, as many sections of it appealed to him and he was always able to find relevance to his own situation. He had long since decided that he did not care for Jonah a great deal, he was one more Old Testament character who left rather a lot to be desired as a human being - and especially as a 'man of God'.

How could The Old Testament always be so honest about the negative characteristics of its heroes? - Adam, Abraham, Jacob, David and even Moses. They were all flawed, often deeply so, and The Bible just admitted it. What a testimony to its honesty and confidence in its own truth this was. Consider the disciples. It was just the same in the New. This was a point which struck him repeatedly and never lost its impact. So why wasn't he a Christian? - He could not put his finger on it at all.

* * *

He lay down on an agreeably hard bed and caught up with the sleep he had missed earlier in the day. He and Lucy had not gone to bed until about two and so he had only had about five hours. He was again perplexed that he was taking what was happening to him in such a philosophical manner. Sleep came easily but deep within his subconscious there had to have been some kind of an internal recognition of his troubles which had simply not surfaced. He dreamed long, difficult and claustrophobic dreams which no psychoanalyst would have had difficulties in interpreting. They recognised more than he could admit to himself, that he was trapped; caged like some zoo exhibit for the rest of his natural life. He had never been too keen on the principle of zoos and his subconscious now latched onto this inner reflection.

He was shouted awake by a Civil Guard, '*Oiga!*' and a smartly dressed visitor of about thirty-five was ushered into his cell accompanied by some senior Police Officer who introduced herself as Martha something or other.

The former was from the Embassy and the other headed some team or other investigating a series of crimes.

A bucket load of ideas ran through his brain. As soon as she opened her mouth he twigged that she was wondering if he had been part of the widely reported vigilante action which had had such a marked effect on life in some of the desperately crime-ridden parts of England. He was sure that she had to have flown out in anticipation of his arrest.

He was amused by the thought and asked her why he should bother talking to her.

The question clearly took her by surprise and she was unable to proffer any reason other than 'he might want to be helpful'.

Mel remembered Jerry's advice and snarled, "I have been kept imprisoned as an innocent man, shunted off to an island hell-hole and when I escape I am captured by these brutal Civil Guards and you expect *me* to help *you*?"

Thenceforth, he ignored her and turned purposefully towards the diplomat, or whatever he was, and asked him what was going to happen next.

"Well, it evidently seems you aren't denying who you are - but with DNA and fingerprints not much point I imagine - so HM's Government will request your extradition at the earliest opportunity. I expect they will transfer you to Madrid. That is often the way of these things until you have exhausted all your appeals."

"There will probably be no appeals," Mel said forcefully and noted that the visitors exchanged knowing and delighted glances. Having raised their hopes, he almost felt guilty about the sting in the tail. "I expect I shall have gained a bit more notoriety with the escape and I shall make you an offer."

Now both looked at him with undisguised concern. He was in control - and for one to whom such things customarily mattered little - he was rather enjoying it.

"I expect appeals would cost hundreds of thousands," he observed. "I want something and if you agree, I shall not fight the extradition. I am doomed to failure, whatever happens." He paused for effect then added, "I want five minutes with the Press, either here or in Madrid. Once my short interview is published in the various tabloids, I shall allow you to escort me to a plane home. I shall of course, be requiring Club Class," he added, tongue very much in cheek, "I expect it would not be the done thing back in Blighty, so we'll have to do it here," he said as if there was no doubt that it could and would happen. And like a salesman with his successful 'assumptive close', he received an uncomfortable promise that he would get what he was asking for.

Mel wondered if they had the authority to organise it and thought they probably had but somebody could well be in for a right bollocking somewhere down the line, at least until the circumstances of his obduracy were pointed out.

The diplomat was no fool. "We agree to the interview but you must announce in the opening sentence that you have been granted the interview only because you have waived your rights to appeal the extradition. I.... I mean we, do not want this biting back at us personally. Agreed?"

Mel assented and everybody was quite happy. Martha had been more concerned than her companion on the question of the interview and was pleased with him. He was quite handsome too.

The diplomat was more aware than Martha that extradition these days from Spain was not all that difficult and he would have faced considerably less fuss over the granting of the interview than she would. She wasn't bad-looking. He wondered if she might respond to an invitation later to dinner in the best restaurant Alicante could offer.

She would.

Mel promptly went back to sleep. He felt slightly ignorant in not wishing them a gracious farewell but he had a game to play through to whatever its conclusion turned out to be.

So he ignored their departure and simply turned his back. Rudeness went against the grain but he would not have to care.

He slept for three hours before being awakened and taken in the same car with his original escort to the airport where he was to be flown to Madrid.

Two of the same *Guardias* accompanied him, still heavily armed, and they were joined on a public flight by his two visitors from earlier who had been forced to change their evening arrangements to dine together, from Alicante, to what would now be in a tiny restaurant just off the *Puerta del Sol.*

They had both been booked into the *Internacional* and Martha wondered what the night would bring. Julian, as he was called, was to the forefront of her thoughts, Mel had almost been forgotten.

The journey took just over forty minutes and they were ushered through the customary checks and waiting areas with barely a pause.

A *Guardia Civil* vehicle was waiting at Barajas to transfer them to a conference room at the *Internacional* where the press conference had already been arranged.

"You'll be on for your meeting with the Fourth Estate in about ten minutes." Mel was taken aback by how fast the authorities could act if they felt they had to.

"You recall our agreement? - The first sentence....."

Mel nodded and tried to think what to say. He would keep it short and see if there were any questions.

He was escorted into the room on cue and was staggered to see at least seven sets of TV cameras and a minimum of sixty journalists. That he was big news was rather obvious. The BBC were represented – thank goodness!

He kept his promise to Julian and was somewhat smitten by his conscience as he stood before an audience of tens of millions and declared his innocence of all charges. He had learned from Jerry to use the word 'innocent' at least once in every utterance.

Once the questions began, it became clear why he was in so much demand. It was not him as a serial killer, nor as an escaper which had captured the imagination, but more accurately because he had fled Muckle Voe and this lifted him into the folk hero category.

He was asked his opinions on the 'vigilante action' and he said that as the father of a murdered child he fully understood the feelings involved but would prefer to comment no further.

Trivial questions in their dozens assailed him. Questions were screamed as desperate reporters tried to make a name for themselves above the din.

After twenty five minutes and a final expression of his innocence he asked for the meeting to be concluded.

The Civil Guards escorted him away and his last sighting of Martha and Julian left him in no doubt that 'Cupid's arrow' - or at least something like that - had struck. Years of teaching others had taught him how to read body language and these two were clearly deeply in lust with each other.

He was taken to Carabanchel Prison to the North of Madrid where he was given a room rather than a cell and was fed a quite excellent repast. He noticed that the door was lockable even so and he was informed that the infamous Francoist, Teniente-Coronel Tejero, had stayed in the same place after his involvement in the abortive coup of the 23rd of February, 1981.

Nobody had told him what was happening but a series of documents was brought and thrust in front of him for him to sign. They were all in Spanish so he read slowly and carefully before adding his signature. The papers were relinquishing his rights to fight the extradition.

Apparently, he would be flying to Manchester first thing in the morning. Speed. What he did not yet realise was that he would indeed be travelling the Iberia equivalent of 'Club Class'. It was apparently easier to maintain good security.

He slept well and felt optimistic, but not for any reason he could readily identify.

CHAPTER SIX

Lucy was in a bewildered state for several hours and was unable to function properly. She was actually suffering from a kind of mild shock.

Eventually, she dragged herself to her feet and made a strong coffee. It was probably not the best of decisions as her over-tense body really had no need of caffeine. On the plus side, it did give her a mental boost but at the expense of the whole of her body beginning a slight tremble which was to continue for the rest of the day.

She could not force her mind to address the problem of the three houses; that was something which would have to be put on hold.

She tried to think about how Mel would be feeling; everything had been working so perfectly - only to be destroyed without warning.

It was so like a bereavement.

She began to wonder how they had been tracked down but surely, neither of them would be able to find that out. All she could conclude was that somebody must have spotted Mel and recognised him. He *had* been a teacher, there must have been hundreds, possibly thousands of former pupils - and what about all those parents who would have known him too? Whoever had sighted him had clearly thought they were doing their social duty. She would have wagered that their excitement would be more than cancelled out by Mel's gloom.

Prayer. What else could she do? She attempted to establish contact with her Lord and could not. Strange how close God could be at so many times and yet now it was as if He wasn't there at all.

She analysed the situation and the stumbling block was easily recognised. She was resentful. She felt that God should not have let this happen and her irritation with Him simply created a barrier she could not circumvent. Where was the comfort?

She knew what she had to do; repent, but was not yet prepared to do so. She was punishing God for messing up her life. At the same time as she entertained these negative feelings, she knew deep inside her that *she* was the one who was wrong and the relationship between her and God would be put on hold until she sorted herself out. She was unreasonably angry that there were so many more spiritual Christians out there who would be able to cope with the situation better than she. What use was it having God in your corner if you were too stupid to access His help, love and succour in a time of genuine crisis?

She was also angry that she was thinking about her own situation when it was so much worse for Mel.

She idly turned on TVE and the arrest was being reported excitedly by a breathless, brunette with absurd blonde highlights, whose Spanish was only slightly faster than the normally registered speed of sound.

It would only be a matter of time before it was picked up on the English speaking channels and sure enough, it was considered worthy of a newsflash on BBC One - the second time Mel had been the cause of one such.

The information was sketchy:

Reports are coming in that the multiple murderer, Melvin Roberts, has been arrested near Alicante following a joint operation by Spanish and British Police. Roberts was thought to have died in the Muckle Voe disaster, so his re-appearance is something of a shock to the authorities.

Our sources inform us that Police are awaiting the opportunity to interview him about possible connections to the so-called 'Vigilante Kings'.

We are told that extradition proceedings will begin immediately.

We expect to have more information on this matter presently, so stay tuned in order to receive updates on our regular news bulletins.

Lucy sighed. Links to the 'Vigilante Kings' were not something she had been anticipating but to be brutally candid, it simply did not matter, however wrong or irrelevant.

She would have to try to see Mel but did not know how this could be accomplished. His arrest had been by Civil Guards so that was different to the ordinary Police. She was not sure what their precise function was but made a rather vague comparison to the French *Gendarmerie* and was no better off for having done so.

And where was he, anyway? Alicante? Valencia was probable. They would eventually take him to the capital she supposed.

Her mobile rang unexpectedly. A Julian Tremlett wanted to know if he was speaking to a Mrs. Roberts. It was no secret so she shed her commonly used maiden name and agreed that it was she.

He told her what had happened and that Mel was to be transferred to Madrid that very day. He could tell her little but promised to keep her informed. She asked if there was any point in her travelling to Madrid and he told her to let the dust settle over a day or two and he would get back to her at the appropriate time or within forty eight hours at the latest.

Lucy had another coffee as she could think of nothing else to do. It was not the best idea she had had. It suddenly occurred to her that her parents would be stunned and she hoped she would able to ring and explain before the news began to seep through to them. The shock would be considerable as they had been to Mel's funeral - or memorial - to be strictly correct. She needed to ring George and Jerry. Jack would also want to know the details. It could all be a little embarrassing, she thought, but as it turned out, everybody was kind but there was no answer when she called Brenda and Jerry.

She left the TV news on all day and the only thing of interest was that there was apparently going to be a press conference from Madrid in the evening. At this point she did not realise that this would be a televised interview with Mel but once she had switched to a twenty-four hour news channel, this point was made and she got excited.

She rang everybody again to update them of this development but still remained unable to contact Jerry and Brenda. She had had the feeling that something was badly wrong when she had last seen Brenda but was unable to put her finger on what precisely.

When Mel came on, he stood easily in front of a bevy of microphones with Civil Guards proudly in evidence behind him. He looked confident, spoke clearly and persistently affirmed his innocence. She thought he had been persuasive and then felt guilty as she was rooting for him to succeed in an outright lie. He was just doing as Jerry had said but this did not ease her conscience.

She learned that Mel was returning to the UK which helped her put together her own plans. She would return to Burton upon Stather for a fortnight while she established what was going on. She would need to check out their financial situation very carefully - she was actually quite keen to go through with the purchase in Cabo Roig. It was La Mata she preferred to lose. The house in Burton would have to come off the market.

She needed to establish what their joint finances amounted to. It was not that they were not extremely well off but that they were going to end up having too much tied up in property. The house in Burton was very much at the expensive end of the local market and the Cabo Roig venture was even more costly.

She booked an expensive flight, by *Easy Jet* standards at least, to East Midlands the following day as there was nothing on offer to Robin Hood.

She began her packing with a heavy heart and for the first time really began to empathise with her husband's plight.

Her first task, after a much needed lie-in the next day, was to check through all of their finances. It was convenient that she now owned everything – or did she, with Mel being found alive? - but she was able to work out precise figures online in less than twenty minutes. Efficient.

She was surprised to learn that if she kept all three houses, she was still able to pick up twenty six thousand pounds a year net after paying tax on investments. There was simply no cause for concern and this made her determine to continue with the purchase in Cabo Roig even though the villa was far too big for just one person. The place was just so perfect. She accepted that she was going to be a very lonely lady.

She felt a need to plan for the life ahead and decided immediately that she would buy a cheap flight to the UK every month from Spain and would spend about a week in Burton coinciding with visits to see Mel.

In England she would drive over to Sheffield on the Sunday to put flowers on Jenny's grave for Mel and then she would visit George and would be able to go to the Church in Sheffield.

Maintenance of two large houses would be a nightmare. It was a must to sell the flat in La Mata. Coping with two oversized dwellings would take effort but to add the flat to that was just too much. Was she being sensible taking this route? Probably not and it was hardly an arrangement she could keep into old age - Mel's prospects of a release in under thirty five years were less than slim. She sighed.

On the day she had flown to East Midlands it had been a nightmare finding her way from there to Burton. By the time she arrived, Mel was already ensconced in Manchester Prison becoming accustomed to their rather strange ways and as yet unaware that Wakefield was to be his final destination.

By the time that Julian Tremlett rang her mobile for a second time, she was in Burton and Mel had arrived back in Yorkshire experiencing the highest level of security he had yet encountered.

CHAPTER SEVEN

Mel never found difficulty with routine and by the time he had been banged up in Wakefield for a week he had become accustomed to the regime. It was well run and consequently more difficult for exceptionally aggressive prisoners to impose their will on weaker inmates here and although he knew that his reputation would precede him and protect him to a certain extent, he felt that this would not have been overly necessary in any case.

He settled down in the many hours he spent alone in his single cell to meditate on his situation.

Was he being castigated by God for past sins, even if he was not quite sure which of the things he had done classed as such - or maybe was he being punished for not accepting God when he knew that God was real?

This did not ring true. Generally, it was clear that God only entered ones life on invitation but did this not mean that people who talk of 'God's plan for their lives' had a problem?

What he did not realise was that he was stumbling into the theological, minefield of debate between the Calvinists and the Arminians. It was food for thought even if he had been unable to recognise one of the most divisive debates in Christendom for what it was and his thought patterns in this area supplemented his extensive studies of the Scriptures.

He was eventually able to ring Lucy and was grateful to be able to update her on much of what had happened and she the same. There was only five minutes allowed him and he was yet to work out how the phone-card system would work out for him.

He had rung the home number and was unsurprised that she had returned to Burton. He agreed with her that she should sell up in La Mata and tried to tell her how to arrange her first visit to Wakefield.

The five minutes disappeared in what seemed less than two and he was upset that he had had no chance to say something loving to her but he did give a clue that their conversation might well be monitored, so she would do well not to say anything to incriminate herself.

She had wanted to tell him that in the last few days, there had been a real upsurge in the actions of the 'Vigilante Kings' or the 'Veekays' as they were known by the criminal classes who might have been targeted by them.

Durham, York and Huntingdon had seen the hangings of two murderous, drug-dealer kingpins in addition to that of a violent, multiple rapist whose court case had collapsed due to his family of 'travellers' having successfully and quietly intimidated both witnesses and jurors, and in the one case, by burning a potential witness to death in his maisonette. Hands tied by political correctness, the detectives on the case had been unable to investigate properly; shackled by their own senior officers who in their turn were answerable to The Home Office.

Beatings by hooded men had taken place in about a dozen venues.

A Police Superintendent in Hull had broken ranks to tell the 'Hull Daily Mail' that crime was plummeting throughout the Humberside Region and reports had reached him that this was the case in every Police Force.

Once this news came out, it was grasped happily by all the original, tabloid newspapers and thrust tauntingly into the faces of all liberal-minded politicians. 'The Guardian' was of course an exception as it lamented the downward spiral in society, conveniently forgetting how its own 'liberalism' had contributed to allowing the criminal classes to terrorise decent people as a number of commentators of a more rightwing persuasion were not slow to point out.

The rest of the 'quality press', as they liked to call themselves, expressed ambivalent attitudes and the new PM was required to issue a statement saying that 'crime had fallen but only slightly' and this was 'entirely due to the new initiatives brought in by his government'.

Lucy was not one to adopt *schadenfreude* as a general rule, but in this situation she was prepared to make an exception. She enjoyed the newspapers as well as the discomfiture of the 'liberals on crime' and their political allies and then promptly felt a sense of guilt about it.

Mel remained well informed and in his rather limited contacts with other inmates, was able to detect tangible fear in their attitudes and discussions. It had not escaped their attention that the 'Veekays' had often targeted those who had been released from prison if it seemed they had been under-sentenced. Some were less happy than usual to be applying for parole as the 'what if' factor kicked in.

Mel was delighted to hear it often stated by fellow prisoners that they would 'genuinely give up crime' if and when released. Nobody seemed to be aware that he was being linked to the 'Veekays' or maybe they were too frightened of him. Certainly, everybody including officers seemed rather kind.

That 'element of fear' had been excised from the social structure. Now the 'parallel justice system' had reintroduced the principle which had been steadily eroded over half a century and the effects were clear to see.

Letters Pages were filled with the delighted crowings of people whose lives, once blighted by crime, were now beginning to enjoy a proper existence once more.

The 'liberals' who wrote in to condemn 'this descent into the law of the jungle' whilst demonstrating apoplectic rage, were roundly trounced by regular contributors to their columns. On Local Radio phone-in programmes, many declarations of pleasure that the criminals, for once, were on the back foot were made by countless happy callers who were often insulted by less than even-handed broadcasters.

Those writers about the 'Veekays' divided all too clearly into 'pro' and 'anti' camps. Mel, with regard to the crimes for which he had been convicted, was mentioned as a 'paragon of all human virtues' in several letters where the writers incorrectly assumed links with the secret organisation. Letters 'voicing reason', stating that 'all of this was only happening as successive governments had abandoned justice thereby creating an undesirable but nonetheless inevitable set of consequences', were sadly rare and Mel was quick to deplore that absence. In a properly ordered society, vigilanteism was anathema to him.

He was truly unhappy that a society should have to be based on vigilante-type principles. It was ironic, he knew, but he was ever clear in his own mind that any nation should be run under 'the rule of Law' but also recognised that once there was a breakdown in will from on high to execute its responsibilities, there would be consequences not unlike what was currently happening. He was hopeful that the new government would realise what was taking place and act to cancel out half a century's social decay prompted by the shedding of such responsibilities by a dozen governments of assorted hue.

The amount of damage done by what he preferred to call 'false liberalism' was inestimable and he was under no illusions that all of the lost ground could be recaptured. He knew it simply could not.

Poor parenting skills, a weak Church, couch potato attitudes, the moral neutrality of broadcasting and the media were all issues which had to be addressed too. Looking at this new government, he doubted that they possessed the moral fibre to take on the task but it would be acceptable if they just started a movement away from political correct thinking and began the move towards the shared, social goals of bygone eras without the jargon of words such as: 'inclusivity' or 'multicultural'. Decent social behaviour towards people different to yourself in attitudes, race, religion or background could never be achieved by either jargon or legislation.

'Loving your neighbour' was the real answer. So simple. One more to God! There was just no good reason to pigeon-hole all poor human behaviour into politically-defined categories.

He could imagine how hypocritical he would be considered by many of these destructive people but did not really care. He was happy enough with his own logic provided that it still met scriptural criteria which, for some reason, were of vital importance. Part of this was because he respected his wife's faith but his own thoughts on this had pre-dated Lucy. It was an integral part of both his psyche and his inherent, personal honesty.

That night he suffered bad dreams but was unable to recall them the following morning. The only memory he was able to retrieve was a vague remembrance of something based on his concern for Lucy and even then, this was in bit of a vacuum. He knew he felt he had let her down and even began to think that he might encourage her to divorce him as he supposed she would then be free to rebuild her life and find somebody new. The dream had merged with reality.

In his heart of hearts he realised that she would be horrified by the proposal - or anti-proposal, as he supposed it was. She was the very epitome of loyalty and would be hurt. He still felt obliged to make her the offer - it was the only fair thing to do.

CHAPTER EIGHT

"The Assistant Governor wants to see you, Roberts," said a buxom, female officer with a lesbian haircut. He wondered if she was a lesbian and then decided that it was none of his business.

He tried to guess what this would be about and was unable to do so. Still, it made a change and he was certain that he was going to derive pleasure from the meeting. He was slightly concerned that he was enjoying being the centre of attention a little too much in some of these set-piece scenarios.

He was ushered into the actual Governor's office. The man himself was away on a conference, learning how to become more efficient. Had Mel known this, he would have been correct in guessing that 'efficient' was a euphemism for politically correct. He had seen it all before in the teaching profession and the stories of such like, received from friends in the Civil Service, could curl hair at forty paces.

"Ah. Martha. I had rather been expecting you," he lied as he spotted the genuinely attractive but otherwise unimpressive Detective Superintendent who was accompanied by a Detective Constable who had the kind of face which looked as if it had been carved out of a particularly unyielding granite. 'I'll bet he's a tough one,' thought Mel.

She had been singularly unsuccessful in their previous chats and he opined that he had won 'by technical knockout' rather than just 'on points'. This man was an ageing DC who looked as if he had seen it all.

"So who's your friend?" he asked.

"I'm DC Gordon," said the ready hewn piece of rock with more than a tinge of menace.

Mel had a huge advantage. When should he use it? There was no saying how it would all break so he sat back, thought of Henry Wilt and decided that real life might still have its compensations.

"What can I do to help you? You can help me of course by obtaining the release of this innocent man." He was growing in confidence.

Should he use his weapon at all? Should the Americans have 'nuked' Hiroshima and Nagasaki? If you are 'on the ropes', to continue the boxing imagery, he thought, do you not use whatever is at your disposal? Like President Truman must have felt, he decided that he would hate himself in the morning but it just had to be done. He was in a war, and in a war there would be casualties and politically correct, Bramshill appointees were fair game. Cannon fodder even. She had not even spotted that she was at risk. 'Fish in a barrel' as the Americans would say.

"I trust your hotel was comfortable in Madrid," he said suddenly and Martha did not move by as much as a quarter of an inch but her face reddened and the tension was tangible. - Ah. He *was* right. Bullseye!

'El momento de verdad', the moment of truth as the Spanish matadors would call it. He raised his metaphorical *estoque* and drove it forcefully downwards, seeking a heart in which to plunge it.

"I trust Julian Tremlett also found the accommodation to his liking?" said Mel and put emphasis on the word 'also' and wondered whether it should have gone onto the 'his'. He need not have been concerned.

The apprehension was like a thick curtain as Martha twitched in embarrassment. Mel looked up and gave a sweet, disingenuous smile.

"It was fine. Thank you," she managed to stutter but the damage was already done. That half second of hesitation was picked up on like a ferret grabbing the throat of a rabbit which had already yielded to its inevitable fate. DC Gordon had spent a career picking up the tiny inflections of a voice and of course, those minute giveaways from body language.

He grasped the situation in its entirety and instantly knew he would have a really interesting topic to bring up in the canteen over many a lunch. He was an excellent and efficient officer in more than just his own mind and had gone too long unpromoted to concern himself with any possible fallout in his own direction and besides, opportunities of this magnitude were too infrequent to be missed. Mel detected the ghost of a smile crease his lips.

It was clear to Mel that he had left one of his interviewers dead in the water and so he decided to stonewall the other.

At this point, there was a little bit of fuss at the door of the office and Mel's much-loved solicitor, Mr. Dawkins appeared, as if on cue.

To be honest, Mel was impressed with this amazing efficiency but it was the purest of coincidence that he had turned up at the prison with such perfect timing, as it were, and had been told by an officer "Your client is being seen by the Police, now." The officer had reasonably assumed that Mel knew about the visit and was expecting to be represented.

It is just *so* agreeable in life when circumstances work out well for no reason other than the possible intervention of fate. Mel was thoroughly enjoying himself and took Dawkins to one side to explain that he was in command of the situation and all he needed was for him to sit there and glower at the officers. He suggested cruelly that Mr Dawkins should peer into Martha's face and give an occasional knowing smile and hint of a nod. He decided not to allow Dawkins into his little secret but to be fair, the man played his role rather well and Martha began to disintegrate and give desperate glances towards the exit.

"Over to you," she said to DC Gordon and it was about as much as she could manage.

Mel hoped that his targeting of such a victim would not be seen as sexist by her in any way. He had no problems whatsoever with women in positions of authority, at least not if this had been achieved on merit, but then he realised again that he should not care how such people perceived him.

He firmly believed that it was individuals like this one who worked to the politically correct agendas set by the 'Champagne socialists' and members of the 'chattering classes' thereby causing immense social harm.

He looked at her and remembered how few Police disagree with The

Death Penalty and just knew that she would be one of those few exceptions.

He did not doubt that she was a very nice lady but he despised her type and when you added the 'vaulting ambition' she clearly possessed, all he could think was: 'It is people like her who are responsible for what happened to Jenny. I blame them even more than I blame Malone.' Equally, what Marner had done to Larry may well be one more to lay at the door of people just like her. His assessments were unerringly accurate.

He naturally recognised that it was possible that both of these foul murders may still have happened even with the possibility of the guilty parties dying on the end of a rope but statistics showed that the risk would have been reduced by some eighty per cent. He had managed to lay hands on Home Office figures some years before and knew how homicide stats had been massaged in a blatant exercise in damage limitation.

He was quite aware, having read the figures in 'The Sunday Times' that in the first year following the abolition of Capital Punishment, the rate for what had then been Capital Murder under the definitions of the 1957 Homicide Act, had seen such slayings increase by 127%. This was deemed 'so successful' by abolitionists they had managed to have the ultimate penalty killed off before the end of the so-called 'experimental period' of five years and the homicide rate had climbed dramatically further, even though figures had been concealed to a small degree by an increased willingness of courts to bring in manslaughter verdicts. Mel was angry. This was why people had to create their own justice, was it not?

The effects of superior medical treatment had surely helped the astronomically high figures from going even higher as more people were managing to survive murderous assaults.

He found it interesting how the figures were published. For many years they had not dared to release them to the public at all and today, they were always played down.

All that hype about Hanratty being 'innocent'? Utter tosh and latterly proved untrue through forensics but nonetheless, cynically manipulated so that some might worry about 'the dangers of hanging an innocent man'. This scenario became less and less likely year on year with the developments of science, so he wanted to know why they could not introduce a 'double verdict' in capital trials if this were a genuine fear?

Still. His despised EU and the so-called Human Rights Legislation would even prevent the people of the UK having a democratic say on the matter in a referendum. Disgraceful.

'Guilty beyond reasonable doubt' as before but a second verdict in such cases would then be required to become capital: 'Beyond *any* doubt'. That should satisfy the worriers - but for most abolitionists, it was not a worry - just a weapon to point at the undecided. *They* found it unsavoury so everybody else had to dance to their tune. Let democracy go hang - because violent killers most assuredly would not.

Besides, why was it okay to worry that somebody innocent might be executed every decade or so but not worry about the thousands - possibly as many as fifteen thousand - extra murder victims since 1965 who by all normal definitions, had to be innocent *all* the time? Whatever happened to balanced thinking?

He realised that today, this was somewhat complicated by what everybody seemed to now be calling 'parallel justice'. The expression was used freely and without irony throughout the prison.

"First of all, we want to know how you escaped from Muckle Voe ," said Gordon abruptly.

"Oh dear. I expect you will be wanting to charge me with escape from lawful custody", said Mel. "This is all very worrying. Just think what that could add to my sentence."

Dawkins smirked at both officers in an exceedingly unpleasant fashion and Mel felt he had scored a second point.

"No. Why should I tell you anything at all?" - It was difficult to see why he should cooperate and both realised that Mel was very much in the driving seat. Again.

"Have we anything to *offer* you?" asked DC Gordon in a most reasonable tone.

"I shall not discuss my escape but I shall tell you everything I know about the 'Vigilante Kings' in exchange for one piece of information," he offered.

"Try us," said Gordon betraying a certain excitement as Martha attempted to keep an extremely low profile.

"I want to know, out of simple interest, how you caught me," he declared.

"You were recognised by somebody who had once worked with you. A woman by the name of Muriel Travers. She was staying in La Mata and passed on the info. She said she recognised you straight away."

"Muriel. Really?" and Martha gave Gordon a sour look for 'putting a witness at risk of harm' but DC Gordon knew better.

"Strange, that. I can't have seen her since she did not return from maternity leave about twelve years ago. And I had changed appearance. It just all goes to show," he stated rather aimlessly. Picking up on Martha's anxiety he added, "Don't worry. I am not a vengeful man. I wish her no harm, she is a super lady and an inspirational Physics teacher. I bear no grudges against people of *integrity*."

"Well," said Gordon, "There we have it. Tell us what you know about the 'Veekays', please."

"I shall," said Mel, "but you won't like it one jot." He paused for effect then added, "I have no connection or knowledge of that group nor have I ever had any link with them. That is the God's honest truth." He waited before reiterating his innocence which was rather less truthful.

His guests stared in disbelief and walked out of his life, hopefully forever.

"Nice," said Dawkins, remembering Mel as a one time gibbering wreck.

"I think that we shall aim to get a second appeal. You never just know."

"I can hardly disagree with you," said Mel. "I am in a desperate situation and really don't know what else I can do."

"So. How did you escape from the island? It has been exciting my curiosity," asked the weasel-like advocate.

"Simple really. I hitched a ride on one of the rescue helicopters. Nothing more to it than that. I saw an opportunity and took it," Mel replied. "It was a truly terrible night but I couldn't let a chance go begging. Please tell nobody!"

Mel was beginning to impress his lawyer who went on to explain the channels he would have to go through and how it was 'quite a long shot'.

"Your publicity was a good thing. A very good thing. What we now have to do is to use your fame to persuade a TV company to make a programme which will prove you were given a really raw deal at trial. You had suffered a breakdown and who gave you credit for that? Did the judge even mention it in his summing up? This is the *real* you not that person who perhaps appeared insensitive to the jury - that was because of your illness. No promises, but it's definitely worth a spin, I think."

"Please go for it," said Mel, "I really hate being away from my wife. She does not deserve this."

Dawkins departed with a purposeful step and a new project to occupy his over-active brain. The chances were not good but perhaps the recent publicity might just produce the desired result. It would certainly be the largest ever feather in his cap were he able to get Mel released. Why! There might even be a book in it for him. It would need to be a very good deal indeed from a publishing house as The Law Society might take an extremely dim view of such a course of self-aggrandising action particularly if he were to betray any trust with a client.

It may well not work but he would take some initial soundings on the basis that there was always a small chance Mel would be released and it would be a shame if he failed to cash in.

He wondered if Max Clifford would be able to offer advice.

CHAPTER NINE

Mel's dreams were often quite devastating nightmares which left him feeling breathless, exhausted and frightened. It could often take several hours into a morning to shake off their effects.

So close to each other were they, he and his much better half, that Mel was not surprised when Lucy told him that she too was suffering similar nights of misery. They were intended to be together; it was their destiny - one which had been savagely interrupted.

Now that he was able to purchase phone-cards, it was a relief to be able to have occasional short chats with his beloved. He explained about the attempt to get the second appeal but would not suggest a possible divorce until he could see her face to face and it seemed that this would be at least a ten day wait.

He meditated for many hours a day and could easily have turned into a serious philosopher as he exercised his mind around some of the great conundrums of humankind. Perhaps he could do a degree in either Theology or Philosophy?

He was pleasantly surprised to find how often The Bible, which he now knew exceptionally well, could come up with solutions to just about everything. Impressive. Now he could understand how there were philosophers such as Kierkegard who had some basis in Christian belief - however unrecognisable that sometimes appeared to be as it emerged and evolved.

Inevitably, he turned and returned to his own actions. He had personally killed one hundred and seventeen people. Was this God's will? - Probably not, but was it part of 'His *permissive* will'? That was not an issue he had covered before. Old Testament Prophets were encouraged by God to kill or at least encourage killing in certain circumstances. But those circumstances tended to be based on the destruction of pure, idolatrous religions with an unhealthy penchant towards the regular sacrifice of infants and young children. He had seen archaeological photos of the earthenware jars in which the pathetic bodies of butchered children had been stored. Purest evil.

Certainly, he was unable to accept that what he had done was fundamentally sinful - with the exception of course, of the killing of Malone as an act of the purest vengeance and hatred. He was prepared to repent that as he was convinced that he had been wrong. The rest? - No. Was there any point in repenting anyway if he was seemingly unprepared to embark on any kind of a relationship with God? Repentance could only have an intrinsic value when seen in a God-based context. Was that not right? Could it exist *in vacuo*? - If that were the case, it was going to be a purely introspective line to follow. Could it have any greater value than say, psychotherapy?

Did he have a conscience, social or personal, that he had taken the lives of all these individuals? - He could only conclude that, as society was a substantially better place without these dregs - then no. But had they been denied their opportunity to repent? Had he committed the ultimate sin of 'playing God', himself? Had he acted with integrity? Was he being unfair to his wife by failing to commit to God as she had? Was this damaging their relationship? What would a Christian make of the idea of divorce?

His conscience was definitely clear as far as the killings were concerned. He was literally more troubled by the self-protecting lies he had found himself forced to tell and the way he had deprived his wife of a second husband.

He wondered on occasions, how the trio of Christians from Muckle Voe were progressing. He missed the times they had spent together. He hoped they had all been shipped to the same prison. These were men of genuine repentance and he held them all in the greatest of respect. What would they make of him if they knew the full story? What would Brian think? It mattered to him. These were questions he had asked himself many times.

He realised that he would never be able to tell the full story of what he had done to anybody. He needed to keep his own counsel and he thought he could achieve this. His bad dreams were more as a result of the physical distance between him and Lucy rather than any deep-seated, unresolved feelings of guilt which was what any passing trick cyclist would have surely suggested to him. No. That was not it.

No hour went by without thoughts of his daughter; the age she would be now, what year group she would have been in, how she would have developed as a person, if she would have a had a boyfriend. He had to admit that if she had lived, so would his wife - he could hardly bear to mention her name. They would have been divorced by now.

That begged a question about him and Lucy. Would they ever have even met? Or was their love something ordained by the hand of fate - or by God?

Somehow, he thought that life was just too random to have had quite that much influence from outside sources. God basically allowed people to just get on with their lives, didn't He? So perhaps this meant that *some* good had emerged from Jenny's death.

He considered the large number of seriously violent people who were no more - that had been a plus point. He thought of Lucy and realised she was the equal best thing that had ever happened to him in his entire life - that too was a plus but there were no others.

It said in Romans Chapter Eight that 'all things work together for good for those who love God'. Some statement. It was perhaps the hardest thing in the whole of the Scriptures for him to believe. But why should it apply to him anyway? - He only *respected* God. He had made no commitment. The 'love' aspect was absent. Would it always be? He could not be sure. He was not sure he wanted God at all even though he recognised that he did *need* Him.

The one thing which seemed possible was that he would perhaps drift into being a Christian. Can people do that? Could he really become 'saved' on the back of his wife's faith? - He sincerely doubted that too.

He was looking into the possibility of setting up a Bible Study group as he had done before. The success of his previous venture as a non believer - no, that was wrong - as a non Christian - better - had quite startled him.

Was he being used by God in that? - Clearly. But he could not work out the principle behind it. This made little sense to him but his outreach had been real and had produced tangible, spiritual results. Odd.

He really would have to take on some serious study of Theology. What if he were to win an appeal? Perhaps he could join the Anglican Ministry, after all, they didn't seem to mind whether you were a Christian or not. Indeed, did you even have to have any belief in God?

No. That was not on. Surely, it had to be all or nothing. How could you be a spiritual advisor not being a believer? The irony of his group on Muckle Voe struck him forcibly.

"God really must move in mysterious ways," he mused.

CHAPTER TEN

Lucy was at home in Burton upon Stather that same evening having just learned from a neighbour that the word 'stather' was of Anglo-Saxon origin and meant 'jetty'. She knew that a little further down the Trent was Flixborough Stather, also. She had met the word 'staithe' before and correctly assumed there to be a linguistic link. Mel already knew this but he had not remembered to tell her.

The phone rang and she was both astonished and delighted to hear Brenda on the other end of the line although she had been hoping that Mel had sufficient phone credit to have called.

"I must see you as a matter of extreme urgency. Tomorrow, meet me in Sheffield in the main car park at The Northern General Hospital, off Barnsley Road. A quarter to ten. You *will* be there?" she asked anxiously.

"Of course, if it's that critical. Yes," and Lucy did not want to pursue the conversation any further. Brenda's tone of voice was not something to be ignored and questions were inappropriate as she had clearly not wanted to volunteer any information.

"Please don't be late. Early is okay. This is of *great* importance. Dress smartly. Goodbye."

Receiving a phone call from a friend of this type is guaranteed to make the mind race. Why hospital grounds? Why smart? Why could she not be told? Why had Brenda and Jerry been so out of touch? All there had been was the briefest of meetings with a Brenda rushing to get away at the fake Memorial. What of Jerry?

Lucy did not know what to think. Nothing made sense as far as she could gauge it all.

All of a sudden, she remembered Jerry's promise to ensure that Mel would not stay in prison. It was not something she had thought about in a very long time. Jerry and Brenda having disappeared from their lives, well hers anyway, had meant that this had eventually withered away as a hope.

No. That could not be it because it was only Brenda she was meeting and she had not mentioned Jerry at all. She gave up and rang her hairdresser to cancel the appointment she had booked for the following morning.

Her curiosity had been piqued and Brenda's serious tone had made her believe that there was no good to come out of this. Smart? - Who was she meeting whom she had to impress? Or was it that they were going on somewhere else and Brenda did not want Lucy to look or feel out of place. Why else was 'smart' of importance?

In the end, she forced herself to stop thinking about it and watched some appalling television in order to take her mind off a mystery which could not be solved. Why bother? All would no doubt be revealed on the morrow.

* * *

Lucy set off very early indeed as she knew that parking could be a nightmare near The Northern General. In the end she found a side road off the Barnsley Road where she left her vehicle with no small amount of trepidation. Perhaps she should have attempted to use the hospital car parking. No matter. She secured her car and double checked it before crossing the busy road and heading towards where she was due to meet Brenda.

It was only twenty-five to ten but Brenda was already awaiting her arrival. I shan't bother to explain. We are going to a meeting. Here's a note pad and biro. I promise you that you will want to take notes. There is a great deal happening today and you will not want to miss anything out at all when you see Mel."

They entered that maze which is a modern hospital and Brenda walked off at so brisk a pace that Lucy was hard pressed to keep up with her.

They ascended several sets of stairs and Lucy had soon lost all sense of where she was and all sense of general direction.

"If we get there for five to ten you can have five minutes with Jerry beforehand," she said.

Lucy began to be extremely worried about Jerry. Surely, he wasn't a patient? Was he? She began to remember previous hospital appointments he had spoken of. What of that nasty cough he had been unable to shake?

She now suspected the horrible truth and as they swept past a sign marked 'Oncology' her worst fears were confirmed.

Brenda ushered her into a large, single ward where Jerry lay on the bed with a sallow complexion. He had always looked thin but never like this. He was linked up to several drips but gave a big, beaming smile as she entered and she almost ran across in order to give him a hug. She did so rather tentatively but he embraced her warmly.

"Sorry to do this to you. We have kept this all a secret from you as we thought you both had quite enough on your plates," he gasped, although his voice was reasonably firm and distinctly audible. "It's lung cancer, I'm afraid. I just wanted to see you before the meeting and tell you personally," he smiled again; "I keep my promises."

"Okay, wheel them all in!" he shouted as best he could.

A side door opened and in trouped a succession of well-dressed individuals apart from a pair of gentlemen wearing extremely scruffy suits. In all, there must have been about fifteen people crammed into the ward.

Jerry was undoubtedly the centre of attention and Lucy wondered if any of the others knew what was going on.

"I insisted on seeing Mrs Roberts first, in order to offer her my sincerest apologies," he began and looked around before speaking again. Lucy was confused but the germ of an idea was beginning to form in her mind.

"I have invited The Chief Constable - my boss, Judge Clayton, Mr.Dawkins, the solicitor of Melvin Roberts" - Lucy spotted him for the first time, "and we have reporters from local and national press. Now, I have here an affidavit which will underline what I am going to say to you all and you will all be allowed to see a copy at the end. Now the bombshell. Melvin Roberts has been wrongly imprisoned. I killed all the six people he was accused of murdering and it was also me who beat the living crap out of that scumbag Toby Meredith on the Manor.

I placed the weapons under the shed next door and relied on the efficiency of my colleague DC Calver to find them. She did not require much prompting. I am not sorry for anything I have done with the exception of what I did to Mr. and Mrs. Roberts. In my defence, I hoped it would not be for too long a time as I have known about the lung cancer for some considerable period. I am not expected to last the week so that is why I have invited you all. I doubt that you will be able to justify arresting me," he said smilingly to The Chief Constable who was looking aghast, strangely pale and totally devastated. "My wife was informed of all this a week ago in order to arrange this meeting; to coerce important people and the gentlemen of the Press to attend. She also brought in my solicitor to help work on the affidavit. I expect the Police Force to honour her widow's pension. She has done nothing wrong." He looked witheringly again at his boss who stuttered: "I'll see if that can be arranged."

"Thank you. I would not have made this declaration if I thought she would be damaged," his voice began to break.

"Order his release, Judge. Today, please. Bail. I want to see him before I go and it could be very soon. I must apologise to him," he sank back onto the bed and fell asleep in front of their very eyes. Only Brenda knew he was faking.

"Here are the copies of his affidavit. You will be especially interested Mr. Dawkins, I expect." Algie Dawkins looked pensive and nodded.

"Judge Clayton?" Brenda asked. He perused the affidavit then nodded.

"Today," he said. He was not actually sure of the procedures as this was not an everyday occurrence but knew all too well how he would be pilloried by the Press if Mel were not to be released immediately. He was above criticism in his decision whether technically within his powers or not.

The Press did not get to ask any questions as Jerry was 'sleeping' after his arduous announcement.

They attempted to ask Brenda questions and she simpered, "I just didn't know!"

Giving up, they turned to Lucy with the inevitable, "And how do you feel about all of this Mrs. Roberts?"

Lucy was not prepared to be drawn and simply said, "My husband is a decent and unassuming gentleman. He did not deserve to be locked up.

I offer thanks to Mr Kemp for not allowing Melvin to languish incarcerated any longer than necessary. I lost my first husband to a killer. My sympathies towards men of violence are not too well developed. As a Christian though, I want it known that I offer forgiveness to anybody who has caused my husband to be locked up so unfairly. I have nothing else to say. Thank you all for your support."

She stood to one side and talked to Brenda. Everybody else exited when they saw there was nothing else forthcoming.

"This afternoon," said the Judge to Lucy as he departed. She nodded her thanks.

The Chief Constable approached her and asked for a contact address so she gave him a business card. "So sorry," he mumbled with feeling as he shook his head in abject dismay. He was all too aware of 'where the buck stopped'.

Dawkins was soon the only person remaining.

"I'll be in touch about the compensation," he said, nodded in a triumphant fashion and also disappeared.

Alone, Jerry 'awoke' immediately and beamed. "Cracked it! Terrific result. I just did not want to add burdens. Sorry again for leaving you in the dark. I *would* like to see Mel while I still can. I suggest tomorrow. I expect to still be here. But not for too much time after that, I'm afraid."

"Have you seen a minister?" Lucy asked in a deep concern for his spiritual welfare.

Jerry smiled and said, "*You* can pray for me if you like. I'd appreciate that."

Lucy remained with him and did just that. He seemed much comforted and she remained for a quarter of an hour before he drifted off into a relaxed - and genuine - slumber.

Lucy thanked Brenda and realised that she had not thanked Jerry as she ought to have done.

"Please. Let him know how grateful we are. We have a life again now. Thank you so much."

She hugged Brenda and headed for Wakefield. She might have to wait for ages while Mel was processed but she was determined that he would not spend one more minute in that place than he had to. She had not yet managed an actual visit here and now, happily, she would never have to.

* * *

Mel was called in to see the Governor and informed that he was to be granted a second appeal. His heart leapt but he was not ready for the next bit.

"Until then, Judge Clayton has granted you unconditional bail. You can leave as soon as the documentation is complete. Your wife is waiting downstairs."

None of this second part registered. How could somebody possibly get bail for six murders? It had to be a sick joke of some kind. Still. Nothing else to do, so he decided to play along and show no excitement - that would just be playing into the hands of any would-be tormentors.

He was escorted downstairs and made to sign for his belongings and several additional signatures were required on documents he could not even be bothered to read. He returned to collect his things from his cell and he was ushered to the main door and invited to rejoin the outside world.

Lucy had been waiting inside initially, on invitation, but as his release became imminent she was taken to the door where they were reunited.

She drove him to Burton upon Stather where they celebrated in the fashion customary since time immemorial for a wife and a released prisoner.

She did not want to tell him straight away why he had been released. She wanted him relaxed first and then she would break to him the extremely unfortunate side of this situation.

At this point, of course, he did not even realise that she knew the reasons for it. He did express his puzzlement on numerous occasions but she preferred to leave it until mid evening.

That late May evening reminded him of the day he had arrived on Muckle Voe almost a year earlier. It was near perfect. Life was nigh on perfect. No. It *was* perfect. He was a free man. He had a seriously wonderful wife. The sun shone deep into the balmiest of evenings and they were able to chat over some Champagne they had been obliged to purchase on the way home.

They would live in this terrific house, indeed he would finally spend his first ever night in it on this momentous day. They would soon be owners of an equally wonderful house in Spain but with added sunshine. What could possibly destroy the idyll now?

Mel sat back and prepared himself for the start of yet another 'brand new life' - the only difference was that this would be spent entirely with Lucy 'til death did them part'.

CHAPTER ELEVEN

As they drove to Sheffield Mel was pensive. Everything now made sense.

Jerry *had* kept his promise so he had to have known for quite a while that he was dying. In fact, the more he thought about it the more he became convinced that Jerry must have known from around the point when they had first become friends.

He had lost all of the previous day's euphoria at the thought of the imminent loss of a man whom he respected enormously for his remarkable integrity. He now knew one reason at least, why Jerry had been so insistent that he never admitted to anything. Superficially, it seemed a simple idea but must have taken considerable, detailed planning. What an impressive man. He would have wagered that Brenda would have helped him too.

Lucy parked in the grounds of The Northern General and paid for several hours of parking. She was all too aware of the small but deliberately inflicted scratch which had appeared, as if by magic, on her passenger door from when she had parked on the side street the day before.

Lucy was unable to direct them to where Jerry was seeing his life draw to a close. They had to ask staff on two separate occasions before eventually finding the room.

Brenda was already there and Jerry was asleep. Lucy thought that he had deteriorated a great deal since the day before. His cadaver-like appearance denoted a rapidly-shortening period of time remaining to him. Even through the drugs his breathing was laboured, hoarse and uneasy. They smiled pathetically at each other across the bed but apart from an initial hug, said nothing.

Mel considered that great issue of 'life and death'. How could you not at a time like this? If ever your mortality was brought home to you, it was sitting watching a friend or loved one depart this life. Mel was pleased that Jerry had allowed Lucy to pray with him. It added a sort of completeness.

So where did this leave him? Did it push Mel any closer to making a 'decision for Christ'? No. He would not be pressured by circumstances, however intense his feelings were about his own mortality.

Believing that all the claims of Christianity were true could not overcome the one thing which he now recognised was his great 'stumbling block'. You can never become a Christian when you are unforgiving.

In his own situation he had established precisely where his lack of forgiveness originated. It is not easy to forgive God Himself when your daughter has been butchered.

One day maybe, but not today.

EPILOGUE

The funeral at the Crematorium on City Road, Sheffield, was heavily attended in spite of the highly publicised revelations about Jerry's 'misdeeds'. Brian Patten took the service - this had been a suggestion by Lucy which Brenda had readily accepted. He spoke well under the most difficult of circumstances and made reference to Jerry having spent time in prayer with Lucy the day before he passed on.

Afterwards, Mel and Lucy took Brenda aside to plead with her to join them in Spain for a month but she refused graciously but agreed that she would come in the autumn.

"I am so sorry that you were not able to *talk* to him before he went," she said sorrowfully to Mel.

"We were just glad to be there," said Lucy, "for you, more than for Jerry because he was unaware as he drifted away." She wiped a tear from her eye and spotted that Mel was doing the same.

"We had been hoping to tell you something that morning," said Brenda, "Something we felt you perhaps even *deserved* to know after all you had been through.

You both know about the 'Vigilante Kings', of course? - Well, they *are* centrally organised as many have suspected but despite what people are now thinking, Jerry was never part of them you know, he was simply not connected - well not in a direct way. The proper title they give themselves is the PJG. The Parallel Justice Group." Mel wondered if this was a phrase he had picked up off Jerry or from elsewhere as it was one which had run through his mind on a number of occasions.

"They contain scores of concerned individuals dedicated to the view that society cannot survive if the criminals start to win. You may not be surprised to learn they contain a goodly number of serving Police Officers, divided into cells in true Maoist fashion in order to avoid the organisation ever being put at risk should arrests of members ever occur. There are a great many former Police Officers involved too - in fact it's a *former* Police Constable who runs the whole lot."

She looked knowingly into Mel's eyes and for the first time on that incredibly sad day, she smiled.

Printed in the United Kingdom
by Lightning Source UK Ltd.
107881UKS00001B/148-315

9 781846 850257